Sweet Destiney

Collector's Edition

Chasing Destiney & Destiney Fulfilled

25 Years in the Making

Plus exclusive Bonus Chapters and Collector's Note

Vivienne Paul

I0590293

Hibiscus Tea Publishing

Contents

And at the very end... a personal note from me,

written just for this edition.

Chasing Destiney

Sweet Destiney Book 1

Cover by ZSW

Hibiscus Tea Publishing

For my husband.

*You've held my heart since I was twenty, and our love
is a dream I could never have imagined.*

Preface

In seventh grade, I began writing a story about a girl named Destiney, who was also in seventh grade. It was a coming-of-age story highlighting the struggles that we Black girls often face during those awkward years: challenges at school, friendship drama, boyfriend troubles, and family issues. I wrote on notebook paper wherever I could and kept those pages in a three-ring binder. My sisters eagerly read everything I wrote, acting as my first beta readers. I worked on the story on and off for a few years but never finished it. Yes, I still have it. I packed it when I moved into my first apartment and held onto it over the years, getting married, attending college, moving to two more apartments, and buying our first home. Over the years, my sisters have asked about Destiney, encouraging me to finish her story.

While the story has evolved, the character of Destiney reflects the young woman that seventh-grade Destiney has become

one

DESTINEY

"It has got to be the most epic wedding kiss! Have you seen it yet?"

"Yes! Just watched it for the thousandth time."

"That's so sweet! Can you imagine a man adoring you that much?"

My sister, Daijah, and my best friend, India, were gushing over a viral wedding clip.

I watched it earlier, getting the feels myself.

The clip had millions of views.

Definitely swoon-worthy.

The clip was less than a minute long and began just as the pastor pronounced the lovely couple husband and wife. When he tells the groom he may kiss his bride, the groom immediately performs several push-ups effortlessly. Wedding guests found it hilarious, and so did his bride. I did, too.

But when he finally kisses her, it's the most passionate kiss I've ever seen. The love and adoration they held for one another was palpable.

Intensely romantic. And beautiful.

How fortunate they were.

As with most viral clips, I watched it several times. Then, I fell into the rabbit hole of watching other wedding clips that were just as passionate.

And I kept watching them.

One after another. I guess I couldn't help myself. I'm a hopeless romantic.

I loved seeing those brides being loved on like that. I figured it has to be an incredible feeling.

"Des, will you come out already?!" Daijah was at the doorway of my ensuite bathroom. "Yassss Sissy! Turn around and show us all that ass!" I guess that clip was long forgotten. Daijah held up her phone, recording as I modeled the white lace jumpsuit timidly. Strappy nude wedge sandals completed the look. "You better werk, Sis!" Daijah had the confidence of ten women, and right about now, it was contagious. I slowly spun, examining my final look in the full body mirror on my closet door.

The jumpsuit was a sheer lace at the top, with capped sleeves and a high waist, enhancing my modest curves and hugging me like a second skin. I wasn't voluptuous by a long shot, but the splicing shorts put my thick thighs on full display. A big ass wasn't something I was blessed with either, but there was a little something back there I could work.

Stepping towards the mirror, I examined my hair a little closer. Daijah had styled the top half of my locs in a high bun, and the back hung freely. I didn't style my locs a lot these days because they'd grown so long. Ridiculously long, but Daijah wouldn't take no for an answer. She said "we were on birthday behavior and weren't doing anything ordinary tonight." The bun sitting high on my head, along with the wedge heels, gave my short ass at least three inches in height.

"Come out here, let me see!" India harped. She was sitting on my bed, eagerly anticipating my emergence. "Destiney! Oh my gosh! You look stunning! You did damn good Day!"

Daijah hand-selected everything I wore tonight, down to the delicate jewelry adorning my ears, neck, and wrists. As great as I looked, I admit I wouldn't have picked any of this for myself—especially this white jumpsuit.

It was absolutely sexy, and I felt sexy in it. But I would have gone with a black one. Hell, maybe even a red one.

I rarely ever wore white.

Daijah and I had tastes and styles that were as different as night and day. Black was my go-to color for pretty much everything. And as much as I tried to object, Daijah wouldn't hear any of that. Anyway, just like I knew it would, everything came together nicely. My baby sister had an eye for great fashion, that was for sure.

"Thank you boo! Come on, let's get a few ussies before we get out of here," Daijah said, taking a place on my right and India joining us on the other side of me. It was my twenty-seventh birthday, and we were headed out to celebrate. I wasn't thrilled about this initially, but these two ladies, as dear as they were, persevered. Honestly, I didn't mind a lounge on the occasion I had the energy, which I did have tonight. Thankfully. The best part was that I'd be spending time with my two very favorite people in the entire world. So, they eventually won me over. I was excited and I planned to enjoy myself.

Daijah and India busied themselves taking pictures for the book, the gram, and snap.

"Oh my gosh, this one is sooo cute!" Daijah gushed. "I'm sending it to Julian!"

"Let me see!" I turned toward Daijah, "Oooh, that is cute! Send me that one."

"I just sent it to both of y'all."

"Girl, Julian is gonna wonder where the hell you're going with your legs and titties all out!" India jested playfully.

"He knows where we're going and won't mind." Daijah cackled. "He'll probably try to come get me and crash our party."

"He better not!" India declared through a chuckle of her own.

"Right. I love Julian, but it's just us ladies for the next couple of days," I said.

"Hell yeah it is, and I am so excited!" Daijah squealed.

I was, too. It had been a long time coming, and I was beyond ready to relax and enjoy the low-key festivities planned. These two knew exactly how I wanted to spend the weekend. Tonight, after the lounge, we'd watch movies, binge on junk food, and have a sleepover. Tomorrow, after we sleep in, we'd have brunch, a spa day, and a little shopping if we got around to it.

Several pictures later, we headed downstairs to wait for our ride. We looked damn good, like a girl group stepping out for a night on the town. The sun had gone down, but it was a moderately warm evening for mid-April, so we had arms and legs out, each showing off shades of melanin.

India was gorgeous as usual, wearing a spaghetti-strap tiered bodice dress with a v-neckline. It was cute and flirty, stopping mid-thigh, and her slim figure was perfect for it. I loved the back; it was a deep scoop open back stopping at her waist. The rich marigold color perfectly complements India's smooth cinnamon skin. Her long black hair was pulled into a sleek low bun with a fresh sunflower tucked behind her ear.

My sister was as beautiful as ever, giving me life in her burnt orange with golden polka dots satin cocktail dress. It embodied Daijah's feminine style with a vintage flair. She'd begun a loc journey with sister locs that were thriving and now shoulder-length. Tonight, she had them styled in two French braids tucked into a side bun. I loved my locs, but I had to admit how much I missed them short. Shoulder length was my favorite phase, and I'd contemplated cutting mine shorter multiple times.

"Indie, you want another shot? The Uber is a few minutes away." Daijah had just tossed one back herself before offering India one.

"Hell yeah."

The girls were pregaming while I was getting ready, and they were already feeling it by the looks of things. I didn't drink often at all—nothing dark and never anything straight. I planned to have my one drink for the night when we got to the lounge. We chilled a bit longer and took a few more pictures, and once the Uber arrived, we were on our way.

***

Chasing Destiney

We entered Torch, a hookah bar and lounge, immediately consumed by the sweet, smoky ambiance. I was a big fan of hookah, and I've been to various hookah bars all over Sacramento.

Torch was absolutely one of my favorites. Black owned, has the chillest vibe, superb hookah flavors, and a bar and restaurant. I love the food here. They have your typical bar food, plus featured menu items you can't get anywhere else. There was a sushi burrito with many build-your-own options, which was pretty good. Then they had Cajun with Asian fusion items. That gave me pause at first. But I ordered some Ragin'Cajun fries one day, and my mind was blown. They're tossed in a medley of Cajun and Asian spices. The fries are so damn good, I get them every time we come here. They had a house sauce too that was so bomb you could eat the sauce on damn near anything. Daijah loves their Ragin'Cajun meatballs and wings.

I took in my surroundings as we headed toward the back of the lounge. It wasn't too crowded for a Friday. The lights were low, and the walls were vibrating with sound. Tonight, the music was on point. The DJ was playing hits from the nineties and early two-thousands. I grooved with my girls on the moderate-sized dance floor, and after a few songs, I returned to our section. I got comfortable on the couch, vibing with the music. Daijah and India stayed on the dance floor, returning soon after. Our hostess set us up with our hookah, and we put in food and drink orders.

Daijah and India ordered a platter of Ragin'Cajun wings and fries.

I ordered a basket of Ragin'Cajun fries. Extra spice. Extra sauce.

"Are you having a good time, Best?" India asked. The music wasn't super loud, and it was nice that we didn't need to yell to hear each other.

"I absolutely am." I smiled. "Thanks for being here."

"Of course!"

"Do I really get to have you for the next two days?" I asked India gingerly.

"I really hope so Best."

I gave her a quick side-hug and decided to leave it at that. India had a lot going on at home, and the last thing I wanted to do was ruin our good vibe.

Our drinks came out first, and I took a few sips, smiling in delight. I loved it. It was a pretty drink—guava-colored with an orange slice in the rim, topped with fresh cherries, pineapple wedges, and fresh mint. The flavor was vibrant and tropical and had banana, pineapple, and coconut.

"A birthday girl in the house tonight?" My face grew warm, but I smiled anyway. I gave Daijah a knowing expression, and she was wearing a sheepish grin. Daijah knew exactly what she was doing, insisting I wear the "Happy Birthday" sash, conveniently surprising me with it once we got out of the Uber. Attention was inevitable. "Happy birthday, beautiful," The same voice said in my ear. He walked around to the other side of our section. Now facing me, he stooped low resting his forearms on the back of the couch, "And I do mean beautiful."

"Thank you," I returned sweetly.

"What you drinking, mama?" The mystery man asked me. The surrounding tables had a mix of men and women, but I hadn't noticed him before.

Not that I was looking anyway.

I shrugged. "My sister ordered it for me." I looked at Daijah, taking another sip. I wasn't as versed in this area since I didn't drink much.

"No idea. I just asked our server for something sweet," Daijah chimed in.

He peered at the contents of my glass intently. Whoever he was. Meanwhile, I canvassed him. I figured I might as well; he was front and center.

And he was handsome, that was for sure.

Likely in his late thirties.

Smooth as hell too.

And he smelled good. I got a whiff of whatever he was wearing as he walked by me a moment ago.

"Hawaiian Screwdriver," he stated matter-of-factly, "I'll get you another one. And another round for these lovely ladies."

"Yes, please!" India chirped.

He chuckled, nodding, "Sure thing."

"Thank you," we all said in unison.

"You're welcome. Enjoy."

Just before Mystery Man turned to leave, he slid me a business card. "That's my cell. Call me birthday girl. I'd love to see you again."

India grabbed the black business card from my hand. "Tyler McBride. Torch Hookah Bar and Lounge...oh my gosh! Destiney! He owns this place!"

My eyes grew wide, "Damn for real?" I muttered.

13

"Yes, for real!" India placed the card on the table, pushing it back toward me.

Daijah picked it up, having a look of her own, "Birthday girl, he wants to see you again!" she said in a singing voice, raising her eyebrows, "Ooh Girl!"

"So it seems," I said absently. I didn't have anything substantial to add.

The girls didn't either because moments later, our server returned with our food, and we dug in immediately. We didn't talk for a while, just let the food fill our mouths. Not long after, our server returned with our second round of drinks.

"You planning to call him?" Daijah segued, taking a long pull from the hookah pipe. I knew she'd make her way back to this.

I had just taken a pull myself, and I loved the flavor. We tried a new one tonight. Royal Raspberry Muffin. It tasted like a mix of vanilla and freshly picked raspberries, perfectly smooth with a balance of sweetness and faint tartness.

I shrugged, somewhat dismissively. "Maybe."

"Oh sissy..." Daijah began, passing back to me, "You get all the cat calls. Yet you never entertain any of these men."

I smirked, my brows knitted. "You guys get hit on too."

Daijah waved that off. "We aren't talking about us right now. You my dear sissy are single as fuck."

After my turn, I huffed my annoyance and passed to India as she chimed in.

"Right! He's handsome. He's polite. Nothing is repulsing about him at all from where I'm sitting."

14

"Live a little for once," Daijah said.

"I don't do one-night stands."

"Destiney! Who said anything about a one-night stand?" That was India.

"I don't know…he just gives me that vibe. He didn't even ask my name." That screams an indifferent lack of regard. To me. "What if that's all he wants?"

"You don't know that." Daijah said, sipping her drink, "Maybe he's keeping it casual and will ask all the vital questions once you talk more." Daijah would say something like that because she didn't know what was out here. Daijah had Julian. Been had Julian. "Call him. Get to know him."

"He may be the perfect gentleman," India chimed in.

Yep. India had a man, too.

I signed audibly. They seemed positive and hopeful and…

I'm no cynic. I swear I'm not.

Taking another pull from the hookah, I gave this more thought.

Meanwhile, my girls were on to the next topic of discussion just that quickly, and I tuned them out. Aside from our lack of a formal introduction, Tyler seemed nice enough to talk to again.

Maybe he was different.

There was only one way to find out.

I nodded, agreeing silently.

I could call him.

two

DESTINEY

So, I called him.

I even saw him again.

In fact, we hung out a total of three times.

Unfortunately for him, it was over before it started.

Pretty much right away it was clear he wanted nothing more than to screw me. I am keenly aware of how many women are moving out here, so I didn't hold it against him initially. He just needed some course correction.

The thing is, I always tell men up front that I would not be having sex with them. Not anytime soon. I informed Tyler of the same. And he told me he was cool with that. But he was lying through his teeth. Tyler saw me as a conquest; he was right back to it days later.

Also, he constantly bragged about the money he had. And he had plenty of it.

I'd imagine he could get just about any woman he wanted with that kind of money. There are women galore out here looking for a come-up.

Also, unfortunately for him, I am not one of them.

You cannot buy me.

Grandiose gestures from the wrong person turn me off. A man pursuing me need not lead with his wallet, especially if we just met and are in the building stages.

But say we've been together for some time, and it's just because of our anniversary or my birthday. Feel free to take me on a helicopter ride or some shit. I really would love that. But please don't pull out a bunch of stops when you haven't bothered to learn my middle name or my favorite color. Because meanwhile, I am making it a point to know yours and everything else about you.

I'm not a grand gesture type of girl when I get to know someone new.

I love sweet gestures, though, and Tyler did not seem to know the difference. He would have figured that out had he been paying attention. Thoughtfulness and simplicity are the way to my heart. And for the record, I like the finer things just as much as the next girl. But it's all in the intent. Buying me something just because you have the means doesn't impress me.

Tyler McBride took issue with the reality that I was unimpressed with his money when really, I was unimpressed with him. He never bothered to get to know me. He was dead set on taking me out, wining and dining me, and tossing me lavish gifts with the assumption that I'd give him the panties.

Once, he called his bank on speaker so that I could hear his account balance. He had a few hundred thousand and was sure to mention that he had more money in multiple accounts. That was the last time we hung out.

But he kept calling me.

Even after weeks went by, he continued calling me. But I kept it moving.

I should have told him to move along, but whatever. I realize now that my handling of that was immature.

About a month after I'd last hung out with Tyler, Daijah and I hosted a girl's night at our place.

Daijah's best friends came. Twins Veronica and Victoria. India came by, and my friend Neeka. On the weekend of my birthday festivities, Neeka met Daijah, India, and me at the spa the following afternoon. India gushed about the owner of Torch giving me his number. When Neeka came to girls' night, she asked how things had been going with Tyler and me.

I told Neeka that I stopped seeing him and why.

Neeka went on and on, criticizing me for unceremoniously tossing him aside. Giving me the third degree, "Girl! Pass him over here if you don't want him!" She was dead serious, too. Informing me she would have gladly taken him off my hands. Daijah rolled her eyes so hard I thought they would pop out of her head.

I didn't care one way or the other. Neeka could have Tyler. Dude was barking up the wrong tree, plain and simple.

The funny thing about it, from what I'd gathered about Tyler and knowing Neeka, that arrangement wouldn't have lasted past a simple fuck.

Neeka absolutely would have wanted to attach herself to Tyler, marry him, and everything else, but he wouldn't have been remotely interested in anything more than sex with her.

three

MICAH

"Come on ref!"

"You can't be missing them travels, man!"

The worst part about this was the nagging parents. I didn't mind officiating games, but they were all convinced their child was the next Lebron. Half were trying to overcoach from the stands, and the other half were yelling obscenities about all the calls we were or weren't making.

The crazy thing about it is that these players were eight-year-olds.

Meanwhile, my partner was tricking off and missing a bunch of calls. Since I was on my shit, it seemed I was calling every little thing. There were a few cuties in attendance, but Terrence needed to chill. I rolled my eyes every time we were paired up. Terrence was the homie, but he stayed flirting with these women.

I was a referee for youth basketball at the Salvation Army in my spare time. They had a recreational league for ages five to fourteen. I coached on occasion as well. I did it for fun more than anything. I got the opportunity to work with kids, which I enjoyed. It kept me in shape, and it was something to do. Most importantly, it was a terrific way to give back. My brother and I grew up playing basketball here, so it was a great feeling to return and pay it forward. I believed in their ministry, and my values aligned with everything they tried to do for the youth and the community. They paid officials a small stipend for each game, but I refused to take the money; I claimed it as a charitable contribution each year. I was glad to volunteer my time because the funds returned to the program.

I blew my whistle for one of the coaches requesting a time out.

"T, man... You need to keep your head in this game," I sighed in frustration, glancing at the scoreboard. "We got about six more minutes. You think you can handle that?" There were many single women at these games each week, but now wasn't the time for Terrence to exercise his many options.

Terrance chuckled, "Man, don't worry about all that. They ain't coming back, no way. This game is about over."

I shook my head. There was more than a thirty-point lead. The guest team was getting hammered, I had to admit. Just the same, Terrance needed to focus on the task. He'd have plenty of time to get at whoever the hell his flavor of the week was. But that was T. not taking things seriously. Well, aside from entertaining the women, that is.

A beat later, Terrence blew his whistle, ending the timeout. "You can chill on all the calls you're making. That way, nobody else can get mad at me," he cracked up, taking off behind the ball as the kids made a fast break.

All I could do was shake my head.
***

About two hours later, I pulled my bag over my shoulder and headed out through the gym's double doors. I'd just finished two back-to-back games and needed a hot shower. The referees ran just as much as the players, especially the older kids.

You could almost stay at half-court with the little ones and still see everything since they're so small. But since the younger kids were still learning to handle and control the ball, things could go all over the place, and we had to stay with it.

When officiating teenagers and adults, the game was more controlled, but we still ran up and down the court. Plenty. Those back and forth and high intensity moments could get to be exhausting. I stayed in decent shape, which helped tremendously, but I was glad to be done for today.

Walking through the vestibule, I waved at Carlos, the site supervisor who hung out at the front desk. Most of the crowd in the lobby had cleared out except for the spectators standing around watching the next game through the oversized windows. I was near the doors leading out to the parking lot when I heard someone calling after me.

"Hey, excuse me!" Her voice was soft and meek, and as I turned around, I saw that it fit her petite stature perfectly. She was bending over to retrieve something, and as she stood to her feet, I realized it was my sweaty towel. It must have fallen from my neck as I approached the exit.

"Oh goodness, you don't want to touch this." I gently took it off her hands. "I just wiped my sweat with it." She was chocolate with a beautiful smile, and I smiled right back at her.

"No harm done." She shrugged. "Just making sure you don't leave it behind."

By now, I was taking in her features. I counted one dimple when she smiled.

Her face was soft and pretty.

No resting bitch face in sight.

I didn't know when that happened, but it would be a great day once that fad was gone. I didn't find anything about that shit attractive.

"Excuse us," A woman with a few children passed me. I hadn't realized I was standing in the doorway. Apologizing, I quickly moved aside. As eager as I was to head out just moments before, I wasn't ready to go yet.

Before I got too carried away, though, I needed to establish protocol.

"Thank you so much," I told the chocolate cutie. She had since turned back toward the glass windows.

"Sure," She tossed over her shoulder.

Her hands were in the pockets of her hoodie, and I couldn't recall if she had a ring on her finger.

Taking the few steps toward her, I held out my hand, "I'm Micah. I'd love to thank you properly. Would you be okay with giving me your name?"

"Sarina. But really, it was no big deal."

"Sarina," I nodded, "Thank you, Sarina. You're very pretty, by the way."

Smiling, she brought her hands out, a bright gold band with a shiny diamond sat snuggly on her ring finger. It was a lovely ring. I don't know how I missed it.

"Thank you," she glanced at me quickly with that smile again. And you're welcome, Micah."

After shaking quickly, her hands returned to her pockets, and her eyes were back on the game.

Meanwhile, I mused for a moment.

I'd heard some unmarried women wore a ring on their ring finger to ward men off, something akin to mosquito repellant. That cracked me up, and I suppose that is a thing for the more conventionally attractive women.

Then there are the men who will pursue a woman regardless. Wedding ring be damned.

That's another conversation entirely.

Anyway, as a gentleman and a straight shooter, there was only one way I could know for sure.

"Forgive me if this is forward, Sarina. Are you married?"

"I am married," She returned with a confident smile. This time, she kept her eyes on the game.

I nodded in understanding, turning toward the game myself. "You have one out there?"

"Yes, my nephew."

"Indeed," I returned, stepping back, "Have a great evening."

"Thanks, you too."

I quickly made my way out of the gym and toward the parking lot.

She was pretty with a kind spirit.

Of course, she was married.

In my experience, women like that didn't stay on the market long.

I was never the type to operate from a scarcity mindset; however, occasional abstractions from the dark side got into my head.

Like right now.

But I kept them in check—most of the time.

I'm a hopeful person.

Perpetually optimistic.

I tossed my bag in the trunk, and as I climbed into my Mercedes, I reminded myself that I wasn't there for that anyway. Before cranking up, I checked my phone for any notifications. Shortly after, I was merging onto Highway 99 South, headed toward home. Traffic was moderately light for an early Saturday afternoon.

The Salvation Army was in the Oak Park area of South Sacramento, and I lived in Elk Grove just about twenty minutes away. As I cruised down the highway, I considered what I would do with the rest of my day.

I needed to restock my fridge. Today was the second Saturday of the month, so I could go to the farmer's market. As convenient as it was to go to a supermarket, I tried to shop small as often as possible. Mentally, I ran over what I needed when a call came in over my Bluetooth. I quickly glanced at my screen, seeing Malachi's name.

"Brother."

"Baby Brother. What's happenin' man."

"Just leaving Salvation Army. Had two games this morning."

"That's was'sup. It's hardly noon. Must have been the little ones."

"Yup. Eight and under."

Mal whistled, "Bet them rugrat's ran yo' old ass ragged."

"Old? Mal, we're the same age."

Malachi cackled, "You have a partner today?" Occasionally, we were on our own, and that was a lot more work. It was always nice having another official. Malachi understood the concept well since he also officiated every blue moon.

"Yeah. T."

"Oh yeah? Bet he had a good time," Mal cracked up all over again, and I couldn't help but join him.

"Man, I swear."

"I'll see you at the Blue House tomorrow, but I wanted to make sure we have you all set for next week."

"I appreciate you, but we gone be straight dude."

"No doubt. Ella wanted to be sure. This is the longest they'll be staying over at your place."

"Well, they aren't babies. And we can drop by your house anytime we need to." I had a key to Malachi's home, and he had a key to mine.

"True."

"You and my sis just go enjoy yourselves. We'll be fine."

"Sure plan too. Got all sorts of ideas. Bout to have a good time rediscovering…"

"Mal, really?" I had to stop him because I already knew where this was going.

Malachi's hearty laughter flowed through my speakers. "We grown man, stop it," he said once he calmed down.

I shook my head. "Anyway. That all you wanted?"

Mal paused for a beat. "Yeah. What you got planned for the rest of the day?"

I preferred the early games because I could still make plans in the afternoons and evenings, like date plans, even though I haven't been dating much lately.

"Shit. Gone hit the shower, get this gym smell off me. Grab some groceries. Nothing else concrete."

"Come by. Jackson and Polsinelli are on to-night." Mal was a huge MMA fan. I enjoyed watching the fights but didn't follow the hype as much since I was no MMA fanatic. Just as well, any time with my big brother was a good time.

"Yeah, I'll come by."

"You have a standing offer to join us for dinner, too. Always."

I smiled at that. "You grilling?"

"Nah. Ella is fixing something."

I already knew whatever she made was going to hit the spot.

"What should I bring?"

"Don't worry about it. You're already doing us a solid."

"Anytime. You know it ain't nothing," and it wasn't. I loved Mal's children just like they were my own.

"Good stuff. I'll see you this evening, baby brother."

"Bet."

I made it home about fifteen minutes later and headed straight upstairs to shower. On my way back downstairs, I gathered my dirty laundry, deciding to get a cycle going when I returned from the market. Back in my kitchen, I used the last of my fresh produce to make myself a green smoothie. I sat on a barstool while I drank it, using the notes app to list everything I would need to grab. I thought over a few meal ideas for the upcoming week and added that to the list as well.

When I returned home, I decided to vacuum and clean the restrooms. My mother taught us young that maintaining the regular habit of household chores always kept your home clean and kept house-work light. That was a habit I continued to practice when I went to college and still do now: making my bed each morning, cleaning behind myself as I go, dusting surfaces regularly, vacuuming high-traffic areas daily, cleaning my kitchen every night, and keeping my laundry done so it doesn't pile up.

I glanced around.

My home was tidy.

It was considerable in size.

It was quiet.

It was empty.

And… I was man enough to admit that I was lonely.

I was ready to fill this home with a family. I've been preparing for a few years now. I yearned for intimacy. Not even sex necessarily, though it had been a very long time.

Coming home to an empty house and sleeping in an empty bed was getting old.

When I had this house built five years ago, I thought I would at least have a wife and a child by now. I wanted to fill my home with a family and make memories.

Create a legacy. To make this house a home.

Beyond the basic things, I hadn't even decorated the place. The walls aren't even painted. I wanted my future wife to decide all of that. Now and then, my niece will playfully tease me about my house looking like the doctor's office with the plain off-white walls.

My cousin gave me the third degree; asking in part, "why I built a big ass house without any prospects."

I felt criticized and defensive as hell at the time.

Now, I'm beginning to wonder the very same thing.

four

DESTINEY

"Best."

"Hey, Indie."

"By the sound of things, you're still down for the count?"

"Yeah, still down. I hope I can return by mid-next week at the latest."

Today was Friday, and it seemed the week was going slowly. Funny, in any case. I was so disoriented just days ago that I had no idea what day it was. I'd somehow caught a cold.

"No rush. We'll be here. Rest up, and let me know if I can get you anything."

"Thank you, Indie." I placed my phone down beside me and turned to my back.

I hardly ever got sick.

I honestly couldn't even remember the last time I had a cold. And this had been a cold straight from hell. I thought it was a cold but shit, maybe it's the damn flu. It had been even longer since I had that. For the past hour, I felt a sinus headache building.

I'm an independent artist, which I love. But it sucks in the unfortunate event that I got sick. I love working for myself and the freedom it afforded me. Having the latitude to do what I wanted. Commission work, freelance. Pick up multiple gigs simultaneously, spending weekdays at one project site and weekends at another. A flexible work schedule. Taking jobs in the next town or city over. Having the choice to work as a part of a team or work independently.

I tried the corporate route, and it just wasn't my thing.

Doing what I loved and with autonomy was lovely.

Working as an independent artist had its cons, too.

Murals were my bread and butter, and although they could be indoors or outdoors, outdoor projects could be more lucrative but were less common during the winter months. Searching for work during the off-season could be stressful when gigs weren't as plentiful.

Another con was contracting out my work and dealing with difficult people. It was reminiscent of corporate America.

Then there was the shitty insurance because it's the best I can afford and that wasn't fun either.

It also meant I wasn't getting paid when I wasn't working. This cold wiped me out, and I was down so bad that I couldn't go to work if I wanted to. I was currently a featured artist working as part of a collective for a beautification project at a charter school. India was also part of the collective, and we often worked together.

Holding a paintbrush would be far too difficult with chills and body aches. I wasn't good for shit. And I appreciated India checking on me. Art was actually how we met. About eight years ago. I showed up at a volunteer opportunity for a community mural project, and she was there volunteering too. And India was the first person to speak. We sketched ideas, and she complimented me on something I'd worked on. Then, she started talking about my hair.

"Girl, oh my gosh, your locs are beautiful, by the way."

"Thank you. You are beautiful, period."

She had an exotic look I hadn't seen before. Her long black hair is what threw me—it was really long and super straight, naturally. Later, she told me about her heritage.

India and I were in college when we met, and right away, India inspired me. She'd shared that she eventually wanted to work with kids as an adaptive arts teacher or an art therapist. That came as no surprise because India embodies the word "artist". She could paint, she could draw, and she could dance. She is so talented. India always says I was the better painter, but I would fight her on that every time.

The community project lasted a couple of weeks. India and I were the only two black girls, and having India there was nice. Even on subsequent projects, there isn't much representation, which we both wanted to change. But we were fast friends, remaining in touch, and I quickly discovered that India is my twin flame. We have so much in common. And she is so much fun to be around. I love her spunky personality.

At first, Daijah was low-key jealous because she and I never made room for other friends. Daijah is my absolute best friend ever. She always will be, but that got in her head at first. Understandably. No one could get close enough to either of us. We had each other, and that's all we cared about. Anyway, she loves India now.

I sat in bed and headed down the hall toward the kitchen once I gathered the strength. I was in desperate need of something to relieve my aches and pains. Searching my cabinets was all for naught. I realized we were out of DayQuil, and no Tylenol was in sight. Sighing, I accepted the realization that if I wanted to rest tonight, I had to make a quick trip to my neighborhood Walgreens.

I went to pee in my ensuite bathroom, making a mental note also to buy more Charmin. I washed my hands, grabbed my wristlet, then pulled on my hoodie hanging by the front door. Once I locked up, I climbed into my hunter green Honda Accord.

It was still raining, and it had been all week. Seeing the heavy overcast, I was especially eager to get into bed and sleep off this cold. Gratefully, my house was less than ten minutes away; I knew I'd be in, out, and home again within twenty minutes.

I parked, headed inside, and made a beeline for the Cough, Cold, and Flu medicine. Using my manners, I squeezed past a few other patrons in the crowded aisle to peruse my options. Deciding on a twin pack of DayQuil and NyQuil, I continued to the other end of the aisle, now on my quest for toilet paper. I was so glad the store wasn't large and I wouldn't have to walk too much. I had hardly any energy, and my headache was gradually worsening.

I continued surveying the aisles, glancing from left to right, recalling the scarcity of store aisles during the COVID-19 hysteria. That shit was crazy.

"Wings or no wings?"

I halted briskly and looked to my left, regarding a tall gentleman, possessing two packages of maxi pads.

Did he just ask me that?

His voice was a deep register—my goodness.

He was absolutely handsome, dressed in a black tailored suit, with a bald head and full beard. His voice stunned me.

I returned a perplexed expression, simultaneously noticing the comfort of his warm brown eyes. I quickly scanned his tall stature. He was over six foot tall and solid, with broad shoulders and milk chocolate skin. Daijah and I would call him a teddy bear.

And dammit, was I a sucker for a teddy bear.

"My niece and nephew are spending the week with me," He explained, "And my niece had an emergency." Nervously, he looked back and forth at each package. "Just trying to ensure she's comfortable and has everything she needs for the next few days. She's twelve, in case that helps."

He smiled kindly. And I was somewhat lost in a trance, partly due to my headache but primarily because of his voice, his baritone flowing smoothly like velvet. I gave a reassuring nod and returned a warm smile of my own.

"Yes, that helps," I said, chuckling lightly. Though I wasn't feeling well, suddenly, I felt an immense calm. Seconds ago, I had been in such a hurry to get home, yet now, I wanted to be consumed in the company of this gentleman who sounded damn good and looked even better. "I'd say wings. Then she can move freely, it stays in place, and she won't have to worry about any...leaks, you know..." I gestured with my empty hand at nothing, sniffing the entire time. I stammered as he intently gazed back at me. He nodded in understanding and appeared entirely engaged in the uninteresting, unexciting subject of feminine hygiene products.

"So, wings it is." He sighed in relief and turned, placing the other package back on the shelf. "You made it so simple. I appreciate your help. Thank you…" Returning to face me, his eyebrows rose.

"Destiney." I offered, smiling widely, "I would shake, but I don't want to give you my cold." Resisting the urge, I offered a fist bump.

"I'm Micah." He returned the gesture and tucked the maxi pads with wings under his arm like a football. "Thank you for being so considerate. I must admit I was overwhelmed by all these options," he laughed.

I laughed too. "It can be overwhelming. Let's say I've had lots of trial and error, you know," I shrugged, "It happens every month after all." After a couple seconds and suddenly unsure of myself, I leisurely took a few steps, pretending to consider bandages and ointments. I felt some kind of connection. That, I was sure of. I returned my gaze, and his warm brown eyes were still regarding me, and I wondered if he felt what I did. I didn't want our exchange to end, so I added, "I'm glad I could help."

"Well, thank you again, Destiney." His smile never leaving, he held my gaze, my name rolling off his tongue as if he'd said it hundreds of times.

"You're very welcome, Micah." After a beat or two, I took a few more steps, finally rounding the corner of the aisle, already wondering so many things about him. For some reason, I was too afraid to turn around and see if he was still there. Was he wearing a wedding ring? I couldn't remember.

No way he's single, I resolved.

But wait, maybe he was. He had to be single after asking me a question like that.

With sinus pressure building, I wandered through Walgreens, all the while contemplating. Men and relationships, in general, have been an afterthought for me lately, but the immense comfort and familiarity I just felt made me want to feel it again. The million-dollar question was, did he?

I certainly couldn't have asked for his number or some shit. I mean, I'd never asked a man for his number before.

Never had to.

I glanced to my right, eyeing the rainbow of nail polishes and various mascaras. This was wild and not my style at all, but I felt a gravitation toward it and wanted to explore it. Still musing, I continued my stroll, and by now, I had passed four or five aisles.

Fuck it.

I wanted to know more.

I spun around quickly and began scanning each aisle I'd passed, hoping to spot him. He was nowhere in sight. Shit. I kept scanning; the drugstore wasn't very large. My pace increasing, I continued scanning. I returned to the aisle with all the pads and tampons. I walked a bit further then surveyed straight ahead. There were two check-out lanes open. The clerks were moving slowly through monotonous scans, and about a half dozen people were in line. He couldn't have checked out that quickly. Spotting one self-service checkout with just one person waiting, I pondered if he'd used it.

Defeated, I slowly turned again and headed back toward the rear of the store, my frequent body aches reminding me I just needed to get that damn toilet paper and take my ass home. I sighed, pissed at myself.

Maybe I'll see him again someday.

Yeah right, that shit only happened in movies and romance novels.

Strolling past more aisles, I heard the deep timbre of a once-unfamiliar voice behind me.

"Destiney."

I turned around, peering up at him.

"I'm so glad you're still here. I thought I'd missed you." His chest softly heaved. "You took off so quickly. I didn't want to seem like a creep chasing after you." His handsome face still displayed that warm smile.

Was he looking for me?

I felt a tinge of embarrassment but smiled back anyway. Unsure of what to say, I asked, "Do you need help with something else?"

"Can I have your phone number, Destiney? In case my niece has another emergency." He reasoned, reaching into his pocket.

I reached out to receive his phone and nodded slowly. My smile was gone. "Sure," I said flatly, not even trying to mask my disappointment. I must have misread everything. That quickly, I had forgotten about my headache, but now it was back and with a vengeance. I briefly considered giving him a bogus number. Do people still do that? I returned his phone. "I'm sure you'll be fine, Micah." Already over the conversation, I began walking in the direction of the toilet paper. I really needed to get the hell out of here.

"And if it's alright with you, I would love to get to know you better," he said to my back. I turned towards him, greeted again by his warm smile. "I'll be honest, Destiney. You are beautiful, and I'm intrigued." he slid his cell phone back into the pocket of his slacks.

I smiled bashfully. "Thank you, Micah. I would love to talk to you again," I stated, slowly releasing the breath I didn't realize I was holding.

"Sounds like a plan." He let out another light chuckle. "Well, let me get back. I'm sure my niece is eagerly awaiting my return."

"Yes, I'm sure she is. Talk to you later, Micah."

"I'm looking forward to it, beautiful Destiney."

five

MICAH

"Destiney."

I couldn't help but repeat her name as I drove from the drugstore.

This detour wasn't planned, but I was convinced I wouldn't have met her otherwise, and I was grateful for divine timing. And eager to see her again.

Relieved to finally be headed home. I turned on my windshield wipers as the light sprinkle picked up. My office was in Midtown Sacramento, and rush hour traffic in this weather meant I was about thirty-five minutes from my destination.

Malachi and Ella were headed out of town to celebrate their fifteenth wedding anniversary. I'm sure they were excited to escape all this rain. Since I'd still be at work, they used their spare key to let in my niece and nephew. I planned to head straight home after work; I was excited to start the week. About an hour before leaving the office, my niece Gabrielle asked if I could pick up emergency supplies for her. Even though I never had to fulfill this kind of request, it seemed simple enough, and I expected it to be quick.

Turned out I'd been standing in that aisle for several minutes. Unscathed, I resisted the urge to call her. I didn't want to embarrass my dear niece by asking sensitive questions. Apart from that, I was determined to manage mission impossible on my own.

Contemplating what to buy and beset with several options, I spotted her, and I was immediately smitten. She neared me, absent-minded and unassuming, carrying cold medicine. She was everywhere but here, as if she had blinders on. I quickly scanned her petite but curvy frame.

She was so beautiful, instantly taking my breath away.

Usually, I'm the type to pursue something I want expeditiously; however, I found myself hesitating out of respect.

I was positive she was married.

Then, it was as if the good Lord above gave me a sign. Almost in slow motion, she used her left hand to brush stray locs out of her face, exposing a bare ring finger. She continued walking with no sign of slowing down, and I knew I had to make a move and quick. Having narrowed my options to two remaining packages, I boldly asked her: *"Wings or no wings?"*. Best four words I've spoken in a while. As expected, she was taken aback by my question, but as soon as I explained, her big, brilliant eyes had a spark in them.

I was charmed by everything I saw and everything I heard.

Her smile was wide and infectious. Despite an occasional sniffle, her voice was melodic, light, and airy. I encounter beautiful women regularly, yet it was clear she was so much more. I regarded her chocolate skin, big, vibrant eyes, the tiny gold stud in her nose, and the locs hanging down at her waist. Her ethereal vibe was my jam. I always appreciated a natural queen.

The crazy thing about it is that I got the impression she was unaware of her striking beauty.

Anyway, I was already pressed to see her again.

I made it home and headed inside, grateful to finally be out of the rain and eager to greet my two loves. I barely made it in the door before my niece Gabrielle squealed, skipping toward me.

"Uncle Micah!" She threw her arms around my waist, and I returned a bear hug. "I'm so glad we'll be here for the week!" Her voice muffled against my chest.

"Me too, Gabby girl."

"Thank you!" She grabbed the bag from me. As she looked inside, her eyes grew wide. "Great choice."

I smiled, responding casually, "You know uncle got you."

She quickly disappeared up the stairs to the guest room she stayed in whenever they spent time with me. I placed my work bag in the foyer, then headed toward the living room to find my nephew playing the game on my big screen.

"Hey, man." We did the handshake we'd done since he was just a toddler.

"Hey unc. How's it going?" My nephew Gabriel was fourteen, smart as a whip, super mature, and cool as a cucumber. Although he resembled my sister-in-law Ella in the face, he inherited his six-foot height from my older brother. He and my brother were so much alike personality-wise that sometimes it was scary. My father, brother, and Gabe, as we call him, are all over six feet tall.

"Pretty good man." I sat down across from him on the oversized sectional. "New game?" I watched him play for a minute.

"Yeah, just picked it up. Trying to analyze what I'm looking at to understand the graphics and framework better," he returned, not taking his eyes off the screen. Gabe was brilliant, and he was such a game nerd and a whiz kid. He'd learned to code by fifth grade and was in the process of developing his own app and video game. He played multiple games, but not for fun as most kids did; he was learning the craft by method of reverse engineering. His intel was amazing, and I was excited to see what he would become.

I headed to the kitchen and looked in the fridge to try and figure out what I would prepare for dinner. After contemplating, I decided to order in to-night.

Still consumed with thoughts of Destiney, I didn't want to waste any more time. Picking up my phone, I texted her.

Hello Destiney. Thank you again for allowing me to stay connected with you beautiful

I grabbed bottled water from the fridge. After taking a drink, I called over my shoulder, "Hey, you two, how does pizza and wings sound?"

"Works for me," Gabe replied.

"Yes, please!" I heard Gabby yell from up-stairs.

I leaned against the kitchen island, opening the pizza app to place an order. After completing the transaction, my phone vibrated in my hand. Seeing it was her, my heart swelled.

Beauty: You're very welcome. Is your niece all situated?

I smiled at her thoughtfulness.

She's fine. Wasn't her first rodeo. I'll keep a stash here for next time

Dots appeared just as I sent it.

Beauty: You're such a great uncle

I thought back to that cold medicine.

How are you feeling?

Beauty: Just a little under the weather. I plan to rest this weekend. Thanks for asking

My response was immediate, and I instantly wanted to take care of her.

I'm happy to bring you soup or anything else you need, please don't hesitate to let me know

Beauty: I can manage. Thank you Micah

I laughed at myself after reading her response. Damn this was crazy. I'd known her for less than two hours, and here I was, coming up with excuses to see her and do things for her.

All I knew was I wanted more of Destiney, and I couldn't wait to see her again.

six

DESTINEY

I woke up late Sunday afternoon to the sun brightly peeking through my drapes. This cold had kicked my ass, and I'd slept for hours. Friday night through most of Saturday, only waking up a few times to pee.

Getting out of bed, I headed down the hall to the living room and drew all the blinds, eager to let the sun in. It rained five days straight, and this much rain was not typical in Sacramento, especially in May.

Stretching for a moment, I basked in the natural sunlight flooding through the oversized bay window. This was one of my favorite places in the house. Daijah and I have lived in the condo for the past two years, and the three bedrooms and two bathrooms have afforded plenty of space for us.

Lately, though, I had the place all to myself. Daijah spent most of her free time at her fiancé's home across town in Natomas. Julian was a great guy, so I didn't mind. Daijah was happy, and they were deeply in love. I was overjoyed for them.

Back in the kitchen, I filled my kettle with fresh water and turned on the stove for a cup of tea.

I wasn't back to feeling like myself yet, but I was glad to feel better. I expected to be back one hundred percent within the next day or two.

I started my playlist, noticing an unread text message Daijah had sent me early this morning.

Sibling Bestie: Good morning sunshine. How are you feeling?

So much better today thanks

Sibling Bestie: There you are! I was about to send a search party!

I giggled at her antics. Daijah was so full of personality and zeal, and there was never a dull moment with her.

Sibling Bestie: I'll be home later to get clothes. Let me know if you want a bahn mi. Grabbing some on the way.

I'd love one, thank you!!!

Sibling Bestie: The usual with extra veggies?

You know it Thank you!

My mouth watered. I liked her thinking—no doubt a bahn mi would hit the spot right about now.

I slept so much the past thirty-six hours; I hardly ate anything. I'm not usually a huge fan of sandwiches, but Banh Mi's are hard to resist. Banh mi is a Vietnamese sandwich. They're made on a fresh baguette with pâté or mayonnaise and a delicious combination of pickled carrot and daikon radish. It also has fresh cucumber, jalapeño, and cilantro. The protein varies; traditionally, it would have Vietnamese ham, steamed pork roll, or other meats. Daijah loves to get charbroiled chicken on hers.

The Bahn Mi's around here are the best in town. In South Sacramento, where we live, there are dozens of Vietnamese restaurants on a 4-mile-long strip called Little Saigon. Sacramento, where we were born and raised, is one of the most diverse cities in the country. The food scene is second to none, with so many diverse cultures and cuisines to indulge in.

I had my very favorite playlist going: R&B slow jams from the 90s. As I prepared my cup of tea, my thoughts returned to Micah.

My thoughts of him have been nonstop since I first met him.

I contemplated calling Micah, but I hesitated. I didn't want to disturb family time with his niece and nephew. Pulling up our text thread, I read his messages over again. I smiled, considering how thoughtful he was, offering me his help if I needed it.

I sent him a text.

Hey you, happy Sunday. Can you talk?

The three dots appeared almost instantly, and my heart pattered a little faster.

Micah: Hey, Beautiful. Playing basketball with my nephew. Can I call you a little later?

That's fine

I smiled heading back to my bedroom to finish my tea. I was absolutely looking forward to Micah's phone call.

I took the final sip of tea and decided to wash all the linen from my bed. Clean sheets and a hot shower would do my body good.

My time in the shower had me thinking.

It occurred to me that for the past few days... I'd been feeling things.

Being honest with myself was important; to that end, I needed to acknowledge that.

It's difficult to articulate, but... it was like emotions formerly lying dormant were beginning to awaken.

We'd only been texting so far. Micah had been checking on me around the clock. I always had a message or two from him when I woke up. He offered to bring me soup. He wished me a speedy recovery. Then, he reminded me more than once that his proposition to help me out was still on the table. I wasn't as responsive since I wasn't feeling my best, but I would reply whenever I woke up to pee. Micah seemed okay with that.

And...it was wild that I liked him before we even had a verbal conversation.

Yes.

I like him.

I couldn't say if that were a good or bad thing.

Honestly.

Being unsure was the worst part about this.

Whether I was okay with this or not.

How I would proceed. If I proceeded at all.

The idea of Micah was absolutely good. But potentially becoming... something.

That, I wasn't sure about.

I closed my eyes as the hot water cascaded over me. I pictured Micah's warm brown eyes. They were sincere and inviting, and there was a depth and comfort there. He was very handsome—a grown man handsome. That got me thinking, too. It's been quite some time since I've been so eager to get to know someone.

And I wanted to know everything about him. I had so many questions.

Chasing Destiney

I quickly finished up in the shower. I was excited to hear his voice again and didn't want to miss his call. This would officially be our first real conversation.

I moisturized my skin and dressed in leggings and an oversized graphic T-shirt. I had slept so much the past few days that I wouldn't lie down again until bedtime if I could help it. After moving my linen from the washer to the dryer, I decided to head to my in-home office.

I was the only one who worked from home, so I converted the third and smallest bedroom into an office space. It was simple but had everything I needed: a corner desk and office chair from IKEA, where I kept my laptop computer and monitors. I did a bit of digital artwork that I wanted to expand on, so I worked on that here in the office when I had the capacity.

Adjacent to that, I had an art desk with shelves for my pens, pencils, paints, sketchbooks, and canvases. The furthest wall had a floor-to-ceiling bookshelf full of my ever-growing collection, some titles I have cherished since childhood. Though I was a full-time artist and illustrator, I was also a voracious reader. For as early as I can remember, if I wasn't drawing, I would be reading; and if I wasn't reading, I was drawing.

I powered up my MacBook Air and checked my email since I'd been off the radar for the past few days. I sent a few replies and pulled out one of my sketchbooks.

My interest in art started when I was a little girl and has now become a fiery passion. I vividly recall only wanting a new set of crayons and a new coloring book for a birthday or Christmas. Reading and drawing are both my favorite pastimes. Depending on the mood I was in, they were equally therapeutic. I could never decide between them; they both created an escape whenever I needed one.

I'd inherited the art gene and my love of reading from my father. He always encouraged Daijah and me to read from the very beginning.

When Dad discovered I had an artistic gift, he encouraged me to draw daily and challenge myself. I took his advice to heart, capturing everything on paper. I'd draw for hours, filling up more sketchbooks than I could count over the years. My father was a tremendous support, investing in me, paying for art classes and summer workshops, and stressing the importance of honing my craft as a creative. And I kept drawing and creating, always carrying a sketchbook with me.

Most artists do. You truly never know when inspiration will strike. A sketchbook is an instant canvas to capture inspiration on the fly. Any creative person would agree that ideas can go as quickly as they appear. I've found that having a sketchbook handy ensures I can get the blueprint down and explore it later on. That's a regular occurrence for me.

Daijah has always encouraged me to share my art with the public, but I am super shy—inherently so. I don't post any of my work on my social media platforms, and I don't have much presence on social media, period. However, I share my gift with the world by being a muralist. Since I started, I haven't stopped contributing in some capacity to more than two hundred murals in the past eight years.

If someone told me that volunteering for a mural those years ago would bring me here, I wouldn't have believed it. One of the project sponsors liked my art so much that I was offered a year-long contract, *on the spot*, doing window lettering for a few major retailers in the area. That was so cool, and I learned so much from that experience. I'll always be grateful because things exploded for me after that.

Humming along to Mary J. Blige, I scanned my assortment of more than three dozen illustration pens. I finally decided on my go-to Pigment Liner. It was my favorite pen to work with. I flipped to the next available page in my sketchbook, and in no time, I was well into the groove of my creative genius.

Several songs later, I faintly heard my cell phone ringing. I looked around, realizing I had left it in the kitchen when I returned for another cup of tea. I retrieved my phone from the kitchen, extremely enthralled to see Micah's name on my screen.

My grin was back. "Hello."

"Hey Destiney. Is this a good time?"

seven

MICAH

"This is a great time," Destiney said. Unbeknownst to her, she was damn near seducing me with the lullaby of her soft voice. I turned to my back and propped my arm behind my head, instantly feeling calm. I was fresh out of the shower since returning from the park, so glad the rain had stopped, and the courts weren't too wet for Gabe and me to shoot around for a while. He was a great basketball player and full of energy, of course. Gabe whooped my ass out there. But if I'm honest, my game was off, consumed with thoughts of Destiney. My face lit up when I got her text, and I was eager to return to the house and call her.

"So, how's the cold?"

"A lot better. I expect to return to work tomorrow."

"Glad to hear that. For your information, my offer still stands if you need me to bring you anything," I reminded her.

She chuckled lightly. "Are your niece and nephew still over?"

"Yeah, my brother Malachi and his wife will be back tomorrow afternoon. I'll take them to school on my way to work in the morning."

"Do they stay over often?"

"Oh yeah, this is their second home. And I love those two with my whole heart." I said that with my chest. They were so special to me.

"They're blessed to have you." Our conversation flowed. "So, are you the older brother?"

"Baby brother. I'm taller, though."

"Are you really?"

"Yeah, since about junior high. Man, he used to hate it too." We both cackled. "But I only have him by an inch or so. And we're only eleven months apart. Damn near twins and extremely close."

"That's beautiful."

"What about you?" I quizzed. "Any siblings?"

"One younger sister, we're a year and a half apart. And she's taller than me." We laughed again.

"Serious?"

"Oh yeah. It happened around the same time for us, too. The summer before I was to start eighth grade, and she was to start seventh grade, she sprouted several inches," she continued. "I'm short, but she's really tall."

"Wow."

"We're close too. She's my best friend."

"Love that."

"Me too."

"How old are you, Destiney?"

"You're not supposed to ask a woman her age." I could hear the sarcasm in her voice.

"You're too young for that rule to apply to you."

She laughed, "I'm joking with you. I just turned twenty-seven. You?"

"Oh, you're just a baby. I'm thirty-four."

"I'm a grown ass woman."

I gasped, my theatrics on display, "No way, you curse?"

"All the damn time."

We both cackled again. "You watch that pretty mouth of yours," I teased.

There was a comfortable silence.

"So why me?" Destiney asked after a beat.

"Why you what?"

"Why was I the lucky customer picked to answer your question?"

I was transparent with no hesitation, "Your vibe. Your energy."

It was true.

Destiney had such a feminine aura—it was clearly one of her superpowers. I was only in her presence briefly, but it was comforting and soft. "I watched you for a second before I spoke to you. You're so beautiful and intriguing to watch, might I add. So why not you?" I stated rhetorically.

"Thank you." I could hear her smiling, and I pictured it mentally. She had a beautiful smile.

"I have to say that I'm so glad you did ask me. I may not have stopped otherwise. I tend to have blinders on when I'm out and about. I've often been told that I need to be better about that. More observant of my surroundings."

"I would agree, especially when you're out alone. A beautiful woman is a moving target."

"You've used that word a lot these past few days."

"What, beautiful?" I asked entirely in jest. I already knew.

"Mmm-hmm."

"Since meeting you, your beautiful face is all I've managed to think about. Now I'm wondering how I'm supposed to get any work done tomorrow." I was serious.

"I'm sure you'll manage, Micah."

Well damn.

I loved the way my name rolled off her tongue.

I loved her voice. It was the most beautiful melody in my ear. Demure and soft. But not in a ditzy, damsel-in-distress kind of way.

Not only was she beautiful, but she also had something else going on.

It was a fact Destiney was channeled into her femininity and that shit was super sexy.

Subconsciously, I felt my primal instincts awaken, and I wanted to handle her as delicately as possible. That may be why I insisted on offering to take care of her.

At least, that's what I was telling myself.

"So."

"What's up?"

"What happened with your last relationship? You are single, right?" I was joking with that last question. Destiney was too classy of a woman to entertain me beyond pleasantries if she already had a man. I could tell that much off rip. I knew she was single; hell, I was glad she was single. But I was curious why any man would let her get away.

Her soft chuckle cruised through the line, "I am very single."

I chuckled too. "Good to know."

"You are too, I take it?"

"Single as a pringle."

"Wow." She laughed heartily this time. When she calmed down, she answered, "To answer your question though… my last official relationship was in high school. I was just a teenager. So… not much to speak on relative to that."

My head drew back; my eyes grew wide. "You said high school?"

Shit. That would mean a decade ago.

"Yeah. I mean, I've dated a few guys since then, but… nothing serious ever really panned out."

"Hmm."

"I sound like a weirdo to you now?"

"No, no, no. Not at all, sweetheart. I enjoyed getting to know you. Everything about you: please know you can speak freely with me. Always."

"I appreciate that."

"Indeed." I certainly wasn't judging her. My last relationship wasn't recent, either. Not even a little bit.

"What about you?" She volleyed.

"My last serious relationship was in college. Like you, I've dated a little since then. But."

"Nothing to write home about?"

"Nope."

"Dating can be a lot." She sighed lightly. "Not to sound like that girl, but... it seems daunting. Repetitive. Bleak. Damn near depressing sometimes."

"Oh, I hear you!" I couldn't help my light chuckle. "And though I don't date often, I try not to focus on that part. Instead, I see it as an opportunity to get to know someone new. I've also learned a lot about myself dating. Learning from my mistakes. My philosophy is not time wasted, but a learning experience. You know what I mean? Life is full of lessons, and they come in many forms. Even crap ass hell dates."

Destiney laughed, "I'm compelled to agree." After a beat, "Typically, college relationships are a bit more serious. What happened with you two?"

I sighed lightly, considering how much I wanted to share. Then, I quickly decided to put it all out in the open. In my mind, it was the best way to establish what I deemed as a new friendship between us.

I could only hope, sincerely, that Destiney didn't run for the hills after my confession.

"We met our sophomore year. Down at Cal Poly, San Luis Obispo."

"Nice."

"Yeah. We found out we were both from Sac, which was cool. Anyway, we were inseparable. And things were serious. We were engaged by the end of junior year."

"Engaged?" She replied, surprised, "What happened?"

This time, I released a heavy sigh. "It seemed like the right thing to do. At the time. Getting engaged. Like a natural progression. My brother was married, and I felt pressure, which I've since realized was all a figment of my imagination. I did care about her. I loved her. Very much. But... we saw things differently. Things that mattered a lot to me didn't mean as much to her." I shook my head. "My mind was a mess. My heart was conflicted. I wanted... I needed to be sure. She deserved certainty. So, a few months before the day we were to be married, I asked for a break. Just to pray and get my head in the right place. You know."

"Yeah."

"I called it all off in the end."

"Wow."

Wow is right.

This shit still got to me. Even now, nearly twelve years later. "I hurt her. But I've made peace with my decision. The momentary disappointment was worth avoiding the severe heartbreak I knew would come later had I gone through with it. I cared enough about her to let her go." I sighed heavily again, but I was relieved. It felt good to share this with Destiney. I hadn't spoken of this out loud in years.

Something else that occasionally crossed my mind: lightning doesn't strike in the same place twice. It's not as simple as just finding another one.

I wondered if I'd fumbled my one.

I certainly didn't toss her aside, thinking that I'd replace her with a better model.

I wondered sometimes if I tried hard enough. There's compromise, and then there are deal breakers. I thought maybe I'd given up on us too soon. And I wondered, if I had sought out counseling to address my inner issues or something, could I have salvaged our relationship?

Destiney pulled me from my thoughts, "Well, thank you for sharing this. I get the feeling it's somewhat of a sensitive topic for you."

"I guess so. Yeah." She had no idea the emotions that had come flooding back just sharing that with her. But I was glad she knew this part of me. Taking a page from her book, I queried, "What are you thinking? I sound like a weirdo to you now?"

Her lively chuckle was back again. "No. No. No. No. Not at all." She sounded sincere. I was convinced.

And.

She was so adorable. A contented "Mmm" is what I gave her. My fret having already melted away.

"I respect you, Micah. Even more so now. Your vulnerability. Your honesty. Your transparency. She isn't here to speak for herself, but your kindness and consideration, despite how things ended with the two of you, speaks to your character."

Well.

Can't say I expected that. But I was good with it; we

could definitely do something here. Granted, she didn't disappear on me after this. For some reason, I didn't get the feeling she would.

We chatted for a while longer. When the time came, I hated hanging up with her, but I had to get some dinner on the table for Gabe and Gabby girl. Destiney had to get ready to head out to work tomorrow. It seemed she didn't want our conversation to end either.

The plan was to chat again tomorrow evening.

And... *I already couldn't wait.*

eight

MICAH

A few days later, I was at my parents' house, putting eyes on them.

The rain and wind we had days ago left the backyard fence slightly leaning. After surveying it, Daddy and I figured adding some reinforcements back there would be a good idea. This prompted a trip to the home improvement store. I'd already made a mental note that Mal and I would replace the entire fence later this spring.

"Let's head over and get some post-ups. Take a ride with your old man."

"I'll be right out behind you, Daddy."

Between Malachi and me, one of us was checking in at home base every couple of days. They still lived in our childhood home. Mal and I lovingly called it the blue house. My mom's favorite color is robin's-egg blue, and that's the color it's painted. With a crisp white trim. For as long as I can remember. We've given the house a fresh coat a few times over the years.

When I made it out the front door, I found my father in the driver's seat of his pickup truck, the engine purring, waiting for me.

"I can drive us, Daddy."

"I got it. Come on here."

I didn't argue, just proceeded around to the passenger's side. Mal and I drove them as often as possible. When they allowed us to, that is. Though Mommy didn't seem to mind, Daddy was holding on tight. I fell back without retort each time he resisted. Daddy was fiercely independent, and I understood.

We made our way to the local home improvement store, driving with the windows down; the fresh air felt good on my face. I loved to see the sun out and all those heavy clouds and rain finally gone, at least for the time being. We cruised toward our destination, and Daddy had talk radio on.

As far back as my memory serves, we were always tuned into talk radio in Daddy's truck. He loved music but not in the car. We listened to music for hours at home, but it was always talk radio in his truck. That was his thing. I didn't mind it though. He mentioned once that had he seized the opportunity to finish college, he would have pursued broadcast journalism and made his mark in sports talk radio somewhere. He certainly had the voice for it. The texture of his voice had only grown richer with age. I'd inherited my deep timbre directly from him.

Daddy and I listened intently to the three gentlemen talking about the latest in the world of sports as we enjoyed the ride. This was how things were with my old man. He was seriously the easiest person to be around. He wasn't a man of many words. But anytime he decided to bestow his wisdom, it was always welcomed.

"I can't believe Mal and Ella are at year number fifteen. That's bananas!" I broke our silence after a good while.

Daddy nodded, and I saw the trace of a smile. "Seems like no time at all, doesn't it? He said they had a great time in Cabo."

"I bet they did. Missed all this rain, that's for sure."

"No doubt." After a few beats, "What did you three Musketeers get into?" Referring to Gabe, Gabby, and me.

I chuckled, "It was a low-key few days, relaxing around the house. But we enjoyed each other's company. Gabby was mostly on the computer, working on something for school. Gabe had a new game we tried out, and that was cool. The rain stopped long enough for Gabe and me to play a little ball, too."

"Oh yeah?"

"Yeah. You know he whooped my butt out there! He's getting good!"

Daddy released a lively chuckle. "Oh, did he? That's my boy. Bet that shut you up!" He continued laughing heartily, and I joined him, shaking my head. Everyone knew full well I could get a little competitive out there.

"Man! I didn't think he'd get away from me, but he showed out!" It seemed a tad premature to tell Daddy I was actually distracted the entire time. The beautiful woman I encountered with the angelic voice had since captivated my every thought and was living rent-free in my head.

Destiney was a beautiful distraction, and I didn't mind it one bit.

Riding shotgun alongside my father on this beautiful sunny afternoon was nothing but nostalgia. If it weren't for my hesitation, I would have told Daddy all about our exchange and subsequent conversations. Sparing no details. As an inquisitive child, I always loved talking to my old man while we took a ride somewhere in his truck. It was, by far, one of my favorite childhood memories. There were so many pivotal conversations in this setting over the years.

I took another route instead.

"Daddy?"

"Yup?"

"I wonder sometimes if I'll ever find my wife. The older I get, the more I find myself wondering. Do you think marriage is in the cards for me?"

Daddy was quiet, as usual. He tapped his thumbs along the steering wheel and took his time musing over my question. Whenever we came to him with a loaded question like this, he didn't rush about it. Every word he spoke was given thought and intention, which I appreciated immensely. I do my very best to demonstrate the same.

"Have you prayed about it?" He finally spoke.

Not sure why, but my head reared back slightly.

I certainly wasn't surprised. I was a man of faith after all. Prayer was an integral part of my life and my upbringing. I gave his question some thought. In true Daddy fashion he cut the radio off as we continued cruising down the highway giving me space to consider what he'd asked. Mal and I used to get so frustrated when he answered our question with a question. We couldn't appreciate it then, but there was so much value in that. In hindsight I realized he was fostering critical thinking. Often, we had the answer all along, we just needed to consider things from another perspective. As I prepared to answer him, I knew I had to be honest.

I hadn't.

"You know Daddy... I can't say I have prayed that prayer specifically."

Daddy nodded and took a few more moments, always exhibiting a gentle approach in his encouragement. "When you get on your knees tonight, call this out. Make your request known. And ask for a sign. Then, you put in the work." I nodded as I listened intently. So glad for this time together and his wisdom. Always there to help, guide and inspire and I loved that so much about Daddy. He continued, "You can dream, wish and hope. But you must put action behind it. Faith without work is dead. Not only must you believe for it, but you work to secure it. Just as you would with anything else you desire to achieve." He quickly glanced at me, and I met his eyes. My same eyes twenty-five years older and wiser. "A man who finds a wife finds a good thing."

Your good thing is out there son. You pray about it, and then you see about finding her."

I knew it was soon. Really soon to feel so strongly.

But I felt like I had found something good in her.

Yes, she was gorgeous and adorable and sweet. And her vibe was fire. But I felt something else. Far beyond the surface.

I couldn't wait to get to know her.

I really couldn't wait to see her again.

Praying silently right then and there I asked God to reveal to me if she was the one.

I hoped she'd be the one.

I wanted so badly for her to be the one.

nine

DESTINEY

"Hey beautiful."

"Hey you," I said casually, trying to play it cool, but I smiled from ear to ear seeing Micah's name on my screen. We'd been talking for a couple weeks now, and it was still happening. And the way he made me feel, it likely wouldn't stop happening.

"I catch you at a bad time?"

"Not at all, this is the perfect time." I sat up straight on the couch, placing my iPad beside me. I was reading the past hour, getting utterly lost in a love story.

And the sex.

Especially the sex.

The indie urban and contemporary romance authors I followed did not play around when it came to this, and I was here for all of it. I suppose it was partly because it was the closest I'd ever come to experiencing the real thing. But I was making do.

All I had to do was dive into a book by one of my favorite indie authors and I was set. The erotic novella I was currently reading was hot! Hot! Hot! I could focus on very little else once I started it. I'm a fast reader and I typically devour title after title. Steamy novellas are my very favorite. My daily streak on record was more than five hundred days. Yup. Almost two years straight. My schedule could get hectic sometimes, but I always find time to read every day. Even if it's just a page or two. I took another sip of my tea. I just made it, so it was still hot, and I slurped a bit louder than I meant to.

"What you got over there?" My embarrassment melted instantly by Micah's playful tone.

"Cup of tea. It's how I relax at the end of the day."

"Definitely a great way to relax. What kind of tea?"

"Chai."

"Chai is a great choice."

"Totally agree. It's my favorite." Chai was always tricky for me. Too much sugar was too sweet to enjoy; too much cinnamon made it spicy. Tonight, I accomplished the perfect ratio, and this cup was everything.

"Indeed. You prefer tea over coffee?"

"One hundred percent!" I replied eagerly. "I don't mind iced coffee on occasion, but tea is my go-to. I can drink tea any time of day. Any day of the week. What about you?"

"Expresso for me. Only now and then."

"I'm always wired when I have an expresso. If you can even imagine. I'm already on ten most days anyway." We both laughed. "So how was your day?" I asked him.

"Productive overall, but busy. Glad to have you in my ear, helping me relax."

Oh shit.

Micah's voice was already beginning to unravel me. Moments before his call I read an explosive sex scene... now his deep voice was in my ear.

Doing things.

"Glad it was productive," I managed, bypassing the rest.

"Yes, it was. How was your day?"

"Productive as well. I met with some high-schoolers this afternoon and they want to paint a mural in their campus theatre. We're brainstorming some ideas."

"Oh yeah?"

"Yeah. These kids are talented with dope concepts. I'm excited to get started."

"Nice. You work with kids most of the time?"

"Depends on the project. Community work will bring in all walks of life. I've worked with kids of all ages. Preschoolers up to high school and college. I've worked with seasoned citizens. Everything in between."

"What's your favorite age group?"

"I enjoy working with them all as long as I get to create something in the process."

"Indeed." That made me smile. I was learning Micah and noticed he said "indeed" a lot. I also noticed how much he enjoyed getting to know me. Things that didn't seem significant about me mattered to him. It was sweet and I felt seen.

And special.

My tea seemed slightly cooler, so I took a few hearty swallows. Warming my throat as it traveled down.

"So. Did I cross your mind at all today?"

I froze. As if Micah could see me. I also damn near choked.

"You alright over there?"

"Ye…" I coughed several times, "Yes, I'm fine thank you."

Once Micah knew I was good he continued, "I'll have you know that I thought about you all day long, wondering if you were thinking of me too. I must admit, I'm constantly thinking of you, Destiney baby."

Baby?

Oh.

Oh. This was a new one. I liked it.

Also, note to self: Micah was a straight shooter. That's certainly a good thing.

But I wasn't ready. And my ass needed to buckle up.

"Really?"

"Yes. Why does that surprise you?" He countered.

I pondered for a moment. "I don't know. You're a busy man. And I guess I didn't think I was that interesting."

Micah thought that was so funny. "You've had me intrigued from the moment I saw you. There are so many things I want to know."

Well.

"What would you like to know? I'm an open book," I said, "You've given me a safe space; I'm comfortable sharing anything you ask me." I was partially honest. It was true. I was comfortable and I wanted to share with him. But I was fiercely shy too. Clearly, I had a crush on him which made me feel... silly? Hell, I don't know. That feeling girls feel when a guy they like is paying attention to them.

Whatever that is. That's exactly how I felt.

"I'm happy to hear I'm doing something right," Micah said.

"Now you sound a little surprised."

He chuckled again. "Come on now, don't leave me hanging. You never answered my question."

I paused for a beat. Then, "Let me put it this way; I'm so glad to hear your voice. I've missed you," I effortlessly shared.

"Hmm." That sounded damn good in my ear, but I pretended not to notice. "Now, to answer your question. I wonder what goes on in that pretty head of yours." He continued, "I said I was intrigued a minute ago. And I am. But that word doesn't truly interpret conceptually what I feel when it comes to you."

My eyes grew wide, and my lips parted.

Shit.

Micah carried on, "Enchanted? That too. But... captivated? That's it. Captivated. You are so beautiful. And... you have a vivid imagination, colorful language, you're so expressive. Passionate. Well spoken. Words aren't big enough for your ideas. Your mind is fascinating." He was silent for a beat, but it was a heavy pause, "Were you the type to daydream as a young girl?"

Somehow, after all that I found my voice, "I was. Always daydreaming."

How'd he even know?

"Mmm." Micah seemed pleased with that. "Destiney, I happen to think you are extremely interesting," he said matter of fact.

"Thank you. You intrigue me too. Deep conversations are clearly your specialty. I enjoy our talks. You should also know you have the calmest, most soothing voice I've ever heard. It's crazy where my mind wanders when you're talking to me." I didn't mean to say that last part out loud. Now I was curious if the arousal I felt could be detected in my voice.

"Is that right?"

Well shit.

Micah didn't wait for a response, "Your voice is also calming. Light. So sweet in my ear. You're likely great at reading bedtime stories," he paused, "And pillow talk."

I giggled nervously. "Never tested that theory."

Micah chuckled. "I also imagine how you might sound when you're being pleased and when something feels good to you."

I definitely felt my pussy awaken. I held my breath, taken aback but turned on by his bluntness. I slowly released the breath I was holding. Then,

"Now I'm curious about the same." Surprised by my revelation.

We had a few beats of comfortable silence. And I desperately needed to change the subject.

And my panties.

"So, Micah?" I seized the opportunity before he said something else because I had no idea how I could possibly handle whatever came next.

"Yes?"

"What do you most look forward to?"

"I look forward to many things. Traveling, making memories, having a family of my own. A wife. Children. These are all so cliche, but the fact is, I have everything else."

"That isn't cliché at all. I look forward to some of those same things," I replied, gulping down the last bit of my tea. I sat back on the couch, resting more comfortably. "At some point we realize what matters most and what will sustain us when all the temporary things are long gone."

"Agreed. I came to that realization a long time ago."

Micah was a beautiful man saying all the right things. I felt so comfortable.

"Now, this is completely off the record. But I'm a pleaser, and I look forward to pleasing you. In all the ways."

My breath hitched in my throat. My face grew warm, and I knew I was blushing. Thankfully he couldn't see me. "Do you really?" I somehow managed, my demure feelings surfacing. I wasn't sure of what else to say.

"All the time."

I took a moment to gather myself. I had a feeling there was more to come on this. But how could he say that so casually? My mind was going a million miles a minute.

"And... whenever you're ready... I look forward to kissing you."

Shit.

I was not expecting that. But I loved that he told me. And he was such a gentleman about it.

Surprising myself I said, "I look forward to kissing you too."

***

So, I've been giving Daijah the latest. A play by play in real time.

And so far, she loved everything she heard about Micah. One afternoon some days ago, she came home in the mood to tease me. I was in the office working on a commissioned design and she leaned into the office doorway.

"Hey Des."

"Hey Day."

"Catching feelings, are we?" Daijah jested.

I spun around in my chair, finding the silliest grin on her face. I knew she was giving me a hard time because she knew I'd built a wall complete with a fucking barbed wire fence around me.

"That's random." I suppressed my smile as best as I could. When Daijah returned a knowing expression, I shrugged my shoulders. "Maybe?"

"Ain't no maybe! I love this for you sissy. Don't fight it. Go with it. You're already there anyway."

67

My brows dipped. Not that I disagreed. That was my exact sentiment.

"You are all smiles lately. You're always smiling and bubbly anyway, but you are beaming so bright these days," she nodded with that silly grin again. "You are sprung sissy."

"Aww man. I guess I am."

"Are you afraid to be?"

"Maybe a little bit. But I trust Micah. He is such a good guy Day."

That shit was crazy because it was exactly as she predicted when I first told her about Micah. And it was very soon after meeting him, but I couldn't contain myself.

"So, I met someone."

"Okay." Daijah was deadpan with that one, returning an empty stare, waiting for the punchline. I always got attention from men, but it was never worth mentioning as I didn't often entertain them beyond a respectable hello.

"I gave him my number."

Her eyebrows went high on her head.

"And we've been talking for the past two weeks. Texting, talking. We text and talk all day long."

"Oh damn," she said, suddenly interested. "You like this one."

"I really do."

"Tell me about him."

"He's thirty-four. Tall, handsome. Incredibly sweet."

"Sounds like he's already made quite the impression on you."

"He absolutely has."

"I'm excited for you."

I smiled wide. "I'm excited too. I've already told him so much about you sibling bestie."

It was her turn to smile. "Aww. I hope I live up to the hype."

"Of course you will," after a beat, "So, what do you have planned rest of the night?"

"Wash some clothes. Julian's picking me up around nine."

I looked at my watch. "You're always leaving me," I whined with a dramatic sad face to match.

Daijah chuckled. "Don't say it like that. In a minute you won't even be worried about what I'm doing. You'll be up under your man every chance you get. I think you forgot how much you like that shit. You're such an affectionate person. You like being close to the people you're fond of. Especially someone special to you. What's his name?

"Micah."

"Oh damn! Look at the way you said it!" Her eyes were wide. Her smile too. "You're getting the feels already. That's a good thing. I'm so happy for you sissy!"

That was weeks ago, and I've already accepted that as a fact.

If I'm not careful I am going to fall in love.

That much I knew for sure.

What have I gotten myself into?

ten

DESTINEY

I was bleeding again.

I was constantly bleeding.

It was as unpredictable as it was painful.

Unbearably painful. Not only that, but I would bleed for several days. Ten days or more were typical. And the pain is so intense that some days I can't get out of bed.

Like this morning. The churning and clamping of my damn uterus woke me up.

And a sanguineous presence akin to a fucking crime scene.

For years, I thought it was just a normal part of everything.

My normal.

I assumed I just had heavy, painful cycles.

I am fiercely shy and get embarrassed easily, so I tend to keep personal and private matters to myself. Mostly out of desperation, I opened up to Daijah, sharing these details, and she told me I needed to see an OB/GYN.

Like, yesterday.

I was twenty-three years old when I finally saw a doctor about it, and that's when I was diagnosed with uterine fibroids. That was four years ago, and back then, it wasn't terribly hard to manage. Uncomfortable, sure. I was living with it as best as I could. Managing. But it's gotten progressively worse—especially these past few months.

Lately, it's been horrendous.

The debilitating cramps.

The bleeding between periods.

These days the bleeding lasts much longer, and it's been so heavy I've had accidents while in public. The blood has ruined my clothing. My current wardrobe consists of cheap black leggings. Black leggings that I have no problem throwing away if necessary.

I've had to set multiple alarms throughout the night, so that I don't ruin my bedding.

I learned that the hard way.

The "monthly curse" has taken a whole new meaning for me. Except it wasn't even monthly. It was all the time, weeks at a time and heavy. All the time. As of late, I spend more time bleeding than not. It's like three weeks on and one week off and it's hardly predictable.

I've bled so much, and my iron is so low, I am now considered anemic. I also had to have a couple blood transfusions. Worst of all, during this time I am often exhausted. My energy can be scarce sometimes. Or just plain nonexistent. And I hate that.

I miss myself.

The old me.

Anyway, since things have progressively worsened my doctor is suggesting surgery. As much as I don't want to get surgery, I'm so desperate I'm leaning closer to making this decision with each passing day.

And... it was the irony of it all for me. When I told Daijah I had to laugh about it. Wasn't shit funny but maybe I laughed to keep from crying.

God really had a sense of humor.

Me meeting Micah of all places in the tampon aisle.

An aisle I spent more time in than I cared to admit.

I tried them all. I settled on a combination of reusable pads, period panties, and a diva cup on the days that had mercy on me and the flow was light enough. I used so many disposable pads that I felt

71

convicted. I had to reduce my carbon footprint and not clog up the landfill.

Also, I'm saying this parenthetically; I remember thinking that I could imagine my father being in the same situation Micah was in at some point. Needing guidance on what to get for Daijah and me.

So, there you have it.

That is the reason I shy away from men. I knew relationships would eventually lead to a desire for closeness. Not just on his part either. We would desire closeness. And intimacy. And eventually, sex.

Sex wasn't something I could offer anyone right now.

Not anytime soon. I honestly don't know if it's something I could ever offer.

My female department did not appear promising. There were a few unknown variables, and I couldn't guarantee much of anything.

And that shit was depressing.

Anyway, it's been ages since I'd been in a committed relationship, but I have dated a few guys.

And I've always dated men a little older than me. I didn't intentionally seek them out, but it always worked out that way somehow. We just got each other. I've been told many times that I have an old soul. And... if im objective, men my age bore me.

I need psychological and emotional stimulation.

Multidimensional. Provoking. Engrossing stimulation.

Without it, my ass was checking all the way out.

Micah had all the above on lock. Micah is by far the sweetest guy ever. He was also seven years older than me. Go figure.

I supposed I would date again, but I know I'm selective as hell. I've had a couple "almost, but not quite".

I could also admit that I could take things a little more seriously.

That's the first thing.

I was too old for this self-sabotage thing. If that's what you even called it.

For example, there was a guy named Zeke that I hung out with now and then. He really had a thing for me. Like he really, really liked me. Once he told me that I was his dream girl. That was incredibly sweet.

And I liked him too. Honestly, I did.

At the time I was twenty-five and he was thirty-one. We hung out several times; sometimes out somewhere, other times at his house. We were never intimate, but we kissed plenty of times.

I remembered him being a gentleman and always sweet to me when we hung out. He always wanted to see me, and it wasn't like I was super busy, I just never really made it a priority.

One Saturday I went to his apartment unannounced, and he was so glad to see me, he hugged me and invited me in immediately. When I stepped inside, I saw that he had one of his boys over and they were watching the game. Zeke was thrilled to introduce us. Since he wasn't expecting me and already had company, I offered to come back another time, but he insisted I stay because the game was almost over.

So, I went to watch tv in his bedroom and at some point, I fell asleep. I must have been sleeping for a while because he'd covered me with a blanket. When I went back to the living room, he hugged me again and took me to the kitchen. He had ordered takeout from a Thai place.

Thai is one of my favorites. Like, top three.

I only mentioned that one time, but he remembered that detail. It was crazy too because as he warmed the food, he told me he was hungry as hell but was waiting for me to wake up so we could eat together. My ass wouldn't have been able to wait as good as that food smelled.

Zeke and I were never official, and had I taken things more seriously we would have headed in that direction. He wanted to be. I evaded that. I don't have any excuses, but I didn't really give things with Zeke my best. I was never mean to him but what I did was mean and inconsiderate. I feel bad as hell thinking back on it. If I ever missed his call, I never made an effort to call him back right away. I avoided making concrete plans with him whenever he asked to see me.

I remember the last time he called me; whatever the reason, I didn't answer so he left me a voicemail. I had completely forgotten about it and didn't check my voicemail till a few days later.

"Hey Destiney, it's Zeke... how you doing? Been thinking bout you... miss you... been wanting to lay eyes on you. I'm trying to give you space because it seems that's what you need... but I don't know because you won't really tell me what you need. Anyway... I guess that's just how it is right?"

74

He sounded frustrated. And I couldn't blame him. I remember feeling horrible, but I never even called him back. He was a great guy, and he deserved love and happiness. I hope he found it. I know he would make someone very happy.

I didn't know how else to maneuver the dating pool. That was a personal problem of mine. I could admit that. I'm a complicated person. And I really needed to stay out of it. Which I generally did. And I guess I wasn't missing out on much. Apparently, the dating pool was full of piss.

I had Neeka in my ear telling me all about it.

Neeka was a serial dater and was tenacious as hell. Her ass was determined to find her husband. I told her she shouldn't have to look so hard, but what did I know? My ass was single too.

My feelings were all over the damn place and I was extremely guarded. I hadn't always been, but over time, something switched somewhere.

And something else crazy was that I had a way of leading someone to believe I would entertain them beyond a conversation, but they'd end up disappointed. I didn't do that shit on purpose. Honest to God. I was just being myself. I'm an intellectual. Apparently, men like that because it always happens that way. It came as no surprise. I am attractive to intelligent men. And I'm extremely attracted to them.

I'm a sapiosexual through and through. Conversations are my specialty and my weakness. Especially deep conversations.

I can converse with anyone about almost anything even if I wasn't doing much of the talking. I'm easily intrigued by many different things. I love to coexist with people opposite me, I'll inquire to the point where I'll eventually ask them twenty-one questions. Those questions would beget more, and before we knew it, we would be waist deep. I especially love to nerd out when we uncover commonalities.

But... those amazing conversations do not lead to any lasting relationships.

Mainly because I don't allow them to. I've done enough introspection to admit that.

Daijah has tried to set me up a few times, but things never quite panned out.

I wasn't taking it seriously enough.

Some months ago, Daijah begged me to double date with her, Julian, and Julian's coworker. He and Julian were good friends, and I'd met him once or twice in passing but didn't think anything more of him. Frankly I wasn't paying him any attention. I acquiesced since he was a nice guy and seemed pleasant enough to be around.

The four of us went to a bowling alley and he and I talked a lot. He had a great conversation, and I genuinely enjoyed his company. When the night ended, and he asked for my number I had to let him down. He brushed it off but had inquired about me again a few times. He also seemed always conveniently to be around for something or another. Twice, I'd gone to pick up Daijah from Julian's house, and she asked me to come in and there he was sitting on the couch in the living room.

Later, Daijah revealed that he'd asked if she could get me to come out on the double date and he'd had his eye on me for a while. By then I figured as much.

Eventually we did have that conversation, and I told him it was nothing personal.

And it wasn't. I was being honest. I just wasn't really interested in pursuing anything right now. To be real, I may have considered it if I was in a different headspace.

And not bleeding all over the damn place.

When he asked about being friends, I had to shut that shit down too. I know how I am. I could never just be friends with a guy. Like ever. Tried that. I don't do opposite sex friendships. They aren't good for me.

Feelings always ended up being involved.

Either the guy would end up liking me, or I'd end up having a crush on him.

It honestly wouldn't take much for me to grow sweet on him. If we were friends, we'd be talking a lot, sharing life moments and being there for one another. I'd end up being vulnerable and before I knew it my ass would have caught some damn feelings.

Anyway, I told him, hypothetically, I'd only be friends with him if we were going to explore a relationship. When he asked for a ballpark timeline, I encouraged him to move on.

I'm not even sure what his relationship status is now. I don't think he's married but who knows.

And that's why things were so crazy when it came to Micah.

Micah was the first man in a while to truly intrigue me. And intrigued I was.

We spoke daily. For hours. And our conversations were fire. We'd even graduated to FaceTime which I loved. I looked forward to our talks each night. And my feelings were growing.

By now, I was so into him. My little crush had taken off full steam ahead.

I was always giddy every time my phone chimed. Hoping it was him texting me. And when it was, my face lit up. Bright as a Christmas tree.

I was absolutely sprung. From our first conversation.

Micah was kind. Intelligent. Charming. And handsome of course but his quiet confidence and awareness of himself just did it for me. He moved with a quiet swag I was into. His wisdom and maturity absolutely had something to do with my attraction. I couldn't even say what it was exactly. We just seemed to have something. A spark. Magnetism. I didn't know… I felt deep in my gut that it would lead to something amazing. I really liked the way he handled me. And talked to me. I loved it. And I couldn't help but imagine being his. And how beautiful it would be.

I'd never given relationships much thought. I didn't even think it was in the cards for me.

But Micah had me thinking about all of that. A life together. Love. Marriage. Babies.

I saw the way Daijah had effortlessly fallen for Julian, and I loved that so much for her. It really was a beautiful thing.

I guess… I never thought I'd get a turn.

As much as I tried to keep those thoughts under control, my feelings were already invested. There wasn't anything I could do to stop them either. But I was hesitant. Hesitant to give it a try. Reluctant to let things go and stop fighting it. I worried that if I did, he would want something more with me.

Something I wanted too, but something I couldn't give him.

That scared me because I didn't want to lose Micah.

In the meantime, I was trying to slow things down.

But that was becoming difficult.

eleven

MICAH

"So. What was your first job?"

"Chuck E Cheese."

"Aww for real? You had to sing that birthday song?" I guffawed.

"Shit. A million times."

Destiney and I had been on the phone for the past three hours. We took a break to shower, and I had just called her back on FaceTime. We were both lying in bed. I was on my back, one hand behind my head, my other hand holding the phone. Destiney was lying on her belly resting on her arms, her phone propped nearby. Her beautiful face filling my screen.

Since meeting Destiney those weeks ago, most of our evenings ended the same way. She was the last voice I heard night after night after hours of conversing. I had to admit it was my very favorite part of the day. We talked about so many things and the more I got to know her the more my fondness grew for her.

It was so easy opening up to her. I had nothing to hide but just the same it felt good to feel safe and vulnerable. Our conversations always flowed so smoothly. Flowing like waves, we maneuvered from one topic to the next. I noticed we reminisced about our teenage years a lot. Tonight was no different and we'd segued into talking about our first jobs.

"Good grief!" Destiney roared with me. "Gabe and Gabby had a many birthday parties there. That place is too germ infested for me. Seems like all of them kids have a runny nose and sticky ass fingers."

"Now that's a fact. What was your first job?"

"Ice cream scooper."

"That's adorable. Baskin Robins?" Destiney squealed filling the screen with her bright smile.

"Yep."

"You try all thirty-one flavors?" She asked playfully.

"Just about. Funny thing about it, I'm not a huge fan of ice cream anymore. Even all these years later. I've had one too many free scoops."

"Oh man! I love ice cream," she gushed.

I lightly tittered, telling her, "I used to love ice cream too. In this case the perks can be a bad thing."

Each conversation was an opportunity for me to learn more about Destiney and I loved everything I learned. I always took mental notes, storing things for later. I found out she loved green, any shade, but her favorite was jade. She and her younger sister were incredibly close. She called her Sibling Bestie, and I loved that.

Destiney was also a Daddy's girl, and she spoke of her father all the time. That made my heart so happy. She never spoke of her mother, and I took the hint not to bring her up. I figured when she wanted to talk about her she would. I was curious though.

Recently, as in just a few days ago, I learned she's a vegetarian which fascinated me. She had my interest piqued there since I didn't personally know many black vegetarians.

But she wasn't overt at all.

She didn't force her views onto me about it. I learned of this detail simply because we were talking on Facetime over our lunch break, and we talked about what we were each having. We did this a few days a week and I noticed the trend that she never had any meat and that's when she casually informed me.

And another thing, Destiney loved all things, art. She was so creative. So talented. And she spoke with such excitement about the things that she felt passionate about. She shared a few pictures of some of the work she had done on murals. It was amazing. Sensational. Her passion for art showed itself in her work and I was beyond impressed with her level of talent. The best part was that she was so humble about it.

Destiney possessed a confidence in herself and was so comfortable in her skin. In a classy way.

Theres a sweet spot for the right level of con- fidence. A level that isn't too much. And Destiney had the perfect amount of self-assurance. I've found that only a select group of women can pull it off.

She liked to mention she was super shy on oc- casion, and I picked up on that too. It was adorable honestly. But her confidence was a constant presence. In the best way.

And she was sweet. So sweet. My gosh.

She'd call me sometimes when she was leaving a work site, and I'd hear how she spoke with people. Peers. Counterparts. Colleagues. Associates. Seniors. Children. Superiors. She spoke the same way with all of them. Kindly. Respectfully. Littered with manners, fluff and compliments.

Destiney was a rare breed.

I could dig it. I was into it.

I was into her.

Hella.

"Let me see if I can guess your favorite flavor." I peered at Destiney with low lids with my hand on my chin. As if in deep thought. "Don't tell me."

She grinned, "You won't guess."

"Rocky road?"

"That's Daijah's all-time favorite. But not mine."

"Hmm." I tapped my chin silently.

"What made you guess that?" She asked after a moment.

"You're multi layered a lot like rocky road. An interesting mix."

Smiling she said, "Aww. That's sweet. Want me to tell you now?"

"No, I want another try."

I looked at her and she looked back at me, keeping a straight face. "Mint chocolate chip."

"Oh my gosh that's my least favorite, eww." Destiney laughed after making a gagging sound.

"Least favorite? Why?"

"This is my humble opinion, but Mint flavor belongs in toothpaste or chewing gum not ice cream. There's a school of thought that thinks otherwise but I could never get into mint chocolate chip ice cream."

"I hear you on that. Like the way people can mix savory and sweet. Not my jam either."

"I'll give you one last guess."

"Hmm. Butter pecan?"

"Oh yum, now that's a good one. But not my favorite. It tastes pretty good, but don't you think there's too many nuts?"

"Oh yeah, there's no getting away from those. Like nuts in brownies." I chuckled. "I'm beginning to think you're more complicated than I thought."

"Hey! I'm not complicated. Good ice cream doesn't need nuts. Something already good, doesn't need anything extra. My favorite flavor is vanilla ice cream. Perfectly sweet, not mixed with anything extra."

"Vanilla ice cream huh? Wow. I should have figured."

"Yup. Extra points if it's French vanilla. My grandmother used to make homemade French vanilla ice cream. It's a bit richer because it's made with a custard base. Perfect on top of warm peach cobbler."

"Yum! I can imagine that!" I mused. After a beat, "I know a place near midtown with some of the best ice cream around."

"Really?"

"Yeah, it's called Gunther's. Ever been?"

"Not yet."

"Well, I'd love to take you there. Every ice cream fan must try Gunther's."

"Hmm." Was all she gave me. No longer looking in my eyes, she was now focused on something in the distance.

It wasn't lost on me that she suddenly grew quiet. This was my second time asking her to meet me, and she retreated then, too. As great as our conversations were, I couldn't figure out what I was doing wrong. We'd been talking for about eight weeks now, for hours at a time. I wanted her to be comfortable, but I was eager, I guess.

"You know Micah..." She brought her eyes back to me, pausing, and I waited for her to complete her thought. "Can we take it slow for now?"

"Take it slow?" That question came out before I could stop it, and it was laced with an ounce of sarcasm.

"Yeah, I mean...for right now, I'd love to continue getting to know you better. If that's alright with you."

I sighed lightly. "Is that not what we've been doing? We've been talking for hours night after night. I just want to see you again. I like you, Destiney."

"That's very sweet. I like you too."

"Yeah?"

"Yeah. And I want to see you again too. I'm just not ready yet. But I'll be ready soon."

After a beat, "Tell me when you're ready, and we won't wait a second longer."

"Deal." Her beautiful smile filled the screen again, and I returned one of my own.

Later, after we'd said our goodnights, I was up. Pondering.

I wasn't sure how I would fare taking things slow. But I didn't have an issue trying to figure it out. I could concede that too much too soon could end badly.

We were both intentional about how we wanted to pursue things.

I appreciated courting a woman. I could be patient. Destiney was absolutely worth the pursuit.

I just knew I wanted her. She was beautiful. She was sexy. But I desired to know her so much more. Share space with her. Learn her intricacies.

Destiney captivated my mind, and my thoughts were consumed with her morning, noon, and night. At the same time, I didn't mind doing things differently.

I'd prayed about this, and I wanted this to be it for me.

I wanted her to be it for me. I'd do everything in my power to ensure I didn't fumble this one.

Destiney was precious to me. All of her. Mind, body, soul. Her heart. I was going to handle her accordingly.

And her heart took priority. If she wanted-needed us to take things slow, we would take things slow. It was imperative that I took the time to show her who I was. I wasn't one of those other dudes who only wanted one thing from her. If that meant slow-walking this thing, I was fine with that. I felt good about us and where we were. Most of all, I was never intimidated by a challenge.

I also knew that once we got to the point where we were seeing each other, I would have a whole new world to explore with her. That shit had me excited.

Taking it slow.

I thought about it.

That meant we had an opportunity to get to know each other intimately before any intimacy whatsoever. I'd never touched her. Never kissed her. Aside from the day we met in that drugstore, I never shared any space with her. And yet, I was so far gone for Destiney.

Yet and still... I was perfectly fine with being so gone for her.

twelve

MICAH

"Okay. So, this may seem like a random question..." I told Destiney, then I cracked up. I couldn't see Destiney, but I heard her laugh along with me. Many conversations started this way between us. By now, we've talked about so many things. But we still had many more things to learn about each other.

I reveled in all of this. I enjoyed the process of learning about each other. My fondness for Destiney growing by the day.

Anyway, we were eating dinner together tonight. Kind of.

We both had dinner in front of us. And we were on FaceTime. This was something we did a few days a week.

"No such thing, baby," Destiney volleyed from somewhere nearby. I chuckled at that. I guess she was right. "Hang on just one quick second."

"Take your time." Her phone had been propped up at her kitchen table. And I had my phone propped up in front of me at mine. My plate untouched.

I was waiting for her to start. We always waited for each other.

"You settled?" I asked her once she came back into view.

"Yup. Thank you, baby. Just had to get my water."

"Of course. It's my turn, right?"

"Yes."

I nodded, then prayed over our meals.

We ate in silence at first.

"Beans must be delicious," I teased playfully. She looked up, and I laughed, "Or you were starving. You're so quiet."

She laughed too. "Both! And these beans are perfect. Thank you very much. My best ones yet."

"Nice." Destiney made red beans and rice. We were on the phone yesterday while she picked through them to soak overnight. And she was pretty excited to have them for dinner tonight.

"How's your salmon?" She asked me.

I made honey-glazed salmon and broccoli. "Great. Thank you love."

After a beat, "So what was this random question?" She reminded me.

I nodded. "Right." I forgot for a second. "Can you eat with chopsticks?"

"Yeah? Can you?"

"Yeah. I only learned recently though. So, I'm not that good."

Yes, I was the guy asking for a fork at sushi restaurants.

Destiney gasped dramatically. "No freaking way. Have we discovered something Mr. Wonderful isn't good at?"

I cracked up and said, "Oh, stop it. There are lots of things I'm not good at."

"Not really." She pointedly nodded. "You're perfect at everything." She took a drink of water. "Except for eating with chopsticks, apparently."

I shook my head.

"I'm kidding, baby. You'll get better; keep practicing." She took a few more bites. "So, you like sushi? I take it?"

"Yeah! Love it. You too?"

"Mmhmm. There's always lots of vegetarian options at sushi places."

Naturally, my first instinct was to invite her to get sushi. I knew of some places downtown where we could get the best sushi. And I'd love to take her.

But I knew better than to ask. Suggest. Or imply.

She'd likely shoot me down.

Just the same, it was great to learn that detail. I'd been tucking these things away. I figured that at some point, in the very near future, I could put the info to use.

I hoped so anyway. I wanted to see her. Be close to her.

And last we talked about it, almost two weeks ago, I agreed I would wait for her.

And I was waiting. Patiently. With much anticipation for the very moment, she would tell me she was ready for me.

I've been ready for her.

Looking at her beautiful face on my screen, she seemed so close… yet so far away.

"Good to know." We segued effortlessly once I thought about something else, we hadn't talked about. "So, you a TV fan? Movie fan?"

"I prefer to read or sketch. So, I don't have time for much TV. But when I do, I love a great documentary. Someday, I'm going to make one."

"Oh yeah? Love a great documentary." I was captivated. "What about?" When I thought I had her all figured out, she'd surprise me with something more. She was so multifaceted and intriguing. I loved it when we discovered commonalities too.

"Not sure yet. I'm interested in so many things. I love journalism and great storytelling."

"Same here. There are some great documentaries out there. What are some of your favorites?"

Her eyes lit up. "There's a few. One is called *Whilemina's War*; it's about a small town in South Carolina where the AIDS/HIV epidemic has ravaged the black female population. I watched it years ago, and it was life-changing. So many of the women die of complications related to AIDS and HIV because there are so few programs and funding for them for several miles. I've seen it millions of times.

There's another one called *Carmen and Geoffrey* about a husband and wife who were trailblazers as black dancers in the '30s and '40s, but their careers spanned decades. I love the arts in general, but especially the performing arts. Their story was captivating because they broke down so many barriers for many of the black and brown dancers known today. Misty Copeland wouldn't be where she is without Carmen de Lavallade and Geoffrey Holder."

"Wow. I'd love to see them both."

"I own them both..." Destiney began. And I'll admit, I held my breath. I lightly exhaled when she offered, "Maybe we can watch them sometime."

"I look forward to watching," I replied, not missing a beat.

She looked up at me and smiled. Real big. Her smile was beautiful. "Thank you," she said.

I furrowed my brows. "Thank you?"

"Yes. For caring. You care so much about everything that is me. You're so interested and intentional." I smiled too. "No one's really done that before. Only my dad. He still dotes over Daijah and me." She looked down. "No other man has done the things that you do, Micah." She shook her head. "I'd find myself caring for someone... and sharing my heart with them, and then it turned out to be one-sided."

"Hey, lift that chin, baby." If Destiney were with me right now, I would have gently lifted it myself. When her eyes settled on mine, I said, "Listen, I'm intrigued by everything that is you. And fortunately for me, those yo-yos fucked up."

She giggled, which quickly became a cackle, "Well, it's nice to know my feelings are being reciprocated. And I'm intrigued with you, too, Micah. Everything about you."

I was pleased with that. And though her suggestion was subtle, it seemed we were getting closer to meeting. And I was very anxious to see her again. To share space with her again. It didn't matter what we did; I just wanted to be with her.

***

I'd been hanging out in the VIP area for the past hour and a half enjoying the band, and this band was hot! Smoke was a five-piece band that did impressive covers of some of the greatest R&B hits from the 90s. Malachi and I went to high school with Solomon, the saxophone player. He was badass at the sax, too. And my best friend, next to Malachi. The other fellas in the band were good guys, and we'd have a chance to shoot the breeze every now and then.

A few patrons were on the small dance floor and dozens more at the two bars on either side. This lounge was a great setting for a night out. Going to the club was never my thing, but I didn't mind a lounge on occasion. I hadn't been out in a while and was enjoying myself. I loved the grown folk's vibe of a lounge. The lights were dim, the music was great, and drinks were flowing.

HomeGrownSol was a black-owned bar and lounge in midtown Sacramento and was a pillar in the black community, specifically in the art space. I read an article covering the tenth anniversary of the grand opening that this was the brainchild of two college sweethearts; "She was a starving artist and passionate chef from humble beginnings, he was a business minded philanthropist from old money. They both wanted to open a space to somehow pay it forward".

Anytime I could support them, I would. HomeGrownSol hosted many benefit concerts over the years and offered their space as a venue, often free for a good cause. They generously opened their doors to up-and-coming artists of many genres to play their music and had indie art shows and weekly open mic poetry nights. It was a great place to spend time and meet great people. But my favorite thing about this place was the food. The chef and co-owner of HomeGrownSol could cook her ass off. The vibrant flavors she could capture were incredibly delicious. Her specialty was Black Southern cuisine with Creole, Caribbean, and African influences. Her passion for great food was evident in all her dishes.

Everything on the menu was fire, but the red snapper and spaghetti plate was my favorite. They also had your typical bar food, so there was something for everyone. And speaking of the food, that was the only reason I'd agreed to come out when Ray asked to meet here. I was overdue for my red snapper and spaghetti fix.

Raymond stumbled back into our VIP section and sat down with a curvy brown skinned chick attached to him. Her dress was too tight and way too short, and it was clear ole girl had one too many to drink. She leaned forward to tell Raymond something in his ear and her titties looked as if they were about to fall out of the top of her dress. I looked the other way, taking a swig from my second glass of brandy and coke.

"You hurry back!" Raymond yelled over the music, slapping her ass. She yelped and almost tripped as she stepped down to exit the VIP area. I shook my head and lightly chuckled.

"What?" Raymond looked over at me, oblivious.

"We getting too old for all that."

"I ain't never too old to entertain a beautiful woman!" He flagged down a cocktail waitress and ordered another round of whatever he was drinking.

"I see that," I returned simply, returning my glass to my lips.

"Man, you better get you some of this. Look at these options. Thick, slim, tall, petite, caramel, chocolate, high yella!" Raymond expanded his arms looking around the lounge, "You can take your pick of the litter in this muthafucka!"

"I'm good," I returned. The truth is, I was mentally somewhere else. A pretty girl came a dime a dozen, and at this point, I desired much more than a pretty face. I wasn't impressed by the infinite options of beautiful women surrounding me. I glanced around the lounge. Tonight, there were many. If I had to guess, the women easily outnumbered the men by three to one. In my peripheral, I could see Raymond glaring at me.

"Man, what's going on with you? You ain't moved since we got here."

Raymond's father is my father's older brother, making Raymond my first cousin. My uncle drove long hauls for a living and was gone quite a bit, so Ray spent a lot of time with us when we were kids. At one point, he lived with us. I didn't know much about Ray's mother besides that my uncle never married her. I think I only met her once, as far as I can recall. I think she was an alcoholic, and Ray didn't see much of her as a child. I believe they have somewhat of a relationship now, but I'm not sure to what degree.

Anyway, Ray is a year older than Malachi, which makes him two years older than me. Mal and I were both close to him as kids. And Ray is hilarious. Always keeping things light. But his ass is wild. Ray chases the ladies like it's going out of style. He may not ever settle down. As we've matured, Mal and I love him from a distance more and more often.

"You seeing someone?" He quizzed, pulling me from my thoughts. Last he heard, I was single as a Pringle. I hadn't brought a woman around in a number of years.

"Yeah. Kinda sorta." I couldn't refrain from smiling as thoughts of Destiney flooded my mind.

He returned a quizzical expression. "Why am I just now hearing about this?" In Ray's defense, we were super close once upon a time. I would share everything with Raymond and my brother Malachi. I haven't shared much with Ray lately; instead, I go to my brother for everything.

I shrugged my shoulders dismissively in an attempt to downplay it. I didn't need Ray in my business. "There's not much to tell right now. We're not actually hanging out or anything like that but talking a lot and getting to know each other." I took another drink, "Taking it slow."

"She in the pen or some shit?"

Here we go. I grimaced. "Naw!"

"She in another country?"

"Land Park."

"Land Park! You bein' catfished my nigga?"

"No Ray. I'm not being catfished," I said defensively.

"How you know that if you've never seen her?"

"I have seen her. On the day we met, we've been focusing on getting to know each other since then. Minus all the physical shit getting in the way."

Ray pondered for a moment. "Exclusively?"

"Yeah. Why?"

"All this pussy at your disposal and you're holding out for someone you can't even see."

"You already know that ain't even my style, cousin."

I'd already told Malachi about Destiney. How amazing she was. How much I enjoyed getting to know her. How much I liked her. From the beginning, Mal wanted the best for us both. And he'd been asking me how things were going. I kept him in the loop, and he knew we were taking things slow. Of course, I couldn't help but share how much my feelings have grown.

"These feelings are just… they're unlike anything I've ever felt. Her beauty is what captivated me, but our conversation, our connection… I like her a lot."

"Sounds like it." Mal chuckled, "I love it, man. Get your girl. Then, once you get her, never stop chasing her."

That was the plan. I wanted her, and I was going to get her. And I planned always to remind her how special she was.

"She probably getting it in with some other nigga," Ray said, bringing me back to the present. I peered over as he smirked, accepting his drinks the cocktail waitress returned with.

"Doubt that." I tossed back the last of my drink and handed the waitress my empty glass. I gave her cash to cover my food and drinks and a tip. The band had just finished their set, and the DJ announced he would be up next. I took that as my cue to take my ass home. Rising to my feet, I extended my hand, "I'm headed out, Ray."

"What man?" He glanced at his cell to check the time. "It's still early! You ain't in your feelings because of what I said, are you? I was just talking my shit. You know how I am sometimes."

What Raymond had to say didn't bother me in the least. What I decided to do didn't need to make sense to anyone else. And what's understood doesn't need to be explained.

Furthermore, I didn't give a damn. I would stand behind my decision ten toes down.

"You good cousin, for real. I'm just ready to get out of here." Ray stood to his feet, and we shared a quick embrace. "You really should be right behind me," I chuckled. His lady friend returned to the VIP section and sat beside him. "Be good aight?"

"Oh, I'm just getting started, Micah." He handed her the drink he ordered as he put his arm around her waist, settling back into the couch and getting comfortable. "I'll holla at you."

"Bet." I turned to head out of the lounge, stepping down into the main section. The DJ started spinning, and the congregants on the dance floor grew. I weaved in and out of the clusters of people, using my manners and keeping my line of vision straight ahead. I was near the exit when I felt a light tug on the hem of my shirt. I turned to my right noticing a tall, slim, cutie smiling. She looked familiar, so I turned completely around to get a better look, but her face didn't register. I was trying to get out of here, but I had already stopped and being the gentleman I am, I obliged her.

She leaned into my ear, "Hey handsome, how about a dance?"

"Can't. I'm headed out," I gingerly told her.

96

"Aww." She placed her hand on my forearm. "Just one dance? I noticed you sitting behind that velvet rope past two hours. I hate I waited for nothing."

Maintaining my gentle tone, I told her, "I'm about ready to go. Not really in the mood for dancing."

Stepping closer and facing me, she placed each of her hands on my shoulders. "I'll come with you," she said with low lids and a sultry voice.

Well, that was forward. I considered it a turn-off being pursued by women, and ole girl was not my type. Not even a little bit. She was cute, but I chased what I wanted when I was on the market. Her persistence meant there were few excuses I could use to get through to her.

"I have someone waiting for me," I said simply. I was partially honest. "Excuse me." I stepped aside and made my way to the exit, leaving her no time to retort.

I texted Destiney as soon as I was back in my car. She likely wouldn't respond tonight, but I didn't care. I just wanted her to know she was on my mind. Destiney stayed on my mind. It didn't matter where I was or what I was doing.

Shifting into drive, I headed back toward my house, ready to call it a night. I couldn't hang like I used to, and my ass was tired.

thirteen

MICAH

It would have been easy to take ole girl from the lounge home with me.

But I was focused on a greater task.

Practicing abstinence was nothing new for me. I was a slow swimmer to begin with, and I didn't start having sex till college. I was damn near twenty-one when I had my first blow job. I had foresight even before I'd physically gotten to that point. I just knew that I needed to protect my heart. I knew how much was at stake in opening myself up to those things. I knew how emotional I was and how easily I got attached.

Ray would always tease me about still having my V-card.

And for every discouraging word, Mal would always encourage me. I appreciated that immensely. People were out here fucking on each other like it was going out of style.

"Don't worry about what everyone else is doing, baby brother. Ain't nothing wrong with holding out. I promise you, sex ain't going nowhere. Fucking before you're ready, ain't gone do nothing but complicate shit."

It was no secret that Ray had a completely different philosophy. He'd fuck anything and everything willing. One time Daddy told Ray, "His dick would fall off if he weren't more careful about where he was putting it."

I remember Mal cracking up at that. I joined in with the laughter but didn't see what was so funny. I do now though.

When I got home, I hopped in the shower, and now I was lying in bed in the dark, staring at the ceiling. I had caught a second wind and couldn't fall asleep just yet, so I'd been thinking.

And for some reason, my thoughts drifted to my ex-fiancé. Ayesha.

There was a time I thought of her constantly. Of course, when we were together and in love, but even after we were no longer together, I thought of her.

After everything with Ayesha was officially over, I was confused with exactly what I would do with myself. I did dumb shit that would hunt me later. For example, I hadn't been in a serious committed relationship, yet I fucked a few times without good reason. I knew better but I did the shit anyway. As a result, it was screwing with my mental. Big time.

I couldn't just lay with a woman if I didn't care about her. I must care about her in some capacity to be intimate with her. That's just the way I am.

I was out at a lounge once with Ray. And Erica, a woman from work, was with a few girlfriends. We'd never spoken at work, but I'd seen her in passing. She's hard to miss. Erica is extremely attractive, and she knows it. A few men at the lounge tried to dance with her and talk to her, but she made it clear she wanted me. She kept approaching me throughout the night and was extremely flirtatious. We did end up talking and Erica was so sexually suggestive, I was convinced she would have let me fuck her right out in the open in front of everyone. I was so turned off that it was over before it even started. Yet, for some dumb ass reason, I left with Erica anyway, ending up at her place.

Erica begged to give me head. I let her.

Then begged me to give her the dick. Against my better judgment, I relented.

That was my first and only one night stand. And as I drove away from her house, I was more than pissed at myself. I was irritated and on edge. I knew I should have stayed my ass away from Erica. When I couldn't shake the repulsive thought of what I had done, I went to Malachi.

I still remember that day. I called him on my Bluetooth speaker as I drove away from her place.

"Baby brother." He greeted me pleasantly and I immediately hated that I even called him with this shit.

"Brother," was all I could manage.

"Come on and see me man." His tone reassuring. "I'm at the house."

All I had to say was one word. Mal knew me frontwards and backwards.

I was so thankful for him and our relationship. Malachi, always the voice of reason was the person I needed to get my ass out of that funk. Next to our father, Malachi was the only one I trusted of this magnitude.

We were eleven months apart and were raised like twins. We were so close.

As close as we were, my parents made a point of always celebrating our unique strengths and accomplishments. We did many of the same things in the early years, yet I never felt I was in competition with Malachi. Since my parents celebrated us as individuals, we were confident in ourselves. We liked different things but enjoyed the things we had in common.

When I was a senior in high school, Malachi went away to Morehouse College. That was tough because we were separated for the first time in our lives. I remember him coming home during Christmas break and telling me how much fun he was having. By then, I'd already committed to Cal Poly in San Luis Obispo on a full athletic scholarship. I had a few offers, but I always knew that was where I wanted to go. When I asked Malachi about the ladies in Atlanta, I couldn't believe what he told me.

"Baby brother, there are beautiful chocolate women everywhere! You almost get used to it," He chuckled.

"Ain't no way man!" I exclaimed.

"I swear!"

When Mommy and Daddy moved him in, I was doing a summer internship, but I may have gotten a sample. But I found out just what the hell Mal was talking about when I visited for my spring break. I really missed my brother, and he was so proud to introduce me to his roommates and new friends. I only stayed 4 days and hated that I couldn't stay longer. But damn! A black teenager from Northern California saw all the good things about the South. The Spelman women he showed me were beautiful and my ass didn't want to come back.

But Malachi wasn't fazed by those ladies. He was laser-focused on handling business and even pledged Greek. And anyway, Ella already had Malachi on lock by then. He only had eyes for her. Quite frankly, in Malachi's world, no other women existed.

I remember when he first met Ella. We went to the same high school. Malachi was a junior, and Ella and I were sophomores. Ella and I had AP Biology together, and one afternoon, he saw us both coming out of class. We weren't walking out together, just exiting at the same time. One second, I saw him standing across the hall; a second later, he ended up right next to me.

"Baby brother!"

"Hey Malachi," I answered with eyebrows high on my head, wondering what the hell he was so pressed about.

"Who is that?!" He pointed at a group of girls nearby talking.

"Which one? It's like six of them over there."

"Which one you think?" I chuckled, already knowing, "Ella is the one in the green dress."

"Wow." That was all he said, but he was saying a hell of a lot more than that. I knew my brother, just like he knew me. I briefly regarded him; I had never heard him speak that way about any girl. Malachi wasn't a playboy by any means; he only dealt with one girl at a time. That was something my father drilled into us. But Malachi never seemed invested; it was more so passing the time, I guess. I could tell off rip, this one would be a little different. As it would turn out, he was smitten with Ella from the start.

"You know her?" He asked, pulling me from my thoughts.

"Kinda," I shrugged. "We have AP Bio together. She's smart as hell. We worked on a group project before. She's nice too," I offered. It mattered a whole lot whether the girl was kind. To me, anyway. If it wasn't one thing I couldn't stand, it was a mean ass girl. And don't be cute and mean. Your ass is damaged goods as far as I'm concerned. Ain't nothing remotely attractive about that shit.

Malachi looked me in the eye. "Brother. If you're already interested in her, I'll back off."

My mother always told us never to let any girl come between us. "There are too many women out here for that kind of foolishness", she would say. We never *expressed interest in the same girl. Plus, I was a slow swimmer when it came to the ladies. There could be a girl interested in me, throwing hints all day, and I wouldn't know if one hit me right in the head. Malachi and Ray would always tease me about it.*

Admittedly, Ella was out-of-this-world beautiful. In a class all her own.

But I hadn't even seen her in that way before.

I hadn't even thought about her like that until now. If I were honest, I wouldn't have minded getting to know her, but I didn't take the opportunity. That was my bad.

"You go ahead. I'm not," I returned confidently.

"You sure?"

"Yes, I'm positive."

They were inseparable very quickly after that. Once we graduated high school, Ella joined Malachi in Georgia. Headed to Clark-Atlanta on the first thing, smoking.

As they say, the rest is history.

When I talked to Malachi following my lack of judgment with Erica, he had to remind me of something.

"That's not you, baby brother. You've never been the casual sex type."

Mal was right, and I'd say that with my chest.

At that point, I was thirty-two years old, and I could count on one hand how many women I'd slept with. Counting my ex-fiancé Ayesha, I had been intimate with four women total.

I made the decision then: the one finger remaining was for my wife. Considering that, I decided to be abstinent.

I'd been abstaining for two years now, preparing my heart and my mind for my wife. I knew I needed to stop with the foolishness and clear out all the shit in the way.

Staying ready is better than having to get ready.

***

I met Ayesha during our sophomore year at Cal Poly. The crazy thing was, I'd been hearing about her since freshman year and had no idea. I still remember my roommate Tyson coming in one night after being out with his girlfriend Laila. He told me Laila also had a roommate from Sacramento, and maybe we should meet each other.

He said it casually, and I brushed it off. On a few occasions, he'd mentioned going to hang out with Laila, and if I wanted to roll, he could ask her to bring her friend. It didn't register that he was talking about the same person all that time. He never told me her name, nor did I ask, so I couldn't have known.

To that end, I guess I was indifferent about meeting someone. That's likely why I wasn't too pressed about it. My spring semester was intense; I was playing baseball and didn't have much free time between practices and my very rigorous course load. I wasn't sexually active either so women in general were an afterthought. Somehow Tyson made time for all of that. Anyway, whenever Tyson mentioned Laila's friend, I'd brush it off.

But then, I finally did meet Laila's friend.

And everything changed.

I remember that night.

Vividly.

Ty and I were chilling in our dorm. We'd been working and training hard for the past several weeks. Non-stop. And for the first time since the pre-season started, we didn't have practice that day or a game the next.

"You tryin to hit M.U.?" I asked Ty. I was eager to get out.

"Yeah! I'm down."

The Memorial Union was a hangout spot just off campus frequented by students. It was your typical college bar scene: cheap appetizers, loud music, pool tables, darts. Once Ty and I arrived, we linked up with a few more friends and shot the shit for a while. We'd probably been there for close to two hours, and Ty walked away from our table at some point. When he returned Laila was with him whom I'd met on several occasions. Laila was cute and super sweet, and I liked her for Ty. After I stood to greet her with a friendly side hug, I sat back down and went back to absently scrolling on my phone.

"Quit being rude man!" Ty snapped.

I looked up in confusion. "I said 'hey'. What are you talking about?"

Ty shook his head. Laila giggled, "Micah there's someone I'd like you to meet if that's alright."

I looked back at Laila. Right beside her stood a young woman I hadn't noticed before. I could see why Ty thought I was being rude. The bar had gotten so loud and so crowded, and clusters of people were moving around our table. I stood immediately but I was speechless. Who-ever she was had me stuck. I held her eyes for just a second, but she quickly looked down. I continued staring at her and noticed her fidgeting under my gaze. I don't even know how long I stood there but I was in awe.

I could not believe how pretty she was.

"Ahem!" Ty said obnoxiously breaking me from of the trance I was in.

Laila giggled again, "Micah this is my friend Ayesha. Ayesha this is Micah."

I took her hand in mine, "Very nice to meet you, Ayesha."

"Likewise." She gave me just a second of eye contact and as she removed her hand, she looked away again. She was shy but that wasn't an issue. I could work with that.

"You and Ayesha probably have a lot to talk about, you're both from Sacramento," Laila offered.

My head snapped in Ty's direction. He smirked at me already knowing and I was floored. This was her.

Anyway, Laila was right. Ayesha and I fell into a comfortable conversation, our segues were effortless, moving from one topic to the next. It was the most effortless conversation I'd had. So easy that hours passed. At some point Ty and Laila headed out, but Ayesha and I stayed at M.U., conversing more and enjoying each other's company.

Close to midnight, I walked her back to her dorm, and we made plans to meet the very next morning.

"Tyson, why didn't you tell me! I would have been met Ayesha!" I playfully punched him in the shoulder. I sat on my bed and began removing my shoes.

Ty shook his head, "Man, that's on you. Ain't like I didn't tell you!"

"Yeah, but you ain't said all that! She's so pretty. And her vibe is insane! We talked for three hours about so many things."

Ty nodded. "Ayesha is cool. Yo ass lucky she was still available."

I couldn't disagree there. I playfully cut my eyes at Ty, "Did you know Laila was bringing Ayesha to M.U. tonight?"

"I may or may not have had an idea."

"Of course, you did!" I threw the t-shirt I had just taken off at him.

"Man get this shit off me!" Ty threw it back just as forcefully. "You should be thanking me."

"I'm just playing. Hell yeah. Good looking man."

Ayesha and I met the next morning at a coffee shop on campus and fell right back in. Talking about everything under the sun. I learned so much about her. She asked the same about me. We discovered that Ayesha and I attended rival high schools. Her dad is a pastor, and my dad is a deacon and since we both grew up in the church we bonded over those things.

It turned out Laila had been trying to talk Ayesha into meeting me too, but she was consumed with school herself. Ayesha was going for her BSN and minoring in Child Development. She loved children and wanted to be a Pediatric Nurse Practitioner. She had such a passion for children and nursing. She mentioned the graduate programs being quite competitive, but she was undeterred, determined to graduate with high honors. I was impressed.

We managed to spend all our free time together. As often as we could, considering. In so doing, we quickly fell for each other.

It was easy to do.

I'd never been in love before, and Ayesha was just my speed. Everything happened organically. She wasn't in a hurry to move faster than we needed to. I never felt pressure from her, nor did I pressure her about anything.

Another one of the many things we bonded over was the choice to wait. We were both virgins, choosing to abstain. It was such a relief learning we were on the same type of time. The craziest thing about college were the women offering me the pussy. Women I hardly knew. Shit was wild. It was the same for Ayesha. She was pretty as hell, and a lot of guys took their chances shooting their shot, only wanting one thing from her. But she was a good girl, and they eventually moved along.

Anyway, Ayesha and I were together more than a year before we went all the way. And very much in love before we even considered taking things there.

I called Malachi one day to talk about it. I told my brother everything and I trusted him with everything. He was in his senior year down at Morehouse and by then he and Ella were already married.

"We're thinking about it. We've been talking about it. A little more lately. Guess I'm just not sure."

"Okay. Why is it that you're unsure?"

"I don't know. I can't really put my finger on it. It's a big step. And I'm hesitant because there's no going back after that. Know what I mean?"

"Yep. No doubt it is. Listen, I know you love Ayesha, but things change when you start having sex. Not necessarily for the better all the time. Dynamics will shift. There's no harm in waiting a little longer. Seriously, baby brother. Think about it more. Keep talking about it. There's no need to rush into sex."

I took Mal's advice, and we waited. When we decided we knew we were ready to make love, I called him then too.

"The most important thing is that she's comfortable. She'll be nervous, she'll be in her head, but help her relax. Tell her you're nervous too. And you will be. Remind her how much you care about her. How much you love her. Take everything slow. That's the key. Hold her and kiss her for a long time. Focus on that. Let everything else happen organically."

"Yeah."

"But I get the feeling you were already thinking this stuff."

"Oh yeah?"

"Yeah. I mean, I've taught you everything you know."

"Man, shut up." We both cackled.

So, I met Ayesha at her dorm, and we headed back, hand in hand. I figured our first time would be at her place because she'd feel most comfortable there. Surprisingly, Ayesha wanted to be at my place. I told Ty about the plans Ayesha and I had, and he agreed to stay away from our dorm, planning to chill with Laila.

I tried to chill out, but my mind was all over the place, especially about what was to come.

This was it.

We made it back, and I checked in with her immediately. "Ayesha." I found her beautiful eyes on mine. "Are you alright?"

She nodded.

"Please use words with me, baby."

"Yes. I'm fine."

Mal called it.

I was extremely nervous. I knew Ayesha, and she was nervous, too. I could tell—likely a little scared even.

I turned on soft music for us, and we kissed on my bed.

And kissed. And kissed.

It was our favorite thing to do, and up until now, it was all we ever did. This was our first time being completely alone like this. Ever. The moment was surreal. Despite our plans to consummate our love, the innocence of it all made everything that much sweeter.

After kissing for a while, we talked a lot—more than anything else—partly to talk through the jitters and nerves.

But also, I wanted to make sure Ayesha was good. I wanted her to relax. I knew that would help when the time came.

So, we talked through everything, and I checked in with her ad nauseam, asking what I could do for her, how she was feeling, what she was thinking, and what she needed from me. Ayesha did the same for me, too. Conversely, I shared what I was thinking, how I was feeling, what I wanted to do before I did it, and what I was doing while I did it.

"Are you comfortable?" I asked her.

"I am. Yes."

"You need anything?"

"No baby. Thank you."

"Do you like what I'm doing?" I asked. I was level-setting. I began with one finger, and now I had two inside of her. My hands were large, and my fingers were thick, so I was careful. Slow. Deliberate. Gently, I worked my two fingers in and out of her.

"Yes, baby." Ayesha spread her legs wider.

After a beat, I told her, "I like it too. Mmm." Her opening was so tight around my fingers. Slick with her essence. "You're getting wetter. Does this feel good to you, baby?"

"Yes." I heard traces of a moan. "Are you... enjoying what I'm doing?" She politely asked. I looked down at my hard dick in her hand. Ayesha was jerking me. Ever so softly. It felt amazing. This was our first time venturing this far, and I was enjoying the feeling. I was relishing the view, too, so much so that crystal clear precum was showing itself.

"Definitely. You're making me feel good, too, baby. So good." It became increasingly difficult to concentrate. But I persevered. Keenly aware of my movements, ensuring she was feeling pleasure and nothing else. "You see what you're holding... that won't feel like my fingers."

"I know."

Resisting the urge to get lost in the moment, I focused on her. Looking for any signs of distress. Nonverbal cues. Anything. I considered her pretty face intently. Ayesha's eyes were closed now, and I let her rock, but I kept mine open. Currently trained on her soft, delicate fingers wrapped around my dick, giving him all the love and attention. She had a nice rhythm—a mid-tempo cadence, yielding flaring veins. The sight alone was sending me.

We'd been indulging for the past thirty minutes at least, and neither of us had brought each other to orgasm — the epitome of callowness. Yet...there was something so beautiful about not knowing what we were doing, that we were learning together. Experiencing everything for the first time. Together.

"So... are you sure?" Still stroking her with my fingers. Still gently moving in and out of her. "You can change your mind. Even right now, you can. I don't mind.

I respect you so much, and I love you so much. I can wait for you, baby." This was the most precious thing Ayesha had, and she chose to share it with me.

I was so pleased she chose me. And I was contented my first time was with her too.

"I know. I love you, too. And I want to. I'm sure."

I held her eyes. Searching. Thinking. I wanted her. But there was no hurry. I revered her virginity just as much as I revered mine. "What's on your mind?" I volleyed after a beat.

She sighed. "The pain."

Yeah.

There it was.

I hated the fact that this would hurt her. I wished it were me instead.

"I know baby. I know. Hold on to me. Squeeze me. Scratch me. Do whatever you need to do."

When things with Ayesha ended, I felt that I'd fallen short because she gave herself to me, and I didn't end up wifing her. That shit messed me up because I knew how much it meant to her.

It also meant a lot to me, and I grieved that loss for us both.

It was one reason I went back and forth about ending everything. That fucked with me for years.

The guilt of it all. I went to Mal about that, too.

"Ayesha gave me her virginity. Something so sacred. And..." I shook my head. "I walked away from her."

"For what it's worth, you gave her your virginity too, baby brother. The fact that this still bothers you means your heart is in the right place. It was then, and it is now," Mal said. "You aren't a bad person. Don't look at yourself that way."

I appreciated Mal's words, and I received and believed them too.

fourteen

DESTINEY

It was a productive Saturday.

I had an appointment with Daijah early this morning to get my locs retwisted. Daijah has been caring for my hair forever—since we were kids. In our teens, she'd do hair for our cousins and friends. She has the Midas touch for real. Doing hair as a side hustle, she stayed booked and busy.

Eventually, Daijah got her cosmetology license, and a few years ago, she walked away from her corporate job and went into business full time. She does all hair types but specializes in natural haircare—locs in particular—and she's one of just a few certified Sisterlocs consultants in the region. I always get stopped on the street about my hair, and I send all inquiring minds her way. Her shop is doing really well, and I am so proud of her.

After my appointment, I went to the grocery store, washed my car, and even vacuumed the inside this time. I never really felt like doing that, so it was a big deal. When I sent Daijah a picture of that giant vacuum at the carwash, she replied with a million laughing emojis.

India and I met at our favorite coffee spot this afternoon and chatted for a good while.

I love cute coffee shops. And I love catching up with India anytime I can. I adore her spirit, and she was a beautiful soul inside and out. I couldn't have been more blessed to have met her. We were literally twin souls. I was often misunderstood, but I never had to explain myself to India. We just get each other because we're so similar. She gives so much of herself, just like I do. I don't know anyone else like me. And then I meet her and I'm like, are you fucking serious? It's like me again.

And India is solid. She's super protective of me and always has my back. I am just as protective of her, and I'll always have hers. Most importantly, I was so glad to be able to get her out of the house so she could breathe. India has a lot going on at home, and sometimes I worry she'll crumble beneath it all. India was my girl. I'd always be there for her.

After chilling with Indie, I went to the grocery store. Once I got home, I finally got caught up on my laundry.

Throughout the day, I'd been texting Micah. As we always do.

This morning, I woke up to a message from him. And it was so sweet.

Micah: My cousin thought I was crazy, being a wallflower at the lounge. But all I could think of the entire night was you baby

When I read that, a silly grin swept my entire face as I quickly typed a reply.

He replied right away, and I grinned even bigger.

You were thinking of me?

Micah: I am always thinking of you. And good morning beautiful

I'm always thinking of you too baby

He'd gone out with his cousin last night and wanted me to know he had been thinking of me. I felt so special. Micah called me beautiful as if it was my name. I was still getting used to it. That was incredibly sweet. Everything he did was thoughtful and sweet.

Micah had so much reverence for me.

As a woman. As a person. It was something I'd never seen.

Not like this.

I was jealous of any woman that had his attention before me. Crazy, too, because I didn't have a jealous bone in my body.

What's for me is for me, and what's not mine isn't my concern.

I don't covet a damn thing that belongs to someone else.

And the truth was I didn't leave room for anyone to get close to me. I filled my free time with commitments and projects, and I preferred things that way. Then, I wouldn't have to face the fact that I was lonely. That I didn't have anyone. No one was missing me or looking for me. But now that I had Micah- well, I didn't have him, but I knew him. And getting to know Micah as I have these past several weeks made me want him for myself. I was breaking all kinds of my "rules".

Where I didn't befriend men, Micah was absolutely a friend. A close friend.

Where I wasn't checking for a relationship, I wanted one. With Micah.

I called him, and we spoke briefly when I came in from the grocery store. He had gone to play basketball, and later, he planned to head over to his parents' house to spend some time. I loved how close he was to his parents. He visited them at least once a week, and they spoke every few days. Family was important to him, and that meant so much to me.

As productive as my day was, I thought of Micah at every moment. As usual. He called me right before I got in the shower, so I told him I'd call him back once I got out.

And there was something else.

I wanted to see him. Badly. So bad I could hardly stand it. I'd gotten out of the shower a while ago. Did my moisturizing routine. Now I was lying on my bed, wishing Micah was here. I felt an overwhelming gravitation toward him that I couldn't even explain. I had only been in his company once, but through our conversations, I was getting attached, and it was becoming increasingly challenging to continue staying away. I felt silly because I wasn't exactly sure how to tell him. He asked to take me out twice, and I'd declined. That was all it took because he hadn't asked me again since. I couldn't blame him, and knowing Micah and his thoughtfulness, he was waiting for me to initiate this next step.

He was more than patient.

I didn't know a man who was more patient.

I was the one who asked to take things slow. I know full well the ball was in my court. And I didn't want to take things slow. I wanted to see Micah. And I wanted to be with Micah.

And I'd come to the realization that it was about time I made a move.

My feelings for him were beginning to become overwhelming. At this point, I was ready to let it all go and let things unfold as they may. That felt right, natural, and like the best thing to do.

I held my phone in my hand, contemplating. I knew I could always be honest with him. I reasoned that, at minimum, I would no longer be suffering in silence.

That was good enough for me.

I exhaled a frustrated breath and opened our text thread. I quickly typed a message and hit send before I changed my mind. I had just placed my phone down when I heard it chime. I knew it was Micah, but now that my feelings had been revealed, I was almost too shy to read his message. I was also much too eager not to read it.

I really want to see you

Micah: You can see me anytime Beautiful

I lay on my back, considering my response. Bearing all, I responded more bluntly this time.

I really want to kiss you

His reply was immediate.

Micah: When?

Oh shit.

I held my breath, contemplating and unsure of what to say next. I couldn't go back on it now.

Not that I wanted to.

My phone chimed.

Micah: Drop your location and I'll come kiss you goodnight

I glanced at the time; it was close to eleven. I didn't want him out this late just to kiss me. I'd feel horrible if something were to happen. I saw dots appear. I started to type some flimsy excuse of a response just as I saw an incoming call from Micah. Likely because I was taking too long to reply. I sat straight up in bed, considering my excuses, and answered just before it rolled to voicemail.

"Hey."

"Hey. You okay?"

I wanted to be near him… and his smooth baritone in my ear at this hour was a dangerous combination.

And…I felt my pussy beginning to purr.

"Yeah. I'm okay."

"You sure? For a second, I thought I'd get your voicemail. And you still haven't sent me your location."

"Micah, it's getting late. You really shouldn't be out this time of night," I said pleadingly.

"I want a goodnight kiss, sweetheart. Or were you joshing me?"

I contemplated for a few beats.

"Destiney baby."

"Yes?"

"I would love to kiss you right now."

Shit.

"We can't kiss yet."

"Why can't we kiss yet?"

"If we kiss, you just may fuck around and fall in love with me," I returned using an ounce of sarcasm.

He roared with laughter. "Is that right? You that kind of kisser?" I could hear the smile in his voice.

Smiling, too, I replied, "I'm certain you want to make an informed decision, Mr. Walker."

Another beat of silence.

"What if I want to fall in love with you, Ms. Evans?"

Pulling up our text thread, I dropped a pin, my smile still wide as I considered my words.

Throwing all caution to the wind, I dared, "Come kiss me then."

Micah paused for a moment. "Seventeen minutes. Or will you fall asleep on me?"

"Tell me when you're outside."

"Bet."

fifteen

MICAH

It was a leisure Saturday.

For once in a long time, I slept in. I woke up around nine this morning, which is sleeping in for me. Most of my mornings begin before six.

Since I wasn't on the schedule for any games, and nothing else was planned, I made a hearty breakfast and then took a walk. It was brisk out, but the sky was clear, and the sun was shining. I lived in a subdivision full of multicultural and multigenerational families. I wasn't engaged with my neighbors beyond pleasantries, but everyone seemed friendly.

My neighbors on one side were a Hispanic family with four small children. We moved in five years ago, around the same time. At that time, they were on baby number two. There's also an older woman living there, who I assume is the children's grandmother. I see her every now and again whenever she walks the children to the playground.

The neighbors on my other side were a middle-aged white couple with an empty nest. I knew they had at least one daughter who came around occasionally, mainly during the holidays and the summertime. I figure she's in college or something.

I made my way toward the running trail that weaved through the park. It didn't take long since I lived just two blocks away. Many people were walking the trail. Some walked briskly, while others took a stroll like mine.

Many people were out walking their dogs. I love dogs. I've considered getting one on many occasions. A bit of company in my spacious home would be nice. They're great companions, truly man's best friend. I've been back and forth on that since I travel semi-frequently for work, and I would have to figure out a dog sitter often. We'll see.

I continued my stroll through the tunnel of trees. I could hear the gravel under my feet as I enjoyed the view of the man-made lake the trail looped around. A woman running with her Lab passed me. I couldn't help but smile.

We had a golden Labrador Retriever growing up. I would get one of those if I decided to get a dog. Mal and I loved her. We named her Tweety, after the cartoon character. Looney Toons was one of our favorite Saturday morning cartoons. Ray would always tease us for giving our girl puppy a boy's name. I think Ray was jealous because we had a dog, and he couldn't get one. We argued back and forth about Tweety Bird's gender all the time. I always thought Tweety was a girl. Ray swore Tweety was a boy. I still don't know the answer to that.

But anyway, Tweety was a great family dog. She was house-trained and affectionate. She learned a few tricks, and we took her with us when we rode our bikes or went to the park. She grew up right along with us, and Mal and I cried like babies when she finally died at thirteen years old. Mommy and Daddy cried, too.

I took my time walking and made it home after about an hour.

Once back at home, I hung around the house for a while. I went into my home office to check my email. Mal and Gabe stopped by briefly, and I told Mal I planned to see the parents later. He'd gone by two days ago. Between Mal and I, one of us was at the house every few days, and both of us spoke with them regularly. My parents weren't the type to text, so we had to pick up the phone and call them if we ever wanted to talk. I was okay with that when it came to those two. I preferred hearing their voices anyway.

After Mal left, I installed a few floating shelves in my bedroom. I put that project off for a while but was glad I finally did it. I had a small collection of books, and my bedroom was the perfect place for them. I talked to my boy Solomon, and we decided to meet up and play ball. Afterward, I went home to shower, and then I headed over to the blue house to see Mommy and Daddy.

When I entered the front door, my dad was walking toward the hallway, carrying a light bulb. He handed it to me.

"Hey Son."

"Hey Daddy."

We hugged one another after I locked the door behind me.

"I need the light in the hallway restroom changed. You mind taking care of that for your old man?"

"I don't mind at all, Daddy. Let me kiss Mommy before I do that." He patted me on the back and headed to his recliner. As usual, I found Mommy sitting on the couch with a book in her lap. She was always in the middle of a book for as long as I can remember. My mother was an avid reader and belonged to the same book club for something like twenty-five years. I leaned down and kissed her cheek, hugging her warmly.

"Hey Micah Bear! How's my baby boy?"

"I'm good, Mommy. How are you?"

"It's been a great day so far, even better now that I have eyes on you."

Once I fixed the lightbulb, Dad and I enjoyed some 7-Up cake with vanilla ice cream. Mom was an excellent cook and a phenomenal baker. She made most of her desserts from scratch using family recipes. She had been teaching Gabby how to bake a few of them, and she was getting pretty good at it.

Dad and I went to the backyard to put his ladder back in the shed. I was in his shed all the time, and one look around told me all I needed to know. He hadn't used the ladder in a while, and I could see he moved a few things around to get to it.

"Let Mal or me handle this next time. You shouldn't be doing too much heaving lifting, Daddy." Daddy drove garbage trucks for a living, and the work did a number on his back after all those years.

He chuckled, "My bride didn't tell me that light was out until a few minutes before you got here. You know I never use that restroom."

I chuckled, too. "I'll take my grievance up with her then." Malachi and I both told them to leave these things for us to take care of. They didn't need to do anything; we could handle it for them, but they still wanted independence. And Daddy could be stubborn.

I understood.

They were in their early sixties and still very healthy and active. God willing, that would be me one day. Mal and I offered to move them into our homes whenever they were ready, and whichever they chose would be okay with either of us. I had a feeling they would likely choose my house because I had a bedroom on the first floor. Malachi's home was larger, but they wouldn't want to deal with those stairs. Eventually, Mal would get tired of those stairs, too. Hell, I was already tired of the stairs in my house.

Mal and I paid off the rest of their mortgage two years ago, and Daddy was able to retire. Now that they have more free time, we encourage them to go away now and then and see some places. But they don't seem interested. Mommy isn't a fan of airplanes, and Daddy wouldn't sleep well in a hotel past a night or two.

I spent a couple hours with my parents then headed home to get my ass in the gym. Mom's cake was so good I had two slices and needed to work that shit off. Of course, before I left, Mommy found a reason to mention my love life...or lack thereof.

"You wouldn't gobble up these sweets so fast if you had a wife baking for you, Micah Bear."

Daddy laughed loudly as I smirked.

"What if she doesn't bake?"

"Then I would teach her, of course."

"Touché Mommy. Touché."

I desperately wanted to tell Mommy and Daddy about Destiney. I was eager as hell to tell them about her. I could hardly contain myself. I liked her so much.

She was so special to me.

But I was conflicted.

Though I felt confident in the connection between Destiney and me, we weren't seeing each other physically. If Destiney was worth mentioning, that meant we were serious. If we were serious, I knew Mommy would want to meet her. I wanted them to meet, and I looked forward to the day I could bring Destiney to meet them. But I didn't even have a ballpark estimate of when that would happen.

I was trying to see Destiney my damn self.

I thought of Destiney all day long—I always did. We text each other throughout the day. Earlier, I spoke to her while I was at the court with Solomon. Now, I was home and settled in, waiting for her to call me once she got out of the shower.

Imagine my surprise when she texted saying she wanted to see me.

I stood from my bed and made a beeline to my dresser, quickly throwing a pair of Nike sweats over my basketball shorts. I headed down the stairs two at a time, my thoughts in overdrive. I felt a mix of emotions. Of course, I was excited and wanted to see her too.

But I almost didn't think the day would come.

I laughed out loud in spite of myself.

Grabbing my keys, I secured the alarm and put on my Nike slides. I sent Destiney my ETA, reversed, and waited for my garage door to close. Just before pulling out of the cul-de-sac, I read her reply.

Drive safe. See you soon

I felt giddy as a teenage boy with a crush. It had been several weeks since we shared the same space, so that was one reason to be excited. I'd also imagined what our first kiss would be like, how her lips would feel on mine.

I mentally replayed the last portion of our conversation. Destiney was probably facetious, but I was as serious as a heart attack. I was convinced I could fall in love with her after a kiss. I was already in very strong like, and I had only seen her once.

Destiney had grown to become a close friend and confidant. We talked and texted all day long. For hours. About everything and nothing. I loved the way her mind worked. She sent me pictures of things she found interesting or links to an article she wanted to tell me about. My favorite part was the end of a long day when we could have an uninterrupted conversation. Destiney was always the last voice I heard each night. She was so open and honest. Funny and intelligent. I shared everything with her, never feeling judged. I welcomed her into the deepest depths of my soul and shared things I'd never shared with anyone. Mal and I were close as close could be, but this was a little different.

More than that, her beautiful face consumed my thoughts day and night.

Destiney was unbelievable. She was incredibly comfortable in her skin, unconcerned with the opinions of others, yet so kind and compassionate whenever she spoke to someone. Everyone who encountered her felt seen and valued, especially me.

It was close to eleven, and few cars were on the road. I was on a mission to get to her, making it from my home in Elk Grove to Destiney's home in Land Park within fifteen minutes. I pulled onto a quiet residential block and killed my engine. No sooner than when I alerted her that I was here, I heard her front door open.

I smiled from ear to ear. My anticipation was building by the second. I immediately got out of the car to meet her. She descended the few steps toward me, her waist-length locs swaying with each step. She had the sweetest smile adorning her beautiful face and I damn near lost my mind fixated on everything before me. She wore black biker shorts and a grey tank top. I'd forgotten how much taller I am. I likely stood about a foot taller. She couldn't have been any more than 5'3'.

"You are so beautiful Destiney," I found myself saying as soon as I reached her. Her face was bare and held a natural glow. Fuck. She had no business looking this good.

"Thank you." She smiled shyly.

Unable to contain myself, I embraced her, and she fell into my arms naturally, resting her head against my rapidly beating heart.

I felt like I was in the damn Twilight Zone. We'd grown so emotionally close that it seemed like a lifetime had elapsed. It was as if one day was a week's time.

"And thanks for coming to see me, but you really shouldn't have." Her voice was slightly muffled as she spoke into my chest. She hugged me around my waist just as firmly as I held her.

"I'll come see you anytime, sweetheart." I needed Destiney to understand that I meant that. I rested my chin on top of her head, and she settled into my embrace. She belonged in my arms. I never wanted to let her go. She belonged to me.

I had missed her, and I told her so.

"If I'm honest, I missed you too, Micah. Something vicious."

I continued to hold her close, savoring the moment. Closing my eyes, I inhaled her fragrance deeply, committing her notes to memory. She smelled like a lovely mixture of citrus and coconut. She was intoxicating. All five of my senses were stimulated by her pheromones, and I could feel my dick coming to life. Damn. I didn't want her to feel the brick in my pants and think I came here for all the wrong reasons.

Wanting another look at my baby, I took a slight step back, resting my hands at the small of her back, mindful not to venture off too far. Her head was down, so I gently lifted her chin with my finger. She looked up, but her orbs evaded mine.

"Hey, look at me." Speaking gently with a fragment of firmness, "Are you good?"

She smiled at me. Her eyes were now trained on my quizzical expression.

"It's nothing personal. I promise," Her sweet voice just above a whisper. Destiney pushed a few of her stray locs over her shoulder. Observing my puzzled visage, she said, "I get embarrassed easily. Especially when I'm around someone I'm crushing on," She revealed, through a confident smile.

I chuckled lightly, captivated by her sincerity yet again.

She was the cutest thing I'd ever seen.

I released my hold and took her hands into mine, threading our fingers. I felt a spark and wondered if she felt it, too.

"No need to be embarrassed sweetheart. I have a crush on you, too. And you know what? I am absolutely crazy about you," I avowed. "And I promise you don't have to miss me so much." I rubbed the soft skin of her hands with the pads of my thumbs. "But you already knew that."

Destiney smiled again. Really big this time, showing all her pearly whites.

Her smile was breathtaking. Goodness. She was so fucking pretty.

Since sharing that detail moments ago, she'd given me her beautiful eyes. And I gave her mine.

I felt pretty damn good, as we stood there, holding each other's hands and each other's gazes. I don't know what she was thinking about, but I was losing myself in her. Her eyes held depth. And curiosity. And vulnerability. And I was drowning. Falling...

"So glad it's mutual," she released a breath followed by a low chortle.

"It is positively mutual, Destiney baby."

We shared a comfortable silence. Eyes on eyes.

Her hands were still in mine, and it felt so good to be in her space. She brought me a calmness I couldn't explain. I hadn't even realized when my erratic breathing had returned to normal. A passerby would see two people holding hands, but there was much transpiring. As a grown ass man, I never gave hand holding much thought, but this shit right now was hitting different.

I noted our interlocked fingers and how her tiny hands looked intertwined with mine. My hands were massive in comparison. As she caressed my digits with hers, I regarded her attention to our mingled fingers. There was an art to this, and Destiney had it down to a science. Her tenderness and affection were on full display right now. Another attribute that truly set her apart.

I could dig it.

I continued stroking her hands, lost in deep introspection.

My mind was everywhere, but somehow, at the same time, it was right here with her.

Trying to figure this out. This intense chemistry. It was Kismet. Synchronous.

The energy was so thick I could feel it around us.

None of it made any sense. Yet it all made perfect sense.

Feeling so strongly for her, after never being near her. Caring for her as deeply as I did, solely on the essence of who she is. I felt this… this gravitation.

And this calmness. It was as if I was exactly where I was supposed to be.

With her.

There weren't any words, but the insurmountable peace I felt with her led me to one conclusion.

Recalling our conversations since day one, my confidence in her, and the peace and serenity she afforded me.

The assurance, devotion, and protection I desired to bestow her generously… I felt this confirmation in my spirit. And I knew right here at that very moment that Destiney was it for me.

Destiney is my wife.

And I had plans to make good on that very soon.

But right now, I really wanted to kiss her.

I gave her hands a gentle squeeze, considering my next move. I didn't want to be intrusive or assume she still felt the same. After contemplating for a moment, I said, "I'd love a kiss before I go. Would that be alright with you, beautiful?"

Gazing into my eyes, and without pause, she said, "I'm good with that."

I didn't waste any time leaning into her, gently pecking her soft, full lips. Slowly, I pecked her lips again, and again and again, lingering longer each time. Destiney hungrily kissed me back. When our lips remained connected, she parted, giving me access. And damn... I loved her taste. Our tongues danced together as we naturally fell into a rhythm we seemed to know by heart.

It was so easy with her.

Destiney was a phenomenal kisser. Gentle but eager.

Her tongue had a mind of its own. Brave and confident, she explored unfamiliar territory. I made my own moves as she welcomed me into the sweetness of her mouth. I couldn't help but wrap my arms around her waist, deepening the kiss. I felt relief when Destiney returned the gesture, wrapping her arms around my neck. I was pleased she felt comfortable doing so.

Light smacking sounds emitted from us, and I held her even tighter, getting lost in a trance. Her block was so quiet, and we were so consumed that a dog howling somewhere in the distance is what broke us from our reverie.

I don't even know how long we kissed, but I enjoyed every second of it.

Kissing her was unlike anything I'd ever experienced.

I loved kissing her.

I could have kissed her all night.

Destiney released her arms from around my neck, bringing them to rest on my shoulders. I lessened my grip around her waist, settling in the small of her back.

"Wow." was all I could say after such an explosive moment.

"Ditto," she said shyly.

"Well. That takes care of that." I rubbed her chin with my thumb. "Have a good night, beautiful." I took a few steps backward and leaned against my car. Never taking my eyes off Destiney as she headed toward her front door.

She was almost to her door when I heard a languid giggle. She turned on her heels. "I should mention... now that we've kissed. I just may get attached to you."

"I'm good with that." I tossed back.

Destiney really had no idea.

sixteen

MICAH

It had been seventy-two hours since I put eyes on her.

Since I had her in my arms.

Since I kissed her lips.

I could think of little else since seeing Destiney and sharing that kiss.

Her beautiful face consumed my thoughts. Remnants of her taste hypnotized me.

That night repeatedly played on a loop in my head.

Being close to her again was surreal. And she was so beautiful—my goodness, more beautiful than I remembered.

I wanted to kiss her all over. Hell yeah, my dick was hard, but I wasn't even thinking about sex. Not right then, I wasn't. I'm super affectionate and express my love and adoration through physical touch, and I like to receive the same. I was cool if she wasn't ready for an affectionate overload. I was willing to rock with her till she got there. Though I got the impression she'd come around pretty soon. Her heart and soul were open and available, giving me a sensual vibe.

None of that took me by surprise. She's an artist, and artists are passionate people.

When I'd made it back home, I floated up the stairs and ended up sprawled out on my bed, my head in the fucking clouds. I don't even remember driving home or pulling into my garage. I went to plug in my phone and noticed a text from her asking me to let her know once I had made it safely. I messaged her back telling her I had, and she replied instantly with her usual goodnight text.

Meanwhile, my dick was hard as fuck in my sweats. I hadn't masturbated in months. I came dangerously close that night. Destiney was such a great kisser. She tasted incredible. I got the feeling she tasted just as delicious between her lower set of lips and that had my shit rock hard.

I eventually fell asleep, enraptured with thoughts of her. Those same thoughts plagued my mind when I woke early the next morning.

I woke up at 5:30 this morning, pushed through my workout, and then took a quick shower. While I cleansed myself, my thoughts returned to her soft hands and the gentle way she caressed mine.

Destiney was showing me something. I never thought a gesture as simple as hand-holding could be so sensual. With Destiney, it was. Her tiny hands were swallowed by mine, but they commanded attention. They were soft and dainty and made their presence known.

I wondered what else her hands could do.

Despite my distraction, I managed to stay on schedule, and after a light breakfast, I was out the door on time.

As I rode the elevator to the third floor, I considered just how productive I would be today. If the prior days were any indication, prospects were meager. I could still feel her soft lips on mine and the groove of her sweet tongue. I couldn't wait to make love to her finally.

Just the same, I could wait.

I looked forward to it but didn't want to rush anything about this. We were going at the right pace, and things were right where they were supposed to be. I was not going to mess up a good thing just to get my damn rocks off. Patience was a virtue, and I planned to exhibit the patience of Job.

I strolled toward my corner office. The floor I worked on was generally quiet later in the week as most of the department worked a hybrid schedule, only coming into the office on Mondays and Tuesdays. After connecting it to my monitors, I sat in my office chair and brought my MacBook to life. Laurie, my assistant, was working from home today and had already sent over her morning email with a few updates. Once I'd been brought to speed, I responded to her email, thanking her for the debrief and wished her a great Thursday.

I opened my calendar and sighed in relief, pleased that no meetings were scheduled until the afternoon.

I decided to look at a project charter for a merger we were considering. I'd already reviewed it several times, but thorough due diligence was critical since we were still in the project planning stages. The numbers looked promising, but I couldn't be definitively sure of any anticipated risks without taking a deeper dive. As System Vice President, I needed to ensure we made the best decision on what to include in our deal terms.

I opened a report, deciding I needed to review an outline of the project scope, resources, and dependencies.

"Knock, knock."

"Come on in." I returned, never looking up from the spreadsheet I was reviewing.

"Where are your glasses, boss?"

I looked up to find Ellington standing before me with his laptop bag slung over his shoulder.

I returned an inquisitive expression.

"You gone look like an old man prematurely scrunching up your face and squinting like that." He laughed. "Put your eyes on and take some of that strain off!"

I returned a boisterous laugh, reaching over and fishing my glasses from my briefcase.

"How's that?" I placed them on my face, peering back at Ellington.

"Much better." He chuckled. "You keep squinting like that, and those wrinkles will set in and never go away."

"You're right, E." I smiled, adjusting them on my face.

"What brings you in? You're normally working from home on Thursdays."

"Baby's teething, and I need peace and quiet. I'll get back and relieve Jayla once I get a few things done here."

"Gotcha. I'll be heading out to lunch after my afternoon call. You're welcome to join me. Or let me know if I can bring you back anything."

"Thanks, but no thanks." He patted his shoulder bag and replied, "She still managed to pack her dear husband lunch with a cranky baby and very little sleep."

"You're a lucky man, Ellington." I returned gingerly.

"You know me better than that. Luck doesn't have anything to do with it." He pointed up toward the sky. Like me, Ellington was a man of faith.

"I hear you, man."

"Well. I'll be at my desk; let me know if you need anything, boss." He said, retreating out of my office.

"Appreciate you, E," I called behind him.

"Yes, sir!"

I continued my analysis and moved on to a Pro Forma I needed to review. Expenses and revenues were critical for future projections, and a Pro Forma was the best way to determine what to expect. These could be cumbersome, but I planned to knock out a significant portion before my afternoon conference call.

"Hey, Micah! Good morning." I quietly sighed, attempting to mask the annoyance I felt at the sudden presence of this individual. "Well, good late morning! It's nearly eleven." She was extra chipper. Annoyingly so. I looked up as Erica padded into my office, uninvited, swaying her hips exuberantly. "I've got Noah's Bagels in the breakroom for everyone. I can grab one for you."

"No thank you." I'd since returned my attention to my computer.

"You sure? There are quite a few everything bagels. I know those are your favorite." She sang that last part, provoking my subtle eye roll. If she saw it, she didn't react.

I looked up at Erica to find her already looking at me expectantly. Erica needed to find something else to do. She was an attractive woman, but this wasn't happening. Mixing business with pleasure was not a good idea. Even under different circumstances, I wouldn't have dated her.

I curse the very day I went home with her that night at the lounge.

I knew better. That was two years ago, and Erica was still trying to make something happen. A constant thorn in my side. Furthermore, she was chasing the men all over the building. She thought I didn't know about it, but everyone knew it.

She even tried it with Ellington and that shit pissed me off. Her ass knew Ellington was married. Erica saw a good thing and wanted to mess it up. Simply because it wasn't hers. Ellington was a good man. Professional. Hardworking. Kept to himself, and he loved his wife and his baby. Erica peeped that and was up for the challenge.

I loathed women like her.

No. Damn. Good.

One day, Ellington confided in me that she spent too much time at his desk. In a particular instance, Erica came to speak with him and had her cleavage out.

Just plain disrespectful.

Ellington came to see me immediately and told me he couldn't continue working with her. She made him uncomfortable, and it was beginning to create an interference. We relied on the Administrative Coordinators when we had to meet with other department heads—namely, C-suite executives. Erica worked magic, securing meetings with people with the most challenging calendars you've ever seen.

Many of the people we worked with were in high demand and critical to the progression of the project timeline. She was vital to our department, and I understand why Ellington hesitated telling me. Knowing Ellington, he just wanted to keep the peace. I immediately made the executive decision to trade administrative coordinators with my colleague. Their coordinator was a recent college grad named

Jackson. He worked well with our team and was just as efficient as Erica, and I was glad to have him.

I expected we would see less of Erica with this change. Maybe we'd even stop seeing her altogether. The other department sat on the other side of the building. Literally, complete with their own bathrooms and elevators... yet somehow, Erica still managed to find her way over here.

I didn't want to take anyone's job, nor was I above it. If I heard one more complaint, I would dismiss Erica, no questions asked. As System Vice President, I had the latitude to do so.

"I'm positive, Erica. Now, if you'll please state your business, otherwise I need to get back to work here."

Erica stood in front of my desk, making a show of straightening out her black dress. I'll admit she looked great. She was tall. Had long, toned legs. Always wearing high heels, she walked impeccably in.

"I did want to ask you. Would you like to have lunch with me this afternoon? Or sometime next week, maybe? We don't have to go far. I'm fine with the café downstairs."

I sighed. In addition to our one-time sexcapade we did have lunch together here at the café on the first floor. It was just the once, and I realized pretty quickly Erica wasn't the type of woman I wanted to continue to build with. I'd even told her so.

Sighing, I said, "Erica. We've had this conversation. More than once." And we had.

She wasn't getting it.

"I just don't get it!" She snapped. "What's wrong with me Micah? Huh? I know I'm pretty. I'm smart. I parade myself around in front of you, and you don't even notice me!"

"Erica. I never said there was anything wrong with you."

"Then what is it?" She was a little calmer now."

"We aren't compatible," I told her for the umpteenth time.

"So, I'm only good for one thing, huh?"

I sighed again. "The way we met each other was unconventional for me. And things happened in an unconventional order. That's not the norm for me, either. I assure you it wouldn't have gone that far if I had formally met you first."

Erica reared her head back as if she'd been slapped. Her face immediately settled into a scowl. Brows connected. She was offended by that. All I did was answer her question.

Furthermore, what I'd told her for the past two years didn't seem to land.

I should have been blunt to begin with.

Erica slowly crossed her arms, peering at me through cut eyes. "Just who do you think you are?" She seethed.

I said nothing. But my antennas were up. She sounded eerily calm.

"For your information, you aren't all that, Micah! I'm an incredibly good catch. Plenty of men want me! And whoever I choose would be lucky to have me! You're crazy for letting me go!"

"I guess so," I said, shrugging my shoulders.

Erica huffed loudly, stomping out of my office.

I sighed again, rubbing my temples. Just that quick, I had a tension headache. I hoped this meant she'd leave me alone for a while.

I sat for a moment, unable to return to the spreadsheets open on my desktop.

I glanced at my wristwatch. It had hardly been about three hours since I arrived at the office.

I sighed another exasperated breath.

I was no good right now, and I was much too distracted. My head was about to explode between Erica's shenanigans and my yearning for the woman I truly wanted.

Thinking for another moment, I exhaled at the revelation. It was simple. Her voice alone was not enough for me anymore.

I wanted more.

I needed more, and sharing space with her regularly was the only remedy. I could only hope she felt the same way.

On impulse, I picked up my phone and called the one woman that had me besotted.

She answered on the second ring.

"Hey, you. Good morning."

I closed my eyes, moved by her soft voice, sounding sweet as a lullaby.

Not wasting any time, I said, "Destiney baby, I want to see you again." I continued, unable to stop myself. "I thought I would just go back to everything as usual, but honestly, I've been enamored with thoughts of you since seeing you. Being in your company. Your beauty. Your scent... your kiss. Especially that kiss. You are all I've been able to think about."

She released a breath I didn't know she was holding and chuckled lightly.

"Me too."

"Yeah?"

"Yeah."

Damn.

We were silent for a few beats.

"Can I be honest with you?" Destiney volleyed.

"You can always be honest with me, love."

"Well... I have longed for you too."

"Have you?"

"Oh yes. Especially the way you kiss me... it's been at the forefront of my mind."

Goodness.

"Why didn't you tell me?"

"A little shy. Embarrassed. Silly, I know, but I'm glad it's out in the open now."

"Can I take you out, baby?" I asked boldly. "If you are comfortable... seeing me again."

"I'd love to see you again."

"Is tomorrow night, okay?

"It's perfect."

"I'll pick you up at seven if that's alright."

"What should I wear?"

"Something comfortable."

"I look forward to it."

"Likewise."

It was no surprise that the rest of my day flew by.

seventeen

DESTINEY

Just got here. Once I've parked, I'll head inside

Instead of letting Micah pick me up for our date, I convinced him I could meet him instead.

Maybe I knew then that I would do this to him.

Micah sent me the address to where we were meeting and texted me once he left home, headed that way. Now that he had arrived, he texted me, letting me know. As each text came through, I shamefully hung my head as if he were standing right in front of me.

I had every opportunity to tell him I wasn't coming… but my pathetic ass didn't have the decency to take it.

About five minutes after his last text, my phone rang in my hand. I saw that Micah was calling me, and I let his call roll to voicemail.

After seeing Micah the other night, I was so consumed; it was ridiculous. I thought I was before, but this was another level entirely.

Like Tamia, I was so into Micah. My feelings for him grew with each passing moment. I liked him so much, and talking to him was so easy.

Effortless.

Being near him seemed even easier. This was wild because I felt like… almost as if… I was falling. I wouldn't know for sure, I suppose. I've never fallen before. Never been there before.

But this feeling was so strong.

And something else. I don't know what it is, but there's something about conversations when it's dark.

Late-night convos are grown, sexy, unfiltered, and unpredictable.

Feelings are bound to be caught.

Any existing feelings are guaranteed to grow deeper.

Assured to develop into something stronger.

Conversing with that special someone... you had the feels for... when the sun went down... and the hour was far spent...was...dangerous. But in the best way.

I was feeling the hell out of Micah. The majority of our deeper conversations happened at night. Nighttime was my favorite time.

And once we kissed, that was it.

I am consumed even more so now. I was partly joking with him when I casually mentioned getting attached after kissing him. But that's precisely how I felt.

All bets were off. You could stick a fork in me. White flag frantically blowing in the wind.

Micah was everything. He smelled good. He looked great. 6'3 and 230 pounds of solid muscle. He clearly took care of himself. When he held me in his brawny arms, I felt safe with him. Protected.

I'd imagine someone of his stature would appear imposing to some people.

But Micah was a gentle giant. A big cuddly teddy bear. And I felt right at home in his arms. Something I wanted to feel all the time.

And when he kissed me, my mind was blown.

First, no one has ever kissed me the way he kissed me.

He captured my lips, cautiously. Gently. And his kisses were so delicate. Tender. Unhurried. I noticed that it was his m.o., taking his sweet time with me. Making it a point to ask me first.

But when Micah kissed me, it seemed he was savoring the moment as if he didn't know when he'd get the chance again. His lips were full and soft.

And his tongue. Oh. My. Gosh...

He took my breath away.

Simply put, it was amazing. Panty wetting.

Micah brought a serenity I hadn't even realized I needed, and I wanted to be wherever he was. I didn't want him to leave. I was seconds away from inviting him inside.

Literally.

I wasn't thinking about jumping his bones.

Okay, maybe I did. Very briefly.

But honestly, I pictured a grown ass comfortable atmosphere. Maybe some wine with some chill music, conversing the way we do. I enjoy an occasional glass of wine. Those elements paired with a good conversation... I imagine that being a risqué combination once you start feeling warm inside. And I wanted that with him.

And Micah has been abundantly clear about his feelings for me. Unmistakably.

That's probably the one thing I appreciate the most. Last night, I was all in my head. Feeling shy. Typical for me. I was so shy that I couldn't even make eye contact. I was comfortable. Very comfortable. But since I liked him so much, I felt bashful. And Micah helped me relax. Effortlessly. Not only with his words, which are unmatched, but his actions. It is absolutely apparent how he feels about me.

And it's nice to know how he feels without needing to ask. I'm not the type to need constant reassurance.

Well, maybe I am. Sometimes.

But, anyway, being reminded how much he likes me. How beautiful he finds me... ineffable. Considering I feel the same way especially. There was a time or two... or three, where I liked a guy much more than he liked me. And I was taken advantage of.

I've even had a few one-way platonic friendships. That shit was really wack.

Wack as fuck. Didn't feel good.

But this was definitely an equal exchange—mutual gratification.

Yeah. Micah was everything.

When Micah asked to take me out, I said yes without hesitation. I wanted to spend time with him. Go on dates like normal couples do. But... once I thought about it, I knew I likely wouldn't go through with it.

I'd been bleeding—a lot.

Last night, I went to sleep dreaming of Micah and woke up to underwear full of blood and soaked sheets. Things with my "issue of blood" were going from bad to worse.

Nonetheless, I felt terrible for flaking. I wanted to see him, but I was in my head. Bad. If I'd met up with him, I'd probably be too damn self-conscious and overly anxious even to enjoy our time together. He would notice, and it would ruin an otherwise lovely evening.

Now I felt immature and pitiful, lying across my bed and wishing I was out with Micah.

He called me again, and I watched the phone vibrate in my hands.

I sighed, fed up with myself. He was more than patient, and I was wasting his time with my teenage shenanigans. What the hell was my problem?

My phone chimed with a text from him.

Micah: I'll head home since you're not coming. Please at least let me know you're okay

I could have cried.

I'm sorry

It was the least I could offer him; besides, I didn't know what else to say.

He replied immediately.

Micah: I'm glad you're okay sweetheart

I didn't deserve him.

And if I didn't get my shit together and quickly, I knew I'd lose him before I even had him.

eighteen

MICAH

I entered my home through my garage, not even bothering to cut on the lights. I grabbed bottled water from the fridge and sat at my kitchen island in the quiet darkness while I drank it.

I was so eager to see Destiney again finally; disappointed was an understatement.

Shit. I was more than eager. I was juiced.

Disappointment didn't seem fitting either. Gutted was more like it.

Destiney didn't give me much to go on, so I wasn't sure how to feel as it related to her. I thought I'd made her feel comfortable. I was confused as to why she agreed to meet me if she wasn't ready. I didn't pressure her. If she had said not yet, I would have been totally fine with that instead of her flaking.

If I'm honest, I was a bit frustrated with her mixed signals at this point.

Destiney hadn't been in a relationship for a long time. Had never been in one in her adult years. I was cognizant of that. During our conversations, Destiney was opening up so much. We both were. And I could see that her heart and feelings were extremely fragile, which was why I was gentle in the way I handled her.

This was the third time I'd asked to see her. I figured after we kissed, we were past that.

I guess I thought wrong.

Maybe she only agreed to meet because I'd brought it up.

Maybe I'd have to wait for her to initiate when this happened.

Maybe I needed to fall back even more so and let her lead.

I just hoped it would be sooner rather than later.

My phone illuminated the room, and I exhaled an exasperated breath, seeing that it was Destiney calling me. I certainly wasn't angry with her, but I wasn't exactly in the best headspace to take her call. I didn't want to snip at her.

While I waited for her at the restaurant, I called her twice and texted her several times, which all went unanswered. Until she told me she was sorry.

I'm not even exactly sure what it is she was sorry for.

Opting to text her instead, I typed a message and headed upstairs to get changed.

I took a shower, changed, then hung out downstairs to watch TV.

The one television I have in my home is in my living room. I haven't had a TV in my bedroom for several years. I had one in my bedroom years ago and hardly watched it. In my opinion, which I know is unpopular, my bedroom was for four things: resting, reading, conversing, and love making.

Malachi always clowned me about that, naturally. His ass had televisions all over his home. His main screen was eighty inches, I think. The shit was huge, but it fit their expansive living area. I wasn't much of a TV person anyway. I didn't even purchase a TV right away. When I finally decided to get one, it was for Gabe and Gabby to have something to watch.

I flipped a few channels and ended up on sports highlights. But I wasn't watching.

My mind went back to Destiney.

It never left her, if I'm honest. I glanced at the clock realizing we'd usually be wrapped in a deep ass conversation by now. It dawned on me that this was the first night in several weeks we hadn't had one. I texted her, asking if she was still up. She responded with affirmative, so I called her.

She answered on the first ring.

"Hello." She spoke softly in my ear.

"Hey." My tone held an element of firmness. "How was your day?" I asked, briefly, disregarding the elephant in the room.

Destiney was silent for too many beats, so I said, "Destiney. What are we doing?" She needed to let me know something. Maybe I was losing my patience.

If she didn't know, she was about to find out. When she was still silent, I continued, "I want you. I want to see you. And I've made that clear to you. But these mixed messages. I just…are we finished, or are we done?" That last line slipped out before I could stop it. More silence filled the line, and I honestly wanted to hang up.

She finally said, "I'm so freaking frustrated Micah."

"What has you so frustrated?" I asked evenly.

"I was too shy to meet you today." She revealed.

"Shy?" I pressed. Chuckling but wasn't shit funny. "I need more than that, Destiney."

She sighed. "I was too shy to meet you today…because… I suffer from severe uterine fibroids, and I'm bleeding. I'm too embarrassed to go out because if I don't go to the bathroom every half hour, I could bleed through my clothes. It makes me uncomfortable and gives me the worst anxiety. I literally have to cancel plans and stay at home because the bleeding is so excessive."

Wow. There it was.

"How long have you been dealing with this?" My voice was tender now, laced with concern.

"Few years now. Since about my early twenties."

I didn't have sisters, but I have a mother, and one day, I got a crash course related to monthlies. I have an impeccable memory- that can be a blessing and a curse. Depending.

Anyway, I vividly recall my introduction to this occurrence when I entered my parents' bathroom searching for my mother. I had to be about six years old. Maybe seven. Ordinarily, when their bedroom door is open, we can come in. When the door was closed, we had to knock first, in case Mommy wasn't dressed.

I walked into their bedroom and proceeded to their ensuite restroom because I heard her in there. I entered the bathroom as Mommy had just stood from the toilet and pulled her pants up. I entered without bothering to announce myself, and in so doing, I caught a glimpse of a toilet bowl filled with crimson. My pure and innocent eyes had never seen so much blood before, and I was terrified.

Within a matter of seconds, I was hysterically crying my little eyes out, convinced my mother must have been dying. Malachi came running when he heard the commotion. He was none the wiser but was just as hysterical once he saw me in that state. After my mother comforted us, she took the opportunity to explain.

"Don't cry. Mommy is fine." She gently pulled us into her arms. *"It's called menstruation, which happens to a woman every month. I promise everything is okay."*

In my teen years, I had girlfriends who would mention the cramps, bloating, and discomfort.

I hadn't heard of uterine fibroids, but based on what Destiney shared with me, I could imagine things must have been much more severe than a monthly cycle. My heart immediately softened for her.

"Is it painful, sweetheart?"

"Wasn't so bad at first. But these past three months have been really brutal."

"Hmm. Is there anything I can do?"

She lightly chuckled. "You're so sweet, Micah, but no. It's just something I have to deal with."

"Thank you for sharing something so personal with me. You really could have come to me love."

"I know, Micah…" Destiney exhaled heavily. "I should have told you sooner. I'm so sorry for flaking on you today. It's just embarrassing. This issue has affected my life in all areas."

"We'll get through it together. And I'm always here, we can talk about it. About anything. Please come to me even if it's uncomfortable. All of you is safe with me."

"Alright."

I wanted to hold Destiney in my arms. Though I couldn't sympathize with her, I did empathize with her situation.

"I need to see you." I proclaimed boldly.

"I want to see you too."

"Can I come to you?"

"I would love that, Micah."

"Have you eaten?"

"No, I haven't."

"Give me an hour, and I'll be right there. I'll bring dinner with me."

nineteen

MICAH

"I absolutely love your lips, Destiney baby."

"I love yours too."

I really did love her lips. They were so soft, her mouth was so sweet, and her tongue was wicked. My baby could kiss. I captured her lips again, gently sucking her bottom one. We'd both been sucking lips amidst messy tongue swirling.

We were in Destiney's living room, lying on her couch, kissing each other into oblivion. I was on my back, and she was settled between my legs. When I arrived, she kissed me at the door, leaving me desiring more of her kisses.

I stopped on my way to grab us sandwiches from Jersey Mikes, and we ate in the living room while we watched Juice on BET. Now, the TV was watching us.

After we ate, we settled on the couch, and Destiney surprised me by cuddling up so close to me that she eventually ended up in my lap. Everything was good in my hood. That's when I asked her for another kiss.

Apparently, we were on the same type of time.

This brick in my pants was bulging against the zipper in my jeans, and Destiney had been grinding against it. We were basically dry humping. She was sending me places the way she snaked her body on top of mine. I knew she could feel how hard I was beneath her.

My dick was hard as steel. But she couldn't truly know how much I wanted her at this moment. I wanted her so badly.

The fact that I was in her home with her lying in my arms, my lips on hers would do for now.

The fact that I was in her personal space was hugely significant. But just the same, I couldn't help but desire to get closer to her.

As close as I could.

I was vigilant and cautious with each move I made. This was chess, not checkers.

When I came by to kiss her goodnight, we kissed passionately. It was a perfect first kiss.

But nothing like this. These kisses tonight were wet and sloppy. Nasty. The kind of kissing that would typically get something started. It had been years since I made out like this, and I was here for all of it.

"I need a break baby." Destiney broke our kiss, bringing me out of my thoughts. She laughed a little, wiping her mouth, then mine. I could agree. We had been kissing for quite a long time. So long we probably should come up for air.

"Whatever you want, love." I placed a peck on the top of her head as she laid on my chest.

"Whatever I want?"

"Whatever you want," I reassured.

"I can't have what I want right now."

"Try me."

She was still on my chest, silent as I rubbed circles in her back.

Finally, she said, "When I'm bleeding, I don't... I don't feel confident. I don't feel sexy. It's holding me back. I feel dirty and gross. Even right now, would you believe me if I told you I'm feeling incredibly self-cautious?"

"Hmm." I continued to rub her back softly, trying to formulate my next statement. I knew this was extremely personal, and I appreciated her vulnerability. Our phone conversations were all over, and we talked about so many things, including intimate topics. She had already shared with me that she hadn't been intimate for a few years.

She also revealed to me that these feelings were awakening for her again. So, I knew what she was referring to. I'd told her it was the same for me, too.

"First, please don't say that again. You are not dirty or gross. You are not. Women bleed. I know this situation is not ideal, but I promise we will figure this out and get you better, sweetheart." I was serious. I meant that shit. The very last thing I wanted was for her to feel this way.

Destiney was silent, and I continued musing over my thoughts. Despite her situation, I had an insatiable desire for her. Her situation didn't deter me. I wanted her better, of course, but establishing my position and making it clear that she was the woman I wanted was my goal.

"Destiney baby?"

"Yes."

"Do you know that I find you incredibly sexy?" I hadn't shared this specific detail with her before, but there was no time like the present.

She lifted her head from my chest. Her beautiful eyes held my gaze. "Really?"

"Indeed. You are super sexy. Beautiful yes. But sexy as hell. If nothing else, I need you to be so very confident in that."

"Wow. Thank you, Micah." She leaned forward, kissing me sweetly. "Never been called sexy before."

"Get used to hearing it, sexy."

She lightly tittered. "You're so sweet, Micah." Her head returned to my chest. Then, "Transparency moment. I find you sexy too."

She was so cute. "Is that so?" I asked, chuckling lightly.

"Very much so."

"Appreciate you." I resumed rubbing small circles on her back. I had an idea and carefully considered how I would approach bringing it to her. "Since we're having transparency moments, can I tell you something else?"

"Of course you can."

"Hmm. Give me a moment to get this together."

"Okay."

I was a straight shooter, but I didn't want to cause her to cower by making her uncomfortable. "Alright. So, I want to get closer to you, baby. Intimately."

She looked up at me again. Eyes wide. "Closer how?"

"You may think I'm referring to sex. But I'm not. I know we aren't there yet."

"So, how do you mean?"

"Shower with me." Destiney averted her eyes, but I continued, "It is incredibly intimate washing each other's bodies." She had a look of hesitancy as I continued, "I promise, it will not lead to sex."

After a beat, she gave me her eyes, nodding. "Alright."

"Are you sure?"

"Yes, I'm sure."

"Alright love. Lead the way."

After Destiney cut off the TV and the lights, I grabbed her hand, following her down the hall into her bedroom. I glanced around. Destiney's bedroom fit her personality down to a T.

It was comfy and inviting with eclectic décor. There were various shades of green everywhere, with purple accents. I was greeted by a coconut scent, which I loved. It added to the comforting ambience of her bedroom. Coconut must have been her favorite scent. I noticed a few coconut-scented body butters and candles on her dresser.

Her bed looked like a place where she got the best sleep. It had a fluffy lime green comforter and lots of pillows. I knew she loved to read, which explained the purple and white polka dot reading pillow. I hadn't seen a reading pillow in years.

Destiney beckoned me toward the ensuite, telling me to go ahead of her to get the shower started, and she would join me momentarily. She probably needed a moment to talk herself through her nerves, and I could understand that. There were few things as intimate as couples in the shower.

Once in the bathroom, I closed the door behind me to give her some privacy.

I removed my clothing, folded it neatly, and placed it on the vanity. I turned on the shower and gave it a minute to reach the desired temperature.

Destiney probably preferred her water to be a little warmer than I did. Women could take incredibly hot showers and baths. I didn't know how that shit was even possible. After a moment, I heard music coming on, and that's when I noticed the Bluetooth speaker in the far corner of the bathroom. It was a slow jam, which was a great idea. Another moment later, I heard a knock on the door.

"Come on in, sweetheart." I was naked as the day I was born, standing there in her bathroom.

Destiney cracked the door, and I saw eyes peering back at me. "Micah…" she said hesitantly.

"Are you alright?"

"Yes. But I'm a little shy," She revealed.

"No need to be shy, love," I told her gingerly. She remained on the other side of the door, and I remembered the hummingbird nightlight when I entered her bathroom moments earlier. "Would you feel more comfortable if we turned the lights out? This nightlight will be bright enough for us."

"I would."

"Indeed." I turned the lights out, and Destiney entered the bathroom wearing a bathrobe. "Is that better baby?" I asked as I brought her to me, wrapping my arms around her. I wanted her to be comfortable; hopefully, she would be since this was her space.

"Yes. Thank you."

"Of course. Anything you need, you tell me."

"Okay."

I reached into the shower behind me, and the water was perfect. Taking her delicate hands in mine, I kissed both of her palms. Went back and forth. I didn't rush the equal peppering of kisses on each of her hands. Humming, I pressed, "Destiney baby…" now kissing the tops and undersides of her soft fingertips. "I plan to kiss you. A lot. If you're good with that."

"Absolutely fine with that."

"Alright. You ready love?"

"Yes, I am." I took note of the shift in her voice. It held a sultry tone, and I was with it. Slowly untying the belt of her robe, I gently removed it from her body. Kissing her all the while. I took my time kissing her lips, then kissing her neck and bare shoulders. After placing her robe on the hook behind the door, I took her hand in mine, bringing her with me as I entered the shower. She stepped in behind me, and only then did I scan her silhouette. Salivating instantly.

It wasn't long before we were kissing heavily again. I took Destiney into my arms, rubbing her upper and lower back as the water cascaded over us. Her skin was so soft. Damn.

We kissed for a good while.

Flush, skin to skin, no barrier between us, and I could feel the stiff peaks of her nipples. She wasn't the only one who was excited. My dick was hard as hell, pressed between us and there was no hiding it. Destiney's arms were around me, and she moaned softly as I continued to caress her body.

"That feels so nice, Micah," She told me.

"My pleasure baby." That shit had two meanings. All in due time. And I looked forward to it. I kissed her lips. I kissed her forehead, her cheeks. Her neck and her shoulders. Her fingers.

When the time came, I planned to kiss and caress every single inch of her body.

When I arrived earlier, I grabbed her hand and didn't let it go right away.

Holding hands was such a thing with her. Destiney is the best hand holder there ever was. And her hands are so soft. I was a little surprised since she works with her hands so much. As an artist. Creating masterpieces. Painting and sketching for hours a day. I figured maybe that meant her hands wouldn't feel so velvety smooth.

I was beginning to love bringing them to my lips. Kissing her fingers was my new obsession.

Destiney's hands were pretty. Petite, matching her petite stature.

Slender, delicate fingers. Perfectly manicured nails.

Evidently, she maintained a top-notch exfoliating and moisturizing routine.

Breaking our kiss, I surveyed Destiney with low lids. Her doe eyes peering right up into mine. "Sweetheart..."

"Yes." An alluring tone in her voice. Still. I'd caught that inflection moments before, which sent excitement rushing to my groin.

The lighting was dim, but I could see the desire in her eyes. The same desire I had for her. I held her face gently in my hands, my lips just a whisper from hers. "Would it be painful if I touched you? There? If you're comfortable. But I don't want to hurt you if you're tender during this time."

She began, "I...you..." Sensing her trepidation, I lowered my hands, holding her firmly at the waist. Continuing my gentle caress of her skin. I'm sure my question surprised her, and she was likely feeling bashful. But I needed her to understand. She had no reason to be embarrassed with me.

"I'm a grown man. I'm not afraid of a little blood, sweetheart."

Destiney shook her head as she chuckled. "Hardly a little." There wasn't an ounce of mirth.

"The water will wash it all away."

She waited a beat then asked, "You sure you want to do that?"

"I am, Destiney baby."

She took a few beats. Then, "Okay."

"Okay?"

"Yes. Okay."

I placed an arm around her waist, anchoring her close to me, then made a graceful motion of lowering my other hand to the apex of her. I gently cupped her. My massive hand covered her in its entirety. She was smooth. And… fuck. There was an intense heat emanating from her.

Destiney quivered softly as I applied pressure, gently moving my palm from side to side. Arching her back, she leaned into me. Her soft moans music to my ears. She was incredibly responsive as I squeezed and palmed her there. Connecting our lips again, I applied more pressure, pushing the heel of my hand against her. It was clear she liked that, so I did it again.

I liked it too. I was so turned on. Hard as hell. To the point that it was painful.

Rocking her hips slowly, she moaned against my lips.

"Destiney Baby?"

"Yeah?"

"Can I put my finger inside you?" Speaking close to her ear, still applying pressure. I could feel her pearl, showing itself. Got damn... using the heal of my hand I applied pressure there too. Connecting our lips again before she could answer me, I swallowed more of her faint moans.

Destiney broke our kiss, giving me her eyes. "If you want to."

"Do you want me to?"

"Hell. Yes."

I released a faint chuckle as I gently nudged her upper thigh. She understood my silent request and immediately spread more for me. I returned my hand to her center, then, unhurried, carefully pierced her sanctuary with my middle finger. There was some restriction. I decided one finger would be plenty.

I held her even closer to me. "Destiney baby." My strokes were gentle and slow.

"Yes?" She murmured.

"Is this okay? Am I hurting you?"

"You're okay... not hurting me at all."

I was back in her ear, "You sexy girl." I'd never been intimate with a woman while she was bleeding, but things didn't feel any different to me. "Everything feels perfect," I told her. I planted a few kisses on her cheek, then moved up to her forehead, remaining there for a moment.

Destiney moaned, and I felt her subtle nod against me. "It feels perfect to me, too."

Ever so slightly, I increased my pace, grazing my thumb over her swollen pearl. I brought my lips lower again, now tenderly pressed to her neck. I could feel the vibration of her vocal cords as she released a faint moan. She liked that.

Yeah.

We'd eventually get around to washing ourselves.

But first things first.

twenty

DESTINEY

"Byyyyeee Miss Destineeeeeey!"

"See you later, Sasha!"

Sasha was such an adorable seven-year-old little brown cutie pie and super polite. I'd taken such a liking to her right way. All of these kids have my heart, but little Sasha was one of my favorites. Likely because she reminded me a lot of myself as a child; she had a big smile and an even bigger personality. She was imaginative and creative and could draw pretty well for her age. Sasha already had something special. And I told her so.

I knew how impressionable kids were and wanted to always speak life over them. You never knew how that would impact their confidence, especially the ones expressing interest in the arts. There was a school of thought that STEMS were significantly more important. Many adults would discourage kids from artistic expression altogether.

I couldn't disagree more. That shit would grind my gears every time. Yes, STEM fields are vital, but the arts also matter. Tremendously. I would continually cultivate creativity with people of all ages, especially children.

"I'll miss you! See ya next week!" She'd come running back to me, grabbing my legs tightly one last time before she took off again behind the other kids, headed across the quad where all their parents were waiting.

"I'll see you next week, my friend!"

It was close to four o'clock now. Thankfully, the weather was great today. Warm enough to be comfortable. But not too warm. Officially summer. And Sacramento had very high digits in the summer months.

The artists and crew had to arrive at eight thirty a.m. and get everything set up. The kids arrived at 10 a.m. This morning, we had fresh fruit, granola bars, and water for them. Around noon, we had sandwiches and chips for lunch donated by a local deli. We were painting the mural outside a Boys and Girls Club in an underserved area of South Sacramento. We extended an opportunity for the kids in the summer day camp to help with the project. About two dozen kids came out today, from age seven to thirteen.

The mural would be bright, colorful, and lively, showing children of various cultures and ages playing together around a large oak tree. Scattered throughout the mural would be phrases in multiple languages. Spanish, Italian, and Portuguese. Japanese, Korean, Yoruba, Swahili, and many others. The phrases roughly translated to the English word unity. The concept was dope, and I loved the diversity it represented.

The key to a lasting mural was good quality paints, which could be costly, especially for larger murals. We secured generous sponsors who provided everything we needed, including supplies and meals. I was willing to sign on even after learning the artists wouldn't get paid much.

But that's the nature of the beast. Some community projects don't pay as handsomely as the others. I applied for a few grants, and if those came through, I could make up the difference that way. Even if those fell through, I would be fine. I eventually planned to secure another gig on the days I wasn't committed to this project. It was such a great cause; I was just grateful to be a part of it. Especially getting to work with these kids. Making a positive difference in their lives meant a lot to me.

It was a productive day considering. Getting the kids to work for extended periods of time can be a challenge. Understandably. They had such limited attention spans, but they're so proud of their hard work and love helping. Collaborating with kids is always a joy for me.

We have to keep a close eye on them, though. If someone isn't paying attention, one of the younger kids can take a paintbrush and ruin something in just three seconds flat! I've seen it happen.

The mural was along the side of the building, facing the street. Such a great place for it. It would definitely be a neighborhood focal point and look great once it was done. This would be a large project. Twenty-four feet by eighteen feet. Approximately four hundred and thirty-two square feet.

There were seven of us, including India and me. Half guys and half girls. All of us were in our twenties. We all worked really well together and made up a talented group, I dare say. Typically, the number of sessions is based on the size of the mural

and the number of muralists. This mural was orga-
nized over consecutive weekends, and today was
session number two of six sessions scheduled.

Even though we'd been out here most of the
day, we couldn't yet call it quitting time. It wasn't unusual for muralists to work after hours when necessary, and today, we would need to stay a little longer
to ensure the project was completed on schedule.
With just the muralists remaining, we could work
with little interruption and really get into our element. I'm sure we'd accomplish a great deal of work
now that the kids had gone for the day.

I successfully mustered up the excitement to
engage with the kids. And I could put my face on
when I was interviewed by the press that came on
site. I was trying desperately to hang on to that excitement. I needed it to get through today.

I was still bleeding. Today made day number
seventeen. That's almost three fucking weeks of this
shit and it didn't seem that things were slowing
down. But I wasn't in that much pain. However, I realized that maybe I was convincing myself that I
wasn't. I know for a fact that my pain tolerance is
higher than the average person's. I was accustomed
to these massive cramps. Someone else would likely
be curled in a ball somewhere. Although I was toler-
ating the pain, I didn't have much energy. Anyway,
I was a little sluggish but pushing through it.

I hated being away from home for hours like
I did today. But I didn't have much of a choice. So, as
always, I kept a change of clothes in my car and a
sweatshirt in case I needed to tie it around my waist.
And made sure to take frequent trips to the ladies'
room. If not, I would almost always have a leak.

I learned that the hard way.

"Yo! This portrait is dope, Des!" India said as she walked up behind me. India and I were working on opposite ends. I'd already gone by to see how her section was coming along. It looked amazing.

Everything India did looked amazing. My bestie was incredibly talented.

"Thank you, girlie. I'm getting better at these. In a minute, I'll be as sick as you are with portraits."

"Girl, stop. You're already there! In the meantime, I'm getting a handle on my lettering. You're the lettering queen! I think Brandi had us mixed up when she assigned us."

Brandi was a hippie white chick, a freaking beast with a paintbrush and Artistic Director-Extraordinaire of this project. Generally, there's a director in charge of the design and execution of the mural. They're tasked with organizing the artists, identifying their strengths, and assigning them accordingly based on their talents.

I was good anywhere, really, but I would have expected to be working on the lines and lettering and India the portraits. Instead, we were flipped, which was fine. But it was still funny.

"Yeah. She probably did." We both cracked up.

Many people got India, and I confused. We worked on multiple projects together, and we'd been mistaken for each other plenty of times. Though I didn't mind. Funny, we didn't resemble one another, but we were always together and had similar personalities. And almost always, we were the only two black chicks. This project was no different.

When we broke for lunch earlier, I called Micah, and we spoke for most of the lunch hour. I sent him a few pictures, and he loved our work so far.

The night he came to my place was the last time I saw him.

That was almost two weeks ago.

I missed him something fierce, and I desperately wanted to see him. Be near him. But I was trying to keep my distance since I was still bleeding so much.

This was the worst. I was beside myself, and I missed him terribly.

But... I just couldn't be near him. Not only was I feeling insecure as hell, but I also knew I couldn't offer him anything physical. All we could really do was kiss, which I loved. I absolutely loved the way he kissed me. The way he kissed me and the way he touched me had me fantasizing.

I should be embarrassed at the amount of fantasizing I'd done these past two weeks.

Anyway, Micah is a grown man. He needed more than kissing. Eventually, it was only a matter of time. And...I wanted to be the woman who satisfied those needs. He certainly deserved it. Micah was so considerate. Thoughtful. Sweet. Gentle.

And Micah made me feel sexy, which is entirely new for me. I feel confident in myself as a woman. I know I'm an attractive woman.

But sexy is different.

Micah just had a way with shit. I can't even put my finger on it, like when we were in the shower. I was so nervous. But my nerves were dispelled immediately.

Micah made sure I was comfortable, checking with me before he did anything.

Everything he did required my permission.

I didn't know if he was being extra conscious because of my situation or if that was just him... ever the gentleman. But my goodness. Even when we kissed, unless I initiated it, Micah was asking first.

He had no idea how much I appreciated that.

My first sexual experience was... not good. I tried to forget about it and compartmentalize it.

And it remains my only sexual experience.

Considering that, it seemed that Micah knew precisely how I needed to be handled without being told.

I loved the way Micah handled me.

And I didn't express it, but I took notice of Micah's prominent erection when we were lying on my couch. Micah's dick was hard as hell. I felt it grazing me multiple times when we were in the shower.

Crazy too, because he didn't even take care of himself. Not in front of me anyway. That shit had to be painful for him.

That entire experience had me in my feelings, not only in the moment but also after the fact.

I concluded that my feelings had grown deeper than before. I attribute this to the careful way Micah handled my situation and me. I can't say exactly what I expected, although I wouldn't dare say I was surprised.

Micah has already proven himself to be compassionate. Sensitive. Hypersensitive to what I'm dealing with. His compassion revealed itself early in our friendship and was a constant presence.

That was just Micah. Compassion came second nature.

But not all my feelings concerning this were warm and fuzzy.

For one, I felt incredibly selfish.

My loudest thought of all, aside from how much I loved everything Micah was doing to me, was that I wanted Micah all to myself. I wanted to be with Micah.

Yet, I couldn't offer Micah anything beyond conversation. And making out.

That wasn't okay.

Something occurred to me a long time ago.

Something I desperately tried to ignore, hoping that by doing so, maybe I could make it go away.

And as hard as I tried to ignore it, I couldn't make it go away.

It was time I faced the music.

The fact of the matter is that I just needed to let Micah go. Leave him alone. Let him be.

That was inevitable. I also felt an immense amount of sadness. I cared about Micah so much. I knew he cared just as much about me. Hurting him was the last thing I'd want to do.

The sudden influx of moisture in my underwear pulled me from my thoughts. It was about that time I went and checked on things.

I put my paint brush down and removed my black rubber gloves. I prefer wearing gloves while working on a mural. I have sensitive skin, and it's easily irritated, so the extra barrier protects me from the harsh chemicals and paint we use. Of course, it keeps the skin clean but also helps prevent accidentally transferring paint or chemicals to other surfaces and accidental smudging. Not all painters wear them. I get a better grip on my brush with gloves than without.

"Indie, I'll be right back, headed to the ladies room." She was back in her zone, working away. She smiled warmly, giving me a knowing expression. I shared my diagnosis and everything I had been dealing with, with India a while back. She was constantly checking in with me, and I didn't feel so alone with this.

Once I was securely in the restroom stall, I saw that my pad was soaked, and I noticed I had passed a few rather large clots. I switched out my pad, and when I wiped myself, I saw another large clot on the toilet paper. I stood up to flush and saw one in the toilet.

Groaning, I buttoned my pants and then washed my hands. I just wanted to go home. It was almost five, and the team would likely work until at least six before packing it up for the night. I felt terrible for bailing early, but I was sure Brandi would understand.

I pulled my backpack over my shoulder and exited the restroom. I needed to find Brandi and let her know I would be leaving.

Taking a few steps, I felt a gush between my legs. I considered going back into the restroom but decided to wait until I got home.

I took another step, and that's when everything went black.

twenty-one

MICAH

"Which hospital?"

"Sutter Medical on Capital."

"Does she know you've called me?"

"No, she doesn't. But she'll get over it. I know she misses you. And she can use some cheering up. The doctor admitted her, and she's scheduled for surgery tomorrow morning. She's not happy about any of this."

"I see. Well, thank you so much for calling me, Daijah. I'll be there as soon as I can. Is there anything I can get you on my way?"

"No thank you, Micah. Julian went to get me something. He should be back any minute. I look forward to introducing the two of you."

"Likewise. I'll see you all soon."

I ended the call, exhaling in exasperation.

Now I knew why Destiney was hiding from me.

She was still bleeding.

When I left her home two Fridays ago, I was confident we'd made progress. We'd gotten so close.

Intimately close.

Shit was surreal.

A fucking fantasy I could have only imagined. A fantasy that somehow came true. A high I was still coming down from.

Seeing Destiney in person was significant in itself. But she let me do more than that. Destiney allowed me into her personal space.

She let me kiss her. And kiss her I did.

Till I got tired.

She agreed to shower together. She let me wash her body. And my goodness, her body was just as beautiful as I imagined. The lights were dim, and my sight was limited, but I could take in everything through my unrestricted touch.

She let me feel her mound. She let me grace her haven with my finger... fuck. That had me painfully hard.

Things went no further than that, but it was all good in my hood. I didn't go to her home to have sex with her. I wanted to show her she didn't have to avoid me. I wanted her to know I still wanted her.

So, when I left her that evening, I felt everything was finally out in the open. From my perspective, I figured she would be comfortable enough to be near me even during that time.

But... since then, it seems we've regressed. In my mind, we'd taken strides forward, only to take several steps back.

We talk daily, as usual. But Destiney continues to have a reason to evade my attempts to see her. Always an excuse. At one point, I considered pulling up on her, then quickly decided against it.

When we spoke this afternoon, Destiney was onsite doing work on a mural. She gushed about all of the cute kids there helping out. She sent me a few pictures, and I was beyond impressed with everything I saw.

But for the life of me, I couldn't comprehend this. She was at a worksite and seemed to be having a great time in her element, doing what she does best.

But she wouldn't let me see her.

If I'm honest, I was pretty frustrated. And I was beginning to take it personally.

Those feelings dissipated immediately when Daijah called me.

Destiney lost so much blood that she passed out at the worksite, and an ambulance was called.

After hanging up with Daijah, I quickly got out the door and hopped in my car to get to my baby.

The sun was beginning to set. It was a beautiful Saturday, and it reached ninety degrees. It's not too warm since Sacramento got a lovely Delta Breeze. Today, ninety didn't feel like ninety. It was close to seven thirty in the evening now. We had about an hour of daylight left. The days were long during summertime in Sacramento.

I merged onto CA-99 Northbound. According to my GPS, I would arrive at the hospital in about fifteen minutes.

As eager as I was to get there and lay eyes on Destiney, I was nervous about walking in on her unexpectedly.

I could only hope she would be glad to see me. If she was worried about surgery tomorrow, I hoped seeing me would lift her spirits.

I made it to the hospital, and once I parked, I entered through Emergency and headed straight for the information desk. They hadn't moved Destiney yet, so they sent me straight back.

As I neared her room number, I spotted Daijah standing in the hallway, speaking to a tall gentleman I assumed was Julian. Daijah and I had only spoken on Facetime, but I recognized her immediately.

Destiney and Daijah favored one another. Daijah is tall, much taller than I expected, possibly

5'9. But Julian towered over her. I'd say he was at least 6'2. He may have had me by an inch if we weren't at eye level.

"Micah!" Daijah whisper, yelling. We were right outside of Destiney's room.

"Hey, Daijah. Thanks again for calling me." I hugged her, then shook Julian's hand. "Nice to meet you, Julian. I'm Micah."

"Same here man. I've heard so much about you."

"Get in there because they'll be back any minute to move her upstairs." Daijah gestured with a nod of her head. "Once she's settled, they'll be starting a blood transfusion. She may not be in the mood for company at that point."

I nodded and headed inside.

When I entered the room, Destiney peered up in surprise. She looked a little tired, but her beauty shined through. Her eyes were red, puffy, and glossy. She had been crying.

I held her gaze, giving her a warm smile. I'm here now, and I plan to help her feel better. As best as I could. I placed the flowers I picked up for her on the windowsill and then made my way to the side of her bed. I leaned over to kiss her forehead.

"Destiney baby," I said, gently taking her hand in mine kissing it. I.V. be damned. I held her hand firmly between both of mine.

"Daijah called you," She stated meekly.
"She did."

Destiney rolled her eyes. "I'm going to get her."

"From there?" I asked rhetorically through a chuckle.

"None of this is funny."

"I agree. I was wondering why you kept avoiding me. Imagine my surprise when I got a call that you were rushed to the E.R. because you'd lost so much blood." I told her evenly.

Destiney looked away from me. "I wasn't avoiding you."

"No? What do you call that?"

"Micah. You wouldn't understand."

"Right now, I don't. But if you open up to me a little more, I may. Or I can at least try. You won't even give me the opportunity." My frustration revealing itself without my permission.

The room was silent, aside from the monitor beeping every few seconds. Finally, she said, "I always feel insecure when I'm bleeding. The smell. The constant wet feeling. The anxiety. It's so unpredictable that I can't even get close to you because I can't guarantee we will ever be intimate."

I saw a tear fall and used my thumb to wipe it from her cheek gently.

"Baby. You're here now. Let's focus on getting you better." I lifted her hand back to my lips, kissing it again. "We'll get through this together."

Destiney shook her head. "You have to move on, Micah."

"What?"

"You're a good man and deserve more than I can ever give you."

"Destiney, what are you talking about?" Dumbfounded, my eyes were glued to hers.

"I'm having surgery tomorrow morning. And after that, I won't be able to have children."

175

Her eyes welled with tears, and my heart broke for her.

"Destiney baby..."

She pulled her hand from mine and snatched away when I tried to reclaim it. "I'm so sorry, Micah." She broke down, weeping so hysterically she could barely speak.

All I wanted to do was hold her tightly in my arms. I pulled up the chair against the wall closer to her bedside. Then I took a seat. She wouldn't look at me. But I proceeded anyway, "Sweetheart, why are you sorry? None of this is your fault." I wiped her tears as they continued flowing down her beautiful face.

"I know how much you want to be a father." She managed, "I'm not the woman for you. We should just stop while we're ahead." Still looking straight ahead.

Still refusing to look at me.

What the hell was going on? How did we get here?

"But I love you Destiney. I'm in love with you," I spoke gently, but insistently. Destiney's head snapped in my direction, giving me her eyes for a few seconds, and I saw something there.

Something I could hardly describe in words.

It was something intense. Something ardent.

Fervent.

It was almost as if... maybe... no. Wait... could she possibly...?

Before I could ruminate any further, Destiney averted her gaze. I probably surprised her.

I was surprised myself.

Not with my feelings. But rather my declaration. I didn't plan to share my heart under these circumstances, but the words came out before I could stop them. And this was how I felt. Truly. And I knew it was soon, but there was no doubt in my mind.

I'm in love with Destiney Evans.

"You're the most important person to me now. You baby. We can always figure out the rest," I told her.

Looking past me, focused on something in the distance, she said, "Just go home, Micah."

My eyes grew wide. "Destiney. Please."

"You already told me you wanted children. And I won't be able to give you any. Just leave." She pulled her hand from mine; I'd since reclaimed it and turned away from me. She covered her face with her hands, weeping. The sight of it pulled at my heartstrings.

I didn't want to leave her. I couldn't, not like this.

"Destiney, baby... let me be here for you," I pleaded. I didn't want to be anywhere else.

I didn't want anyone else.

"Get out, Micah!" She said firmly, her voice at least two octaves louder.

Daijah must have heard her because she entered the room wearing a concerned expression. Julian didn't come in behind her, so I assumed he'd gone home.

A few nurses came in a moment later and began preparing to move Destiney upstairs. The room suddenly grew loud and crowded. I stepped back,

177

rubbing my hands over my head, unsure of what else to do.

Daijah silently nodded toward the door, and I followed her out into the hall. Sighing, she said, "Go on home Micah. I think that's best for right now. You won't need to worry. I'll stay with her tonight, and our dad will be back first thing tomorrow."

I rubbed my forehead. "Did you know she was having that surgery?"

Daijah nodded. "Yes. But she needed to be the one to tell you."

"I understand. Will you please text me tomorrow with an update? I just want to know how she's doing. I won't come back if she doesn't want me here."

"Of course I will." She smiled warmly.

"Thanks, Daijah. Please let me know if I can have a meal delivered tomorrow or if you need anything at all."

"I will. Goodnight Micah. Get home safely."

"Thank you, Daijah. Goodnight."

Walking down the hallway and out toward the parking garage, I was beside myself.

I'd just poured my heart out to Destiney. Professing my love for her for the first time.

I didn't expect her to say it back, but breaking things off was the very last thing I had in mind.

She avoided my eyes and didn't want to discuss things first.

We certainly could have at a better time.

I thought we had something.

Was all of this a figment of my imagination?

No. There's no way.

twenty-two

MICAH

I left the hospital with no particular destination in mind, merging onto the CA-99 Southbound freeway.

I didn't feel like going home.

I certainly didn't want to bother Malachi with this. Not right now.

Just before I cranked up, I texted my boy Soloman to see if he wanted to get into something. Play some pool. Get a drink. I realized he may have been occupied. Probably at band rehearsal. Or playing at a gig somewhere.

The freeway was full of vehicles.

People were enjoying the warm evening and were likely headed out to their prospective locations for whatever plans they made for this Saturday night. It was still fairly early. Sunroofs were open. Droptops down.

I just kept driving, eventually passing the Florin Road and then Sheldon Road exits.

I'd cut the music off, so it was dead silent in my car. I needed the quiet because my thoughts were loud as hell. Running rampant in my mind.

I felt like the rug had been pulled from under me.

Destiney hadn't lied.

We talked at length about children. Children in general. We both worked with children.

We often talked about future children.

I was always up front with that. I pretty much told her from the beginning that I dated with the intention of marriage and a family.

179

I hadn't realized that I belabored the point so much she thought her new reality would cause disarray on my part. Create divergence.

And as much as I wanted marriage and fatherhood, I was almost settled with the idea that maybe it wouldn't happen for me.

Until I met her.

Now, those dreams were dashed. Again.

No. This wasn't the first time.

Marriage and fatherhood were things that seemed just out of my grasp.

This sudden change of circumstances was another situation that seemed to confirm that.

Another situation... concerning a child I almost had, who never got the chance, was something I thought about often. They would be about thirteen now, right between Gabe and Gabby.

My wife to be, at the time. My now ex-fiancé, Ayesha, aborted our baby. That was the beginning of the end for us.

We'd gotten engaged, but she wanted to finish school and get her footing before we got married and started a family, which I could understand.

But the way she went about it all...

She didn't tell me she was pregnant right away. When she finally shared the news with me, she'd already decided she wasn't keeping it.

Yeah. That was the beginning of the end.

***

My phone vibrated with a text from Ayesha.

Can you meet me in front of Kerr? Really need to talk

I was surprised to hear from her because she'd been distant for the past couple of weeks. Although it was a pleasant surprise.

We were kind of in a weird space. We hadn't seen much of each other lately, and the last couple times we'd hung out, I could tell something was off about her. Of course, I asked her about it, but she kept saying she was overwhelmed with her course load.

She doubled up on her science classes in preparation for grad school, and it was taking its toll on her. Her physics class in particular was kicking her ass. Her words, not mine. I'd never taken physics, but I took chemistry, and that shit was almost the death of me so that I could understand.

I offered to take her out to a movie or something, but she said she was too tired. At that point, I didn't know what else to do besides give her space.

Needless to *say, I was glad to hear from her.*

I gathered my things as I shot her a reply. I wasn't a far walk from Kerr Hall.

Yep, 20 minutes

I wasn't sure what she wanted to talk about, but I was glad to get to see her.

When I arrived, she was sitting on our bench, and the sight made me smile instantly.

This was the bench we would always choose if it wasn't taken. Kerr Hall was a place we met often when we first started hanging out because she had many classes in that building.

We had our first kiss two years ago, right on the front steps.

It was the sweetest kiss.

Literally and figuratively.

I can still remember the cotton candy bubblicious flavor of her tongue. She'd been popping her gum nervously right before I asked if I could kiss her. My nerves were just as bad, but I was ready to feel her lips on mine finally. She was on the same type of time because she was throwing hints right at me, nerves and all.

Ayesha looked up at me as I approached. She was smiling, but it didn't reach her eyes.

"Hey. You good?"

She shrugged her shoulders. "Depends."

"Depends?" I halted in my tracks. "You want to talk right here?"

"Sure."

I sat beside her on the bench and took her hand into mine. Once I threaded our fingers, I kissed her softly on the lips. "Something's been up with you, baby. Please talk to me."

She regarded me for a moment, and I held her gaze. Her eyes were different today.

Empty. Dark bottomless pits.

Ayesha began talking, and I regarded her pretty face, still searching her eyes. For what, I wasn't sure, but I needed to make sense of all this.

I was so preoccupied that I wasn't registering whatever she was saying. I was so caught up in my thoughts, but I swear I heard her say she was pregnant.

Pregnant? I had to be mistaken.

"What did you just say?" At this point, we'd been love-making for a while, and we were always careful. There were only a couple of times I hadn't strapped up, but I pulled out in time.

Regardless, here we were.

"I said I'm pregnant, Micah." Her tone was vague. I couldn't get a read on where her head was.

"Okay." I nodded. "Do you know how far along we are?"

"Just left the campus clinic. Exactly eight weeks today."

"How long have you known?"

"About two weeks."

Ah. Now I knew why she'd been avoiding me.

"Why are you just now telling me, Ayesha? I would have gone to the clinic with you."

She shrugged.

"You could have told me when you found out. You know that." She said nothing. I pressed forward anyway. "How are you feeling?"

She chuckled, but it wasn't in amusement. "Sick. Always nauseous. I can hardly eat anything. Nothing stays down."

"Yeah. I can imagine this first trimester will be tough." I rubbed her lower back. "Hang in there baby. I can get you whatever you need. Please tell me what it is. I want you comfortable." She looked away from me as I asked, "How are you feeling about our baby? Being pregnant." I wasn't sure how I felt, but I'd have to think about that later. Ayesha and our baby are my sole focus right now.

She shook her head. "Shocked. Stressed. Terrified." She finally revealed.

"I'm shocked too," I told her honestly. "But try not to stress. It's not best for you or the baby. This is a little scary, and I can understand you feeling terrified. But we can handle this together."

We sat for another moment in silence as I processed everything. This was a lot and would no doubt change our lives.

"I just don't know how I will explain this to everyone." She said after a moment.

"Who said you had to?"

She grimaced. "Micah. I came out here for college. Not to get pregnant! I'll owe people an explanation!"

"What people? Aside from your parents?" I evenly asked, more so rhetorically.

I already had an idea. The fact that Ayesha was a pastor's daughter inherently made her a spectacle. I understood because the church we grew up in was no different. Mal and I were good friends with our pastors' kids growing up, and I knew the troubles they experienced all too well.

People with nothing better to do were watching and waiting, always running back to tell the pastor and first lady something they saw or heard.

I understood the shit firsthand because it was similar for Mal and me. Daddy was chair of the deacons, and Mommy was an usher and taught the children's Sunday school class—practically our entire lives.

The gossiping women in the church irked my damn nerves. Half the ass whoppins Mal and I got were behind some shit they ran back telling. We were only being kids, but they just wouldn't leave us alone.

I could understand Ayesha's position to a degree, but we were in college now, hundreds of miles from home.

We were also grown.

I didn't give a damn what someone back home thought of what I was doing now.

She was still walking the line. I wished she would free herself from all that pressure.

Especially since she didn't have to yield to that anymore.

"I thought about it, and I can't go through a pregnancy, Micah."

"Everything will be fine, and we'll get through it."

"I can't."

I gave her a quizzical expression. "You can't, or you won't?"

She said nothing.

"Ayesha."

"I need some time... alone. I need to figure all of this out. I just need a few days, Micah."

Alone? The hell. "Why are you running from me?"

"People will talk..."

"Ayesha... people will talk regardless. You're a grown woman." She said nothing.

I realized then exactly what the issue was.

If I'm honest, I realized this a long time ago.

Ayesha cared too much about the opinions of others. Entirely too much.

To further complicate matters, Ayesha didn't have a spontaneous bone in her body.

She had to plan every single thing down to the smallest detail.

Anything that happened had to be planned.

It was as if simply thinking about doing shit on a whim made her uneasy. Even the smallest, most trivial things.

Back during our sophomore year, I heard about a poetry slam at a spot just off campus. I wanted to surprise her with tickets and make a date night out of it. We are both fans of spoken word poetry, so I thought it would be something chill to get into.

Anyway, I texted her, telling her I had a surprise for her. That was my first mistake.

Initially, she asked for hints. When I wouldn't give her any hints, she began begging me to tell her.

She finally wore me down because she wouldn't stop insisting. Once she knew, she casually laughed it off, saying she didn't like surprises, and they gave her anxiety.

No shit.

I never did that again. If I wanted to do anything nice for Ayesha, I needed to tell her well in advance so she could plan for it.

So, things like finishing graduate school, establishing her career, marriage, and having kids had to go in that order, and there was no room for a change of plans. No wavering.

Her compulsive desire to micromanage everything had been a point of contention in our relationship. Honestly, it was the only one, but it was major.

She had no idea, though.

As significant as that was, I kept it to myself, which was another mistake. I knew I couldn't change her; nor did I want to. It was who she was.

Part of me wondered if that shit would change even if I did say something. I'm such an easygoing, laid-back person. I'd tried all for naught to encourage Ayesha to try to let things just be.

Why be so type-A and meticulous about everything?

That seems exhausting.

Her micromanaging, stringent, and compulsive traits made it extremely difficult to exist in the moment because she was always in her head about everything going perfectly. Shit was wild.

Conversely, there were benefits to her extremely detailed planning.

I could concede that my time management and study habits had improved significantly since having Ayesha in my life.

Being a student-athlete was a beast. Quite honestly, it was a balancing act and not for the weak.

Especially at the collegiate level.

I figured my high school habits were going to work in college, and I was sadly mistaken.

I wasn't the most disciplined to begin with, and incorporating the additional responsibilities along with my habitual procrastination was a disaster waiting to happen.

Shit wasn't good.

I didn't have enough time in the day for much of anything. I wasn't sleeping well because my mind was cluttered with all the shit I had to do. I was exhausted at baseball practice. Fatigue significantly impacted my performance and my coaches weren't happy.

Shit, neither was I.

Naturally, things in the classroom were no better. I was always playing catch up on papers and cramming for exams. I knew shit was bad, but I couldn't seem to free myself from the funk I was in.

When midterm grades were pulled one of my coaches called me in and told me I'd be dropped from the sports program if I didn't improve. That shit was a reality check.

A few nights later, I revealed to Ayesha that my scholarship was on the line. Simply put, she helped me. With everything she had going on, she still managed to help me.

Foremost, Ayesha was instrumental in helping me get my time management together. When I finally started *prioritizing what I had to do, it left more time for the things I wanted to do.*

Ayesha had excellent study habits, and she kindly shared those with me. Consequently, my grade point average improved. I went from a less than stellar student to an excellent student. I wasn't on the dean's list, but I was damn close.

I owed all of that to Ayesha.

"We aren't even married." She pulled me from my thoughts, rising from the bench. Taking a step, she turned back to face me.

I stood too. "Then let's get married."

"Micah. It's not that simple."

"It's not?"

She sighed, "That's impulsive."

"We're engaged. What difference does it make?"

I closed the space between us, taking her hands into mine. "Look, I know you wanted a beautiful wedding, but we can do that later. Be my wife. Then let's handle the rest of this together. I got you. Always."

She shook her head, undoubtedly in disapproval. "That's not how this was supposed to go...we had goals."

"Ayesha." I hung my head trying to gather my thoughts. I wasn't getting through to her. "Sometimes things don't go according to plan. That's life. We can't control everything."

"I can control if I'm a mother."

My eyes grew wide.

There it was. "Meaning you kill our baby?" I huffed in frustration. "You can accomplish your goals and some with me as your husband. I won't keep you from fulfilling your dreams. If anything, I'll do all I can to help you and support you. I'll take care of you. And our baby."

She pried her hands from mine. "I have to think about this."

"Us getting married or the baby?" I pressed.

She paused for a while. Longer than I liked. "The baby."

"What is there to think about? I want our child."

"I don't know if that's what I want right now."

Growing desperate I said, "You can sign them over to me. I'll raise it. You won't even have to be involved."

I saw a look of surprise which faded just as quickly as it emerged, "Carrying this baby is my choice, Micah."

I took a step back. "I'll get with you later Ayesha," I said that in defeat and really that's exactly how I felt.

It dawned on me at that very moment: she'd already decided.

She called me here to inform me of that and probably didn't expect the reaction I'd given her. "I'll see you around. I guess." I quickly walked away with my mind going a million miles a minute. If she had anything to say I didn't hear her. My thoughts were in disarray, much too loud for me to hear anything anyway. Walking away from this conversation was my best move for now. I needed to stop while I was ahead before I said something I'd regret.

It was her choice, but her ass was being irrational. I couldn't believe this.

She was seriously contemplating killing our baby. To make matters worse, I got the impression she wasn't concerned about considering my feelings in her decision.

This wasn't the Ayesha I fell in love with. The Ayesha I knew adored children and now she was going to kill ours. All for optics. At least that's the impression I was getting.

It was clear we saw this differently and I didn't even know where we stood.

One thing I did know; if she decided to go through with this decision, I couldn't confidently say we would survive this.

And we didn't survive it.

We drifted apart.

We finished up at Cal Poly. Graduated. Came home. And I immediately put some distance between us, asking for a break to figure it all out.

I think I already knew it wouldn't happen.

Marriage.

I prayed. I even fasted.

Bringing myself to officially end things was the difficult part.

So, I consulted with the three people I knew wouldn't steer me wrong.

"You know son, there's no easy way to let her down but there is a respectable way. This is a woman you deeply cared about once upon a time," Daddy said.

I nodded. "I still care for her."

Mommy said, "Please be gentle with her. Do not do this in a text message and not over the phone. Meet her and tell her. You owe her that much."

"No one should marry someone they are not one hundred percent sure about. As much as I hate to say this, it sounds like she isn't the one. For you that is. If you're questioning things you can't work through, you certainly aren't the one for her. She deserves a man who would marry her with no hesitation." That was Mal.

***

After driving aimlessly, I exited Elk Grove Boulevard, arriving at Elk Grove Regional Park.

The park is huge, more than a hundred acres. It's a nice family park, and I've been here many times over the years. Lots of birthday parties. Family barbeques. Little league Baseball games. Music festivals.

A Saturday afternoon in July was a great day to spend at a park like this. There was a big city pool. Mature trees offering lots of shade. I could see people packing up and headed home after what I'm sure was a great day making even greater memories.

There was a miles long walking trail that weaved through the park. It had a lit path at night and quite a few people were walking along the trail. After pulling into a parking space, I shut off my car and I sat for a moment watching people come and go.

A small bridge straight ahead came into view. I sighed.

This was the very place Ayesha, and I met when I'd made the decision to walk away from her.

I guess now I had some idea of how Ayesha must have felt that day.

I arrived promptly at the appointed place and time. Ayesha was already waiting and spotted me as I made my way to her.

She was leaning against the railing of the small bridge that went across the lake.

She smiled brightly. I returned a smile and as I approached her, I knew she could see my smile didn't reach my eyes.

"Hey." *I reached in for a hug.*

"Hey."

We walked along the lake in silence. I suppose neither of us were sure what to say.

I hated this shit.

We'd been on a break for the past few weeks and today was the day I needed to officially end everything.

I knew this would crush her.

But I was here for one reason only and I didn't want to delay things any further.

I just wasn't sure how to begin.

"How are you?" I asked after a while.

"You kidding?!" Ayesha stopped walking to face me. "Micah, I've been a mess lately. Beside myself. I should be the happiest woman in the world, knowing in a few months I'll be marrying the love of my life. But instead, I've been consumed with... this uncertainty. I thought you loved me." She hung her head in defeat.

I stepped closer and gently lifted her chin. "Ayesha. You're an amazing woman. I fell in love with you for so many reasons. Your kind spirit. Your sweet nature. Your heart for children. Your passion for equitable health. You're smart. You're pretty." The corner of my lips lifted, and she smiled weakly. "I'll always love you. But...I can't marry you."

I saw the warmth leave her eyes.

"Is there someone else Micah?"

"No there isn't."

"Well...do you need more time? We can push back the wedding," her tone was hopeful.

My gaze fell away from hers as I sighed, "I don't need more time. I want to end this. Here."

"So that's it?" She yelped on the verge of tears. "How could you do this to me!" she belted when I didn't answer. She hung her head, covering her eyes as she wept audibly and uncontrollably. I went to wrap her in my arms to console her, and she snatched away from me. "Micah don't touch me!"

"Ayesha, I'm sorry."

"Micah, I can't believe you!" She managed through her tears. She pushed past me, but not before roughly forcing her ring back into my hand. I hadn't even noticed when she took it off.

She walked back toward the parking lot, and I followed her at a distance to ensure she made it to her car alright. I could still hear her crying and by now she was hysterical. I watched as she put her car in reverse and slowly drove away.

I'd never felt as low as I felt in that moment.

I hated myself for the pain I caused her. I looked down at the ring and chucked it into the water. Then, I continued along the path surrounding the lake with my hands in my pockets. I had nowhere else to be, so I took the time alone to process my thoughts.

I knew I'd broken her heart, and it tore me up inside.

But just the same, my heart was broken for another reason entirely.

She'd killed our baby.

This was one detail I hadn't told anyone. But I knew I needed to let her go if I couldn't move past that. She didn't deserve having her decision held over her head. Least of all, entering a marriage where I held that against her.

Ayesha deserved a man who would love her uncondi-
tionally.

A man who would move heaven and earth for her.

I prayed sincerely they found each other soon, and
she could forget about how much I hurt her.

One random afternoon after a handful of
years, Mommy told me she saw Ayesha's mom out
shopping, and they spoke briefly.

Ayesha had gotten married and had two
daughters. I was genuinely happy to hear she'd been
doing so well. But that was the last I heard. I never
bothered to keep tabs on her after that.

I felt that it was for the best.

twenty-three

DESTINEY

"Would you like children, Destiney baby? I'd love to create
life with you. If that's what you want to do."

"I absolutely would."

"Would you?"

"Yeah."

"Indeed. If it were up to me...I'd love a son first."

"Oh yeah?"

"Yeah. That way, whoever came next will have a
big brother looking out for them."

"Hmm. I like that! I never had a brother. Big
brothers seem so cool to have."

"For sure! I can confirm it's as cool as it seems."

"Yeah. Then we'll need one more... boy or girl, it
wouldn't matter. But our son will need a partner in
crime."

"Oh, for sure! I need Mal. I'll always need my brother."

"I hear you. I need Daijah. I don't know what I'd do without her."

***

I woke up early the next morning, feeling exhausted. The events from the night before played on a loop in my head. I was drained. Physically and mentally.

I hardly slept. Since I'd had the blood transfusion and needed to be frequently monitored, the nurses came in several times. To that end, I was also trying to process my new reality, and I'd been crying nonstop.

I noticed Daijah in the chair across from me, knocked out. She probably hadn't slept well either.

I was so angry at her yesterday when Micah walked in, but I knew she was only trying to help cheer me up. I reluctantly admitted to her that I'd been avoiding him. She was furious with me. Saying I was being irrational and ridiculous. Quickly, she realized how much I missed him. She also knew I wouldn't have called him myself. I felt terrible for the way I spoke to her.

I felt even worse for the way I spoke to Micah.

I'll never forget the sadness in his eyes when I demanded he leave. He was trying to be here for me and support me, and I pushed him away.

The shocker was when he spoke those three words.

For the briefest of moments, I felt that maybe, just maybe, everything could be okay.

It would be okay.

With Micah, love seemed to be enough. The way he made me feel left me without a doubt that it would. But... he would only be settling with me.

But he loves me.

I love him too.

It was so soon. But there was no way I could control that.

We'd been acquainted all of about four months. Saw each other three times, counting our initial introduction. Actually, I counted four times, including yesterday.

We weren't even officially us. Definitely friends. Close friends. But Micah wasn't officially my man. I wasn't officially his woman. Though in my head, we were. Micah didn't make me feel any less than his. We never had that conversation, and establishing things crossed my mind a couple of times over the course of what we were doing, which was basically talking.

We talked night after night, but it was never mundane. Ever. We did so much more than talk. So many topics were uncovered. No subject was off limits. And we got right to it.

Conversing. Musing. Discussing. Debating. Analyzing. Commentating.

Articulating. Reflecting. Joking. Laughing.

Shooting the breeze.

Learning from and about.

Teaching to and about.

Mastering each other's idiosyncrasies.

Getting all caught up in one another.

So caught up that we messed around and fell in love.

Wild.

Guess none of that mattered now anyway.

I would likely never get to tell Micah I love him, too. That made all of this so much worse.

As awful as I felt, I tried convincing myself that this was best. In a matter of hours, I will have a total hysterectomy. I would never be able to give him any children.

Micah made it clear from the beginning that he wanted a wife and children. Meeting Micah made me realize I wanted that too, and children came up often during our talks.

We'd somewhat unofficially decided that two children would be the perfect number.

I couldn't expect Micah to be with me if he wanted children I couldn't give him.

Glancing at my cell phone, I saw it was nearly seven a.m. My father would be here soon since my procedure was scheduled for nine a.m.

I glanced at my phone again, for the umpteenth time. Despite everything I'd said to Micah, I held a glimmer of hope that I would hear from him. I had no new notifications, so I laid back, closing my eyes.

Each morning began with a good morning text, and our conversation would continue throughout the day. I wanted to text him, but I felt awkward and embarrassed after what I said last night. I couldn't simply reach out as if nothing ever happened. After analyzing my behavior, I knew that my emotions had been all over the place, and I'd made the mistake of reacting in the thick of it all.

Now, here I sat, covered with a heavy cloud of remorse and regret. The shit was suffocating.

I wish I hadn't told Micah to leave.

I really wish I hadn't told Micah to move on.

A nurse came in—a different one than last night.

"Good morning, Destiney," she said warmly. "I'm Trisha, your new nurse. Your night nurse is off shift. I'm going to check all your vitals, and then in about an hour, we will get you prepped for your surgery, alright?"

I nodded silently as I felt tears welling up again.

I was only twenty-seven years old. I couldn't believe I would lose the ability to carry children.

I don't even remember passing out.

My mind went to India.

I learned that India came searching for me when I hadn't returned for a while. Once they called an ambulance, India called Daijah. India came to the hospital yesterday when I first arrived, but she couldn't stay long because she needed to get back to her parents.

I sent her a text message.

Good morning, Indie. Thanks again for having my back

As the nurse finished and headed out, I glanced at Daijah. She was still asleep. There was so much commotion as the nurses came in and out pulling their cart through that loud ass door. I was surprised it didn't wake her. Daijah had to be exhausted, but I was eager for her to wake up. I needed to apologize to her. Last night my stubborn ass had an attitude with her even after she told me something selfless and beautiful.

"Des, if you can't have babies, I'll just have babies for the both of us. I'll be your surrogate as soon as you and

Micah are ready. And we'll raise our babies close. Just as close as we are."

When she mentioned Micah, I grimaced, though she couldn't see.

Daijah and I had our heated exchange just before her declaration, and by then, I had turned away from her.

Of course, she hadn't a clue that everything with Micah and I had gone-to-shit.

Who knew what the future would hold, but I didn't even thank her for the offer.

It was bad enough; my pathetic ass wouldn't even look at her.

I saw my phone illuminate and grabbed it quickly, hoping it was Micah. It was India.

Indie the Bestie: I love you and I'll always have your back. See you later this afternoon

Leave it to India to bring positivity to a fucked-up situation. I smiled despite the disarray I felt surrounding me.

I returned my phone to the table beside me, quickly dozing off again…

***

"Good morning, Daijah."

"Good morning," she returned flatly and expressionless as she folded her blanket and began straightening up the corner she had slept in.

I woke up about fifteen minutes ago. My nurse had just returned to tell me they'd start my prep. My father called me a moment ago, letting me know he was here and parking and that he'd be up soon.

"Thanks for staying with me. You sleep okay?"

"Sure. And I slept as best as I could sleeping in a chair." She placed the folded blanket in the closet. "I'm headed down for a cup of coffee and need to call Julian. I'll be back."

Daijah made her way across the room and was almost out the door before I said, "Daijah... wait." She halted and slowly turned to face me. "I'm so sorry about last night. I was mean to you, and you didn't deserve that." I let tears fall from my eyes. "You're my best friend. I can't believe I let my emotions lead. I'm so sorry. I've been praying, and if this is God's plan for me, then so be it. It could have been worse. I was thinking, what if I had passed out while I was driving? I could have killed someone."

"Or yourself."

"Yeah."

"But you didn't. You still have your life and so much to look forward to. You won't have to deal with these fibroids anymore, and you'll be back to feeling better soon." Daijah came to my bed and hugged me warmly. "All is forgiven. I love you, Des."

"I love you too Day."

"Let me go call Julian. Have you already talked to Micah?"

"No, I haven't."

She returned a quizzical expression.

"I can't call him after the way I spoke to him yesterday."

She sighed. "Just tell him you're sorry. You've been through so much in the past twenty-four hours. I'm sure he'll understand."

"I can't. Yesterday, I told him to move on... I broke things off with him."

"You did what?!" Daijah gasped in surprise. "Why?!"

"When I found out about the surgery, I figured he's better off without me. Micah wants children Day. In case you forgot, I won't be able to have any in just a few hours. My lady parts will be taken from me, and I'll resemble a fucking blown out cave." I laughed despite it all. Maybe to delay the inevitable tears.

"Des, Micah cares about you. Have you talked about it? Do you even know if that's a deal breaker?"

"He's tired of me." I sighed, deciding to evade the question.

"Here's an idea; start with I'm sorry."

I shook my head. "Then what? I still can't give him what he wants. I need to leave him alone. It's better this way." I didn't truly believe that. But I was trying to convince myself it was. I cried softly as Daijah sat on the edge of the bed holding me in her arms.

"Ssshhh. Don't think about it right now. Once we get you home, we can talk this over more."

I continued crying into Daijah's shoulder. I'd cried so much I was surprised I still had tears left.

I got the feeling that Micah and I were officially finished.

That had the waterworks going full blast.

twenty-four

MICAH

It was after eleven when I woke up for a second time. I had been up since seven this morning although I didn't sleep much at all last night. Of course, my mind was on Destiney heavy.

I almost texted her out of impulse.

We both normally greeted each other with a good morning text. Most mornings we would have a minute to talk after we got our day going. We would text back and forth all day long and in the evening, we would end our night talking for hours until Destiney was falling asleep on me.

Just one day off that routine threw me off kilter.

Emotionally, I was in shambles.

A mess.

I was heartbroken. Simple as that.

This was the most heartache I've ever felt in my life.

Interestingly, I didn't feel this way when things ended with Ayesha. Not even close.

But I imagine that's how she must have felt. I'll never forget the sound of her cries as she walked back to her car that day at the lake. Especially since it was all because of me.

There was something else, too; I didn't like the fact that I seemingly compared these moments with Destiney to the parallels I had with Ayesha. But somehow, albeit subconsciously, I still found myself doing it. It occurred to me that maybe it was happening because that was my only other serious relationship and therefore my only point of reference.

Either way I didn't like that shit.

These were two very different women. Two completely different relationships, with polar opposite dynamics. And I've changed. I've matured of course, but beyond that, I was in a place where my decisions were made consciously and with foresight. Back in college I can't say I was thinking my present decisions would have an impact on my life five, ten or fifteen years from now.

I threw my legs to the side of the bed, but I didn't get up for a while. Just sat there. Thinking.

I glanced at my phone again. I expected to hear from Daijah shortly. Destiney would probably be out of surgery in the next hour if she wasn't already out. Daijah texted me this morning as promised after they'd taken Destiney back. She said the surgery was expected to last up to three hours. Daijah, Julian, and her father planned to stay there most of the day and her friend India would be staying the night since Daijah stayed last night. I offered to have a meal delivered but she assured me Julian would be taking care of them.

Julian seemed to be a chill dude. I would have loved to converse with him more and I would have under different circumstances. Hopefully we'll cross paths again.

That was solely based on how Destiney chose to move.

When I woke up earlier at seven, I got the feeling Destiney's mind was in shambles, just like mine. I would have loved to comfort her, but she didn't want me. I was hoping she would text me just to open that door, but that was too hopeful. I said a prayer for her and sent her positive thoughts anyway.

Even still, I cared for her so much. She was crazy if she thought I would just move on with a flip of a switch, simply because she asked me to.

I love Destiney.

I knew I did for a while.

Whether she could carry my children or not made no difference to me. I still want her. She's my wife and being forced away from her had me quickly becoming unraveled.

We hadn't experienced each other yet sexually but I already knew she was the woman I wanted. Just in these past few hours I was becoming a shell of myself pinning after her.

I glanced at my cell. Again. Somehow, I missed the notification of a missed call from Daddy. I also had a couple unread messages from Solomon. He was likely responding to my messages from last night. I'll check in with him later.

I called my old man but got his voicemail, so I called Mommy. She was likely the one calling me from his phone anyway. She used dad's phone more than her own. Mommy's cell phone was hardly charged half the time because she used it so infrequently. If I didn't reach her on her cell, I would call the house phone. My parents still had the house phone connected with the same phone number since Mal and I were in middle school.

I called Mommy's cell and surprisingly she answered.

"Micah Bear!"

"Good morning, Mommy. How are you?"

"It's a great morning! How are you son?"

"I'm alright Mommy." I tried my damndest to hide the sorrow in my voice. I likely failed miserably though. She was quiet for a moment which let me know she knew I wasn't being honest. And I was grateful she didn't press. But knowing her, she would bring it up again. "Is Daddy nearby? I missed his call this morning."

"He's down at the church for the men's coffee and bible study." My parents still attended the church we grew up in. Daddy had been a deacon there for many years. Now that he was retired, he had more time to participate in the various men's fellowships. They met for a coffee, prayer and bible study a few times a month and he seemed to enjoy attending.

"Come by today when you can. By the time you get here maybe I'll remember whatever it was we needed." Mommy laughed and I did too.

"I'll likely go to the store before I head that way. Need anything?"

"How about a few lemons? I have a taste for lemon pound cake."

I smiled at that. Mommy knew exactly how to cheer me up.

Her lemon pound cake was delectable. She captured a true lemon flavor that was so delicious. Her secret was to use fresh lemons. The fresh squeezed lemon juice made a lemon glaze that was incredible. She used extract whenever she was in a pinch but not often. Her presentation alone was award winning; that beautiful citrusy perfection looked too good to eat with the lemon zest sprinkled on top. Her lemon pound cake was my very favorite dessert of hers.

"You're the best."

"I do okay." Mommy tossed back laughing.

"See you in about an hour."

"I'll be here, my Micah Bear."

***

"More?" Mommy asked, gesturing toward my now empty bowl sitting in front of me.

I'd just finished my second serving of pot roast, with red potatoes and carrots. It was seasoned perfectly, tender and so delicious. Daddy was still at the church, but we expected him home any minute now. "No thank you. I've had plenty. Plus, I don't want to eat all Daddy's food," I said through a chuckle.

"Oh nonsense! He'll be fine. There's always plenty," Mommy assured me, but I already knew.

My mother was an excellent cook and kept the three men of her life fed past satisfaction. As early as I can remember, there was always a warm meal for us on the table. Always a freshly baked cake or pie to go with it. Our friends wanted to come by just to get a taste of something Mommy cooked. And there was always plenty to go around. None of them were turned away. Ever.

"I can't take another bite Mommy." I was beyond full, and I made it a point not to do that often.

"I'll pack some up for you."

There was no reason for me to argue. Mommy wasn't going to hear any of it.

We both stood from the table at the same time, she made her way to the stove, and I headed to the sink to wash the few dishes in there along with the bowl, spoon and glass I used.

"Hmm! Looks great!" I peered over my shoulder as Mommy removed the pound cake from the oven placing it on the cooling rack. "I'll let this cool off and I'll get started on my glaze in a little while."

"Yum. It smells even better. I need to let this food go down before I can eat anything else." We both laughed.

Mommy moved in beside me at the sink, rinsing the dishes I'd washed, placing them in the dishrack to dry.

"So, who is she? Tell me about her."

My movements instantly stilled, and I slowly looked over at Mommy.

She was already looking at me, smiling expectantly. Eyebrows high. Warmth in her eyes.

My mouth opened slowly but I couldn't find my voice. I pressed my lips together, quickly opening them again. "How did... what are you talking about?"

"Micah Bear." She gave me a knowing expression. "Only a woman would have you behaving this way."

My jar dropped. "What way?"

"I know you. Someone has your heart," she said gently. There was still a smile there too.

I was heartbroken at the moment, but I smiled too anyway. I couldn't help it if I tried. That was the effect Destiney had on me.

"When did you plan on telling me about your sweetheart?" This was a legitimate question, and I wanted to tell Mommy about Destiney a long time ago.

I sighed, "Well... that's complicated."

"Complicated how?"

I proceeded to telling Mommy everything. From meeting Destiney back at Walgreens, to our nightly conversations.

How amazing she is.

How beautiful she is.

I confirmed her suspicions, telling her I'm in love with Destiney. And she listened intently.

Then I told her what happened just yesterday.

"Try to imagine where she's coming from. She's been bleeding on and off. Lost so much blood she goes unconscious. Wakes up in a hospital. Gets the news she's having an emergency surgery. A surgery that will leave her unable to bear children. My mind would be in disarray too, I can't even imagine."

I could appreciate all of that. I understood.

Mommy continued, "She may have been saying things she didn't mean in the heat of the moment. Sometimes we hurt the people closest to us just because of proximity. It isn't always personal." I continued to wash, and she continued to rinse. "You know Micah, I don't think she really meant that. To end things. She probably misses you and needs you but doesn't know how to say so. Especially now. She's made a mess of everything and probably doesn't know how to fix it."

"Mommy... I get it. But I'm starting to lose it. It's like we're going in circles. We take a few steps forward only to go backwards. She keeps pushing me away from her and I keep coming back expecting things will be different. As much as I want them to be, maybe she doesn't know how to handle this. She's never been in a committed relationship. She hasn't entertained a man beyond surface level conversation in years... she's also nearly a decade younger than me. What if we can't figure this out?"

"But son, what if you can? The two of you care a great deal for each other. That much is obvious. Give her some space. Some time. For now."

I nodded but I said nothing. I finished washing the dishes and now I was leaning back against the counter. Pondering everything Mommy was telling me.

"At some point you'll need to have a conversation. To find out what she needs from you to make this work. And you tell her what you need."

"What if we can't give each other what we need?"

"Then you part ways. But at least you discussed it. You don't want to go through the rest of your life wondering 'what if'."

I nodded. *That*, I could agree with.

twenty-five

DESTINEY

"Everything, everything Princess?"

I was visiting my dad at the house Daijah, and I grew up in. My dad and I were sitting in the backyard under a big tree. I found out just a few years ago, it was called a Blue Oak Tree. It was our favorite place to hang around when Daijah and I were little. It was huge. It had an expansive trunk, sturdy branches and lush leaves. Had the best shade. We loved to climb it. Bravely venturing as high as we could go until we were too afraid to go any further. Climbing down again.

My dad built us a playhouse right beside it. Now there was a hammock in its place, perfect to lounge in on a warm day like this one.

I leaned my head on my dad's shoulder as we ate our popsicles. "Yeah. Everything is everything."

"Good, good. How was your appointment?"

I had an appointment this morning. Six weeks post-op and I'd finally been cleared by my doctor. I'd still need to take things easy in general. I planned to go back to work in a few days. No heavy lifting for a while longer. No strenuous activity.

Slowly but surely, I'd ease back into my pre-surgery routine. I was cleared to drive again, which I was very excited about. It wasn't as if I had too many places to be as of late, aside from my appointments. Daijah and India were giving me rides whenever I wanted to go somewhere. I appreciated them for it. Immensely, but there's nothing like your own independence.

Speaking of surgery, instead of a hysterectomy I had an abdominal myomectomy. There were a number of fibroids, some larger than four centimeters, relatively large considering, but they were able to successfully remove them all. Still leaving my lady parts intact. I would continue to get a menstrual cycle and though I had a leery feeling about still getting a period, I could live with that. My doctor would keep an eye on everything as I continued to follow up with her.

All in all, I had a smooth speedy recovery. I already felt so much better. My energy was returning to normal. I wasn't in pain. I felt like a brand new me.

The best part of all, I can still have children. It was the best news I'd gotten in a long time.

"It went great! All cleared."

"That's great news princess! Thank God!"

"Yes. Thank God!"

"How's Micah doing?" My dad never formally met Micah, but by now he'd heard a good deal about him. There wasn't anything to report as of late. I think my dad figured we reconnected by now. A significant amount of time had passed. Six weeks to be exact.

"Not sure dad. Haven't talked to him."

My dad nodded. After a beat, "Can your dear old dad tell you something without upsetting you? I'm not choosing sides; I just want to share my thoughts."

That was something dad did a lot. With Daijah and me, he had a gentle approach whenever he wanted to express something he thought contrary to how we felt about the matter. Especially during our teenage years.

"Sure, dad."

"From what I can see, Micah has proven himself worthy of you." I sat up straight, urging him forward. "No one deserves you at your best if they aren't for you at your worst. You were down pretty bad Princess. But Micah came running as soon as he heard. That man loves you. It's clear."

I nodded in agreement. And understanding. "He does. He told me so. I love him too, dad. Except he doesn't know that I do. Never told him." I shook my head, still dealing with the residuals of my shitty decision.

"What are you waiting on?"

I shrugged my shoulders in lieu of a verbal answer.

"If this man has proven himself worthy and he wants to be there for you, wants to be with you, let him. No reason to fight it."

I nodded, "I don't know if it's that simple."

"One way to find out. Call him."

I sighed, "Just like that?"

"Sure." Dad shook his head. "Must you kids insist on complicating everything?"

We both laughed. I guess he had a point there.

"Just give him a call. Have a conversation. Share your heart. Promise you'll think about it?"

"I promise dad."

"That's my baby girl." He leaned over and kissed my forehead. I giggled at the way his cold lips felt.

"Dad!" I screeched, wiping off the moisture he left on my forehead with the back of my hand.

He cracked up at that. "Thanks for having a popsicle with me, Princess."

I smiled big. "You're welcome."

I headed home shortly after my conversation with my dad. He lived about ten minutes from Daijah and me. Not far at all. Close enough for us to get to him quickly should he need us.

When the lease ends in a few months I've considered moving back home. Daijah would be moving in with Julian and there was no reason for dad and me both to live alone. He was getting older, and we were growing more protective of him.

We were all he had.

My mom passed away almost seventeen years ago, after an aggressive breast cancer ravaged her body. It all seemed to happen so quickly. I was ten years old; Daijah just nine.

I remember them telling us she was sick, and it seemed very quickly after that she was gone. It's still such a raw place for me, emotionally. I try not to think about it. Some days just visiting my childhood home is difficult for me. All these years later. My mother's memory is very present there. Daijah took her death pretty hard. She was incredibly close to our mother.

Anyway, it's one reason I don't speak of my mom as much. I like to think of her as away on a trip somewhere. It's my way of coping. I've gotten ridicule for that, but I don't care. When I speak of her, especially to someone unaware, I have to acknowledge she's no longer here. Physically. And I have to speak of her in past tense. I don't like to do that.

And my dad. He's my hero.

As cliché as it sounds, he really is. I always admired the strength he had, raising Diajah and me while extremely heartbroken. He and my mom were high school sweethearts. Together since they were fourteen. I was so young when it all happened, some of it is a blur. But I remember hearing his cries from our bedroom. Late into the night when he thought we were sleeping. That went on for years.

I can remember the women who tried to come in and play on my dad's heartbreak and vulnerability. They seemed to come out of the woodwork.

From all directions.

The women at our school, or at our church. Single moms of kids on our volleyball team, or girl scout troop. Those women had no chill. Swooped in and tried their hand when he wasn't even emotionally available. Trying to convince my dad of all the reasons why he needed them. Impressing upon him why he needed to move on. Tried to persuade him that marrying them was a good idea and insisting we needed a mom. Especially once we arrived at pubescence.

But my dad wasn't interested. Not even a little bit. No one could get close enough. His sole concern was Daijah and me.

Once I got home, I hung out on my bed. Thinking about everything my dad said. He approved of Micah. Site unseen. I couldn't blame him. Micah was everything. And I missed him so much.

We still hadn't spoken. Or seen each other.

When I learned I could still have children, all I could do was thank God. I was so grateful. Beyond words. I cried. And I felt like this was a sign. Confirmation that maybe Micah and I could still possibly work things out.

My next dilemma was figuring out the best way to approach him. I wanted him back. Desperately. I worried that each passing day I didn't reach out, my chances of reconciliation were dwindling.

And I didn't know how I would go about doing it but I was sure going to try.

I just hoped it wasn't too late.

So, it was the end of August now and summer was coming to an end.

I was over this heat. Been over this heat. Sacramento has very warm summers. So yeah. Over the summer and ready for fall. Fall is my favorite time of year. Fuzzy socks. Apple pie. Pumpkin flavor galore.

I couldn't wait.

I felt my phone vibrating beside me. It was a text from Indie.

Indie the Bestie: Yay!! We're going to hookah tonight. Need to celebrate your good news!!

After my appointment, I updated India, letting her know I was all good to go.

Hell yes!

Indie the Bestie: I know you're clear to drive but I'll pick you up. How's seven?

Perfect

Indie the Bestie: Daijah coming?

If we can get her from up under Julian LOL I'll ask. Probably will. We're so overdue for a girls night

I texted Day in the group chat, checking to see if she wanted to join Indie and me.

Sibling Bestie: I am there!! Plus Roni and Vic

Indie the Bestie: FUNNERS!!!!

I laughed at that, then I started my playlist.

Throwback slow jams were my go-to any day of the week. I got comfortable on my bed letting the smooth grooves of Avant mentally take me away. "Read your mind" was an oldie but goodie.

Micah could read my mind.

Damn. I couldn't help but think back to the intimate moments Micah and I shared. I thought about those a lot. I didn't need any music.

I missed him. So much. I missed our talks. His text messages. His voice in my ear. His laugh.

These six weeks I had been home recovering from my surgery, I felt like I was damn near on house arrest. And since I couldn't do much aside from reading, and sketching; I was forced to sit with myself. Sit with my feelings. Face my lackluster decisions.

And I wasn't pleased at all with what I had done.

I wondered also if Micah missed me as much as I missed him. Or if he thought of me at all.

After what I did, from the beginning leading up to yelling at him forcing him away from me... I wouldn't be surprised if he told me to kick rocks.

But. I still hoped. Wished. Maybe, there was a chance we could be we. Us.

I wanted that so much. More than anything.

My mind began to wander thinking about things I probably shouldn't. Like, I thought about whether Micah was giving it to someone else now. I felt a tinge of something akin to jealously thinking about that. I tried to move on to something else.

For reasons I do not understand my thoughts ventured to my first sexual experience. Which I tried not to ever think about.

Normally I can keep those thoughts back. But today... I was no good. Thinking about my dad. Thinking about my mom. Thinking about Micah. Wondering if he was still thinking of me, or if he was on to someone else. Someone else more deserving.

My mind was a mess.

I'm so glad India and I would be going to smoke.

I needed to decompress.

But these fucking thoughts were so fucking loud.

I turned to my stomach pulling a pillow over my head. Trying in vain to block them out. It was past time I talked to someone about this. A professional. I should have a long ass time ago.

I wasn't raped, but I was pressured. Regardless it was an encounter I do not like to think about.

Daijah had been hanging out with this guy. Since Daijah and I did everything together, whenever I took Daijah to chill with him, I'd stay and chill too. We went often. A couple days a week at one point.

We always hung out at his apartment and had the place to ourselves. Daijah's guy was an only child with a single mom that worked two jobs. She was never home.

At the time I was seventeen and Daijah was sixteen. Anyway, Daijah's guy had a cousin that was always over whenever we came by to hang out. The more time Daijah and her guy spent together, the more his cousin and I saw of each other. He was seventeen too and he liked me. He asked me to be his girlfriend right away. He was cute I guess, so I considered it. The first time he asked I told him it was too soon. I didn't know him like that. As I got to know him, I wasn't interested in actually being with him. He asked me more than once. Saying shit like, "I'm just wondering when you gone stop playing and be my girl."

Obviously, I said no. His personality wasn't my type. But it was chill kicking it with him.

And he was a good kisser. Whenever Daijah and I went over, the cousin and I made out. Which was a mistake. I've had a damn decade to think back on that situation and I really shouldn't have been kissing him.

Once, Daijah and I were over, and the cousin and I had been making out for a while. Eventually we were dry humping. I could feel how hard he was through his jeans. I'd let him touch my boobs a couple times, but that was the extent of it. Before Daijah and I went home, he said something like, "We won't be kissing forever." I remember being confused, trying to figure out just what he meant by that. We'd never talked about having sex. Actually, we didn't talk much at all. Not that I would have agreed to that anyway. I was still a virgin. We were only kicking it, and that's all we were doing.

I should have ended everything right there.

But I didn't. And the very next time Daijah and I went there, things happened.

It started like all the others. The four of us hung out in the front for a while. After some time, he stood and put his hand out, silently asking me to follow him. That's when we'd go be alone, also giving Daijah and her guy time alone. I looked at Daijah, and she smiled at me. I smiled back then he led me down the hall to his cousin's bedroom. He lay on the bed and invited me to join him. I did, and we proceeded with our making out. At some point, he started going for the button on my jeans, and I stopped him.

"I just want to finger you."

I thought about it for a second. We'd never done that before, but I didn't see the harm in it. "You gotta wash your hands first."

He jumped off the bed with haste, going to wash them.

Once he returned, he made quick work of unbuttoning and unzipping my jeans, but I kept them on.

He didn't waste any time putting his hand inside and went straight for my center, moving my panties to the side. I was jolted in surprise when he quickly forced his pointer and middle fingers into me.

"Damn you wet. This shit sexy as a muthafucka." He pointed upward a few times and swirled and swiped his fingers around inside. "I need to feel you for real."

I pulled his arm out of my jeans. "You said you just wanted to finger me."

He gave me an incredulous glare. "We both damn near grown. People our age been past that."

My expression was blank. I was unsure of what to say. He had a point. I knew many people my age who were having sex already. However, since that day, I've thought of so many things I should have said. Should have done it. And I certainly could have walked out of that room. But I didn't have a handle on my voice back then. I look back with so much regret, which is one reason I don't like to think about that day. I would rather keep it compartmentalized and forgotten, buried deep in my brain.

He stood and began unbuckling his pants and pulled them down along with his boxers. "You got me so hard; I could shatter concrete. And you so wet because you want it." He retrieved a condom from his wallet in the pocket of his jeans. "Besides…" he returned to the bed, pulling my jeans over my hips. "… We at the point of no return now, baby. Can't stop something we done already started."

When it was all over, we both went back to the front. Daijah and her dude were watching Martin reruns.

He slapped hands with his cousin, and I concluded that was their unspoken way of confirming what we had just done.

I sat on the couch, trying to pretend like nothing had happened.

I was confused and angry, mostly with myself. I should have said no.

"Hey, Des, you good?" Daijah asked me.

"Yep," I returned as nonchalantly as I possibly could, through a forced smile.

Meanwhile, I tried to ignore the ache between my legs. He wasn't exactly forceful, but he was certainly not gentle. I took my phone out and busied myself absently scrolling. I decided at that moment that I wasn't going to tell Daijah.

I just didn't know how. Plus, I was embarrassed. And ashamed.

That was the first thing I ever kept from her, and I told her everything.

To this day, I still haven't told her.

I felt guilty for keeping something so significant from her and carried that guilt for a long time. I didn't talk to anyone about it. Daijah was my best friend, and if I couldn't tell her, who else was there? My dad would have murdered that asshole. I hid that away and never spoke of it again.

Ironically, we never went back to the apartment after that. Daijah's dude said his mom's work schedule had changed so he and Daijah hung out in public places like the mall and the movies and shit after that.

And I never saw his cousin again.

The cousin got what he wanted.

twenty-six

DESTINEY

We decided on Torch.

I haven't been here since my birthday weekend. I wanted to let some time go by before I came back, considering everything with Tyler, the owner.

220

But it was still my favorite hookah place. And I needed my Ragin' Cajun fries fix. I couldn't get them anywhere else.

Indie picked me up, and not long after we got settled in our section, Daijah and her besties, Veronica and Victoria, met us.

We put in orders for some drinks and a few appetizers and got two hookahs. We ordered two new flavors, and I was so juiced to try both of them.

The lounge was jumping with people tonight; the walls vibrated with music and chatter. I was glad we came in when we did. Had we waited just fifteen minutes later, we wouldn't have been able to get a hookah section. I heard our server telling someone there was already a wait.

The five of us were making small talk, and when we heard the distinctive bounce beat followed by Juvenile's intro *"Cash Money Records taking over for the 9-9 into 2000..."* everyone in the lounge went crazy. Including us. "Back That Azz Up" was a banger.

"We're going to dance. Y'all coming?" Daijah asked. She, Roni, and Vic had already stood up, making their way over.

"Yeah, we are! Come on Des!" India grabbed my hand, and we followed them. I usually don't dance on the floor, opting instead to groove to the music from my seat. India can dance her ass off. She and Daijah would usually go dancing, and I'd watch our drinks. But I didn't resist. Not this time. We'd barely put in our order moments before. It would be a while. Plus, this was a somewhat of a special occasion, and my girls turned out to celebrate with me.

I was trying to focus on enjoying myself. And I continued to remind myself that I certainly had a reason to, despite today being an emotional one, with Micah on my mind... heavy. I could dance with them to one song.

We stayed on the dance floor for two songs, then decided to head back, and I was glad. The dance floor was crowded. I was hoping our food and drinks would be out momentarily. I was already hungry, and now I was thirsty. And I wanted to smoke.

The entire lounge was dimly lit, and we were in a single file line as we returned to our section. Daijah was at the front, Roni and Vic were right behind her, and India was in front of me. I grabbed India's hand and followed her, holding up the rear.

We were off the floor and now near the back of the lounge where the hookah sections were. We were almost back to our seats when I heard my name being called. My name is distinct, and not many names sound like mine. So I'm certain I heard it.

Also, there aren't that many Destineys.

I heard it again; it was closer now and coming from behind me.

Shit. Maybe it was Tyler.

I squeezed Indie's hand, and she halted, instantly looking back.

"You okay?"

"Yeah, someone is calling me."

"Tyler?"

"I don't know," I still hadn't turned back to look behind me.

"You scared he's going to do something to you?

"No… I just don't feel like talking to him. But I guess I should get this over with. Clear the air."

"Well, I'm right here. You're good. Where is he? India looked over my head, which was easy for her; she was taller than me, even with my heels on.

I was still facing her and heard the voice again, directly behind me. And it wasn't Tyler.

Since the lounge was dimly lit, I took a moment to register the face standing right in front of me when I turned around.

The face spread into an easy smile. Decorated with two deep ass dimples.

Zeke.

"Destiney. Wow. So, it is you! I saw you out there dancing, and I thought I was seeing things." A smooth chuckle left his lips. "You never wanted to dance in front of people."

I shook my head laughing right along with him. "Yeah, I was outnumbered. Got dragged out there."

"Come here, girl. Give me a hug. You look great!"

I dropped India's hand, willingly falling into Zeke's open arms.

And he hugged me like I was a long-lost love he was finally reuniting with after walking thousands of miles.

Through a desert. Barefoot. With no water.

"So do you Zeke. Really." Rapidly shaking my head, I said, "My bad… You remember my best friend India, right?"

"Of course I do. Hey India. How are you?

I'd told India about Zeke. Everything.

And she was always telling me about myself. Seeing how I left things, everything went in one ear and out the other.

"I'm great. Good to see you Zeke." They gave each other a quick side-hug.

"So, you here with your boyfriend?" Zeke didn't waste any time. "Should I be looking over my shoulder?" He dramatically looked around, feigning fear.

I laughed. "No, I'm not. Just out with my girls."

"So, he's at the house waiting on you." It wasn't a question.

"No man to speak of. I'm single if that's what you're asking."

"Really?" His eyebrows high.

"Yeah. Wouldn't lie about that. Why?"

"I mean, come on Destiney. You are beautiful, for starters. Sweet as pie. My Pie Sweetie." I giggled at the nickname he gave me. A silly giggle that turned into a light chuckle and eventually a deep belly laugh.

I hadn't been laughing much. Not lately. And it felt good to laugh again.

I still remember Zeke saying I was his Pie Sweetie. Telling me, "No one was as sweet as me, and that was the only thing fitting since Sweetie Pie was already played out".

Wow. I totally forgot about that.

"Des, I'm going to sit down," India said as she returned to our section.

"Okay. I'm right behind you." That quickly, I forgot India was standing there. "It was so nice seeing you again, Zeke," I said, starting to follow India.

Zeke grabbed my hand. "Destiney, wait." I looked down at our connection, quickly looking back up at him.

He released my hand as quickly as he had grabbed it. "I apologize. I didn't mean to grab you… so suddenly."

"It's okay." I gave him a warm smile. He was always a gentleman.

"Can I talk to you a while longer? Please."

I thought about that. I guess it was okay. After the way I left him hanging, I felt that I owed him some kind of explanation. "Sure." I turned around, and India was almost back to our table. I caught up with her, telling her I'd be talking to Zeke and I'd be back shortly.

"Let's head this way. It's a little quieter." Zeke led me to one of the bars furthest from the dance floor and closer to the entrance. It was much quieter. And a lot less crowded.

He found us two seats and stepped aside as I moved in front of him to sit down.

"Can I get you anything?" He asked, sitting down and turning to face me.

I shook my head. "No thanks. I have a drink waiting for me."

He nodded, smiling. His dimples were on full display again. I was always a sucker for Zeke's dimples. "Still one-and-done pie sweetie?"

"Yeah," I wore a smile too. "One is still plenty for me."

His smile remained as he looked me over.

Checking me out.

I could tell that's what he was doing. Guys aren't so subtle with that. He had no clue that I was looking him over, too. He wouldn't either, unless I told him.

He was dressed casually in dark washed jeans and a polo shirt. J's on his feet. Still rocking a goatee. He always kept it trimmed and neat. Low cut fade with a little more at the top. He smelled nice too. Fresh like body wash with a tasteful splash of cologne.

"Your locs are gorgeous. At your waist now."

"Thank you, Zeke." I last saw Zeke two years ago, and they were long, but they certainly weren't this long. He always loved my locs, too.

He nodded. "You're welcome." Then, "I'm liking your whole get down." He nodded toward me, moving his head down, then up again. "You look amazing."

I was wearing a sage green, one-shoulder body-con dress. It was slightly ruched and stopped just above my knee. My tan peep-toe booties had three-inch heels, giving me some height and a little pep in my step. I felt good about coming out tonight and wanted to look even better. It was sweet to hear Zeke approve. I didn't need it, but just the same, it was nice to hear.

"You look great, too," I told him genuinely.

"Thank you."

"You're very welcome. So," I sighed deeply. "I'm surprised you're being so nice to me. I mean. I didn't exactly say goodbye properly." I'm not even sure why I said that. But it was out there now. No taking it back.

"Honestly Destiney… I let that go. Initially, I figured you needed space. But even after I gave it to you, I didn't hear from you. I kept my number the same. I thought maybe, eventually, you'd call me. But when you didn't, I figured it just wasn't our time." He shrugged. "I thought someday maybe we'd cross paths again. I've searched for you."

My eyes grew wide. My mouth was agape. I quickly closed it, realizing how ridiculous I must have looked. "You searched for me?"

"Yeah. I mean, social media. I found you, but you aren't active there. I let it go, leaving the rest to the universe. Whenever I passed a mural, I thought of you."

Damn.

"Zeke… I…" I shook my head. "Please don't tell me you put your whole life on hold for me."

He chuckled. "What if I said I did?"

I rapidly shook my head at that. "No. That's… Zeke. You're a great guy. You'd make someone so happy."

"Tried that." He shrugged. "It didn't work. But we got a little one out of the deal."

My eyes went up in surprise. "You're a dad?"

"I'm a dad. A little girl." He lightly chuckled, nodding.

"That's so sweet. Can I see pictures?"

He pulled out his phone and handed it to me after a few quick swipes. It was a candid shot. The sweetest pair of eyes were filled with so much happiness. No idea how her mom looked, but she definitely favored Zeke. She had his dimples and his copper skin, hers shining like a brand-new penny.

"She's beautiful."

"Thank you."

"What's her name?

"Eden."

"Oh my gosh. That's perfect for her. She's adorable." I handed Zeke his phone back.

"She's almost a year and half. After you, I... seriously, I tried to wait for you. Then I tried to move on." He shook his head. "And it wasn't fair to her — my daughter's mother. I couldn't really give her myself fully because you were in the back of my mind. I had to be honest with her. And myself. It wasn't... I'm not blaming you, Destiney. It just wasn't meant to be. And she's a great mother. A great woman." He sighed lightly. "I'm just doing the single dad thing for now."

I nodded. "I get it. I'm sure you're a great father, Zeke. Eden is so lucky."

He smiled at that.

We chatted for another few moments. Then I told him I needed to get back to my girls. I came here with them and didn't want to abandon them.

Before we parted ways, Zeke asked for my phone number.

And I gave it to him.

He asked if I'd be up for hanging out. Trying again.

I said, sure for some reason.

At that moment, it didn't seem like a big deal. It was nice catching up. I guess I got wrapped up in it all.

But now, I don't know.

India told me how she felt. Right away. As soon as I sat back down. Couldn't even get comfortable before she felt compelled to share how she felt.

"Zeke is cool and all, but I'm team Micah." She shrugged, taking a sip from her straw. "Sorry."

I sighed. My fries were cold. My drink was watery.

"Hey, Des. *Nice of you to join us.* And I'm team Micah too," Daijah said, pulling from the hookah closest to her.

I shook my head.

And meanwhile, Vic and Roni were cracking up.

The twins were solid. Daijah met Roni in beauty college years back, and they were fast friends, even securing an apprenticeship at the same hair salon.

I was cool with Roni from the second I met her. Her twin was just as dope. Daijah calls them both her best friends, but she's a little closer to Roni.

"I hear you've been plain ole miserable, Des. When you gone call that man?" Victoria asked. She was pulling from the other hookah.

Since Vic was sitting immediately to my left, I beckoned for the pipe. I needed to hit this shit and calm my damn nerves. I took a deep pull. "Vic. Micah hasn't even texted me," I offered. I knew it was bullshit. "I like this one." I took another pull. It was a sweet citrus blend.

"Me too!" Veronica offered. "It's called Ambrosia Fruit Salad."

"Roni, she's trying to change the subject!" Daijah snapped. "Des, you told him to move on. He's respecting your wishes. That isn't fair, and you know it."

"Girl, *really?*" Roni was cracking up.

"How does he even know I'm alive?"

They all peered at me, deadpan.

"He knows you're alive. Stop it." India sneered.

"I'm a complicated person," I whined, shaking my head. "Can I try that one, Indie?" When she silently passed me the pipe, I asked, "Are you mad at me, Indie?" I took a deep pull, closing my eyes. This one was bomb too—a cross between a lemon lime soda and a watermelon jolly rancher.

"Pirate's Cave," Vic supplied.

I took another pull. I liked it a lot but liked the Ambrosia fruit salad a little more. That was a mix of orange, cherry, pineapple, marshmallow, and coconut. I think I have a new favorite.

Opening my eyes, I looked up to find Daijah and India peering at me. They both looked at me for a long time.

"Why are you making this so damn complicated, Des?" That was Indie.

I returned a blank expression. "I don't know."

"Falling in love is a natural thing like breathing, and pissing. Resisting it and fighting it like you're doing is not normal! He's not the forbidden fruit or some shit. He loves you back!" Daijah was furious with me. "Don't let this slip through your fingers. You'll never forgive yourself. I won't forgive your crazy ass either." She shook her head and returned to a basket of chips and guacamole.

"I'm not like these other women. I'm complicated. Weird." I sighed, sipping my drink. It tasted like juice since all the ice had melted.

"He doesn't want to change a damn thing about you Des. He loves you just like that. Has he not shown you?" India pressed.

"He has… I just. Maybe I'm stalling. Trying to delay the inevitable. For a woman like me, it wouldn't last. I don't know anything about relationships. I'm still trying to figure my life out. I'm not sophisticated. Micah's older. Established." I looked up, realizing they were all peering back at me again. Daijah and India clearly annoyed.

"The fuck are you even talking about? You are a beautiful queen. Classy, regal, feminine. Men love that. You need to stay out of your head." That was India talking.

"I feel like such a fucking contradiction. He makes me feel safe and open and free to be myself. He loves everything about me. I've never had that before."

"Then let it be Des. Just let it be. Please let it be," Daijah sighed, rolling her eyes.

"Don't think about it, just feel it. Love is a natural thing and you're fucking it up worrying," Roni offered taking another pull.

"You deserve happiness. And he does too," Vic said.

"Go get your man sissy," Daijah said through an exasperated sigh.

"*She absolutely will.* I got her from here," Indie said. "The jig is up."

twenty-seven

MICAH

It had been almost two months since the day Destiney broke things off with me.

231

I hadn't tried to call her, and she hadn't called me either.

I constantly thought of her though, as usual. This time, though, it was from afar. I missed her so much. I wondered if we'd ever have a conversation, for at least the sake of closure.

But I wanted her. I wanted to marry her. And I wanted a child with her.

Only her.

Desperately, I think.

I wanted to tell Destiney that we could explore other paths to parenthood. Blood relations and biology wouldn't make any difference. It wouldn't matter at all.

I thought about my conversation with Mommy right after everything happened. She raised some valid points. I was just conflicted on how I would go about it. And I thought about it. A great deal. It wasn't just as simple as reaching out to Destiney. It had been difficult not to, but I respected her wishes and left her alone.

I decided that if Destiney extended an olive branch and reached across the aisle, I would fight for us. If she opened that door, even slightly. But only then.

In between time, I tried to fall back into my routine. But I couldn't even remember what that was like. Destiney had become such an integral part of my life. I felt incomplete without her.

So, I filled my time with things to keep me busy. To stay distracted. Threw myself into work a little more. I hung out with Mal pretty heavy. And Solomon. And it was mostly working.

I talked to my boy Tyson yesterday. He's good people. We were roommates all four years in college, eventually getting an apartment off campus as upperclassmen.

Ty planned to come to Sac in a couple of weeks, and I looked forward to that. After we graduated, he moved back to San Jose, his hometown. San Jose is about three hours from here.

We've remained in touch over the years. Ty has some family here, and I always try to catch him whenever he comes to visit. I've gone to San Jose to catch a couple 49er's games at Levi's stadium and he's always a great host. Ty did really well for himself. He's an aircraft engineer by profession.

I reminisce about our college days now and then. We had some good times being knuckleheads. But we handled business. Made it out alive. Graduated.

When Ty met Laila, those two were crazy about each other. They clicked immediately, and their relationship blossomed just as beautifully as Ayesha's and mine. The four of us did everything together, always going on double dates.

Then Tyson and Laila got engaged.

Naturally, I followed suit, proposing to Ayesha. And it was a beautiful time until it wasn't.

When I broke things off with Ayesha, it created a delicate situation with Ty and Laila. Ayesha and Laila were friends. Ty was like a brother and one of my closest friends and my very best college friend. When everything was fresh, I was bound to see Ayesha whenever I made an appearance at anything Ty and Laila would be hosting. Oftentimes, I decided

233

not to come at all to preserve the peace. Ty seemed to understand that.

About a year after we graduated, Ty and Laila got married. Their wedding was the last time I saw Ayesha. I hadn't seen her for a few months, and she looked beautiful. She was a bridesmaid. I was a groomsman. Thankfully, they didn't pair us. We kept it respectful, keeping our distance. We didn't speak.

Anyway, about six months ago, Ty and Laila separated. When I talked to him yesterday, he said they would likely be filing. Ty is pretty messed up behind that, and I understand. He mentioned possibly moving up to Sacramento at some point in the future, just for a change in scenery. I guess we'll see.

I'd been out and about most of the day and couldn't wait to get home, wash my ass and relax. I had three games to referee at the YMCA. Lately, I've been picking up additional games just to stay busy. Stay distracted.

Sometimes it didn't seem like the shit was working but…anyway. After leaving the Y, I went to Mal's to help him work on this deck. I was there for a few hours, and Ella fed me when I first arrived. When I left, it was just past five. I made a quick stop and ordered some dinner because I knew I wouldn't have the energy to cook anything once I made it home.

After paying for my order, I headed out to wait in the car for the curbside.

On my way back to the car, my phone vibrated. It was an unsaved phone number, but I recognized it. The same number had called me twice prior, and I hadn't answered. Whoever it was didn't leave a voicemail.

I started to silence the call, but I answered anyway. Maybe I'd finally find out who had been trying to get ahold of me.

"Hello?"

"Micah?"

I stopped abruptly in my tracks. I could never forget the sound of her voice.

Her soft, raspy voice was distinct, and I would always recognize it, regardless of the time passed.

"Ayesha."

"Hey… I know this is a surprise." She chuckled. "Do you have a second?"

Back when things were still fresh, I wondered what I'd say if I ever got the chance to speak to Ayesha again.

But that was before.

I was in a completely different headspace at that point. Today, right now… I was slightly uncomfortable with this; I'd much rather let sleeping dogs lie.

"Uh… yeah, I have a few minutes." I took the remaining steps to my car, then got inside. I placed the phone on the middle console beside me on speaker. Keeping my tone neutral, I said, "What's up? How are you?"

She sighed, and then there was a long pause. "I realize I'm likely the very last person you expected to hear from…" She paused again, and then I heard light whimpers and sniffling.

"Why are you crying?" I asked with care. Gingerly. I hoped everything was alright. When things ended between us, I wished her well, and I genuinely meant that.

She gathered herself then said, "Do you ever think about you and me? What we could have been?"

Wow! My eyes had to be bucked, my eyebrows high on my head. Sure, I had. Plenty of times. But sharing that with her likely wasn't best.

"Ayesha." That was all I could manage.

"Tell me," She pressed. "We had something so beautiful, Micah."

"I had," I revealed after a brief pause, "But that's fruitless for many reasons. Least of all, you're married. You belong to someone, Ayesha."

"Things aren't what they seem."

"How do you mean?"

"Well, for one, my husband and I are separated. I plan to file for divorce soon."

"What?"

"Moved out almost a year ago."

Wow. "I'd offer you sympathy, but somehow I don't think you need it." I used an ounce of sarcasm, but I was serious. Marriage was something I saw as sacred and ordained by God. I didn't speak ill of a person's marriage. Ever. It wasn't my place, and it wasn't my style.

"After things ended with us, I married right away. For all the wrong reasons. Partly out of spite because I was so angry and hurt. To that end, I ignored red flags and figured things would eventually get better. They didn't. They got worse. Much worse."

"Are you talking abuse, Ayesha?"

"Not physically, no. He was controlling and possessive. I couldn't work. My passion was nursing, and children and I never got the opportunity."

Shit. "Well, I'm happy you're free from that."

"Thank you. Me too. It was a dark time. Treacherous. But I overcame that. I have two little girls who mean the world to me. They make life worth living."

"Indeed." I heard my phone chime, and it was a picture of Ayesha with two Mini-Mes standing on either side of her. "My goodness! They are beautiful! It's like your same face three times." I let out a hearty chuckle.

I didn't say so, but Ayesha looked great herself. Still pretty. The years had been kind to her. I couldn't see the pain she'd described. That was a good thing.

She chuckled too, "Those are my babies. I couldn't deny them if I wanted to. Do you have children?"

"No... not yet. I'm the cool uncle, and it's a great gig."

"Of course you are!" I could hear the smile in her voice. After a beat, "For what it's worth, you'll make a great father when the time comes. You were so attentive. Sensitive and loving with me. Affectionate. No one has come close to the way you treated me. Cared for me. I figured out a long time ago the grass wasn't so green." As flattered as I was, I didn't know what to say. "I think back on those days all the time." She continued as an airy chuckle left her, "You were so good to me, Micah. Is there a possibility we could explore things again?"

I sighed, "Ayesha, you killed our child. A child I wanted so much. An innocent child I offered to raise all on my own. You made that decision without me. I realize it's your body and your right to choose, but I couldn't get past that."

She was silent. Then, "Micah... there's something you should know. I...I didn't have an abortion."

My breath caught in my throat.

"Wha...how is that possible? You had my baby and didn't tell me? Where are they?!" I pressed frantically.

"No, no. I didn't. I'm saying I never had an abortion because I didn't need to." After a heavy sigh, "I went back and forth on the decision for two weeks. By the time I went in, I was supposed to be twelve weeks along, but the baby had stopped developing at week nine. There was no heartbeat."

"Oh no... Ayesha..."

"Wild." She sighed, "I certainly didn't expect it to affect me the way it did. But I cried like a baby getting that news. Funny huh? I couldn't even decide if I wanted them and had no clue the decision would be made for me." She chuckled. "Once it was confirmed that the pregnancy was no longer viable, they sent me home with a prescription to prepare my body to pass the pregnancy tissue."

"Wow."

"I had to decide between that or a procedure where they clean everything out. The irony is that's the same way abortions are done. In this case, our baby was long gone."

There was silence for a few beats.

"Were you alone?" I asked gently. So gentle that I hardly recognized my own voice.

"Yes, I was. But... I feel like I got what I deserved. I was so adamant that the life we created was an inconvenience for me that I ate those words when it was all said and done."

"You couldn't have told me this? I would have been there for you."

"It was another one of my bad decisions. You're absolutely right. I should have told you, Micah. And I'm sorry for springing all of this on you now. You didn't deserve the pain I caused you. You deserved the truth a long time ago."

She really had no clue. "I cried for our child just like you did," I shared. "I still think of them. All the time."

"I think of our child too, Micah—all the time. When I had my girls, I thought of them even more. I wondered if she was a daughter who looked like them. Or was it a son who favored you? Super tall and handsome."

We shared a chuckle.

"I am so sorry you were hurting all these years. You didn't deserve the pain I caused. Can you find it in your heart to forgive me?"

"I already forgave you, Ayesha. To move on and heal from that, I needed to forgive you. Now, though, I have a completely different perspective. All things considered," I paused for a moment before continuing, "I can also admit my culpability in the breakdown of our relationship. I should have been more vocal about my feelings. At the very least, I should have told you how that affected me. Who knows... in my being vulnerable with you about it, you may have felt safer in telling me your truth. Back when it all happened, I was angry with you... so angry... turns out I didn't have to be. I thought I'd gotten over it, but now I'm thinking I just compartmentalized it. Pushed it deep down somewhere. Never actually dealt with it properly. Harboring that did so much damage. That damage took root, and it festered. I started to shut down and shut you out… That was ultimately the demise of our relationship. I checked out long before I officially ended it. When I decided to break off our engagement, I should have told you the entire truth as to why I ended things. I was so selfish. And I'm sorry. I felt terrible for hurting you. I hated hurting you, Ayesha."

"Don't do that Micah. We're equally to blame. And you were hurting too. I hurt you, Micah. And I'm so sorry. I'm so, so sorry."

"Please don't keep apologizing. It's all in the past. And all is forgiven."

"I can do that."

"Indeed."

"Micah?" Ayesha jested after a few beats of silence.

"Yeah?"

"Everything's on the table, out in the open. Everything. Can we try again?"

Shit. Could we?

I mean… I didn't know she lost the baby. "You know…" I paused, "Ayesha… I'm flattered but…"

"Are you married?" She asked abruptly.

"Not married. No."

"But you're seeing someone," She stated.

"I'm not. Not at the moment."

"Tell you what. This is my cell. Maybe think about it. There's a lot to process. Anyway, I'd love to see you. Catch up a little more. Maybe grab some coffee or something." Her soft chuckle cruised through the line. "Our very first date was at a coffee shop. Do you remember?"

"Of course I remember." A small smile made its way across my face. "I can think about it, Ayesha."

"Well." She seemed pleased with that. She laughed again. "I hope to hear from you, Micah."

"Yes, and Ayesha... I'm glad you called me. Thank you for this. I guess I needed this."

"Yeah."

"Well, you take care of yourself and your two beautiful daughters. I'll maybe text you or call you, and we can see about catching up."

"Alright, sure. Have a goodnight."

I hung up and sighed. Talk about a blast from the past.

I needed to talk to someone about this. Ayesha unearthed raw emotions, and they were much too heavy for me. I certainly wasn't going to internalize them. I needed the people I trusted most: my father and my brother. If I couldn't sort through these feelings with them, I would call my therapist for an appointment first thing Monday.

I went inside to grab my food and got back to my car. Before cranking up, I sent a text to the group message Mal and I had with Daddy. It was an emoji that worked as a bat signal—every time we needed to congregate on a serious topic, one of us sent it.

Malachi responded first, per usual.

Brother: Now?

Yes please. I'll be at the blue house in twenty
Brother: Right behind you, baby brother

I started my car and headed toward my parents' home. Their home was my haven and my safe space. I appreciated my tribe every day, especially on days like this.

Twenty minutes later, I walked through the front door of my parent's house and headed straight toward the living room to find Daddy and Mal sitting on the couch. As I entered the living room, they both rose to their feet immediately. Mal embraced me, and Daddy wrapped his arms around us.

No words were spoken, but I knew Daddy was praying. He did that a lot. He had no idea what this was about but had the mind to pray about it.

Prayers didn't always need to be spoken out loud. God is all-knowing. Aware of the situation inside and out. Our job is to bring our burdens to him, leave them there, trust him to handle them, and walk in that authority.

They were both patient as I gathered myself, acting as two pillars, giving me the strength I needed.

I knew exactly where they drew their strength. I knew I could draw some from the same source, and I knew there was an infinite amount of it where that came from.

When I was ready to let go, they released me, and we all took a seat.

And I hesitated because I'd held onto this all these years.

But after taking a deep breath, I got right to it.

"My senior year at Cal Poly, Ayesha and I learned we were expecting."

Daddy and Mal's eyes were wide in surprise, but they said nothing. I sighed. "Ayesha wanted to end the pregnancy, but I didn't. I wanted our child. I even offered to raise it alone. My understanding was that she decided to terminate. I respected her right to choose, but I just couldn't get over that. Eventually, I ended our engagement." Daddy and Mal nodded in understanding but remained silent. "Well, she reached out to me today. I hadn't spoken with her in years. Haven't seen her either. Turned out… she'd lost our baby. She didn't even need to go through with the procedure. And learning that has me thinking about all these possibilities. Like… had she told me that back then… maybe I wouldn't have shut her out… maybe…maybe…"

"Maybe you'd still be together? Maybe you'd have married her?" That was Daddy.

I sighed. Then I shook my head adamantly. "I wished she'd told me this back then."

"What's going through your mind now? Right now?" Mal asked.

"Destiney." After a heavy pause, I said, "But. Ayesha too. Once she dropped this bomb, I've been consumed with these thoughts of what if and what could have been. Ayesha wants to talk to me again. You know. And I'm not totally opposed to talking to her. I don't know… before I was, but that was when I thought she…" I sighed.

"Had that series of events not occurred, you likely wouldn't have met Destiney. Now, imagine that possibility," Daddy said.

I said nothing. But I did consider that possibility and didn't like how I felt.

twenty-eight

DESTINEY

"I love you best, I really do. But you don't seem to know what you want," India told me through a frustrated sigh. She shook her head as she continued stirring the pan on the stove. "Zeke is still fine. But. That's beside the point."

India was over at my place, and we hung out in the kitchen while she cooked us dinner.

"I know, right?" I said, sighing to myself. Yeah. Zeke was F-I-N-E. *Fine.*

We weren't out at Torch super late; I was home before ten. He called me that very night. He texted me first, asking if I made it home safe, and then he called me. We've spoken twice more since then, but I was still unsure of what it all meant.

And... I wasn't thinking I would be calling him back.

We talked for a while that first night and had an incredible conversation. But the two subsequent conversations weren't so stellar. It was like we didn't have much to talk about. It was strange. I don't remember it being that way back when we were seeing each other.

There wasn't much chemistry at all.

He was still very clearly into me.

Zeke is attractive and a gentleman. But that was the extent of it, on my end. The fact of the matter is that I'm not emotionally available.

I can admit that I didn't open myself up with him like I would with Micah.

Micah.

"I know exactly what I want. I want Micah."

"So why are you sulking about it? Call him! He misses you just as much as you miss him since you told him to stay away. He obviously respects your wishes. But I guarantee he misses you." India paused long enough to look back at me. I stood against the counter watching her, and we'd been discussing the Micah situation.

A situation I created and managed to piss her off in the process. India insisted we would come up with a game plan. Clearly, this wasn't my strong suit, and I was willing to do anything at this point.

She gestured for me to toss in the cubed potatoes and water, then immediately began stirring them in with the spices. She peeled, boiled, then chopped the potatoes earlier, setting them aside, and now that they were added in, the dish would be ready pretty soon. I couldn't wait. Before adding potato and water, she heated the fresh onion, garlic, curry leaves, turmeric, and a few other spices in a little oil over low heat. "I've heard that men will wait for the women they want. But they won't wait forever." She continued stirring. "Especially with options. We both know Micah has options."

I sighed heavily, mumbling, "Don't I know it."

Indie and I spent the whole day together. We're working on a mural at an Elementary school in Midtown. After we were done for the day, she asked to spend the night, which I readily agreed to. I knew she likely asked to come by to get a little more rest than she would at home. She's still living with her parents, and she told me that sometimes she just needs a break and a little privacy.

Even though we're in our late twenties, India isn't married, so she is expected to still live at home. India is first generation with very traditional immigrant parents who depend on her quite a bit. That's why I kinda sorta felt bad asking her if she wouldn't mind fixing us something. I don't ask her for favors often, but I'm so glad she agreed. She brings me food from home all the time. I love her food.

"What's this called again?" It smelled delicious.

"Aloo Palak."

Yeah, that. It's spinach and potato curry, and it's one of my favorite dishes she makes. She cooks two variations: a dry one and a gravy one. Today, she was making the dry version per my request. I like this one best. Once this is done, she'll make fresh roti to go with it.

India has an Afro-Guyanese mother and an Indo-Guyanese father. She can cook many of their traditional dishes, and many are vegetarian. India is what I call flexitarian. She eats meat, but you'd swear she's a vegetarian. Anytime we eat together, she's strictly plant-based.

"You really should be watching me, Des; then you can make this whenever you want." India joked. "I'm leaving all these spices here. Make use of them."

"Why, so I can burn the place down?" India released a peal of laughter.

Everyone knew I'd burn water. Daijah can cook, but not me.

"It's about time you learned, Best. What are you going to cook for your husband?" I knew Indie was asking in earnest. India was my girl, and I loved her to pieces.

Before I could answer, the doorbell rang.

"That's probably Neeka. I'll be right back." I made my way to the front door.

On the way home from work, we stopped to get a few things India would need from the store. A Boba shop was in the same plaza, so we went to grab a drink and ran into Neeka. I told Neeka she was welcome to join us for dinner.

I opened the door and greeted her excitedly, then went in to hug her.

"Chill, Des. I just saw you."

When she stepped over the threshold, I closed the door and noticed Neeka eyeing me skeptically.

"Okay. Girl. Where are you getting your clothes from?"

I looked at her, unassuming but curious as to where this random question came from. "Uh… different places." I shrugged.

"But where, though? What places specifically?"

"All over." Shrugging again, I looked down at myself, then back up at her. "I mean… this, what I'm wearing now I got from a thrift store. I like vintage clothing."

"Makes sense." She hotly informed me. I couldn't get a read on whether that was a good or a bad thing. I could only assume it wasn't good when she didn't follow up by telling me anything positive about my clothes.

Not that I needed her to.

At least I didn't think I did.

Her following words stung like hell, though.

"I'd dress much different than you if I had a body like yours."

My brows knitted as I looked down again at my faded destructed overalls. "What's wrong with the way I dress?"

Neeka laughed lightly. "I mean… You have such a cute figure. You'd look so much more put together if you cared a little more about your appearance."

I thought about what she said for a second.

I didn't need her backhanded compliment, if that's what it was.

I did care about how I looked. I liked being comfortable, for starters. I also didn't want to ruin any clothing between painting and bleeding all the time. I didn't owe her an explanation. I did love vintage finds, but thrifting was a great way to make sure I didn't go broke replacing clothes because I'd ruined them with blood stains. On the off chance I wore jeans, they weren't designer. I didn't own anything designer. My everyday wardrobe mainly consisted of black leggings, graphic T-shirts, and some kind of sweater. I'd be wearing it, or it would be around my waist. I was wearing a sweater right now. I was cold a lot, more than the average person. Since I bled so much, I was anemic and on iron supplements. Now, post-surgery, I was hoping to get off of those soon. And maybe I will get a new wardrobe.

But it wasn't at the forefront of my mind.

"Just a thought." Neeka absently tossed out.

I was perplexed. Why did she care so much anyway?

I tried not to let Neeka's words ruin my mood, but who was I kidding? I tried not to cry either, but that never worked. As sensitive as I am. My sensitive ass was always crying. Fuck me.

Neeka hung out for a while, and after she left, India and I got ready for bed.

India called her boyfriend and then her parents to check on them. Now, she was in my bathroom, brushing her teeth. We'd already taken showers. I planned to read for a minute but would be knocked out soon. India was a night owl, so she would probably be up for a while longer.

Anyway, I was sitting on my bed while she was in the ensuite, and India told me something peculiar.

"Best, did you notice how quiet Neeka got when we started talking about Tyler?"

"Hmm. Now that you mention it, I did notice that."

Earlier, the subject of Zeke came up again. We talked about Torch and how we'd gone there a few nights ago. I said something about being glad I missed Tyler, and India mentioned that I was bound to run into him eventually if I went back, seeing as he owns the place and all.

India shook her head, "She's fucking him."

"Woah! Indie, you have no facts to back that up."

"Girl, please. This is Neeka we're talking about."

"That's ridiculous."

"Not for her, it's not. She had so much to say, but then the subject switched to Tyler, and suddenly, she was quietly looking around, acting occupied. She doesn't fool me."

I shook my head. Tyler wasn't my man. He could fuck whoever he wanted. So could she. Neeka didn't have be so damn sneaky about it though. We're grown.

"What happened anyway?" India asked. She exited my bathroom and stopped in front of me, firmly putting her hands on her hips.

I knitted my brows. "Your mood took a nosedive as soon as she got here. What happened Best?"

"Nothing happened…. she just…"

India sighed. "She say some slick shit to you, didn't she?"

I nodded silently. My eyes began to well up, and I couldn't stop the tears if they wanted to fall.

India has seen me at some of my lowest moments, on some of my worst days.

And likewise, I've been there for some of hers.

"I could feel your energy was off a little bit. And I was waiting for you to tell me. What happened Best?"

"Is there something wrong with the way I dress?"

She narrowed her eyes. "No! Not at all. Are you kidding?" I remained silent and India crossed her arms as she spat, "The fuck Neeka say about the way you dress?!"

"I mean…nothing specific. She just alluded that I didn't dress like she thought I should and that I would look better if I cared more about my appearance."

"I love the way you dress. You have an eclectic personality with the style to match. You mix earthy and bohemian, and the aesthetic suits your spirit."

I gave her a weak smile.

"Don't let Neeka's words bother you. I know they hurt, but they're just words. There is nothing wrong with your style. Always be you, bravely. Always. Fuck what Neeka or what anyone else thinks."

She took me into her arms and hugged me.

"Thank you, Indie." I hugged her back. I loved Indie. I wish I were as confident as her. People didn't fuck with India. She was sweet. Probably sweeter than I am but she didn't let people fuck with her.

It's the same with Daijah. People did not try India Rampersaud or Daijah Evans. And they didn't try me either when either of them was with me. Neeka said her whole mouthful while we were in the living room, away from India. Also, Daijah wasn't home.

Girls who would bully me in school learned real quick to leave me alone. Daijah would handle them with the quickness. Especially in high school. Them girls were some bitches, and Daijah took her turn fighting each one up for the challenge. They never messed with me again. The ones who didn't want Daijah's smoke would take the message and move along. Daijah and India are both tall women. I'm short and wondered if that had anything to do with it.

"My pleasure." India sighed, "Freaking Neeka. She's probably jealous you're brave enough to wear what you like. She's so busy trying to maintain that image. All her unnecessarily high-end clothing, perfumes, purses, fancy ass car and all that damn makeup. Then that superior complex." India rolled her eyes hard. "She calls all that trying to bag a husband. She's failing miserably."

I cackled. Damn. India was right about that. It was a fact that Neeka had a great sense of style and fashion if you were into that. Always dressed to the nines. Like always. Hair always impeccable and not

251

a strand out of place. Makeup on fleek. She looked like a runway model.

She had a great career and could afford the finer things. She had an expensive lifestyle. A lovely high-rise apartment in expensive ass downtown Sacramento. And she was pretty outspoken about her desire for marriage. She was constantly speaking of her future husband and seeking him out.

"But she's got her priorities all wrong. Her personality needs some serious work. No one will wife her behaving that way. Not a man with some sense. Why sign up for that? Neeka is the type of woman a man would put in the fun category. She's good for fucking and that's it. She's jealous of you. Best. She wants your freedom. Your carefree personality. And men flock to you and throw themselves at you. She had to hear us talking about Micah and then talking about Zeke, and briefly, we spoke of Tyler. She doesn't have those options. She desperately wants to be someone's wife, but her vibe... I'm done talking about her." India looked at me. "I'm sorry for coming for your friend like that. But she pissed me off coming for you, pretending the shit was a compliment."

"Don't worry about it, Indie."

India wasn't the only one. Daijah didn't care for Neeka. At all.

Not long ago, Daijah told me that when I introduced them, she wasn't even impressed with Neeka. She got a bad vibe from her and couldn't really put her finger on it.

Daijah is better at discerning than I am, so I figured she was onto something. We never told each other to cut friends loose, but I knew what she thought whenever Neeka was around. It had been a while since the four of us had hung out. Daijah adored India and was always glad to see her. Neeka would hang out with India and me, but I rarely invited her to anything Daijah would be at. Also, I only invited Neeka over if I knew Daijah would be over Julian's house. Daijah was saying one time, *"Neeka ain't never getting wifed. Don't nobody want to marry her! She wouldn't even marry her!"* India and I were rolling.

I couldn't agree more. Her attitude needs work, but something tells me she couldn't change even if someone paid her. She wasn't sweet, and nothing about her personality was soft or feminine. Anyhow, I wasn't as close to Neeka these days. When we first met, things were cool. Now, I feel on edge anytime she's around.

"Enough about her. It's time for a come-to-Jesus talk. If you mess this up, I'll never speak to you again."

"You wouldn't!"

"Don't try me." India waved her hand dismissively. "Now, let's discuss this plan I've got for you getting your man back." India chirped.

twenty-nine

MICAH

"If Destiney is heavy on your mind, despite all of this, that tells me you're right where you're meant to be. Sleep on it. And then talk to Destiney."

Mal nodded in agreement with Daddy. "Give yourself some time before you make any rash decisions.

253

Either way, I think it's a good idea to have a conversation with Destiney. So you know where her head is. And tell her where yours is. I know you were giving her space, but this is a good reason to give her a call."

When I got home from my parents' house the other night, I lay on my bed thinking things over. And I had a lot to think about.

That day was much more eventful than I could have ever anticipated.

As I lay on my bed, my cell in my hand, I tried to conjure up a text message to send to Destiney.

Hey. I hope you're well. Thinking of you. Truth is, I never stopped thinking of you. If you aren't busy tomorrow, do you mind if we chat?

I hovered over the send button, of what I thought was a suitable message, but I hesitated.

I just couldn't hit send.

Why? I wasn't exactly sure.

Was she even thinking of me anymore? Even just now and then? Lord knows I was still thinking of her. You don't just fall out of that. Or climb the fuck out.

Not after what we've built. I still cared for her. Immensely. I was still very much in love with her.

I thought Destiney would reach out to me at some point. Especially now. But as more time has passed, I've somewhat begun to accept the possibility that she may not be.

I thought about it more that night and decided not to text Destiney after all. Figuring I'd take Daddy's advice and sleep on it. That was likely best, anyway. That way, I had a clear head.

The fact of the matter was that this conversation between Destiney and I needed to happen, waiting for her may not be the best route. But I still wasn't a hundred percent sure. I would see.

***

"Malachi, you been with the same woman twenty fucking years! And I know you're being faithful. How you even know what's out here?" Ray sucked his teeth through a smirk.

"I'm more qualified to speak on this shit than you nigga!" Malachi rolled his eyes.

A few days later, I was at Malachi's house watching the game, chillin'. He grilled some tri-tip. Mal makes the best tri-tip. Ella made some macaroni and cheese and some homemade rolls to go with it. Also, a green salad I was sure to eat a hearty helping of.

It was almost time to head out; we'd been here for a few hours. Mal's frat brother Jakobi came by. He's the homie and such cool people. He has a son who is the same age as Gabe. They took off a little bit ago, and Gabe headed upstairs.

Now that it was just the three of us, our conversation ended up on Raymond's favorite subject: women.

And something about men not being vulnerable with women and only women being vulnerable with men.

I mentioned that men are often willing to be vulnerable with the women close to them: their mother, sister, aunties, grandmother, maybe a close female friend, and the woman they eventually fall in love with. Of course, there are always exceptions.

That was all I could really add because it turned into a debate between Mal and Ray. I was just here for the entertainment.

A moment ago, they segued again to the different types of women, what women want, and how to satisfy them, not only sexually but in general.

"How? You been married half yo' damn life! Married when you were just barely old enough to buy you a damn beer."

I couldn't help but chuckle at that.

Ray continued, "You been out the game a long ass time. I ain't even mad at that. I have insight as to what's out here in these streets, and you can offer intel on married life."

"Ray, you be lying to these women," Mal said.

"Man, listen, men don't have to lie to women. If a woman likes you enough, she'll start lying to herself. I don't got to lie about shit."

"Nah. Yo ass still be lying." Mal shook his head rapidly, peering at Ray, deadpan. "Anyway," he turned to me, "Check it, I *objectify* my woman. She has everything I need. Women aren't all the same. Learn your woman. Study her like the art she is. Be intentional and curate things to whatever's best for her. Just because you like something doesn't mean she will. Learn what gets her going. You spend enough time with her and pay attention, you'll discover exactly what she needs from you."

"Man…" Ray shook his head and mumbled something under his breath, but Mal kept going.

"When you manage to get to a point where she feels like she can bare her soul, there is not a thing you cannot ask her for. But you must get to the point where she'll open up to you.

Make love with the lights on. Keep them lights on. That shit is a beautiful sight. Not only that, but she'll also get comfortable because you're show-ing her she *can be comfortable.*" Malachi glared at Ray for a moment. Finally, he turned to me and said, "Brother, eat the meat and spit out the bones. Re-gardless of who that shit is coming from." I nodded. Most of this information wouldn't apply to my cur-rent situation. But just the same, I could store it in my arsenal for later.

"I'm going to find my wife. I'll be back." Mal-achi stood and headed toward the stairs.

Ray and I both chuckled, and I took a sip of my drink. We knew exactly what that meant. He was probably about to get a quickie in or something. Mal-achi stayed, pouncing on Ella. It wasn't any of our business, but he always made it known. Ella seemed to be keeping up with his nasty ass though.

One thing Malachi did was take good care of his wife. Ella was always looking beautiful and vi-brant. I recall our conversation around year eight of his and Ella's marriage. He said men at his job con-stantly complained about their wives for one reason or another. A common one was that they always seemed to be sexually frustrated. Mal said he couldn't relate to that because Ella rarely turned him down. Because of that, he wanted to ensure he al-ways poured into her just as much as she poured into him.

"*I owe it all to my wife. She keeps me satisfied. That's why she's so spoiled. Ain't no way in hell I could just take, take, take from her.*"

Malachi has always been transparent about his marriage with me. They were married young, and I had a front-row seat to all of it, Malachi and I being as close as we are.

I still recall the evening at dinner when he told Daddy he wanted to marry Ella. They were home from college on summer break, and he planned to ask her father for her hand. At the time, Malachi was twenty, and Ella was just nineteen. Relatively young to want marriage so soon by some standards, but here they were fifteen years later and still going strong.

"Marriage is serious business. Ain't nothing to play with." My father's voice was stern. His authoritarian command was in full effect.

"I know that, Daddy."

"Malachi."

"Yes, sir?"

After a long pause, he said, "If you're not done playing games, you leave that sweet girl alone."

Mal had his choice of women as a standout basketball player, and the ladies flocked to Malachi. All I know is everything changed when he and Ella got together. He only had eyes for her seemingly overnight. Ella had no shortage of suitors, either, as striking as she is. But their choice of each other was abundantly clear.

"I love Ella and want to be the man who makes her happy for the rest of her life. I know what I have, and I'm not letting her get away. Furthermore, Ella isn't the type of woman that would last long out here. She's mine." Malachi's tone was adamant and resolute.

Daddy chuckled, nodding his head. "Oh, it's like that?"

Mal and I both chuckled, too.

"Gone get your wife, son."

I'm sure Daddy was confident in Malachi's words. Mal was always determined. Wise beyond his years. Focused. I admired those qualities about Malachi. Anything he set his mind to was a done deal. He was always the type to make what he wanted happen. Irrespective of naysayers, and there were always those. Naturally, many people gave them both the third degree for wanting marriage so soon and so young. But the two of them weren't remotely concerned.

Ray and I took off at the same time. I'd just walked in the door when I got a text *from Ayesha.*

Ayesha: Hey Micah how was your day?

We'd been texting a little bit.

Well, she mainly texted me. I'd feel bad just leaving her on read, so I would reply. But she was mostly driving the conversations. It wasn't something that gave me the feels like whenever Destiney would text

And we met up. A few days ago, at a café. About a week after, she called me.

Ayesha looked great. Had a few healthy pounds on her. Very pretty. Still.

We fell right back in it seemed. Caught up on so much. She and Laila were still thick as thieves. As it turned out, Ayesha got my number from Ty. She knew we were still in touch and insisted she had something very important to talk to me about. Obviously, Ty gave it to her. I chuckled at that. He wouldn't have done that if I were in a relationship, so no love was lost. And Ty is my boy, but he still could have given me a heads-up.

Anyway, when we met at the café, we talked for hours. We were there so long that breakfast wore off. I felt bad offering to take her across the street for lunch or something, but she needed to get back to her daughters.

I realized pretty quickly that Ayesha was serious about giving things another try—so serious that she was already trying to set up another meeting within the week. I told her I'd let her know once I checked my schedule.

And I walked away from that feeling certain.

Sure, that I didn't feel anything. That spark. That something.

It wasn't there.

It just wasn't the same—not that I expected it to be. We are a decade older now. So much has happened in life, but we didn't have any chemistry.

She's still as sweet as I remember. A bit more chill. And so proud of her beautiful little girls. And speaking of, I'll admit I pondered how I would fit into her life now, with them. I'm aware she's a packaged deal. I considered how she'd fit into mine. She already had children, and seemingly, it would be a feat fathering children of my own. I mulled over that for a minute.

But no. As far as there being anything between us, it wasn't going to happen.

I planned to let her know—probably this evening. I didn't want to string her along.

And in other news, I still hadn't reached out to Destiney.

She hadn't reached out either.

thirty

DESTINEY

I timidly entered the expansive lobby of the high-rise building. The elementary school India and I were working at was just six blocks from here.

I knew exactly what building Micah worked in. He told me a long time ago.

When we took the gig around the corner, I mentioned it to India. So when we talked over the plans, she suggested the brilliant idea that I come here.

I was sure to come on a day when I knew he'd be in the office because he worked from home part of the time. I glanced at my watch. It was exactly one o'clock, and I knew Micah would be going on his lunch any minute now. He usually had his assistant block out the lunch hour. He had to do that to ensure he actually took a lunch break. Sometimes, he would get so wrapped up in whatever he was doing that he would forget to take it. Once we started talking, he'd gotten so much better about that. I hoped he would continue that even though we weren't talking.

And I hoped this conversation today would change that.

Maybe this wasn't such a bad idea.

On Tuesdays, we had a ninety-minute lunch instead of the normal sixty. This would give me enough time to meet with Micah and talk to him.

Tell him how much I missed him and wanted to be with him.

Tell him that I was in love with him, too. Granted, he still felt the same.

And beg him for another chance.

I stopped at a deli two corners over and got lunch for him. He always went there when we would talk over lunch on FaceTime.

It was a mom-and-pop that had been in business for something like fifty years. It was family-owned and apparently had some of the best sandwiches in town. I knew his order by heart, so when I stopped in, I rambled it off just like it was nothing.

I left the deli and noticed several sandwich shops as I walked toward my destination. There were many restaurants, period, with choices galore. Whatever you were in the mood for. The business district of Downtown Sacramento was bustling. Not quite like New York City, but it's certainly a fast-paced part of town. I had to circle the block a couple of times to find parking. The Golden 1 Center, where the Sacramento Kings played, wasn't far from here either.

I felt sorely out of place as soon as I entered the lobby.

First of all, everyone was wearing a suit and tie.

The women were dressed the part, too.

I had on my painting clothes since I left the site and came here directly.

Painting clothes that were stretched, faded, and covered in splotches of random colors. That had me second-guessing this whole thing.

Fortunately, no one seemed to be paying me any mind. I focused ahead.

Gripping the bag containing Micah's sandwich, I took a deep breath and proceeded to the directory adjacent to the elevators. I realized I had left my cell phone in the car when I got to the deli, but this should be simple enough. I knew the department Micah worked in, but I just couldn't recall what floor.

"Hey, *cutie!* Can I help you find something?"

Cutie was an interesting word choice.

The infliction threw me just a little, too.

I'm a grown woman. It almost sounded like she was referring to a puppy in someone's arms.

Sighing lightly, I looked to the right and up into the eyes of a gorgeous woman.

Thirty something and dressed to the nines in a burgundy dress and stiletto heels. She looked like a damn lawyer or something. Or like she belonged on the morning news. Her smile was perfect, and her hair was styled in a cute French roll. Damn. I hadn't seen one of those since the early two-thousands. She was rocking it, though, and not a hair was out of place.

"I'm Erica, and I'm on the third floor if that's where you're headed." She spoke pleasantly.

"Thanks! I'm Destiney. And I *think* it's the third floor." I nodded. "I left my phone in my car, but I think that's it."

"Who are you looking for? That may help us out."

"Micah Walker."

"*Oh.*" Her demeanor changed instantly. "How do you know, Micah?" She asked curtly. Her bright smiling eyes now shrunk into slits and suddenly she wasn't so friendly anymore.

Nope. Not a trace of her friendliness from seconds before.

I smiled anyway. As best I could, despite this sudden energy shift. "We're... friends," I provided, shrugging casually. I wished I'd said it confidently the second it left my lips. She sniffed out my trepidation and seemed pleased with her discovery—traces of something akin to a snarled expression showing itself.

"Friends? Oh! Well, Micah and I are quite acquainted. We have been for years. Funny, he's never mentioned you."

"Acquainted?" Why did I even ask?

"Yes. *Very much so.*"

Okay.

So they're fucking.

"I see," I mumbled, suddenly reconsidering this whole thing. My confidence was shot to hell.

Micah wasn't mine. But. What was I doing?

This wasn't me. I couldn't do this.

I didn't belong here.

The elevator announced its arrival with a loud ding. The doors slid open as a handful of people stepped off into the lobby.

"Going up?" I can take you to his office. "I'm headed there now myself, matter of fact."

"Uh no. That's alright." I turned on my heels and made my way outside.

Who was I kidding? I couldn't compete with her.

I wouldn't compete with her.

She could have Micah. I knew this wasn't a good idea.

I'm not good with these, and they aren't good for me. Here I was trying something new, all for it to blow up in my face. This is the big league, and I'm just a rookie.

I walked back toward my car down the block, passing a homeless man.

"Hey, would you like a sandwich?"

thirty-one

MICAH

"Thank you for the updated analysis on the proposed market value. We'll need to take a closer look at their financials from last quarter to get a better idea of their Proforma. Let's meet next week after you've had a chance to review."

We were swiftly approaching a charter meeting with our mid-West market, and Ellington was instrumental in helping ensure the Fair Market Value and Proforma were completed on time.

"Good stuff. Appreciate you, Boss," Ellington said, saluting me. I chuckled lightly; he always did that.

"I appreciate all of your hard work." I glanced at the time, and it was just after two o'clock.

"Go ahead and get a head start in your evening with your family. Then take another look with fresh eyes tomorrow." Ellington had a beautiful wife and an adorable baby daughter. I was so thrilled for him and the legacy he was building.

"Don't mind if I do!" E chuckled beaming. "Thanks!"

"Have a great evening, Ellington." I did the same salute and ended our Zoom meeting.

I enjoyed working with Ellington.

I had about a decade on him, so he was like a younger brother I was proud to have around.

As my senior Financial Analyst, E was my right hand. He is brilliant and impeccable at what he does. He's also hungry to learn and eager to exhibit his skills. He's grown tremendously over the past two years he's been on my team, and I was glad to have him.

Ellington has continued to exceed my expectations, earning the maximum merit increases and bonuses I'd given him.

I planned to promote him early next year, and I was chomping at the bit to deliver the good news. It was still a couple of months away, but after a final review of our department numbers, I knew we'd have room in the budget to do so. I would see to it that he succeeds anywhere he deserves. I wanted nothing less for anyone on my team. If I had anything to do with it, it would happen.

I emailed my assistant Laurie, requesting that she schedule the follow-up meeting for next week and then told her to log out for the afternoon afterward.

I allowed them both to work from home and only requested that they come into the office when necessary. They were free to do so as long as they could remain productive remotely.

Work-life balance mattered a lot to me. I didn't want anyone who reported to me to get burned out or become too overwhelmed with work, which inevitably had a negative impact on home and family time.

I planned on heading out shortly myself.

Mentally, I was exhausted. I had a pretty hectic day, with meeting after meeting. I still had one more meeting, and then I planned to leave for the day.

I began gathering the paperwork on my desk so that I could take off as soon as my meeting was over.

I couldn't believe it was already two o'clock. I'd worked right through lunch. I sat back in my chair and sighed. I tried not to do that, and usually, I was pretty good about it. Since Destiney and I didn't talk over lunch anymore, it was something I had to be intentional about.

Destiney used to call me every day on FaceTime at one o'clock sharp.

I loved that. And I miss that.

"Knock, knock." I rolled my eyes at the voice I desperately wanted to ignore. And if we were anywhere but here, I most certainly would have. Since that notable conversation, I really hadn't seen much of Erica. I wonder what she wanted now.

"Hello, Erica." I offered, not even looking over at the doorway.

"Hello," She chirped. After a few moments of me saying nothing, she chuckled lightly. "Well, aren't you going to invite me in?"

"Come on in."

"Thanks." She crossed the threshold, and after quick strides, she was right in front of my desk.

"Figured you haven't eaten yet. So, I picked this up for you." She held out a white bag. I recognized the logo. And the smell.

"You didn't have to do that."

"I wanted to."

I rolled my eyes, but subtly enough that she couldn't see. When I didn't reach out to accept the bag, she placed it on my desk.

"It's your favorite."

My eyebrow went up, and I didn't bother hiding that.

"Smoked turkey, pepper jack, and fire-roasted tomatoes on toasted ciabatta."

I sat there. Silently. Giving her a blank stare.

"That's your favorite from Specialties, right?" She managed around her plastered smile. It was more like a statement.

It was.

And honestly that sounded delicious right about now. I was starving too.

But I couldn't trust Erica. Not that she'd do anything to my food, but she had an agenda. An ulterior motive. Everything she did concerning me was transactional and I didn't want a damn thing from her. At minimum, she just wanted an excuse to come to my office. I could have saved her the trouble.

Instead of a response, I shook my head rapidly.

"Erica, really you shouldn't have." I picked up the bag and tried giving it back to her.

"It's no big deal, Micah. I insist."

"I brought leftovers." I lied. "Was about to go warm them up now."

"Have this instead, and have your leftovers for dinner."

"No thanks, Erica."

"What am I supposed to do with this sandwich? I already ate."

"Eli will be glad to take it," I said, referring to our security guard. Each floor of the building had its own, and Eli had been with us for a number of years. We blessed him with extra food from catered lunches all the time. He was always grateful to have whatever we offered.

She huffed a frustrated breath, snatching the bag once she realized I wouldn't take the sandwich.

"Fine, I'll give it to Eli then." She snapped.

"Great." I stood and walked around my desk to see her out. "Thanks, Erica. Please close my door behind you if you wouldn't mind."

She took a few steps, then turned to me, and I looked up expectantly.

"Oh yeah…" Erica's top lip curled, and I already didn't like where this was going. "Someone came by for you earlier." Her voice was strangely friendly now. "She only made it to the lobby." Erica offered.

"She?" My brows furrowed. Most of my meetings these days were via Zoom, but I racked my brain trying to figure out who it could have been.

I wasn't expecting anyone.

"Hmm… what was her name?" She tapped her chin as if deep in thought. "Odyssey? No." Erica shrugged dismissively. "I forgot her name, but it was something strange like that."

My eyes narrowed.

"She was cute... in an awkward way. Looked like she walked in off the playground or something." Erica cracked up at that as if she'd just heard the funniest thing ever. "Chocolate with locs. Short." Realization hit me, and my blood boiled. "She said she was your friend." She seethed that last part, and I noticed Erica wore a smirk now.

Maintaining my poker face and my cool, I asked, "Destiney came to see me?" I added a pleasant smile for good measure. The first smile she'd seen since she came in here.

Thinking of Destiney did that to me. But I couldn't let on that my mind was in shambles right now. I knew Erica said something nasty to Destiney. And I was frantic at the endless possibilities.

My smile wiped the grin right off her face.

Erica folded her arms. "What kind of friend is she?"

I crossed my own arms. "That isn't your business, Erica."

"Well. I told her we were quite acquainted. She seemed surprised. Guess you didn't tell her about us."

"There's nothing to tell."

"You sure about that?"

"Positive."

"I'm sure she'd beg to differ."

Fuck.

"Was there anything more I could do for you, Erica? I'd like to get to lunch now."

"There's plenty you can do for me, Micah. But we can talk about that later. I won't keep you." With that, Erica pranced out of my office and down the hall. I closed my door and couldn't grab my phone quickly enough.

I called Destiney.

When Destiney didn't answer, I called her again. When she didn't answer that call either, I texted her.

Then I called her again.

Then I called her again. And again.

I was beside myself. I needed to talk to Destiney immediately, and knowing Erica, I needed to do some serious damage control.

***

"We went on two dates. That's it."

"Have you slept with her?"

I sighed.

"Micah. Just tell me."

I frantically tried to get ahold of Destiney for the rest of the afternoon. Unsuccessfully.

Then, I had to facilitate a meeting I could hardly focus on because my mind was so preoccupied. I worried she'd call me while I was in the middle of my meeting, and I couldn't answer.

Eventually, some hours later, I got her on the phone.

Begrudgingly, she was willing to answer me on FaceTime. I knew I was pushing it, but I had to see her. I needed her to see me. I felt things would land better if she could see the sincerity in my eyes.

"I did sleep with her. One time. Worst decision ever."

Destiney nodded. "How long ago?"

"Two years."

"Two years?"

"Yes. It didn't mean anything. Honest to God. But she's still hanging on to that as if there's a possibility of something more."

"Have you given her reason to believe there will be?"

"Absolutely not. I've told her numerous times there won't be. No matter what I tell her, she can't seem to get that through her head."

"That's wild."

We were silent.

More than a few beats went by.

Destiney looked away and never brought her eyes back.

"What are you thinking, Destiney baby? Give it to me straight." I couldn't get a read, and I needed to know. I wanted to fix this, and I wanted us to be okay.

"I'll be honest." She still wouldn't look at me. "I felt jealous. But I remembered I had no right to feel that way. You aren't mine." She said passively.

Her words stung, though it was true.

We weren't officially us. But in my head, we were. Pretty much immediately, Destiney was the only one I wanted. For a while now, she was the only woman in my world.

Initially, she tried to give the impression she was unbothered by the situation, but I called her bluff, in a manner of speaking.

I insisted it was perfectly reasonable for her to be upset at me. Not feeling anything meant she didn't care; we both knew that wasn't the case. I cared immensely, and I felt confident that she did, too.

"Destiney baby. Look at me, please." I gave her a moment, and those big, brilliant eyes were back.

I wanted more than anything to have her in front of me. In my arms. To hold her and reassure her.

"You have nothing to feel jealous about."

She sucked her teeth. "I mean. I was intimidated. That woman was just gorgeous. Picturesque. Like a model. I'm not that."

"Well, it's a good thing she isn't who I want. I want you. And you are beautiful, Destiney. And do you know what?" I waited a moment. "I guarantee she was jealous seeing you, even before she knew you were there for me."

Destiney sucked her teeth again. "Oh, please."

"I'm serious." You roll out of bed looking like you do. Naturally beautiful. She looks nice all made up, but she doesn't look that way underneath all that. You're also just as beautiful on the inside. She isn't. Not even a little bit."

"That's nice, Micah. Thank you. Listen. I um… I need to think about this. I'll call you, alright. I promise I'll call you."

I nodded. "Okay. Alright. Please call me, Destiney baby."

She said nothing more and disconnected the call, and I hung my head in defeat.

***

I dozed off but woke up immediately when I heard my phone vibrating on my nightstand. I grabbed it quickly, hoping it was Destiney calling me, but it was Ray.

I already knew he was calling with his usual shenanigans, but I really didn't feel like talking, especially to him. Against my better judgment, I answered his call anyway.

"Whassup?" I let out a breath.

"Cousin?"

"What's good dude?"

"Shit. Thinking 'bout Seals tonight. You trying to slide through?"

Seals was a cigar lounge in West Sacramento. I didn't smoke a cigar, but maybe twice a year, but it was definitely a chill spot. There was always a great vibe, good drinks, and good music.

They had premium cigar options and an extensive drink menu to pair them with, everything from top-shelf whiskey and bourbon to dark, roasted coffee brewed to order. No doubt it would be a good place to hang out and forget about shit for a while.

I didn't even need a whole cigar; a contact high would be good enough with them strong shits.

"Uh yeah... what time you headed that way?"

"About an hour. Can you roll with that?"

"Yep."

"Bet."

After hanging up, I sighed audibly.

I thought about it for another second and changed my mind. I just wasn't feeling up to it.

I called Ray back, and he answered on the first ring.

"Hey, Ray, I'm not really feeling like-"

"Man! I already know! You in a funk behind ole girl ain't you!?" Ray snapped, cutting me off.

I was stunned into silence.

I didn't appreciate his tone or attitude for one and two. Three, he needed to mind his own damn business.

As if that wasn't enough, he continued, "I been saying that bitch ain't worth all this trouble man. She real cute, but that's it. You stay in yo damn feelings since she been around."

My eyes grew wide. "You know what Ray? Do not fucking call me again!" I ended the call and tossed my cell across my side table.

I was so sick of Ray and his bullshit.

Mal distanced himself from Ray a long time ago, and as I matured, I could see why, though Mal was always civil whenever they were in the same space.

It had literally been years, and Ray didn't even have Mal's number. The two of them would always talk through me. It was mainly from Ray's end, though. Malachi didn't have shit to say to Raymond in the time between them seeing each other.

Ray always seemed jealous of Mal and me for one reason or another. Jealous of us as individuals. Jealous of our relationship with each other. Mal and I were incredibly close and always had one another.

I think Ray envied that as an only child.

Ray's mother wasn't in his life at all, and he envied our relationship with Mommy. Despite the fact that my mother was so kind to Ray and was sure to always love on him, I think he longed for his own mother to love him.

I couldn't blame him.

Then there was my uncle, Ray's father.

He was always gone since he drove long hauls. Uncle Marshall missed so many things concerning Ray, and Daddy picked up much of the slack.

Ray played sports like Mal and me, often on some of our same teams. But Uncle Marshall didn't make time to come to anything. Maybe it wasn't a priority. He missed plenty of championship games because "he had to work."

We never saw the fruits of that labor, though.

For one, Ray was living with us, and two, they had a studio apartment in a shady part of town.

Daddy always said Uncle Marshall could afford a nicer place in the 'burbs, and he must have been tricking off his money.

Who knows.

My phone vibrated. Thinking it was Ray calling me back, I snatched it up and answered quickly.

"Man what? I said don't fucking call me!"

"Yo, baby brother! It's me."

"I'm sorry Mal. I thought you were Ray calling me back." My voice calmed.

"What his simple ass do now?"

I told Mal the latest.

Ray was always trying to find shit to get into and always had some shit to say. I was over it all a long time ago. Maybe this was confirmation that I needed to leave Ray and all his bullshit alone finally.

"Don't pay him no mind, baby brother. He had no business calling your woman a bitch, but Ray don't like to share. His ass was wildin' when Ella first came around. Nigga was beside himself." Mal let out a lazy cackle. "He got over it once he realized Ella wasn't going nowhere."

I shook my head. "I remember."

"He ain't had me for years, and now he's afraid he'll lose you once you settle down. He's feeling threatened, but he can get the fuck over it. And he owes you an apology."

"Right. I told him not to call me. But we'll cross paths eventually."

"Rays ass ain't going nowhere. He'll probably be at the blue house tomorrow trying to eat Daddy's food. Oh! Mommy made lasagna for Daddy to take to the church. Why did Ray go over there and eat off it? Didn't even stop to ask, just helped his greedy ass to it."

"You lyin'!" I shook my head. "Mommy told you that?"

"Hell no! You know Daddy did."

"Fucking unbelievable."

"Shiiiittt! I was hot. But Daddy was pissed so you know Ray had to hear his mouth. That's worse than either of us getting on his ass."

We both cackled.

"Mommy probably told Daddy to leave him alone." I surmised. Mommy always seemed protective of Ray whenever Daddy would get on him.

Honestly, I think she felt sorry for him. She was always that way when we were kids and even now.

"She likely had something else she could throw together just as good as her lasagna."

"True."

"What's up though brother?"

"Yeah. Can you meet me at the blue house this weekend? We need to pull some stuff out of the garage for Daddy. I'll have Gabe with me, but it'll be faster if we had two more hands. Ray's ass need to be over there helping too, but I don't want to deal with his mouth."

I laughed again. "Yeah, that's no problem at all. What time?"

"Let's knock it out early. How's nine?"

"I gotchu."

There was a beat of silence. I decided to forgo giving Mal the latest with Destiney and me for the moment. There were still a few uncertain things.

Then Mal said, "Thinking about barbequing. Ella and Gabby are meeting us there after Gabby's soccer game."

"Bet. I can bring some drinks. What's Ella fixing to go with the barbeque?"

"Any requests?"

"Seven-layer dip?" Ella made a seven-layer dip that was so delicious that you didn't even need the chips to go with it. Sometimes, she switched it up and made it with shredded chicken in place of ground beef. I loved both ways.

"Hang on brother… Queen!"

I heard shuffling in the background, then Ella's muffled voice, "Hey."

"You mind making your seven-layer dip for us to take to mommas this weekend?"

"Yeah, I can definitely do that. Gotta get to the store though. I'll need a few things."

"I'll go, don't worry about it baby," Mal said.

"Please tell my sis thank you."

"Micah said thank you."

"You're very welcome, Micah."

Within seconds, I could hear giggles and smacking noises, and that was my cue to hang up.

Nasty asses.

thirty-two

MICAH

"I'm not perfect. I may even let you down. But I'd never do it intentionally, Micah. And I don't want to be on a pedestal." Destiney looked away from me. "I'm not so great with relationships. I don't have the experience, first of all. This is just a lot of pressure, and I don't want to disappoint you." She sighed, then, "I'm rambling at this point."

"Nothing done in good faith will ever disappoint me. I'm not expecting anything. Except what you are ready to give me. I'll receive that with open arms. Nothing more. Especially nothing less. You can expect the same from me too."

"Yeah," Destiney paused for a beat. Giving me her eyes, she said, "I thought you'd already moved on."

"I haven't moved on sweetheart."

I was at the office, and Destiney and I were on FaceTime.

She hadn't called me back last night, so I texted her as soon as I woke up, telling her good morning.

She said good morning back.

Much to my delight, we continued texting throughout the day—just like old times. We didn't miss a beat.

At one o'clock, she asked if I wanted to talk. Instead of texting her back, I immediately called her on FaceTime.

We had an unfiltered conversation. Got caught up on everything that occurred over the past two months.

I told her about Ayesha.

She already knew of Ayesha but not those other details. So, I filled her in on everything, including that I met with Ayesha. I told her all that and then assured her that that situation was over.

Days ago, before Destiney and I reconnected, I told Ayesha how I felt. I told her as gently as I could that I didn't wish to continue with things. I wished her well. She seemed to take it alright—much different than last time.

Destiney told me she'd spoken to a guy from her past. They hadn't gotten together, but she saw him while she was out with her friends. They had a few subsequent conversations. I worried for a second that she had moved on, but she didn't. She told me that it was over and done with as well.

Her eyes were back on mine now. Her beautiful face filled my screen.

"Do you trust me?" I asked after a beat.

"Yes," she said softly.

Her brilliant eyes bore into me as I spoke earnestly, "Is there any doubt? Or uncertainty…hesitation? Anywhere?" I searched her eyes and continued, "I want you to know if there is, I assure you it won't upset me. We're still building. But I need an opportunity to show you; you can trust me—one hundred percent. You'll always have me. Always. And that you're safe with me. All of you is safe with me. Your mind, spirit… dreams, fears…your body."

"Okay," she declared. She wore a bashful expression and tried to look away.

"Eyes on me, Destiney baby."

"Micah. That was so beautiful. I don't even know what to say. If you haven't noticed, I am a ball of emotions. How would I even follow up after something like that?"

"I'm not even finished."

Her eyes grew in surprise.

Dramatically, I inhaled a deep breath, then opened my mouth, finally saying, "I'll leave it there for now, though." I gave her a silly grin, and she laughed for a while. I did, too, and it felt good — really good.

"Oh my gosh! You're a mess, you know that?" she said after she finally calmed down.

"That I am. A mess over you."

"Hmm." Is what she gave me — a sweet, contented smile to match.

Man, I was so sprung off her.

Gone.

And I needed her to be mine.

Fast, quick, and in a hurry. Like yesterday.

I could hardly stand it.

"Can we give this thing a try?" I more so stated than asked.

"What thing?" She knitted her brows, a confused resolve in her voice.

I paused for a moment. Considering the best way to proceed. She made it so easy to be open and transparent with her, but I didn't even know how to formulate my words.

I quickly decided I'd just put it all out there.

"Destiney baby, I want you and you only. A committed relationship. Official. Exclusive. I don't want anyone else to have you. Mind or body. And when you're ready, and you'll have me, I want to marry you."

She held my gaze but was expressionless and silent for several agonizing moments.

"I don't want anyone else to have me either. I only want you to have me," she returned confidently.

I released the breath I was holding. "So, are we really going to do this?"

"I'd love to do this with you."

I smiled real big. "Yeah?"

"Yeah." She gave me a Kool-Aid smile of her own.

And something else. I didn't plan to bring up children again. Ever.

I was fine discussing it with her, but she'd have to bring it up first.

I always saw myself with children in my future, but maybe God had another path for me.

For us.

If she still wanted them. I was unsure of that specific detail, but I didn't want to bring up anything that would trigger her in any way. She had already been through so much, and I was fine leaving well enough alone.

I guess this was one of those things we'd eventually get around to hashing out.

In the meantime, I was glad to have my wife back and so excited that we made things official.

"When are you going home Destiney baby?"

"I can leave right now."

"You sure?"

"Hell yeah."

"I'm leaving now. Coming to get you."

I still had another meeting scheduled, but I could take that at home. I needed to get to my baby.

Finally.

Destiney Fulfilled

Sweet Destiney Book 2

Cover by ZSW

Hibiscus Tea Publishing

For the hopeful romantics.

And for my real-life sibling bestie.

One

DESTINEY

"Can I kiss you, Destiney baby?"

"Yes."

Micah captured my lips with the softest of kisses, making my eyes flutter. Then he kissed me again, and neither of us held back this time. It was a hungry kiss —frantic—so very fitting for a moment like this. And our tongues seemed just as happy to be reunited as we were.

He drew back, leaving only a whisper of air between us. "Baby?"

I was breathless. "Yeah?"

"Pack an overnight bag. I want you to stay with me. Will that be alright?"

I nodded, agreeing without hesitation. "Yes. Come on in. I'll just need a minute."

He softly kissed me again.

And I didn't have the slightest clue why the hell I ever *spent a moment away from him.*

I was up in my room now. I threw a few things in my bag. I hardly paid attention to what I was grabbing. I wouldn't need much anyway. I'd just need some panties, night clothes, and something for work tomorrow. That was easy. I could show up to work in whatever. I didn't mind getting paint all over. We hadn't yet discussed what would happen after that, but I wasn't even worried about it. I knew I'd be with my man.

My man.

Nothing else mattered.

When Micah arrived, I'd barely just got home myself. And I couldn't open the door quickly enough- couldn't get to *him* quickly enough. Once nothing was separating us, I closed the space instantly. I was swift, throwing my arms around Micah's waist. I held on tight. Inhaling his scent. Basking in his warmth. Losing myself in his refuge. Micah embraced me securely and just as frantically. Rubbing my back softly.

And we stood just like that.

Right in the front doorway.

We held each other for a long time. No idea how long it was exactly. It seemed like several minutes. We didn't need to talk. There would be plenty of time for that.

Damn. It felt so good to be back in his arms. Any reservations I had at one time now seemed... *so trivial*. Frivolous. Nominal. Unnecessary. I had it in my mind that I would make up for all of the time wasted. Time *I* wasted.

Reunited with Micah, I felt... *all* the things. Certitude. Familiarity. Serenity. And, also, I felt sexy. Free. Powerful. And significant. I loved everything I felt with him. I wanted to be with him all the time. I wanted to see him as often as he could stand to see me. I wanted to be in his space and his arms. It felt like no other place I'd experienced. This was precisely where I was meant to be.

With Micah, everything was right in my world.

He's such a gentleman. Damn... so thoughtful. To a fault. Earlier, I kinda needed to remind him that he didn't ever have to ask for what was already his.

Including me. I was his.

He asked for another kiss before I descended the hallway to pack my bag.

"Beautiful Destiney baby... can I kiss you? Please?"

"Yes, please." When we broke apart, I said, *"Mi-cah."*

"Yep."

"Kiss me anytime. I don't mind." My sweet Micah, ever the gentleman, had asked for permission each time he wanted to kiss me. It was so sweet and incredibly thoughtful, but we were way past that now. *"Anytime you want to, you can."*

Micah nodded. *"You **sure**?"* He had a sly grin, and I couldn't help the cackle that escaped me.

"Yes, I'm sure. I love it when we kiss."

"You gone eat them words, girl!" If you can imagine, he said it in an overly exaggerated Southern accent, and we laughed at that. He could be so silly sometimes.

I returned to the living room, and Micah was sitting on the couch, his phone in his hand. He appeared immersed in whatever he was reading, but as soon as he saw me, he stood, greeting me with an-other kiss.

I could get used to these.

"Everything good?" I checked.

"Yep. Just looking over a document, but I can get back to it once we're home." I didn't say so, but I liked the way he said "home" so casually as opposed to "my house." He gently took my bag off my shoul-der, tossing it over his own. "Ready?"

"Baby. I want to tell you something. First."

"Indeed." He nodded. "Should we sit?" His brows high expectantly.

"Uh...no. No. This will be quick." I took a deep inhale to calm my nerves. I was all over the place but desperately wanted to share this with him.

Right now.

This moment felt like the perfect time to do so.

I was feeling super-duper shy, so I reverted to what was familiar. "I'm going to close my eyes."

I saw that his smile grew before I closed them. "Okay."

My eyes closed now; I prepared to reveal my heart to him. I took another moment, and finally, forging ahead, I told him, "I'm in love with you. I love you, Micah."

There was complete silence between us.

I didn't need him to say it back, not right now, at least. After all, I derailed everything we'd built the day he told me how he felt. I didn't take for granted or even expect him to return the sentiment. I just wanted him to know where I was and how I felt. I figured, eventually, we would find our way back.

Anyway, my eyes were still closed, and I was too shy to open them and face Micah now that everything was out in the open.

I heard him put my bag down, and he reached for my hands. Capturing both, he began a gentle caress of my fingers.

Still nothing, but *damn*, if I knew Micah like I thought I did... *any* second now, he'd say...

"Open your eyes, baby." He gently squeezed my hands, patiently waiting.

I opened them to his comforting gaze, and before I could look away, he said, "I love you too, Destiney baby."

I smiled real big. "You still love me?"

"Indeed. I'm still in love with you."

"Wow. Okay." It was music to my ears. For reasons I cannot explain, my eyes started welling with tears, falling before I could stop them. I've always been highly emotional. Some days, I can be so moved by things. Crying at the drop of a hat, hearing a song. A movie. A tender moment between loved ones reunited at an airport. Add to that, I'm so damn sensitive. Got it all from my father.

"Why are you crying?" Micah wiped a couple of my tears and then held me close. "These are happy tears, I hope."

I nodded my head. "You're just so amazing. And I'm so happy." I didn't have my wits about me, and there wasn't nearly enough time to pour my heart out. Instead, I told him, "I'm so glad you're mine."

"I was always yours." He gently held me in his arms. After he kissed my forehead, he said, "And you were always mine. We just had to find each other." He kissed my forehead again. "And now that I've found you, I have so many plans for us, baby. This is only the beginning. I plan to give you something so special. I love you, Destiney baby."

"I love you too, Micah."

two

MICAH

"Thank you for the analysis. Based on that, I'd suggest rebranding is best. An acquisition wouldn't be ideal with this practice."

A team of executives and I were trying to decide how we would move forward on a proposal. A struggling Urgent Care approached us, hoping for an acquisition. They were in serious financial trouble and at risk of closing their doors- *after* going bankrupt. We never wanted to see medical facilities close, especially in the more rural areas. Which this one was located in. Access to quality healthcare mattered a lot, particularly for the vulnerable communities. I was tempted to move forward on that strength alone. And though we could make all of *their* financial problems go away, *we* would garner significant financial problems of our own if we moved forward with an acquisition. Essentially acquiring their debt where there was no return. After my analysis, rebranding and a potential partnership, like a joint venture, would help them get to a better place financially. Possibly, then, we could revisit depending on how the numbers looked.

My hard work and dedication to building my expertise had truly paid off, and my opinion was considerably valued and not just due to my position.

When I joined the company about six years ago, I didn't set out to climb the ladder per se. I just wanted to gain experience, use my MBA, and build my savings. I really wanted a family, and I figured securing these things would put me in the best position to obtain that.

Just over two years ago, I was approached to apply for the System Vice President position. I was the System Director of Mergers and Acquisitions then, which kept me fairly busy. I was hesitant because I wasn't interested in adding unnecessary stress to my life. Though *very* enticing, the money wasn't worth it to me. Not entirely. But after talking with Daddy and Mal about it and praying about it, I decided to apply and leave the rest to God. At thirty-two years old, I was the youngest person to have reached this level in the company's history. It was a lot of pressure initially, but thankfully, things have gone pretty smoothly. I am incredibly grateful, as I know things can be quite different for a young black man in corporate America in a position of leadership and authority. Not many people take so kindly to that. Especially my contenders.

Anyway, it's been about two years now. I've been focused on leading my department to accomplish great numbers, close successful acquisitions, and continue to grow and develop professionally. In my personal life, I've been saving my money, being the best steward possible, and preparing for the wife and family I desire and for which I've prayed.

And now, here she was—just a few feet from me.

I peered over my shoulder.

Destiney was dozing off on the loveseat I had in my office. Guess baby girl was tired. She wouldn't be comfortable sleeping there, and I had no clue how long I would be. We'd already passed the thirty minutes scheduled, and they were still talking. I had to jump on a conference call when we walked in the door, so I didn't get a chance to give her a tour. Besides, she'd been stuck right next to me like white on rice. I didn't mind either, but it was clear she wasn't comfortable enough to venture off on her own. That was fine with me, and we'd get to that.

The director of our region started going into another spiel, and I took that time to encourage her to head upstairs.

I tapped Destiney on her thigh softly. She gave me sleepy eyes. "You head upstairs and rest, baby. The room at the very end of the hall. I'll be up to join you as soon as I wrap this up."

The call lasted another half hour. When it finally ended, I informed my assistant that I'd be logging out for the day.

Then I changed out of my suit. I kept a few things in the closet in my home office, which worked out perfectly.

I headed upstairs to my bedroom to find Destiney sleeping on top of my comforter. She was likely hesitant to get underneath the blankets, but we would work on that.

I took in my sleeping beauty and couldn't get enough of the sight before me.

I couldn't even move.

It wasn't so much that she was so beautiful; it was the fact that she was finally in my bed. Mal told me years back that he'd stand by Gabe's crib and watch him sleep once they brought him home from the hospital. Maybe this sentiment was something similar.

This shit was fucking with me.

In the best way.

Destiney was the first woman to be in my home. In my bedroom. In my bed.

She would be the last. She was the only one worthy.

Earlier, I told her I had so many plans. And I do. For her. For us.

Seeing her in my bed, was… a mind fuck. It was arousing, of course, but so much more. Hell, I don't even know how long I stood there watching her.

Destiney stirred slightly before opening her eyes.

"What?"

Destiney didn't have the slightest clue. I shook my head. Then I laughed at myself—I tended to do that a lot. "You have no idea how special this moment is for me, do you?" I finally spoke.

"Tell me," She said around a lazy grin.

Shaking my head, I struggled to form a sentence. "You… being here. *In here.* This is…this is like…" I chuckled. "Damn. I'm so glad you're here, baby. That's all."

A beautiful smile spread across her lips, her captivating eyes blinking slowly. "You make *every-thing* so sweet, Micah."

"It's easy to be sweet whenever I handle you, baby." I stepped closer to the bed, asking, "Any room for me?"

Destiney flashed an incredulous glare. "This bed is huge, Micah." Glancing on both sides of her and looking back over at me.

She was right. I had an Alaskan King. I'm a big man. I wanted to ensure I had plenty of space to stretch out and that my wife would still be comfortable. I even thought that babies or toddlers would eventually like to or need to join us in bed some days. For example, if they weren't feeling well, I know they sometimes feel extra clingy when they're sick and fussy.

When I had this home built, I made every customization, every detail, and every decision with my wife and children in mind.

"But can I join you?" I could always sleep in one of my guest rooms. I was just glad to have her with me under my roof. I could wait on everything else.

"Of course, you can," she said sweetly. "This bed is *yours*."

Ours.

Nodding, I made my way to my side of the bed and sat down, exhaling a breath. I was beginning to get hard, and his ass needed to chill. Laying back, I turned my body towards her, leaving plenty of space between us, about an arm's length. "Please go back to sleep if you're still tired. I won't disturb you."

She turned her body toward me. "I'm good for right now. That cat nap helped."

"Indeed."

Destiney was lying on her side, facing me. And we held each other's gaze for a while. I wanted to hold her in my arms badly, but we would get to all that. We had been affectionate while we were vertical, but horizontal would take a little time, I was sure. I would keep my hands to myself until she made it crystal clear she was ready.

"Tomorrow after work, I want you to come back." I quickly continued because I didn't want to scare her. "Or I can come stay with you. Whatever you're most comfortable doing. I just don't want to be apart." I meant that shit. I wanted to stay up under her. I wanted her to be under me. I just liked being near her. I loved it. Her energy. Her vibe. Her essence radiated from her. Destiney would have to put in some serious work to get rid of me.

Destiney bashfully gave me a real big smile. "I don't want to be apart either."

"You don't?" I volleyed playfully.

She shook her head. "I don't."

"And you are sure you ain't gone get sick of me?" I asked sarcastically.

She released a hearty laugh, and I swear it was the cutest thing I'd heard in a while.

"I'm the one you're gonna get sick of. I've warned you that I have attachment issues, and I can be real clingy."

"That's cool with me. I want to be close to you. Once you're comfortable enough, I'll *always* be up on you. You just wait, baby." I'm incredibly affectionate but I knew how to control that shit. Especially since there was a lot at stake. The last thing I wanted was to come on too strong and scare her.

"It's going to happen soon. I'm getting more comfortable with you, Micah. You've been amazing." She reached her hand out to mine, and we threaded our fingers. "And I appreciate you being so patient with me."

"My pleasure baby." That shit had two meanings. All in due time.

"We can stay here." She said after a beat.

"You sure? I promise I don't mind."

"I'm sure." Destiney nodded in agreement.

"Alright, that's cool. I don't plan on trying anything, but I can sleep in a guest room if you need me to. I want you to be comfortable."

That must be the word for the day. Comfortable.

That was probably the fifth time I said it in the past hour alone. In the grand scheme, I'd said it *ad nauseam*. But I was serious about this. I was handling Destiney like a rare, delicate flower. I wasn't going anywhere, and we didn't need to rush anything.

She shook her head. "We can sleep in here together."

Damn.

"I trust you. Besides, your bed is huge. There's plenty of space for us without worrying about personal space. And I'm not a wild sleeper."

That bashful smile of hers was back and I could feel my dick rising. *Chill man. Chill. Not right now.* I nodded my agreement. "Alright. So, we're staying here, and we're both sleeping here?"

"Yes."

"Yeah?"

"Yeah."

"Sounds good to me," I said casually. I think I did a convincing job containing my excitement. I was beside myself. You'd think I had never shared company with a beautiful woman before.

But this wasn't just any woman. This was *my* woman.

Destiney.

No one compared to her. "You can shower in here, and I'll take one in the bathroom down the hall. Not sure exactly what you packed, but Gabby has some shower stuff and body lotion she keeps here whenever they stay over. You're welcome to use it. Unless you want to smell like me, you can always use mine."

She laughed. "Thank you."

There was comfortable silence between us. We were still facing each other. Eyes on eyes.

I continued my soft caress of her fingers. She was doing her own thing to me with hers… can't put into words the things she be doing with her soft, sexy fingertips. Yep. Those were sexy, too, simply because they were *hers*.

"Can I feed you?" I pressed.

"Yes please!"

I chuckled. "You sound excited."

I felt the vibration of her quiet titter. "What can I say? I love food."

I thought over the ingredients already in my fridge. I planned and prepped meals when I knew I'd have a more hectic week. So, I didn't go too far with groceries unless I knew I'd have Gabe and Gabby over. If everything went according to plan, all of that would change soon. My ultimate desire was to have Destiney with me all the time.

"Remind me. Is dairy alright?"

She beamed. "Yes baby. And thank you for checking. I'm vegetarian, not vegan, so dairy is fine."

"I got you. How's pasta sound?"

"I love pasta. That sounds perfect."

"Indeed. I'll head downstairs and get started. I want to give you a tour, so you know where everything is. But you're welcome to stay up here if you want. Or you can hang out downstairs with me. Either way." I stood to my feet and rounded the bed. She stood too, coming into my arms and placing hers around my waist. I kissed her forehead and remained there for a moment.

"Can I help you with anything?"

"Not a chance."

She cackled and lifted her head, kissing my lips softly. Then I spoke into her ear, "You just relax and look beautiful." She threw her head back, blessing me with low lids and a lazy grin.

Yep. I was already growing even stiffer in my joggers.

"If you insist."

"I sure do."

"Actually, I'm gonna sketch while you do that, so I'll be at the island. I like being close to you."

I smiled in contentment. "I love being close to you."

After giving Destiney a tour, I was in the kitchen, pulling out the pans I would need.

Moments before, Destiney padded down the hall to use the restroom, and I watched her till she disappeared. I was sure to take a moment to adjust myself. Destiney was unbelievably sexy, and I wanted her bad. When we were lounging in my room earlier, she looked amazing. She'd changed into some biker shorts and her thick ass thighs were on full display. Most of all, she appeared relaxed and comfortable. That's exactly what I wanted for her. She was worth every ounce of the restraint I was practicing. We shared intimate space while upstairs, and I swore I could smell her. She always smelled like coconut and vanilla, and I loved that scent on her. But I could smell *her* too. I was convinced I'd end up with blue balls for real. While I showed her the place, I was hard as fuck. To the point that it was painful. Then, while she was changing, I had it in my mind to stroke one out in the toilet downstairs. I locked the door behind me, and I was seconds away, but I restrained at the last minute. Honestly, keeping my hands to myself wasn't as difficult when I kept my distance, so cooking for her was a welcome distraction.

"I'm back." She announced sweetly as she walked around the kitchen island.

"I get another kiss?" She was already walking into my open arms, and I pressed my lips to hers.

"You get as many as you want, baby." She managed around a smile. A few closed-mouth pecks and she was off again, sauntering into the next room where my home office was. When we arrived from her place earlier, I told her she was welcome to use my office space to work in anytime she needed to. I didn't work from home as much as I had the latitude to. I was home alone so much that it was almost depressing. Anyway, Destiney's eyes lit up, and she retrieved a canvas backpack from her trunk. The bag was teal with a funky, whimsical floral pattern that fit her adorable personality perfectly. And it was filled with at least two dozen paintbrushes. Tubes of paint. Pens, pencils, markers, and a few sketchbooks.

After bringing out the pans I would need, I washed and then filled a stock pot for the pasta and set it to boil on my back isle. I mulled over options in the pantry, finally deciding to go with linguine. I was out of penne, which was my preferred choice of pasta whenever I made Florentine. I had a little rigatoni, but not enough for both of us. Linguine would do just fine. I grabbed the other ingredients I needed and headed back to the kitchen.

I found Destiney sitting at the island with her sketchbook open and a few pens spread out neatly in front of her. She was deep in thought, adding detail to an elaborate peacock feather.

"That's amazing," I said, placing the ingredients on the counter and then turning on the water to wash my hands.

"Thanks, baby." She said, her head down as she continued working. "Just a little doodle that turned into something I'm actually beginning to like." She cracked up.

"Do you take your sketchbook everywhere?" I placed the pasta in the boiling water and then pulled out my cell to start my playlist.

"Anywhere and everywhere. I never know when I'll be inspired. Second, if I need to pass the time, it is a fantastic way to do it. You would not believe the amazing things I've created waiting around in the doctor's office and in that damn DMV."

I released a deep chuckle at that. "I bet." I pulled a few more things from the fridge. The smooth sounds of Goapele surrounded us as I whisked together some flour, vegetable broth, milk, salt, and pepper and set it aside. I minced two garlic cloves and then rinsed and sliced some portobello mushrooms. In a large skillet, I added some olive oil over medium-high heat, and once it reached the desired temperature, I sautéed the sliced mushrooms. I added fresh garlic a few minutes later and sautéed it until it began to brown.

"Mmm. Smells good!" She said, looking up from her sketch.

"Thank you, love."

"Do you cook often?"

"Yes and no. I like to cook, but it's no fun dining alone. I mainly cook when I have Gabe and Gabby girl over fairly often. Now and then, Malachi and Ella will come by too, and we'll all enjoy a meal together."

"Same. Daijah is hardly home these days. She spends every free moment with Julian, so it's always just me, eating by myself. My best friend India comes by every blue moon. But she's always busy."

"Well, would you look at that?" I casually said after a beat, adding my whisked flour and broth mixture with the mushrooms and garlic. I lowered my fire to a simmer.

She furrowed her brows. "What?"

"We're both alone most of the time. Sleeping alone and eating alone. I think we just solved that problem." I pretended to play it cool and never looked at her directly, wondering what she thought of my comment. Now that we had shared space, I wanted to do it as often as possible. If I had it my way, Destiney would never leave my side.

I loved having her under me. I loved having her in my arms. I loved the peace and calm she brought. I loved the sight of her sitting at my kitchen island, looking beautiful. I loved talking to her face-to-face.

I stirred the sauce and checked on the pasta as Kem's soulful voice came on, and I grooved to the tune. I was a huge fan of his.

"I'm not much of a cook, but... we should take turns hosting. If you're down... I'd love that," she said, seemingly out of nowhere. I did my best to hide my grin as I headed to the fridge to get the gouda. After locating my cheese grater, I added some to the sauce.

I looked over at her. "You like a lot of cheese?"

"Yes!"

She was so cute. "Indeed." I grated a generous amount into the sauce, then stirred. "And... I would love that too." I walked around the island and kissed her forehead.

I returned to the stove, removed the pasta from the fire, and strained the water.

"You look like a professional moving around this kitchen."

I chuckled. "I do okay. Pasta and me, we go way back. I always asked Mommy to fix me pasta when I was little. When I was about seven, she started teaching me to cook. Pasta is one of the first things I learned. Been hooked ever since. I could easily eat it every day. Easily."

"That's me, but with rice and potatoes."

"Carb city on your plate? Sounds like my kind of party."

We laughed.

"Hell yeah. Where you think these thighs came from?"

Destiney's thighs were perfection. I really wanted to be between them.

I mixed fresh spinach with the sauce and then tossed the sauce in with the linguine. It looked and smelled great. Mushroom Florentine was an excellent choice tonight, and everything worked out perfectly.

three

DESTINEY

"Would you like wine with your dinner, love?"

"Yes please."

Micah strolled over to a wine chiller against the far wall of his living room. I could see it from where I sat. He called over to me, "Red or white?"

"Hmm. You pick. A little sweeter if possible."

Micah and I had been wrapped in each other for the past few hours.

Not literally. But we'd been side by side, hand in hand, since he met me at my house earlier.

Honestly, there was nowhere else I'd rather be.

He was taking such good care of me. Emotionally and physically.

When he started cooking, I had to go to the bathroom. And my panties were just as wet as I expected. Micah was talking sexy in my ear, and I was getting so worked up. My ass was about to lose my resolve, if I'm honest. He was about to be my undoing.

I had never felt this way at this intensity before. It was as if things were beginning to wake up. And I wasn't sure what I would do with it. It didn't surprise me that Micah wasn't trying to get into my panties. He was so respectful, keeping his hands to himself. He didn't imply or allude to sex. But it was all over him. The energy. The way he kissed me. The way he moved with agility. I was convinced he was a sensual lover. The artist in me saw that. I was excited to experience it.

When the time came.

I sent a text to my group chat with Daijah and India. I had to inform them that I was at Micah's house. And I would be spending the night.

I'll see you at work tomorrow, Indie. Girls, I'm spending the night with Micah!

Sibling Bestie: Well, well, well... Don't do anything I wouldn't do Sissy

Indie the Bestie: YASSSSSS!!!! Let him blow your back out Best!

These two were just too much. I'd have to respond later.

"How about I open both. You can try a glass of each." Micah approached the island with two bottles.

"Which one are you having?" I asked.

"Red. But either of them pair nicely." He placed a tall-stemmed wine glass in front of me and poured a generous amount of white wine.

I sniffed the contents, swirled briefly, and took a quick taste. "Mmm."

"Trebbiano di Lugano." He said, handing me the wine bottle. I always admired the design of imported wines. As an artist, I've always seen beauty in everyday things. It was the way I viewed the world.

Micah opened the red wine and poured a hefty glass before handing it to me. "Try this one."

I took a sip and closed my eyes as it went down slowly.

"Oooh, I love this one! What is it?"

"Nerello Mascalese."

"I love it! I'm not as versed with reds, but this one is lovely."

"I thought you'd like that one."

"What other bottled goodies you have over there?" I asked, referring to his stocked wine chiller.

There were at least two dozen bottles of mixed reds and whites. "I didn't take you for a wine drinker, Mr. Walker."

He chuckled. "Funny, I'm not. I'll have a glass of wine on occasion here with my dinner. I love a glass whenever I want to grill a steak. But I rarely have more than a glass or two, and I end up tossing the rest of it out."

My eyes grew wide. "So why the stocked wine chiller?" It was state-of-the-art and quite impressive looking.

"It was a housewarming gift from Malachi and Ella when I had this home built. They also added a wine club membership, paid for two years. Every month, I'd get a shipment with six bottles. I filled the chiller, and the rest started to pile up so quickly I had to start gifting bottles as Christmas and birthday presents." We both laughed at that. Then he took a drink from his glass. "You take some home; maybe Daijah would like a few bottles."

"That's why you were so eager to open both of these," I concluded.

"That's part of it. But I already told you. You get anything you want from me. Anything baby."

"You're so sweet."

"You make it easy being sweet with you." He leaned in, placing a kiss on my forehead right before he headed back to the kitchen. After a moment, "It's ready."

Micah pulled a chair out for me, and after I was settled, he brought our bowls to the table, gently placing mine right in front of me. He topped off my wine before taking his seat. There was even a candle lit in the center of the table. I wasn't sure when he managed to do that. But it was so thoughtful. I'd say romantic… and it was *very* romantic. But romantic is too cheap of a word to describe everything he had been doing for me. Especially this.

Thoughtful is the best word I can think of.

Everything he does is with so much thought, intention, and consideration.

Aside from the fact that this was the first candle-lit dinner I ever had, in the history of ever... no man had ever cooked for me. Aside from my father, of course. I don't know... it may not have been a big deal to him, but it was a *massive* deal to me.

"Wow, Micah, this looks amazing." I eyed the creamy sauce with the hearty amount of portobello mushrooms. I couldn't wait to try it. It smelled just as delicious as it looked.

This man.

This *man.*

This man.

Damn.

"Thank you for all of this."

There was a light titter. "You thanking me before you even have a taste?" He teased.

I didn't even try to stop the wide grin that quickly spread across my face.

Micah didn't understand. It wasn't just the food. It was everything.

He was everything.

"It's my pleasure, love. Thank you for joining me." He grabbed my hands and prayed over our meal. Once he was done, I took a forkful and blew. When I finally tasted it, I was blown away by the flavors exploding on my pallet. The pasta was cooked to al dente perfection, and the mushrooms had a smoky, umami flavor. I could have eaten a whole plate of mushrooms by themselves.

But the sauce. It was delectable. I was amazed because I watched him make it entirely from scratch. I was the person who bought my sauces in jars.

Micah must have seen my facial expression because he asked, "Good?"

"Superb!" I gave him the chef's kiss. Then I took another forkful and blew. "Let me find out you're a chef."

"No way, but I can cook a thing or two. I've made this many, many times. I'm sure that's why I'm so good at it. I love pasta. I'd eat it every day, but I had to scale that back and only eat it in moderation."

"Yeah, I hear you. Pasta can be dangerously addictive."

"Like you." He returned with low lids.

I took a sip of my wine.

Because, well, honestly, I didn't know what to say to that.

I also crossed my legs tightly under the table because *she* was starting to do that thing she did whenever *he* said the things he said.

And in other news, I couldn't wait to thank his mother for teaching him to cook so well, among many other things.

I needed to meet this woman. I wanted to wash her feet in gratitude. Seriously.

***

My first night staying with Micah couldn't have been more perfect. It was so perfect that I went to work the next day, barely even present. Just going through the motions. Distracted the entire time. Counting the minutes until I could be back in his arms. My thoughts were saturated. Musing over the day before.

We enjoyed the finely prepared dinner he made us. We watched part of *Hustle & Flow*, then took showers and got ready for bed.

He had a playlist going, and we were chilling, just being together. We lay in his bed; he held me in his arms, and we talked and talked and talked. And kissed too. A whole lot. Wet. Sloppy. Nasty. And I was having the time of my fucking life. I'd like to think Micah enjoyed himself, too.

No, we didn't have sex.

Which was fine. It was perfectly fine.

There was this unspoken thing. This understanding. It was like neither of us expected the other to move like that. Not quite yet anyway.

It was close to midnight when we finally fell asleep. I'm pretty sure I fell asleep first.

Yeah.

All of this was surreal.

As soon as I woke up, I was keenly aware of my surroundings. I was at Micah's house. In his bed. Waking up to the gloriously distinct aroma of French toast. My *very favorite* thing to have for breakfast. Micah told me he remembered that detail from a long time ago.

I remember the conversation well myself. It was one of our late nights. We laughed so much, getting lost in the newness and bliss of learning more about each other. We were asking each other *this or that* questions.

Mini-golf or bowling.
Movie night or game night.
French fries or onion rings.
Comedy club or poetry slam.

Scavenger hunt or escape room.

Then Micah said, "I have a good one! Pancakes or waffles?"

"That's easy. French toast."

I remember him cracking up at that. *"That's not how you play! Gotta pick between the two options!"* But I was firm on my answer.

Anyway, I remember Micah telling me that his mom taught him the French toast secret, and I just *had* to try it.

He hadn't lied. Micah makes the most decadent French toast I've ever had.

My favorite part was that he had me sit on his lap and he fed me. Then we fed each other when we made a plate of seconds.

And Micah was such an early riser. I always knew that about him, but observing it firsthand was another thing. After we ate, he informed me he'd already finished his workout. He had a home gym just off of his garage. Talk about discipline. Micah got up early enough to work out, shower, and fix me French toast and an egg white omelet for himself.

And now that we were kissing, we kissed all the time. We can't seem to stop kissing.

Always in make-out mode.

Being with Micah was the most organic thing. Seriously. As natural as breathing. I could not believe how easy it was. He made me feel so comfortable. Right at home.

I realized he had seamlessly curated an environment where I could express myself with exuberance. Free of inhibition. That was perfectly fine with me, too.

When we parted ways to head to work, we joked about just playing hookey and spending the day in his bed. And hell yeah, I was with it. But I'm glad he acted as the person responsible at that moment. Left up to me, we'd be laid up right now.

I didn't like being away from him. I wanted to lie under him and never move. He made me feel *so* at ease. Relaxed. Contented.

I wanted to give him *all of me*. I knew I would be ready soon. And I appreciated that I didn't feel any pressure from him.

While we lay in his bed, he'd had his hands everywhere, caressing me all over. Micah had to know each of my curves by now. My breasts were the main attraction for the time being, especially my right one, which was the one with the pierced nipple. Daijah thought I was silly for only getting one nipple pierced, but one was plenty for me. I liked a little variety. I remember the day India and I went together; she got one, and I got the other. That fucking pain man. One was all I had in me. I had no plans to get the other one.

Micah discovered my piercing the night those months ago when we were in the shower. I remember he ran his fingers over my breasts then stopped abruptly, rubbing my nipple again and again. I heard him gasp, followed by a low growl. Later, he told me in my ear that he was pleasantly surprised and that *"I was a gift that kept giving."* That shit turned me all the way on.

And speaking of being turned on, Micah had been touching me everywhere, rubbing all over my ass but stayed away from my pussy. I sensed he wanted to go there but was waiting for me to tell him it was all right. I knew he was getting aroused just like I was. His bulging erection made that abundantly clear. I could feel the stiffness, girth, and weight through his basketball shorts. We were chilling for now, but I came close to taking a hold of it—a few times. I got the feeling Micah wouldn't mind. We got really close and very familiar without going all the way. I was either sitting on his lap, lying between his legs, or him lying between mine.

And. Yeah. I wanted to feel his hard dick in my hand.

I wanted to do things. Things I'd never done, but I wanted to do them with him. I had grown so comfortable in his space, all thanks to Micah ensuring so.

I couldn't believe I was running from this.

Being with him, even in silence, was so easy. And I would miss his absence even if he was just in the next room. I loved being around him, in his company. I couldn't quite describe how I felt. It was just... there weren't any words. I felt special, and I could feel his desire for me. But not in an aggressive or over-sexualized way. He respected the hell out of me, and I respected him, too.

And he was hyperaware, asking about my mental state all the time. That was so thoughtful.

The way he got me going when we kissed. My pussy would ache and thump and get wet as a damn faucet. I was always wet for him. My. Freaking. Goodness.

Generally, doing things impulsively wasn't my style- for the most part. That would all depend.

Destiney Fulfilled

And anyway, there was a conversation we needed to have. I knew Micah was waiting for me. To say something. The fact that Micah was waiting so patiently somehow had the opposite effect.

Subtlety and gentleness go a long way with me. And lately, I've been feeling like I want to forget the talking. I wanted to take my damn panties off.

No one had ever made me feel the way he did.

Like, Micah oozed sex appeal and BDE. Yet never alluded to trying to persuade me to give up the drawers. I've concluded that he was waiting patiently for me to make a move. He would follow my lead, only going as far as I did. And from the beginning, he communicated everything so there was no room for confusion. I realized that he needed me to offer him the pussy.

And I planned to.

On a silver platter.

Soon.

Anyway, his home was beautiful—expansive, immaculate, and tidy. I loved his living area, which had high ceilings with black wood beams, a fireplace, and a wet bar. Plush white area rugs over white wood floors and a deep grey velvet sectional.

I'm no cook, but I love his kitchen, which had gunmetal appliances and white cabinets.

I loved the smell of his home, too. It smelled pleasant, like fresh laundry. It wasn't what I expected, but I don't know exactly what I expected. There was minimal décor, which added to the charm and beauty of his home. His neutral walls were bare. Free of hanging pictures and artwork. Of the entire house, only two art pieces were hanging. An

315

oversized black Lord's Supper hangs over his dining room table. Then, an oversized, black and white close-up of two hands embraced in the foreground with a sunset in the background. I'd say maybe twenty-four by thirty-six inches. My first time in his downstairs hallway, I was struck. It was breathtaking. Later, Micah told me it was his parents. Micah took the picture on his phone, which was so beautiful that he had it blown up.

But his bedroom.

First of all, it was huge, the size of two of my living rooms. It was tastefully decorated but the opposite of mine. Minimal décor, just the essentials. No television.

The smell was an aphrodisiac. Masculine and clean, a woodsy mix of cedar and mahogany teakwood. His enormous bed sat against a wall he painted black. It was the only wall painted in his entire home. Some oversized pillows. I love pillows. An ottoman at the foot of his bed. Dark cherry oak side tables. Black sheets, a black down comforter, and a blackout curtain.

When I noticed how big his window was, I was beside myself. I love big windows. There was a sitting area in front of the window with a black leather couch. The couch in his bedroom matched the loveseat in his home office. Two doors, one leading to a walk-in closet, where I assumed the entirety of his wardrobe was as his bedroom didn't have any dressers, and another to the ensuite.

The ensuite was oversized too. His and her sinks. A huge jacuzzi-style bathtub and a separate walk-in shower.

Something else that caught my eye were the floating shelves in his bedroom. The lower one had about ten books across genres, including memoirs, autobiographies, and self-help books. But then, the upper shelf was lined with what appeared to be journals.

Get the fuck out of here.

"Micah." I softly called out to him.

"Hmm?" He came to stand beside me.

I pointed at the shelf. "Are those..."

"Journals? Yes. All of them." There had to be at least a dozen hardcover journals lined neatly.

"You... you keep a journal?"

"I do. I have since I was a kid."

Wow. He really couldn't be more perfect.

"Me too." Journaling is what got me through the loss of my mother. I still have many of those journals from that time in my life.

"That's amazing. I think it's a great idea to journal often. I try to as often as I can."

"Totally agree."

I did my morning pages in my journal to clear my head and balance myself—not every day, but several days a month. I loved *The Artist Way*. I bought the book back in college, and it remains one of just a few self-help books I own.

Anyway, I was so in love.

Micah was a whole vibe. Like, the entire thing. It really made no sense. I was convinced this amazingness we had was unlike anything I would ever have with anyone else.

I didn't want to find out either. I was all the way in this.

I loved everything about Micah, but his personality was just unmatched.

Seriously had the dopest personality ever.

I couldn't believe he'd been single all this time. And knowing Micah as well as I do now, I'm not surprised. I know he has options. He's an attractive man with all the things women want. A great career, fancy cars. A big ass house. Child-free.

But Micah's the type to take his time and wait for what feels right. He doesn't rush about anything. He doesn't mind waiting when things take time. But not in a fuck boy way.

He practices active listening. He accepts what he can't change and rolls with it. Extremely humble.

Even-tempered. Incredibly mindful. His mindfulness shows in every space he dwells.

He was perfect. Quite literally.

Handsome. Charming. Respectful. Thoughtful. Sweet.

He encouraged me, especially when I was dealing with my situation. That was tough. But Micah never made me feel like a freak or pity me. I never wanted to be pitied. He made me feel sexy and desired, which was huge for me.

Simply put, Micah was a great fucking catch, and meanwhile, here I was still trying to figure out what the hell I ever did to deserve this. Imposter syndrome was wildin, fucking with me for real.

I love myself. I know I'm unique and proud of that shit. But there wasn't anything *extraordinary* about me.

A man like Micah could have any woman he wanted.

And he wanted me.

He wouldn't dare let me forget it either.

And I wanted him too. *In all the ways.*

four

MICAH

We helped Daddy pull quite a few things out from the garage. The church was doing a rummage sale and swap, and Mommy wanted to donate a few things they no longer used. Mal, Gabe, and I knocked it out within a few hours.

Now, we were hanging out near the grill talking, and I was quite distracted. I tried my damndest to at least seem engaged in the conversation Mal and Daddy were attempting to have with me. In any case, Mal knew what was up. He'd been brought to speed and sent us all the good vibes.

Just last night, he texted me to check in. At that exact moment, I happened to be lying in Destiney's lap.

Brother: Everything good in the hood baby brother?

Perfect. She's been rubbing my head for the last hour

Brother: Which one?

I fell out at his clowning ass.

CTFU man stop!

Brother: Lol

Anyway, shit felt so good she put my ass to sleep while ago. She's invested

Brother: I just fell out laughing. Got my wife asking me what's so funny. I'm asking her to rub my head too but unlike y'all we ain't on restriction

Goodnight

Brother: Yes Lawd it will be

Malachi was a damn fool.

So, the women were inside. In addition to the seven-layer dip, Ella made spaghetti, and Mommy made a peach cobbler for dessert. It was the end of the summer, and it had been such a lovely day out. We planned to eat in the backyard once the food was ready.

Destiney was on my mind the entire time I was working. We talked all night and kissed just as much. Actually, we may have kissed more. She went home last night, and I told her I might not be able to see her today. We'd seen each other four days in a row, and we were both bummed that today may not work. I would still try, but that depended on when I left here. I was busy helping with all the work in the garage and whatever else Mommy and Daddy needed.

One of the nights she stayed over, I can't re- member which- I watched her sleep.

She's extremely beautiful. She hypnotizes me. Gorgeous. Graceful. Soft spoken. With the sweetest soul and the kindest spirit. I was enchanted from the start. Then I thought about how much peace she brings me just being in my presence.

Her aura is soothing. Mesmerizing. Blissful.

The way she sits while she's creating art. The way she draws you in when she's telling you some- thing she's passionate about. The way her eyes light up when she's sharing something that interests her. Her laughter and her voice.

I study her. Every little detail. She's very sexy. So cute. Adorable. A genuine goddess.

I love her so much. Destiney is the jovial spirit we all appreciate in any space she dwells.

This morning, after my workout, I took a shower and called Destiney to say good morning. I told her that I'd be taking her out tomorrow night. I couldn't wait either. I may have been more excited than she was.

It would be our first official date.

Anyway, I was bricking up just thinking about our conversation this morning. I definitely missed her. That, and the intense chemistry we had. All the kissing she was doing to me last night. All the kissing she was letting me do to her. Had she been in my bed and not on my phone, I may have asked her... no... maybe I wouldn't have. My mind went there though. Plenty.

When I called her this morning, I was convinced Destiney felt just like I did. Her voice was extremely telling. I picked up on it immediately. When I told her I missed her, she told me she missed me too, and I took a chance calling her on it.

"You're in rare form right now."

Her light chuckle cruised through the line. "There's something about you... how can I put it? You do things to me, Mr. Walker."

"Yeah?"

"Oh yes." Her sultry voice brought my dick to life. I loved it whenever she called me Mr. Walker.

"Good things?"

"Great things."

"Yeah?"

"Yes."

"Tell me, baby."

She chuckled again. "I'm always wet when you're near me."

"Is that right?"

"Mmmhmm."

"Mmm."

She faintly groaned in my ear. "You don't even need to be near me. It's the way you handle me and the way you talk to me."

"Yeah?"

"Oh yeah. My mind starts to wander... thinking about all the things I want to do with you."

I growled. After a beat. "She wet right now?" I quizzed.

"Yes."

"Hmm. You do the same for me, beauty."

"Hmm. You hard?"

"Hard as a brick."

"Yeah?"

"Yes baby. Only for you."

"It's such a shame we can't take care if each other right now."

I growled at the thought. "Soon."

"Not soon enough. I can hardly stand it."

"I hear you baby." More comfortable silence encased us. Regarding her words, I desired to explore something different with her, and this was the opportune time. No doubt my baby was making strides. That shit was evident even right now, but she still held a level of trepidation. I was good with that when it concerned anyone else, but I didn't want her to feel she needed to hide from me. Her sex kitten was living and breathing underneath these layers, and I planned to bring her all the way out to play. "You been touching your pussy?" I spoke gently with candor. She held in a breath. "It's just me and you talking baby. Have you?"

An audible sigh escaped her. "No. I've come close but haven't in a good while."

"Hmm." Hesitating, I went back and forth the more I pondered.

Fuck it.

"Touch her for me baby."

"Okay." I heard shuffling on her end, followed by a slight moan a moment later. I listened as she continued moaning lightly. Meanwhile, I was hard as fuck thinking about how swollen her bud had to be by now. Nonetheless, I resisted the urge to take hold of my shaft.

"Destiny baby?"

"Yeah."

"I'm connecting us on FaceTime. I want to watch you while you please your pretty pussy."

"Okay." Moments later, her face filled my screen, her bright doe eyes looking back at me.

"Hey Beautiful."

"Hey." She smiled shyly and looked away.

A throaty chuckle left me. "Don't do that. I already know you're getting bashful on me."

"You had to see me **right this second**?" She quipped with a smile.

"You were just talking a big game a second ago!"

"Yeah, but you weren't watching me!" Destiney was so damn sexy. In a class all her own.

"Try not to feel shy. It's only me watching, baby."
I reassured.

"I'll try."

Her sweet smile bore into my soul. *"Put your phone nearby so both of your hands are free."*

She propped her phone on something beside her and lay on her back, giving me a full side view.

"Remove your t-shirt and your bra."

Sitting up, she pulled her shirt over her head, tossing it aside, then reached behind her back to unclasp her bra. I licked my lips, observing the way her heavy breasts fell freely.

Damn.

"Take your panties off." I softly commanded. She lifted her hips, pulling them down, then discarding them. And returned to her back, looking over at me, naked from head to toe.

"You are so beautiful, Destiney baby," I murmured. *"You know that? So beautiful."*

"Thank you, baby." She softly purred.

I could see the gears shifting. My baby was nervous. *"I know this is new for you, but I want you relaxed and comfortable. I hope I've proven that you're safe letting go when it comes to you and me."*

"You have. Thank you for being patient with me."

"It's my pleasure baby."

Leaning back against the tufted headboard, I placed an arm behind my head, holding my phone in my other hand. I needed to keep both hands occupied before I got any ideas.

"Spread your legs apart and rub your clit beauty."

She closed her eyes and got to work rubbing slowly.

"Rub your breasts with the other hand."

I growled, watching her and getting harder by the second. "You keep your sexy ass just like that. Don't speed up either. Take your time, alright?"

"Yes baby." She murmured.

Fuck. I watched her intently as she pleased herself, rubbing over her nipples and grabbing and squeezing both of her breasts. I wanted to be inside of her. Bad. My dick was throbbing. It was so hard. Still, I didn't touch it. I needed to focus on the site before me. "Keep rubbing her baby." I could hear how wet she was, noting how freely her fingers slid back and forth over her slick center. I wanted to eat her pretty pussy like a peach.

She released low moans, and it drove me wild.

"Tell me how it feels."

"Feels so good." She purred.

"Yeah?"

"Yesssssss."

"Put a finger inside."

"Mmm."

"Add one more finger." I almost blasted in my boxers watching her. "Taste yourself, baby," I instructed a moment later. I watched her suck and lick her fingers. Got damn. She sped up her strokes, and I saw her facial expressions shifting. Her moans grew in succession and volume, and I knew she was close. "Make her cum for me baby." As if on command, a beautiful sound emitted from her as she reached her peak. "That's my good girl."

She tittered, covering her face with both hands.

"Let me see you, Destiney." After a second, she rolled over on her stomach and peered into the camera with a look of satisfaction.

"Better?"

"Much better." She sighed, "But you're not. I just know you're hard as fuck right now." Her mellow voice brought me the calmness it always had.

"I'm a big boy. I can handle myself."

Her eyes widened, and I saw a subtle grin lifting at the corner of her mouth. I chortled, "Not like that."

"Go head." She purred. I almost lost my resolve right then.

"I can wait baby. I'll only release if I'm deep inside of you... as soon as you're ready for me."

"Oooh. Is that a fact?" She asked me with low lids.

"It is." I reassured.

She sighed again. "I don't like being apart."

"I know baby. Me either."

"I just want to be with you. I'll follow you anywhere you lead me."

Destiney had no idea. I planned to lead her to ecstasy and beyond.

Something else on my mind; especially after hanging up with her... sexual tension was mounting. And maybe we needed to talk about this.

Going all the way. Or not.

From the moment we reconnected there was an intense sexual energy between us and the intensity was growing very quickly.

This was not going to be an off-the-cuff, spur-of-the-moment situation we somehow stumbled into. I had way too much discipline and resolve, plus an insurmountable level of respect for her. And I loved her way too much. I like spontaneity, but this wasn't that.

I planned to only make love to the woman I married. I told her I wanted to marry her. Although I hadn't yet officially asked, she said she wanted that, too. We were on the same page there.

I wanted *her*…wanted to *give it* to her. Make the sweetest love to her.

But I wanted to do it the right way. Marry her first.

We could mess around… though that also gave me pause. But penetrating her, I wasn't so sure about. Yet.

Shit, I didn't know. I was having an internal battle.

Ultimately, I decided to hang back on broaching the subject. Should Destiney come to me, we would talk about it.

"Uncle Micah! It's time to eat!" Gabby brought me from my thoughts.

Mal laughed heartily at me, shaking his head as Gabby and I walked back toward the picnic table.

"Sorry Gabby girl. Just a little distracted."

Everybody else had already taken their seats. The food was brought out from inside just as Malachi's famous ribs came off the grill. There was barbecue chicken as well.

"Oh, we figured that!" Mal jeered playfully from his seat at the table next to Ella. Everyone laughed but I didn't mind.

Just after Daddy prayed over our dinner, Ray walked through the back gate. *How ironic.*

Mal and I shared a glance but didn't say anything.

"Hey Uncle." Ray gave Daddy a fist bump. I stole a glance and Daddy looked just as irritated as Mal and me.

Ray walked around the table speaking to Ella and then the kids.

"Momma Josette!" Ray didn't call her aunt anything. Ever since forever she's been "*momma Josette.*"

"Hey baby! Nice to see you. Already eat? We're just about to have dinner."

"No, I haven't. Glad I wasn't too late." He took an empty seat and promptly began filling his plate. Generously.

I rolled my eyes and didn't bother to hide it.

"You mean you ain't still full off that lasagna?" Mal shot.

I snorted under my breath biting back a laugh.

Ray looked up at Mal in surprise, and Mal gave him a look daring him to say something. Ray probably didn't know we knew about that. I don't know why he was so surprised. We would have found out eventually.

A moment later, Ray said, "I'm glad I get to have some of your spaghetti, Ella. This seven-layer dip is good, too. Too bad you didn't fix any of your macaroni and cheese. That would have gone perfect with this barbecue."

Mal snapped, "Man... don't go putting in requests with my wife! The fuck out of here with that!"

"Malachi Walker! Do not use that language in my presence. You know better." My mom spoke sternly as she could, though she spoke delicately.

"I'm sorry Mommy." Mal said immediately.

"Mal, you know my bride doesn't like those words." Daddy kissed Mommy's cheek. "Try not to forget that whenever she's near."

Mal nodded.

"Ray." Daddy said sternly.

"Yes sir?"

Daddy took his time proceeding, *"You need your own woman,* if you call yourself wanting anything specific. In case you forgot, these two are spoken for. That includes anything in my fridge. Your name ain't on shit so be grateful for *whatever* you get. You can always take yo tail on down to McDonalds."

"Yes sir." Ray sounded like a scolded child.

I looked up and Mal was already looking at me. Stifling chuckles, we tried our best to keep a straight face.

Ray was quiet after that.

After dinner we all enjoyed some peach cobbler. I loved Mommy's peach cobbler and was lucky enough to get one of the corners today. We all loved the corners and if you did the math, there weren't enough of those to go around. Today was my lucky day though.

Mommy told us all goodnight and went to her room to lay down. I couldn't blame her. We worked hard today getting that garage cleared out. Once the kitchen was straight Mal decided they would head out so I figured I would head home too. I needed a shower and my bed. Gabe and Gabby had gone out to the car after hugging everyone and saying their goodnights. Ella, Mal, and I had congregated by the front door and Ray was still sitting on the couch looking comfortable. Guess he missed the hint.

Mal cleared his throat. "Ray, we're all about to head out. You need to be leaving too, so my parents can enjoy the rest of their evening in peace."

Without a word, Ray meandered toward the door.

"I also need you to apologize to my baby brother," Mal said expectantly.

Ray glared at Malachi with a quizzical expression.

"You don't call his woman a bitch. *Ever.*" Mal was eerily calm, talking through clenched teeth.

Ella gasped in surprise, and Ray shot me a look expressing the same. I gave him a look of indifference. I was so done with Ray and all his bullshit. I knew Mal would bring it up at some point, but I didn't expect him to do it in front of Daddy and Ella. Oh well.

Daddy cleared his throat. "Now Ray..." Turning in his direction from the comfort of his massive recliner. "I'm hearing a lot of things concerning you as of late. Things that I'm not too fond of."

Ray hung his head.

"Apologize now, and don't let me ever hear that again. You are about to have a problem with me. *I promise you don't want that.*" Daddy was calmer than Mal and that shit was scary even to me.

Ray turned to face me. "I'm sorry, Micah. I was out of line." He put his hand out. I briefly glanced at it before returning mine.

"Apology accepted." All I could do was shake my head. *Freaking Ray man.*

Mal and I exchanged glances, and I just shrugged. I did accept his apology, but whether things would change remained to be seen. I wasn't holding my breath. It was always something with him and I planned to take a page from Mal's book and finally leave Ray the fuck alone.

I walked out to the car, and Daddy followed me, stopping at the porch. Mal, Ella, and the kids had just taken off; Ray left right behind them.

"So, you've found her." It didn't sound like a question.

Looking back at Daddy, I couldn't help the grin that swept my face.

Daddy cackled. With a nod, he said, "That's my answer. That. Right there."

I couldn't help but laugh myself.

"When do you plan to introduce your sweetheart to Mommy and me?"

"A couple weeks?"

Dad's eyebrows were high on his head, coupled with a sly grin. "We'll be here."

"Indeed." I was sporting a grin of my own.

I guess Mommy decided to keep our conversation between us. That was fine.

I knew Daddy would tell her they'd meet my sweetheart the second he reached their bedroom.

That was fine with me, too.

five

MICAH

"I don't know what I was thinking, ordering potatoes." Destiney laughed while taking a drink of her spiked lavender lemonade. As she lowered her glass, she yawned real big, then rested her brilliant eyes on mine. Her eyes were glassy after her yawn yet bright and brilliant as always. I loved her eyes. "I knew they would knock me out. But I love potatoes and just couldn't turn them away."

Holding her gaze, I quipped, "You ready to get out of here or what?"

"Oh no! I'm loving this band way too much."

I was so pleased she was having such a good time. I knew this was an excellent choice for our first date. "Close your eyes for a few."

She moved closer, resting her head on my shoulder. I put my arm around her, pulling her even closer to me. After settling, she said, "I hope you know you're stuck with me."

"I want to be stuck."

"Well, that's good. I love it here. With you. I'm never leaving."

"You're so cute, baby," I told her, kissing her forehead.

We'd been having an amazing time together at *HomeGrownSol*, enjoying the vibe and grooving with the band, Smoke. This band was bad. My boy Solomon was on the Saxophone doing his thing. He was incredibly talented on the Sax, having played since middle school, I believe. I was so glad we got to hear them tonight. We had great seats, too. Sol came by to say hey earlier, and we spoke briefly. I took the opportunity to introduce him and Destiney as well.

We had dinner when we first arrived, and Destiney raved over their rosemary balsamic baby potatoes and Brussels sprouts. It smelled amazing, and I knew it tasted just as delicious as it looked. Their entire menu was a hit. Anything you ordered would exceed your taste buds. There were quite a few vegetarian options for Destiney, too.

The band was on a break, and we'd been chatting for the past fifteen minutes with an older couple sitting beside us. I'd say around my parents' age.

"Alright, young man. Enjoy yourselves, and you get your lady home safely, " the older gentleman said, tipping his hat toward me. They'd decided to call it a night but said they thoroughly enjoyed themselves. Like Destiney, this was their first time at *HomeGrownSol.*

"Yes sir. You two get home safely as well."

"Actually, Micah, I'm going to use the ladies before I get comfy. If our waiter returns, please ask for more water?" Destiney asked, standing.

I stood with her. "Sure thing baby."

She smiled sweetly at me. "Thank you."

Destiney looked so lovely tonight. Stunning.

She wore a black halter dress; the top of her back was open. I loved that detail. Her dress was perfect for this setting. Long, and sleek, about to her ankles with thigh-high slits on either side. Her thick thighs would peek out with each step she took. Very sexy. Had me licking my chops.

I was beginning to grow obsessed with her thick ass thighs.

She returned as the band picked up again, and I stood to greet her.

"You good Destiney baby?"

"I'm all good baby." She settled beside me again, grabbing my hand and threading our fingers. I kissed her forehead again, sighing in contentment.

"For this last set, we're going to slow it down for all the lovebirds in the house tonight." Cheers and applause erupted all over the place. "Thanks for hanging with us here at Home Grown Soul and always showing Smoke so much love," the lead singer said into the microphone. Various couples began making their way to the dance floor. The band played a few great ones: Babyface, Kem, and D'Angelo. But when the band started playing a cover of *Slow Wine*, I *had* to get closer to her. I kissed the top of her head again. "Dance with me, beautiful."

She peered up at me, eyes wide. "I'm not much of a dancer, Micah. I have two left feet."

I chuckled. "Slow dancing is easy. Just hold on to me, and I'll handle the rest."

She hesitated for a moment with a look of doubt. "I'd only embarrass you."

"You could never embarrass me, baby. You trust me, right?"

"Yes."

"Then you have nothing to worry about. Come on." I led her to the dance floor, which wasn't too crowded. Just a few couples enjoying themselves. I embraced her, and we swayed together, quickly falling into a natural rhythm like we'd done this many times before. I held her close to me, leading us in a gentle glide. She was doing well and seemed like a natural at this. I'd be sure to let her know that later. I knew telling her right now wasn't best. I didn't want her to get bashful on me.

I closed my eyes, and I wondered if her eyes were closed, too. I held her even closer and got lost in her reverie. I deeply inhaled her scent, which I'd grown to love. Destiney felt so right in my arms. Everything about this felt so right. It had been such a long time coming. And the lead was killing it, just like D'wayne Wiggins. The band was grooving, and I loved this song.

> *Slow wine gotta keep it nice and slow*
> *Slow wine gotta use your body and soul*
>
> *Slow wine, so fine if I can wine you in my arms*
> *From left to right slow wine*
>
> *Slow wine, so fine hey girl all my body's yours*
> *...now it would be, now it could be, so nice*
> *If we could...*

In my interpretation, the lyrics were an ode to sensuality. They spoke to letting the mood of slow music take control of your body and moving and feeling whatever came naturally to you. But most of all, they spoke to embracing intimate moments, existing in them, and focusing on deep emotional connections.

As I held Destiney close to me and slow-wined with her, I got to thinking that I've heard this song millions of times. I played it repeatedly, but this hit differently with Destiney in my arms.

'Cuz I've finally built up the nerve to just slow wine with you...

But slow plus a four-letter word is the one thing on my mind
Slow wine, so fine if I can wine you in my arms
Yeah, just let your body flow

"You enjoying yourself, baby?"

"I am. Thank you for bringing me here, Micah."

"It's my pleasure. Thank you for joining me."

It was a sultry song, but it wasn't about sex. Yet and still, Destiney turned me on so much, and the mood was set just right. I knew there was no way I could hide the bulge in my pants. His ass was showing out, growing by the second. I tried not to focus on that too much as we swayed. I heard a slight moan, and in my mind, that was confirmation she felt the brick in my pants.

We danced to the next song, after which I led us back to our seats.

We'd been sitting for a short while when she asked, "Can we go home, baby?" Her question held a sultry tone.

I looked at her as she peered at me through low lids. It was then that it dawned on me that her question had a double meaning.

It was difficult not to go there. This place was thick with lust, heat, and passion. There was dry humping going on all over the dance floor. I'm willing to bet most of these folks were gone get some tonight. No doubt in my mind. The lights were dim, candles were lit, the music was right, and drinks were flowing.

"Yeah, we can do that."

She gave me a smile, blinking slowly. She was so fucking beautiful. Irresistible. Best of all, *she was mine.*

I wasn't sure what she wanted to do once we got back to the house, but the way I was feeling right now, I was willing to give her whatever she wanted from me. I'd follow her lead; all she had to do was say it.

We both stood to leave, and I could have nutted in my drawers right then. My shit was hard as hell and growing in anticipation. Before I could even take a step, I had to adjust myself. The strain against my zipper was intense. My mind wandering. Especially if Destiney was telling me what I thought she was telling me.

six

DESTINEY

I caressed Micah's fingers as we cruised through downtown Sacramento, headed back to his place.

I was floating.

I could not believe I had been slow dancing on a dance floor. I *never* did that. Daijah and India would get a kick out of this when I told them.

337

All I know is, Micah had me wide open for him, ready to receive whatever the hell he wanted to give me.

When Micah told me he would be taking me out, I was giddy with excitement.

He asked me to spend the night, so I packed a bag and headed over. Then I showered and got ready for our date at his place. He was ready before me and waited for me downstairs.

When I came down, he marveled at me. At my dress. How nice I smelled.

Then he pulled out a gift bag with a signature bright blue box inside. My eyes grew wide. I told him I felt bad because I didn't have a gift for him, but he insisted it was no big deal.

I opened the box, and it was a beautiful Tiffany Bracelet—sterling silver links with a heart tag. I love it. It's so cute. I wore it on our date, and I planned to wear it all the time.

And then we go out, and Micah was so… he's just a gentleman. Well beyond the things like opening my car door and pulling out my chair. I'm talking all *new* stuff. New for *me*.

He asked me to sit next to him instead of across from him. He confirmed what I wanted and ordered for me. Micah stood when I left the table and stood again when I returned. It's the little things. They defy everything, in my opinion. Little things are in the everyday. He held my hand the entire time or had his hand resting on my thigh. He kissed my forehead about a million times. I love his forehead kisses.

I loved HomeGrownSol. The food was so good, and the vibe was grown and sexy. The band was top-tier. I met his friend, Solomon, from high school. He was cool and so talented at the saxophone.

Meanwhile, my mind was gone in the gutter, and my panties were soaked. That sexy ass song we danced to was my undoing. I don't know if I'd ever heard it before. If I had, I wasn't paying attention. I loved the lyrics; they were beautiful and flowed like poetry. I knew that *Smoke* was a cover band, and they did a fantastic job, but I *had* to hear the original. I only remembered a few words, so I pulled out my phone and went to Google to search for *slow wine song*.

I gasped. *Tony! Toni! Tone!*

I should have known. I added it to my playlist immediately.

"I like that song too."

I looked over at Micah, who had an adorable grin.

"Same. Just added it to my playlist."

"Was that your first time hearing it?"

"You know… I can't say. I feel like I'd remember, so I think so."

"You spend more time at my house, you'd have heard it eventually."

"You're a fan?"

"You kidding me? They're one of the best to ever do it."

I nodded in agreement. "Ever seen them live?"

"Yeah. Mal took me to see them at Yoshi's in Oakland for my thirtieth birthday."

My eyes grew in surprise. Yoshi's was a well-known jazz club and restaurant right on the water-front of Oakland. It was right in the heart of an entertainment district called Jack London Square. The club couldn't have had more than about three hundred seats. I could imagine it was a task snagging tickets to see them. "Wow. That must have been a great show."

"It was. I never enjoyed those big arenas, but I enjoy smaller venues. It seems so much more intimate and personal. It was wild, too, because they only did one show, and it sold out within a couple of hours or something ridiculous like that. Mal earned big brother of the year for getting us those tickets."

I laughed, "Absolutely. I know they usually do something special for their hometown whenever they have a show in Oakland. Whoever got a seat that night will never forget it."

"Yup. We had a great time and made great memories."

We pulled into his driveway and chilled after he killed the engine.

It had been a beautiful day earlier, and the evening was turning out to be just as lovely. The sunroof was still open, and I sat back content. I had such a great time tonight with Micah. I looked at our hands still intertwined, then to my left to find him smiling.

"What?"

"Nothing. Just admiring you."

"Aww." I smiled back, squirming just a little under his gaze. "So, you're still into me?" I asked, trying to talk myself through my jitters.

"*Hell yeah*, I am."

He lifted our hands and kissed the back of mine. Leaned over to kiss me on the cheek and gently turned my chin, kissing my forehead. I leaned in closer, meeting him halfway as our lips connected. We pecked sweetly on the lips a few times, and I was sure he heard the light moan escape me. After our lips parted, I leaned forward, connecting our foreheads.

"Baby?" I crooned just over a whisper.

"Yes?"

"Can we do stuff?" My embarrassment was stifled by a mischievous grin. I had a tiny bit of liquid courage from my spiked lavender lemonade, which was delicious, by the way.

I could feel the furrow of his eyebrows. "Stuff?"

"Yeah. *Grown folk stuff.*" I returned

"You're so damn cute." He released a boisterous chuckle. "Grown folk stuff huh?"

"Mmmhmm..." Sitting back, I gave him a bashful smile.

"So. Tell me. What does one do exactly when they're engaging in grown folk stuff?"

My hand was back in his. "Things with their mouths?" It came out as a question, though I didn't mean for it to.

Micah nodded. So, I continued, "I want to do more than kiss you. I want you to do more things to me. But I'm not the most experienced."

Micah reassured me, peppering kisses into my neck. I know that's what he was doing. Murmuring, "We can absolutely do things with our mouths, sexy girl." He held my face in his hands. I felt his smile against my neck. "I'll learn from you, and you'll learn from me. No experience necessary." Still kissing my neck and gently sucking there too. "That cool with you?"

"Yes."

"Indeed. Shall we go inside?"

"We shall."

seven

DESTINEY

"Can I taste you, beautiful?" Micah kissed me softly, trailing down my chest, kissing each nipple and down to my navel. Lingering there, he rubbed his thumb over my heated center from the outside. My panties were done for. I was sure he'd have to peel them off me.

We entered the house through the garage, and Micah took my hand, leading me up the stairs and to his bedroom. His home was dark, with the faint glow of a few plug-in night lights along his hallway.

Now we were in his expansive bedroom in his huge bed. The room was semi-dark; he had a lamp on at the lowest setting. I was laying on my back with Micah settled between my legs. We kissed for such a long time; our tongues were always happy being with one another. I could seriously kiss this man for hours. Vivid thoughts occupied my mind as he lifted again, hovering his frame over me, kissing my neck and my chin. The sounds of smacking and light moans were the only things piercing the darkness. I was incredibly anxious when he first brought me into his bedroom, but making out like we had was a great way to calm my nerves. Micah spoke softly in my ear, "Destiney baby." He pressed, patiently awaiting confirmation.

I had five incisions on my abdomen. They were quite visible, but my doctor said they would fade in time.

Honestly though, I'm most insecure about my vagina. It was the source of all my issues at one point. Having Micah down there between my legs was tripping me out. I told him about my insecurities once we made it to his bedroom, and he got me out of my dress. I told him that I was feeling self-conscious.

In response, he kissed me all over my body, from head to toe. They were open kisses—my favorite kind—the ones that left light moisture in their wake. He spent the most time kissing my stomach, gently scattering kisses all over it, his strong hands securing me around my waist, humming softly as he did it.

"Your body is beautiful, Destiney baby."

"Thank you love."

"I want you to always know that. Whenever you feel insecure, remember how much I adore this temple."

I smiled as I peered down at him.

He kissed each of my scars. "These are a sign of your strength and resilience. And I'm so proud of you, sweetheart."

Damn.

"Micah."

"Yes baby?"

"I want you." I could hardly wait anymore. I moaned as I reached for him. "Can I touch it- can I touch *you*?" I wanted to feel him. Please him. Had to. Even though he balanced his weight while on top of me, I felt his erection brush against me a few times.

"Mmm. I want you too. And you never have to ask. But you know me better than that..." He resumed kissing me, descending lower. "Ladies first." More kisses. "So, can I taste you now?"

I'd never felt a man's mouth on my lower lips before. But I'd fantasized plenty.

Lately especially. My desire for Micah saturated my thoughts.

I wanted him.

And I wanted him to have me.

"Yes."

"Yes, what baby?"

"That's alright with me." I knew he wanted to make sure I was comfortable, but all this talking took me out of the zone. I'd finally gotten to where I was ready for the taking. But now, my thoughts were in overdrive again, and I was losing the battle of calming my nerves. I pulled at his arms, gesturing him up to kiss his lips again, keenly aware this was the best remedy. He understood, taking my bottom lip into his mouth tugging gently.

Micah broke our kiss to lift his shirt over his head. When he got me out of my dress right before he laid me on the bed, he removed my bra too. I was still wearing my black lace panties. Within seconds, we were connected again, skin to skin. Now his large hands ventured upward, cupping my breasts. I had more than a handful, but they fit perfectly in Micah's massive hands. I loved how warm his hands felt. The gentle callous of his palms, his thumbs teasing my nipples into stiff peaks. His periodic murmur articulating his delight. He lowered himself again, caressing me all over, his large hands kneading my skin like a skilled masseuse. Moving down to my stomach, kissing and caressing, then my inner and outer thighs. Repeating the same.

Shit. His touch, his lips. It was intoxicating.

Settled between my legs again he deeply inheld then kissed my pussy from the outside. He growled, and I noticed he did that when he enjoyed something. That shit was hot. I propped myself up on my elbows, watching as he moved in front of me, coming to a rest on his hunches.

"Lift up for me, beautiful." I did as I was told. Unhurried, Micah pulled my panties off, then leisurely parted my legs, surveying with low lids. He carefully spread my legs further, and I was promptly overcome with a sense of self-consciousness. Fully aware he was now facing *her.*

Completely unguarded.

"Hmm." Micah moved closer, emitting a gruff, animalistic lumber. Just as he descended, my nerves got the better of me, and I jolted upward, inching back on the bed and out of his grasp.

I could see that his expression immediately shifted from perplexity to apprehension. I knew he could see the brief expression of apprehension on mine. "Am I moving too fast?" When I said nothing, he asked, "Should I stop?" His tone even and definite. There was comfort there too.

"No, no, not at all." I sighed, flustered with myself.

He regarded me, composed, awaiting an explanation.

"I'm just wondering... is it okay?" I sat up straighter, peering directly at him. He was still back on his hunches. "Am I okay... my area..." I gestured. "Is it what you expected?" Shit. I was rambling now. This was the most intimate thing I had ever done, and I was in my head. Bad. I felt vulnerable, and I wasn't sure how to process it.

Great way to kill the mood.

Micah held my eyes with those warm brown orbs of his. His voice was tranquil and soothing when he asked me, "Have you been pleased this way before?"

I was speechless and certain he could sense my anxiety. I didn't feel an ounce of judgement but certainly abashed by my inexperience.

"Tell me."

"No. Never." I sighed audibly. "I feel so silly. My inexperience is always in the way. I feel like an inexperienced teen. This is weird, and I am too damn old to feel this way." Micah's eyes were trained on me, and in this moment, they were the kindest eyes I'd ever seen. So, I continued, "With my condition, there was so much I couldn't let happen. No one has seen me down there. *Ever.* I worry about it, and I'm self-cautious." Embarrassed as *hell*, I looked away.

Micah waited a beat. Then, "Destiney."

"Yes?" I found his eyes peering back at me.

"I need you to always tell me how you're feeling and what you need. Don't be shy with that.

Please. *Don't ever be shy with that shit.* Whatever you're feeling, know that they're totally valid feelings, and you aren't *weird* for having them."

I silently nodded.

"Aside from when you're self-pleasing, have you had an orgasm before?" I knew Micah wasn't judging me. But... I was... *mortified*. And I felt so pathetic.

"Tell me." He reassured, soft yet firm.

I was silent. Unable to form the words. "I'm embarrassed," I revealed.

"Don't be embarrassed, beautiful."

I said nothing.

"So, you said you felt a safe space with us. Am I right, sweetheart?"

"You're right."

"It's only you talking to me. I would never ask you a question, I wouldn't be open to sharing with you myself. And every single thing we discuss will remain between us."

I sighed, nodding my understanding. "No. I haven't," I returned simply.

Nodding, Micah said, "I'll change that."

My eyes grew wide.

"Being intimate with you is a privilege. And a man doesn't leave his woman unsatisfied."

"You always know what to say, don't you?" I chuckled leisurely, suddenly feeling immensely comfortable. "You have it all figured out, Micah."

"Just being honest, sweetheart."

Micah gently grabbed my chin, caressing it with his thumb, "All I want to do is please you Destiney baby. But if you need more time, please say so."

"I don't need more time."

"Indeed. If at any point you want to stop, you tell me. We can always try this again." He grabbed my hands and interlocked our fingers. "Promise you'll tell me, sweetheart."

"I promise."

Micah grabbed his cell phone from the side table, and as soon I heard the unmistakable melody of the angelic songstress, I recognized the song immediately. "Hold on", The Internet. The music was at the perfect volume, setting the mood just right. It was loud enough for us to hear it if we were completely quiet, so low that I knew the sounds would eventually blend into the background.

This song was made for this moment, and I was absolutely Micah's for the taking. My anxious ass was going to lay my head on this pillow and relax.

Micah was on this same type of time. "Try your best to relax for me. I'll take care of you, baby." He settled on his knees again, carefully spreading my legs. And I did as I was told, tensing up again in anticipation but I instantly mellowed when Micah said, "Mmm...such a pretty pussy Destiney baby."

His voice was smooth and laced with comfort. I felt his warm breath. I heard him inhale deeply, and when he connected us, I felt the wetness and warmth of his tongue. I stifled a moan, but he heard me loud and clear.

"How's that feeling, baby?" He licked my folds as I slowly rocked my hips.

"It feels good." I managed.

"Hmm. You are *delicious* baby." He continued to feast on my pussy and still trepidatious, I fought the urge to express my pleasure. I was failing at that; whimpers and erratic breaths escaped me anyway. And it was no wonder. I was on a cloud high above any place I had ever gone. I had no point of reference, but it seemed Micah was very, *very* good at this. My breathing and rocking increased, and eventually, I arched off the bed as he increased the speed of his tongue.

Micah took his sweet time kissing my pussy with his tongue like she was kissing him right back. Fuck. It felt incredible.

"Does it feel good to you, baby?" He murmured against my pussy.

"Oh yes." I purred.

"Mmm. Don't be shy. Let me know baby." Micah sucked and licked.

Flicked and slurped.

Sucked and licked some more and kept going. Flicking and slurping.

Goodness, his tongue game was vicious. I was in euphoria, releasing a drawn-out moan.

"There's my good girl." He continued feasting. As if he was famished. Hell, I clearly had been.

"Mmmhmm…" He slowly pressed a finger into me. "Damn. You are *so* wet baby."

Micah was right. I was embarrassingly wet. Between my moans, his grunts, growls, and wet sounds from below that music had *been* drowned out. His playlist was going but we couldn't even hear the music anymore, we were making our music now.

And another thing; I *loved* how he talked to me while he was eating. That shit was sexy as hell. Micah had been strumming me like a guitar. His finger felt amazing stroking me. Gently he rubbed his thumb over my clit too. That shit was... fuck.

His tongue, his fingers, his kisses, moans, murmurs.

I felt a sensation. My legs began twitching. "Micah." I managed. My voice was thick with pleasure.

"Yes baby."

Moaning, I repeated his name.

"You're ready to come for me." He stated between sucks and licks and kisses. "Go head baby. Give it to me." Talking me through it, Micah's deep register sent me crashing over the edge. As if on cue, I released, feeling the most intense orgasm I'd ever had. A wave of ecstasy taking over my entire body and I moaned in satisfaction.

"Mmmhmm. There you go, my sexy girl. Give me what I want. I got you." *Fuck.* I was in pure bliss. Everything felt so good.

As I came down, Micah gently licked a few more times. Aware. Methodical and calculated. *Gentle.* Much gentler than he had been. I didn't even need to tell him I was extra sensitive there now.

Micah ate the entire fuck out of my pussy.

He slowly moved up the bed, and I felt his hardness as he brushed me.

Embarrassed to face him now, I turned the other way, burying my face in a pillow. "Oh my gosh."

He chuckled, moving closer. "Look at me baby."

I hesitated.

"Don't be embarrassed," he stroked my shoulder. "Give me your eyes."

Finally turning to face him, he wrapped me in his arms, kissed my nose and lips, and lingered there. I could smell my essence on his lips. I closed my eyes and heard him whisper, "Destiney, baby, you turn me on so much."

"Really?" Still shy but so relieved hearing those words.

He kissed my forehead, "Oh yes, sweetheart. *So much.* You taste amazing. Just as amazing as I thought you would."

"You *felt* amazing," I revealed. "No way I would have expected *that.*" I cuddled closer. "Your tongue... where the hell did you learn tricks like that?" Seriously. His firm tongue felt amazing, better than any battery-operated toy.

Micah laughed. I felt him shrug against me. "Can't say. Just good like that. You have a wicked tongue too. Since we've been kissing, I've learned a few things from you."

I giggled as a memory came to mind. "Daijah and I read in a magazine; I think *Cosmo Girl-* we were teenagers- that if you unwrap a Starburst in your mouth, it will improve your French kissing skills." I cracked up. "We'd buy Starburst specifically for that purpose. I don't even want to admit how many we unwrapped."

Micah cackled too. "For real?"

"Yep. I'd say it worked. You have to unwrap it with your mouth only. So basically, just using your tongue. We got pretty quick. Could do it in just a few seconds."

He released a light titter sarcastically saying, "It's *all* making sense now."

"Hey, don't judge me! We were teenagers." I playfully nudged him with my left shoulder.

"No judgment here baby. You like it I love it."

***

I stirred, restless and unable to find sleep. I felt Micah's arm tighten around me. He moved closer and I felt his hardness poking against my back.

We stayed up talking for a while, and then I eventually dozed off. Now I was up again and couldn't fall back asleep. It had to be at least three a.m.

I knew exactly why.

"You okay?" Micah inquired his deep voice, nocturnal and husky. We were both pretty light sleepers.

"Yes baby."

I was more than okay.

Micah had been so gentle with my heart, my feelings. My body.

He'd left the bed to get a warm towel to clean me up. We'd made a mess. I didn't have to move. Eventually I did, because I needed to pee. But he took such care, probably more than I would have.

Earlier when I alluded to touching him, he evaded that. Albeit with a persuasive distraction. *Well played Micah*. But I wanted to. Still.

I desired so much to please him too. It had been on my mind since we left HomeGrownSol.

To please him.

And right at this very moment, Micah wasn't playing fair, pressing his hard dick into me.

I wanted his dick. At minimum, I *finally* wanted to hold it. Feel it... maybe even...

Anyway, there was only one way to quench my thirst. I wanted to please my man. But I also wanted to satisfy this urge.

Fulfill desire.

Return the favor.

We were under his blanket. And it was completely dark in his bedroom. I honestly didn't know if- wasn't sure I was feeling extra bold because of that. Or if I was driven by desire. Still high off the satisfying orgasm he gave me. My clit was still tingling.

Who knows and who the hell cares.

Now it was his turn.

I turned, facing him, and without warning, I moved my hand down and into the front of his basketball shorts. Gently taking hold of *him*.

He was velvety smooth. Thick. Long. And *heavy*. I could feel prominent veins as I slowly stroked him, getting acquainted.

"Destiney baby..." Micah groaned. His voice thick with desire. He shifted his body just a little and I heard another deep moan. I maintained my soft grip and continued stroking as he came alive in my hand. Growing harder than he had been just seconds before.

Yeah. I kept going. And so did he. Growing harder and moaning louder. *Sexy.* I stroked his dick for a good while and my man liked that.

I knew it was time so I moved into positioned and in one swift motion, pulled him into my mouth before he could react. I couldn't take much, but I gripped him with both hands as I began sucking slowly.

I was glad the room was dark. I'd never done this before and may have been too self-cautious otherwise.

He seemed to like it. His deep glutaral moans left me no doubt this felt good to him. Micah moved slightly again shifting from his side, now laying flat on his back.

Feeling even bolder, I gradually straddled him, never removing him from my mouth.

I took as much of him into my mouth as I could, using both hands I gently twisted and squeezed, maintaining a moderate tempo. I felt him lifting his hips beneath me. I placed both hands on the bed on either side of him.

He had this under control.

"Mmm." Micah sounded pleased and that's what I wanted. His moans of pleasure drove me wild. I moaned too as he moved faster, his hard dick gliding in and out with a mixture of my saliva and his precum. Resisting the urge, I kept my hands planted at his sides. A deep rumble escaped him as he moaned in satisfaction.

I liked that.

"Yeah... suck your dick baby girl." *This dick was mine alright.* I moaned in agreement. "I hear you beautiful. You enjoying yourself?"

"Mmmhmm."

Yeah. He kept going.

"Baby..." he growled fucking my mouth with deliberate strokes all the while moaning with pleasure.

"Hmm?" My sloppy mouth dripping each time he lifted his hips.

His moans growing louder, he gently placed his hands on the sides of my face tugging softly.

"Baby..." he sounded pressed. His hard dick sliding in and out of my slick mouth. "Destiney...I'm bout to cum in a minute. You must move baby." His voice was laced with pleasure, and it was incredibly sexy. I was so turned on; my pussy getting wetter by the second. I brought my mouth as close to him as I could, now feeling him hit the back of my throat, saliva dripping down his shaft, and my chin.

"Fuck. Destiney, I'm close. Where you want it baby?" His voice was husky and resolute. "Where?" He urged.

I broke away for just a second, "You know where love."

"Baby... you sure."

I wasn't going anywhere. I wanted all of him.

He emitted a low pleasure-filled rumble, which had to be the most beautiful sound I'd ever heard come from a man.

Milliseconds later I felt his warm squirts at the back of my throat.

I swallowed every drop.

I was just as satisfied as he was and so pleased I could please him. He grabbed me with both arms as I climbed back to my spot beside him.

"Come here beautiful." Micah kissed me with incredible fervor.

I lay on his chest as he asked. "I take it you couldn't sleep?" Content laced his voice.

"Nope. Way too distracted."

eight

DESTINEY

The mural at the Elementary School in Downtown Sacramento was completed. It looked amazing. The theme was growth, and it came together so nicely. We painted flowers, butterflies, vines, and trees. The star of the show was a big vibrant sun with various shades of yellows, oranges, whites and reds. That was my favorite part of the mural; it was front and center, lively and colorful. The sun is lifegiving and went perfectly with the growth theme. We added a few quotes from some of the students. I loved the way everything came together. Of course, it was hard to say goodbye to everyone at the end of the project. We'd often become like a family. It's easy to do. Spending hours together day after day, working toward a common goal.

So, this week I started a new project, a gig in Roseville, California. About a forty-five-minute drive from Land Park where I lived.

This was a different clientele. Not a community effort.

A brand-new state-of-the-art childcare center had been built. Privately owned. In an upscale neighborhood. The proud owner, a *privileged* white woman, wanted an ocean theme. The rooms inside would have mural art with exotic fish, bubbles, some submarines, and scuba divers. You get the idea.

This project would take a while.

Fortunately, *and* unfortunately. It was a large childcare facility, twenty-five hundred square feet. The team of artists was much smaller than I would have suggested for a facility this size, but I wasn't the Artistic Director. I was just here to do my thing with a paintbrush.

Anyway, the owner was already on my nerves, and this was only like day number three. She was constantly coming in and interrupting us. Asking us to redo an entire sketch because *"it doesn't quite fit what she had in mind."* The thing is, the Artistic Director will run the designs by the client first. Once it's approved and to their liking, we sketch them out on the wall and then paint them. The sketch on the wall is more than ten times the size of a draft we'd show her for review. It sounds like she shouldn't have approved the sketches. It wasn't as simple as just erasing it and starting over. That would only delay the project.

I can't work like this. Respectfully, I don't have to.

If *Becky* wouldn't let us do our thing, *I'm* not the artist for her.

When I complained to India, she reminded me that it would pay handsomely. And to *get the bag.* That's to be expected with these private clients. But...

I didn't revel in working with private clients. Especially these privileged ones. Not even a little bit. I took on private clients *sparingly*.

This constant over-the-shoulder micro-shit is precisely why.

And I'm not sorry.

I almost passed on this gig when I was contacted and asked to join the team. I saw the writing on the wall. The promise of a nice check is what sold me, especially since my past couple of gigs were community projects on much smaller budgets. Meaning smaller payouts.

And India had to pass on it. She couldn't commit to a gig outside city limits for an extended period. Not right now. Her parents took priority, and they needed her nearby. I was so bummed about that. I loved working with her.

India and I planned to pick up a three-day project for fun doing sidewalk art for *Chalk it up! Sacramento*. I couldn't wait. It's an art and music festival, Labor Day weekend, right around the corner. *Chalk it up! Sacramento* happens every year, celebrating local artists and the artistic community. It's been a Sacramento tradition for more than thirty years. I've participated a few times over the years. It's so much fun. Artists get three days to create artwork on two sidewalk squares, and then, during the festival, people walk around the park's perimeter to see the art. I've seen some incredible work. Artists of all levels are encouraged to apply. It's even open to kids. You only have to be in seventh grade to enter. You can join for free, and premium chalk is provided to the artists to use to their heart's content. It's always held at Fremont Park in Midtown, a prime location for an event such as this. There's plenty of shade, thanks to the mature oak trees. There's usually a live band, food trucks, vendors, and a kids' area for families.

I left the childcare center, stopped for gas, and hit the road. The commute was a pain in the ass too. Anyway, the gas station was in a bustling plaza, so I had to wait a few minutes. I looked up and swore I saw a man come out of the gas station resembling my dad.

That couldn't be him.

He was with a woman.

And they looked pretty familiar. I saw his hand at the small of her back.

There was no way that was my dad. He didn't date.

So many of our friends who had single moms inquired about him over the years. It never failed. Dad is handsome. Kind. Turning fifty-three at the end of this year. And he looked great for his age. I was never surprised that the moms on our sports teams always asked about my dad. Women at the church. Every damn where we went.

The more I looked, the more he looked like my dad.

It *was* my dad.

I saw them approach his car. After he opened the passenger's side, he climbed into the driver's seat.

My chin hit the floor, and I felt a dagger piercing straight through my heart. I frantically dialed Daijah, my heart pounding in my chest. It rang three times before she finally answered.

"Day!" I yelled before she could even offer me a greeting.

"Hey Des- you, okay?"

"Dad! I saw him coming out of the gas station with a woman! They were close and holding hands! I mean, *who the hell is she?* And what the hell is going on? He never mentioned he was dating! How can he do that behind our backs?" There was silence on the other end. I pulled my phone away from my ear to make sure the call was still connected. It was. "You there Day?"

"Yeah." She was oddly calm, and that's when it clicked.

Oh, ain't this some shit. "You knew."

"Yes. Dad told me he'd been seeing someone. I also met her briefly when I went by the house to pick up some mail he had for me. She's a nice lady and sweet. They seem to like each other."

"Wow! So, you knew and didn't tell me? I would have told you immediately!" I said through tears. At this point, I felt betrayed by both of them.

"I couldn't say anything Des. Dad swore me to secrecy. He wanted to tell you himself."

"Oh please! Like that shit *ever* mattered. We've always told each other everything Day." My eyes were full despite the heavy crocodile tears falling one after the other.

"I know Des. I'm sorry."

The line was quiet.

"Don't cry Des."

"Too late for that," I said through a forced chuckle, though wasn't shit funny. "Dad still hasn't told me, yet he introduced *you* to the woman. How is that supposed to make me feel?"

"It seems that way, but it could have been either of us. In his defense, I went by the house a day earlier than I said I would. He wasn't expecting me."

Daijah had a point. We both had keys to the house and came and went as we pleased. Dad had a predictable schedule, and we knew his comings and goings. We didn't even have to call first, but most times, we did anyway. I guess all that would change now that he was entertaining a woman.

I wonder if they were…never mind.

"Des, please don't take this the wrong way…"

"I'm listening."

"Knowing Dad, he's been a mess over having this talk with us. *With you especially.*"

"With me? Why?"

"Come on Des. You know you're Daddy's girl."

"You are too!"

Daijah laughed. "Not like *you*. You two have such a sweet bond."

I smiled and got emotional all over again.

"Yeah. I guess we do."

We had a few beats of silence, and I knew she was thinking of Mom.

"You had something special with Mom. I figured if either of us, he may have been a little more anxious to share this with you."

"Maybe so."

Silence filled the line again.

"I want him to be happy, Des. You know? He's a great man. So selfless. He gave us so much of himself. Aside from losing mom, we never wanted for anything." Daijah sounded emotional now too.

"Yeah. I want him to be happy too. I guess I didn't think the day would come when we'd have to share him with another woman. It never seemed like a concern of his."

"Maybe it wasn't. But we've got men now. Great men, who will move heaven and earth for us. I think he feels like he can focus on himself again."

I nodded. "Yeah."

After a few seconds, Daijah said, "Call Dad now."

I let out a boisterous chuckle. Daijah knew me well because that's exactly what I planned to do as soon as I hung up with her.

***

"Hey Dad!" I waited for him to lift the garage door for me. His two-car garage wasn't for parking cars. He had a pretty cool setup in here. A flat-screen mounted to the wall, a pool table, and two vintage arcade game machines, *Pac-Man* and *Street Fighter*. Off to the side was a table that sat six people.

"Hey Princess." He kissed my forehead as we embraced. When I felt his arms loosen around me, I held on tighter, burying my face into his chest. Before I knew it, the waterworks began, and I didn't bother trying to control my shaking or sobbing.

I didn't need to. This was always a safe space.

When we first lost Mom, the grief was as unforgiving as it was unpredictable. Daijah and I had taken the loss so hard and had cried so much. The crying only seemed to stop once we finally had no tears left.

But that took years.

Years of patience with ourselves and years of grief counseling and therapy.

Dad held me in his strong arms, rubbing my back as I cried. He'd always done that since Daijah and I were little, and I swore that always made everything better.

When I finally gathered my bearings, I stepped away, wiping my tears.

"Has something happened, princess?" His voice was laced with urgency, and I felt terrible because he was always the fixer. I knew he was on high alert now.

I shook my head. "No. But... can we sit down? I want to talk to you."

"Of course we can." Dad pulled a chair out for me and pushed me in. He consistently demonstrated exactly what a gentleman looked like for Daijah and me. Grandiose things, the little things, and everything in between. "Is there time for tea?" Dad asked, and I immediately smiled real big.

Over the years, we have had many talks over tea, sometimes over two or three cups. My love for tea was all thanks to Dad. He was a tea enthusiast who exposed me to the infinite world of many delicious and vibrant teas. He always says there's beauty, history, and culture behind each cup of tea.

"Yes! That's *always* a yes."

He turned on the electric kettle he kept in the garage, then reached overhead, pulling down his stash of options. "What are you feeling like princess?"

"Surprise me. You have so many that it would take me too long to decide." He had an elaborate variety and constantly added tea bags, loose-leaf mixtures, and whole tea leaves.

He chuckled lightly. "Alright."

After gently placing my favorite mug in front of me, he joined me at the table. "I think you'll enjoy this one. May become your new favorite." I looked up as he winked at me.

I cracked a grin. "You always say that."

Dad chuckled again. "Taste a sip of mine, too." He offered after he steeped and stirred in a few cubes of sugar. I took in the steaming aroma. It was *lovely*.

I used my spoon to ladle out a sample. "Oh my! I love this one! Lavender... and peppermint." It was heavy with spice, my favorite notes for warm tea.

He nodded. "Very good." I'd been getting better at identifying notes in teas. My dad is an expert at it. He told me we mainly taste through smell. Professional tea tasters smell the dry leaves before and after steeping.

I took a sip of his, "Yes. *I love that one! Chamomile?*"

"Yep. Chamomile, rose petals, and white sage. Wait till you try that one iced. Even better."

"I bet!"

"Alright princess. What was that about earlier? Is everything, everything?"

I stirred my tea as I nodded slowly. "Yes. Everything is everything. Just had a moment, I guess."

Dad nodded in understanding. He was one of the most understanding people I knew, and I loved that so much about him. Over the years, Daijah and I have always been able to come to him *about anything and everything.* If he didn't know the answer, he'd say so and promise to help us figure it out.

That was tricky sometimes because there were things he may not have understood as a man. Regardless, he never made us feel bad. Or weird.

We always had an open relationship. He was our human diary, and we shared so much with him. It was a fact that Daijah and I talked with Dad about things many girls wouldn't typically talk to their fathers about.

But nothing about our relationship was ordinary. He was a widowed father of two growing girls right at the start of adolescence. Dad had no choice but to rise to the occasion. No topic was off-limits. Boys we had crushes on, bras, periods. Friendship drama. The whole nine. Even when I fucked up, he was the first person I wanted to talk to. He'd always say, *"I'm glad you told me."* We kept occasional secrets from Dad, but we shared so much.

After talking with Daijah, I headed home, planning to call Daddy when I arrived. I was mid-route when I decided to go see him instead. I'm so glad I did, too. I felt better already.

This conversation was meant to be face-to-face.

Daddy pulled me from my thoughts, "You said you wanted to talk."

I regarded Dad's warm smile, all the reassurance I needed. Holding Daddy's gaze, I bravely said, genuinely, "Today, I saw you coming out of the gas station. And I saw you with a woman. Since you two were holding hands… I would love it if you told me about her. And I would love to meet her."

Seemingly disarmed, Dad sat back a bit in his chair. He put his face in his hands a moment later, and I was sure I heard a slight whimper. Once I heard a sniffle, I knew he was crying. "Dad, please don't cry." He willingly gave me his hand as I reached for it. He looked at me with eyes full of tears, but he had a smile on his face. "These are tears of joy, that's all Princess."

"Tears of joy?" My brows furrowed. Dad nodded as he stood and walked over to a corner where he had a few shelves. He kept a handful of tools in here, though most of that stuff was in the shed out in the backyard. After rummaging through a few boxes, he brought a shoebox and placed it on the table. Removing the lid, he took out a few Polaroid pictures. He glanced through them, stopping at one, and then handed it to me.

My eyes grew wide, my hand flying to my mouth. I gasped, and just that quickly, I got emotional again. It was a picture of my parents decades ago. I'd seen many pictures of my parents back in the day and old pictures of my mom, but this was a picture I had never seen. It was a bright sunny day, and Dad was sitting in a lawn chair with Mom on his lap. They were young and vibrant. I could see the love in their eyes, appearing not to have a care in the world. Daddy looked handsome as always, with a head full of dark hair and a small goatee without the salt and pepper. But my mom. *She was gorgeous.* She had her hair in long braids and wore a green tank top and a pair of shorts overalls. I chuckled. She had a very nineties style. Her smile was breathtaking. It was bright and beautiful. Her big brown eyes sparkled, and I saw Daijah and me all over her. We were her daughters. I hadn't realized how much we favored Mom. I'd always heard we looked like her, and I seemed to hear it more the older I got. Yet, I still hadn't realized just how much we did until I saw this picture. I continued to study the picture. Everything about it. There was something special about this one… it was ineffable like she had a glow. "Dad… wow," I said, finally finding my voice. "Where was this picture hiding all this time?"

He smiled at me as if he knew everything I had been thinking. "There's a few you two still haven't seen. I'll share them with you in time."

I nodded. I was good with that.

"This is one of my favorite pictures of your mom."

"I can see why. My goodness, she was so beautiful." I kept studying the picture, committing it to memory.

"She was. You know… we'd just found out we were expecting you."

My mouth formed into an *O*, and I looked over at Dad. "Really?" My eyes filled with tears again.

"Really. She was so happy. We both were. We'd been trying for a while, and when we finally had you, it was like you came at the perfect time. It's the reason she chose your name. *You were Destined.*"

I knew there was something about this moment. The lightly tattered and aged photo somehow exuded so much radiance.

"We lost her so suddenly, but I promised her that even in death, I would continue to be the best father I could be and raise you two the way we said we always would. Along this journey, I made Mom a few promises. You two were most important to me. More important than anything or anyone else. And all I wanted to do was make sure you two were happy and safe. As you've gotten older and you've met gentlemen I would have drawn up, I finally felt like I could release that. They're good men. I know they would look after you two, love and care for you. You'd be moving from my covering to theirs."

"I talk to Mom in my dreams, and sometimes she comes to me briefly. Or I'll hear her voice. Over the years, Mom has urged me to find love again. But I didn't want to. I still love Mom very much. She's the only woman I've ever loved. And I felt this pressing thing as if she was urging me forward to move on. Even visiting me less. I didn't like that. Some months ago, I went back to counseling. And then I prayed, asking that God give me a sign. I needed a sign and confirmation from God and a sign from both of you girls to let go of my reservations.

So, two weeks ago, when Daijah came over unexpectedly and saw that Natalie was here, I knew I still needed one more confirmation from you. I wanted to come to you and tell you. But I think part of me knew what that would mean. Especially if you are open to this. As much as I wanted to avoid those thoughts, part of me knew you would be. I've had such an internal battle with all of this. I love Mom. And I miss her so much. But the fact you saw us earlier clear across town, then came here to tell me you want to know more about her and meet her, gave me confirmation. So, the tears of joy were because God and Mom answered me. That was their way of confirming."

Wow. This was all so much. My dad had been dealing with this, and Daijah and I had no idea. I wish he'd shared this with us. It seemed it was a lot. So much so that it sent him back to therapy. Maybe we didn't give him a safe space to share with us. I felt horrible about that. Today was a new day.

"Yes Dad. I talked to Daijah, and you have both our blessings. We want you to be happy. You deserve it. You gave us so much. And I'm sorry if we didn't give you a safe space to share how you have been feeling openly."

"I had reservations, and they had nothing to do with the two of you. Quite the contrary. You've both done so much for your dear old dad."

"Are you sure?"

"Positive. This is all so new for me. And it's a process that I'll continue to work through with God's help, my therapist, and the two of you."

We stood and hugged. "I'm so proud of you, Dad, " I said into his chest.

"I appreciate you, Princess."

We retook our seats, "So, Ms. Natalie, is it?"

Dad tried to suppress his smile, but it was too late for all that. "I see that grin, Dad! It's alright."

"Ms. Natalie is wonderful, Princess. We've spent some time getting to know one another and I enjoy our time. I look forward to introducing the two of you."

"Tell me when."

"Hmm. I'll check with her to see what works. We can all have some dinner. Maybe the end of the month?"

"Wouldn't miss it. I'll pass the details to Daijah and Julian too."

"Alright. I'd love to have Micah join us. Is he also vegetarian?" Daddy asked with furrowed brows. I brought Micah to formally meet Dad several days ago. They're pretty fond of each other. They talked for hours, jumping from topic to topic. Later, Dad said, "He loved Micah for me."

That made my year!

Micah also got to hang out with Julian. Those two fell into lockstep like old friends. Of course, I wasn't surprised. Julian is a great guy, and Micah is too. I got the feeling they'd get along well.

Some days before bringing Micah to my childhood home, I told him about my mom.

Specifically, that she was no longer here. Physically. That was an emotional conversation, lots of tears, for sure. And Micah held me until I was ready to let go.

"No, he isn't. He'll love your beef kebabs if that's what you plan to put on the grill.

"He's my kind of man."

I chuckled.

"Thank you for coming by and having tea with me."

"Of course. I'm so glad we can always talk, Dad." I'd probably hang out with my old man a little longer. And have another cup of tea while I'm at it.

nine

MICAH

Glancing at the time, I decided I was done for the day. I closed the document I had been reviewing and shut down my computer. I was reviewing it at the office and decided to take another look when I got home from work about an hour ago. I think I'd been staring at it for too long because the numbers were beginning to run together. That wouldn't work for what I needed to accomplish.

I've been working from home much more lately; I considered going remote full-time. Destiney was coming over almost every day after work. Sometimes, she spent the night too, and I loved having her nearby. I couldn't go anywhere in this house without smelling her scent, *especially my bedroom*, which was fine with me.

I went to the kitchen to get some water and found Destiney leaning against the counter. "Hey. You, okay? I asked, taking her into my arms and kissing her lips and then her forehead.

"Yes baby. How about you?" She embraced me around my waist. Since I was so much taller, that was where she mostly held me.

"I'm good, Destiney baby. Thank you." I loved this. Having her in my home. Being near her all the time. Indulging in her sweet kisses whenever I wanted them. Passing her in the kitchen and smacking her ass. Holding her hand when we shared space. I never wanted to go back to life before Destiney.

I had to go to Glendale, California, for work at the end of the month. One of our corporate offices was out there, so I went there a few times out of the year. It wasn't far, only about an hour-long flight, and I'd just be gone for four days, but still. I wasn't looking forward to being away from Destiney. I considered asking her to join me, but I knew she'd just started a new project. Anyway, I was planning to take her to San Luis Obispo soon. Once I confirmed her schedule for her current project, I would get something planned. One night, we talked about a few places we'd like to visit, and she mentioned seeing the central California Coast. That was easy. And no doubt, it was breathtaking. I loved living there when I was down at Cal Poly during college. I'd love even more to take her there.

Destiney stepped to my side to put her water back in the fridge. After she closed it, she hugged me again and let me go on her way out.

"Hey, come back here baby." I pulled her back to me, then quickly picked her up, placing her on the kitchen counter right in front of me. I planted my hands on the counter on either side of her, dipping my lips to her neck, smothering her with sloppy kisses. She loved it when I kissed her neck but was extremely ticklish there.

She squealed in delight, *"Micah!"*

I went for the thick band of her leggings. She squirmed in protest, placing her hands on top of mine. "Micah!" She had a silly giggle, and her tiny hands were no match for mine.

"What? Is it shark week or something?" I asked her. Destiney told me she called her menstruation shark week.

"No, it isn't."

I resumed what I was doing, ready to get a taste of her.

"Baby." It sounded like a plea, but she moaned too. "I just took a shower."

"Okay." My mouth was still pressed into her neck, and my hand was in her panties. Cupping, then swiping.

"Micah…mmm. We have to leave soon. I won't have time to take another… mmm…"

My fingers were inside of her now. I used my other hand to yank her leggings off gently but with haste.

"I'll be quick."

She laughed. "Micah."

I lowered myself in front of her. Arriving at my final destination, just before I pressed my face into her wetness, I said, "Mal's house is a ten-minute drive from here." Destiney leaned back, resting on her hands. "Mmmhmm." I went to work with my tongue, and she moaned in satisfaction.

"We'll just make a… *messsss*… You know how wet I get. *Baby*…mmm."

"Don't I know it." I was right back at it. Licking her clit, sucking her lips. They were both swollen. I hummed again. Once I'd ridden her of her leggings and panties, I noticed she was already glistening for me.

Yeah.

We've opened Pandora's box.

I got in that pink. Tasted her honey. And it was *on* after that.

Destiney's pussy was beautiful. Fat and meaty with a clit peeking out the second she got excited. Once I got her aroused, I wouldn't have to go searching. I planned to always keep her aroused. It smelled delicious, and it tasted even better. Her clit was long, and I loved that shit. I took it between my lips and tugged it gently. She must have enjoyed that because I got a reaction out of her. Audible and physical. "You like that baby?"

"Hell yeah. Shit, that feels nice."

"Good. Keep telling me what you like sweetheart." I captured her clit again, humming this time as I tugged, and she writhed in response. I wrapped my arms around her thighs to hold her in place. "You stay right here, baby."

The first night I tasted her, I focused on pleasing her. Simply appreciating her. It was a big deal. Monumental. She was in her head so bad, and I didn't want that for her. I wanted her to enjoy it just as much as I was. And man, *was I*. Enjoying. Relishing. Appreciating.

I'm a pleaser, so pleasing her had me painfully hard. I was gentle with my tongue but also intentional. Deliberately licking and sucking and slurping, thoughtfully at a slower pace so she could savor the moment. I was savoring it right along with her, audibly expressing my satisfaction. As pleasure-filled as the moment was, I didn't take any of it for granted.

This was a sacred space.

The gateway to her womb, and I knew this was a privilege to be able to please her in this way. This was the most intimate part of a woman, not just physically but emotionally. So much more than what's on the surface is connected to the apex of a woman. In my mind, this was a step above the level of intimacy than penetration. It was much more personal. It was easy to get your dick wet, but taking the time to please a woman orally was beyond that as far as I was concerned. I was totally fine being the only person who had that opinion.

Before that moment the other night, I used to try to imagine how she would sound when she was pleased or whenever something felt good to her. Destiney exceeds my wildest expectations. She wasn't very verbal *yet*. She spoke back whenever I talked to her, which was sexy as hell. But my baby was a moaner. And my goodness, those moans drove me over the edge *every single time*. And feeling her, no-watching her pussy contracting as she came. That shit… *fuck*.

Like right now.

I'd brought her to orgasm, then helped her down off the counter once she gathered her bearings.

"I'm gonna clean up real quick. *Again*." She playfully told me as she headed back toward the stairs.

"You're welcome." I tossed back in a playful tone of my own.

Then, later that night, after I tasted her for the first time, I felt her lips around me. It was a *very* pleasant surprise. I let her know how much she satisfied me. How great it felt. I didn't hold back telling her any of that. I knew she had to be incredibly brave to do that for me. And I wanted her to know precisely how I felt. Sparing no details.

And speaking of penetration, we hadn't gone there yet. We'd just been putting mouths on each other, which seemed to be plenty for now. *Shit.*

**

We headed to Malachi's house, holding hands and listening to music. Destiney turned it up when Anita Baker's "Angel" came on. "I love this song!"

"You're an Anita fan, huh?"

"Oh yeah. My dad loves Anita. I grew up listening to her."

"Same here. She's a legend."

By the way, I met Mr. David Evans some days ago, and he was such a great man and an incredible father. I couldn't imagine having to raise two daughters while grieving the sudden loss of your wife. He was laid-back and funny. He was just a great guy and easy to be around. I looked forward to getting better acquainted.

Destiney will meet Mal, Ella, and the kids tonight, and then my parents this weekend. I was so excited for them to meet her finally.

"You know what, baby? As nervous as I am, I look forward to meeting Gabby girl the most, I think. Gabby girl is my best friend in my head."

"Best friend in your head?" I lightly chuckled.

"Yeah."

"Can't say I've heard the expression."

"I just like her a lot, even though we haven't met. Just based on what I've heard. Which are all great things."

I nodded.

"Plus, I owe her *big time.*"

"Do you?"

"Uh-huh."

"Why's that?"

"Had she not asked you to stop for supplies, I'm not sure I'd ever have met you. I don't think we would have ever crossed paths. We don't frequent any of the same places. Our circles aren't connected at all. Our meeting is all thanks to her. Sac is small but not *that* small." She leaned in and kissed my cheek.

"I've never thought of that. You're right. I owe her too."

Destiney smiled brightly. "Are we almost there?"

"Yes. About three minutes."

"Okay."

I looked over at her, already knowing.

"What is it baby?" I asked her.

"Just nervous. I'm excited to meet them. I know how special they are to you, but I can be awkward as hell around new people. Shy too."

"No need to worry. They'll love you. Just like I do." I pulled her hand to my lips, kissing it softly.

I rang the doorbell and quickly heard the locks disengage.

"Brother."

"Hey, you two."

Malachi and I slapped hands and shared a quick embrace. Destiney stood closely beside me.

"Come on in." Mal stepped aside, and we crossed the threshold.

I grabbed Destiney's hand and led her through the entryway. We followed Malachi as he headed through their spacious living area into their expansive kitchen.

"Ella and the kids should be back any minute now."

"Indeed."

He checked one of the pots simmering on the stove. Whatever it was smelled amazing. Malachi leaned back against the kitchen island. His eyes were trained on me with a knowing expression.

"Destiney, I'd like you to meet my *shorter*, older brother, Malachi. Malachi, my lady Destiney." I hoped to lighten her mood, albeit at Malachi's expense. He was always a good sport. Mal rolled his eyes playfully, lightly punching my arm. I punched him back, and he followed with dramatics, grabbing his arm and feigning injury.

Destiney giggled. "Nice to finally meet you. I've heard so much about you." She put her hand out to shake, but Mal immediately pulled her in.

"Come here, girl, we some hugging folk!"

Destiney continued to laugh.

"Pleasures all mine, baby sis. Can I offer you anything to drink?"

"Water is great, thank you."

"Of course."

I retook Destiney's hand, pulling her back to me as Malachi retrieved the bottled water from the fridge. She opened her water, taking a long drink. I rubbed her hand gently with the pad of my thumb. I think her nerves were calming since Malachi was carefree, but she still had three people to meet.

"It smells great in here, Malachi! Thanks for hosting dinner."

"*Anytime.* Our home is your home. You know that baby Brother."

I smiled. I was so grateful for my relationship with Malachi. I looked up to him. He always inspires me. I appreciate and love him, and I'm proud of him.

The beauty in all of that was *everything I felt*; I knew he felt the same way for me, too. We always told each other we loved each other. We always hugged each other. Our brotherhood is truly amazing. If God blessed me with sons, I wanted nothing more than for them to be as close as Malachi and me.

"Yes, brother, I know. And likewise."

"I know this well." Mal returned.

A moment later, the side door swung open. Ella and Gabe entered the kitchen from the garage, with Gabby following closely behind them.

"Hey, Uncle Micah!" Gabby exclaimed, darting her way to me and falling into my embrace.

"Hey, Gabby girl."

"Ms. Destiney! I'm so excited to finally meet you!" Gabby left my arms, falling straight into Destiney's, hugging her like they were old friends.

"It's very nice to meet you too Gabby," Destiney replied.

"So that's our daughter Gabby. No introduction needed." Mal shook his head, chuckling. Gabby had enough personality for all of us.

Malachi held Ella in his arms and kissed her lips slow and nasty. I stifled a laugh when I caught Destiney trying to play off her look of surprise. Her eyes had grown wide as saucers. I meant to warn her about those two, but it was too late for all that now. That would have taken all the fun out of it, anyway. Destiney would learn quickly just how incredibly affectionate Malachi and Ella were. They didn't give a damn where they were and who was around.

My parents are the same way. After nearly forty years of marriage, my father still called Mommy his bride and always kissed her on the forehead or the hand. Destiney was quite affectionate, just like I am. She'll fit right in once she gets over her shyness. We were incredibly affectionate with one another.

Finally breaking the kiss, Mal said, "This is my wife, Ella. The queen of this castle."

After pecking Mal several times, Ella stepped over to Destiney, hugging her warmly.

"Destiney, *in the flesh*! Well, aren't you beautiful! Thank you for coming to our home and sharing a meal with us."

"Thank you so much. And for the invitation. You're beautiful, too, and so is your home."

"Thank you!" Ella returned.

"This is our son Gabe," Malachi said. "He's pretty chill. Sometimes we forget he's there."

"Hello, Ms. Destiney," Gabe said, hugging her as well. Gabe had been standing there observing, per usual. He was a man of few words, the polar opposite of his sister Gabby.

"Destiney, would you mind helping me get everything together so we can get dinner on the table?" Ella turned on the kitchen sink to wash her hands. "I don't know about you, but I'm starving."

"Of course I can," Destiney answered as she went to wash her hands too.

"Do you need my help too, momma?" Gabby asked Ella.

"I think Destiney and I have it. Thank you." She kissed her on the cheek and sent her on her way. "All right, everyone. Give us about fifteen minutes, and we'll be ready to eat." Ella said.

Gabe and Gabby disappeared from the kitchen as I followed Malachi to their back patio.

I took a seat, and Mal sat right beside me.

"She's a beauty, Micah."

"That she is. I tell her so all day long. But she's so much more. *Destiney is incredible*. I'm already *so* in love with her. Shit is intense, and it's only been about six months. She's the one. I want to marry her."

Mal's eyebrows were high on his head. "Do you now?"

"*Dead ass.* I'll marry her tomorrow if she'll have me. I had already met her father and her sister. They're great people. Gonna get her over to meet Mommy and Daddy this weekend, but those are just formalities. I know they'll adore her."

Malachi nodded. If anyone understood, he did. Not only did he and Ella marry young, but they also married quickly.

"There's a strong connection between the two of you. I see the way you're looking at her."

"Brother. It's something I can't even explain."

Mal released a deep chuckle. "Been there. You know I get it. Baby brother," Mal sported a wide grin, "If you're already talking marriage, it sounds like you've got your nose open."

"Wide open." I returned with resolve.

Mal roared with boisterous laughter.

"Handle it, man."

ten

DESTINEY

I knew Micah was close to his brother, but this was a completely different level. It was beautiful to witness just how close they were. I'd been observing their closeness and banter this entire evening.

I can't say I've ever seen such a thing. Daijah and I were close. The best of friends. I suppose I thought sisters had a different type of bond than brothers. I'm not sure where I even got that idea. They called each other "Brother" and "Baby Brother". These men were in their thirties. I prayed that they would be close like this if I had sons.

Malachi and Micah were so alike, yet different at the same time.

They looked alike. They had the same deep voice and eerily similar mannerisms. They really could have been twins. They were twins damn near. They are just eleven months apart.

They had the same milk chocolate complexion and the same warm brown eyes.

Malachi was a bit stockier, maybe just an inch shorter. Just as handsome and charming. Malachi was bald with a goatee. Micah was bald with a full beard.

We sat down to eat at their dining room table. Micah was right beside me, Ella was directly across from me, and Malachi was right beside her. Gabe and Gabby sat on each end. Everything at the table looked and smelled delicious. It was so considerate of them to have so many vegetarian dishes. Most times I went to dinner at someone's house, I'd end up eating bread, salad, or chips. I filled my plate with yellow rice, red potatoes, and smothered cabbage. There was also tri-tip and ribs that Malachi barbe-cued. Once Malachi blessed the food, we all dug in.

I started with a forkful of yellow rice and cab-bage, and my palate exploded. *Everything was so fla-vorful*, and the rice was fluffy and cooked to perfec-tion. I ate a few potatoes, chewing in delight with my eyes closed.

"Good?" Micah asked me. My eyes shot open to his silly grin, and everyone looked back at me. I immediately felt my cheeks growing warm. I couldn't believe he asked me that in front of every-one. I gave him a look, and then I heard Malachi lightly chuckle as he said, "You good baby sis. We can all concede that this shit is bomb. Ella was so happy to cook for you when she learned you're veg-etarian. My baby can cook, but she is flexing to-night." Ella smiled brightly, showing dimples I hadn't noticed before.

"My compliments to the chef." I nodded in agreement.

"I'm so glad. It was a challenge for me to nail great flavors using plant-based ingredients, but I'm pleased I was successful. And girl, I'm going to need some ideas! I've been trying to get them to eat a little cleaner or cut back on the meat."

"My wife wanted tonight's meal to be plant-based, but I wanted me some ribs," Malachi said, taking a bite of the ribs in his hand. "Maybe someday. Today ain't it. *Sorry*." He took another bite.

I couldn't help the laugh that escaped; Micah and Ella laughed right along with me.

***

We'd all finished eating, and I was helping Ella clean the kitchen. Gabe and Gabby had headed upstairs. After the men helped us bring the food in from the dining room, they talked about catching some of the basketball game.

"You good, sweetheart?" Micah stood close to me as I was preparing the sink for dishes.

Looking up at him, I nodded my head. "Yes baby."

He kissed my cheek softly. "Alright. I'm going to the restroom, and then I'll be in the living room with Mal if you need me."

"Okay."

I started washing the dishes, and in my peripheral, Malachi brought Ella to him and said something in her ear. After she giggled, he kissed her lips for a good while. This was the third time they'd indulged since I'd been here. When they were in the middle of their second lip lock, Micah told me they were excessively affectionate and always had been from the start. I hadn't realized he meant it like this, but I was all for it. I loved that for them and found it incredibly sweet. Once I was comfortable enough, I knew Micah and I would fall in the PDA line. Maybe not to the same degree, though.

"You really don't have to do that Destiney," Ella said as she joined me at the sink. "It's your first time in our home. I'm a terrible host to have you do the dishes."

"Oh, no worries. It's the *least* I can do. Please allow me to help. Besides, I ate so much more than I should have! If I sit down, I'll fall asleep!" We both laughed.

"How about if you wash, I'll dry?" she offered.

"Sure."

"Alright."

"Thanks again," I told Ella. "Everything was delicious." It really was, and I really enjoyed myself. Malachi and Ella had a beautiful home. Though it was grand and expansive, it was cozy and inviting, and they made me feel so welcome.

"My pleasure. I have some cheesecake if you have any room for dessert."

I shook my head rapidly. "As great as that sounds, I am stuffed. But thank you."

"Same. I had too many potatoes." Ella chuckled. "Next time, let's save some room," she said sweetly.

"You've got a deal." I returned.

"So, Destiney. I have to say that you must be someone incredibly special to Micah. He hasn't brought a woman around for a few years."

I couldn't hold back my smile. "Micah is special to me, too."

"I see it all over the both of you. After hearing so much about you, it's great to put a face with the name. You're so sweet and gorgeous. I love your locs."

My smile had grown. "Thank you, Ella."

"Aww! You're blushing! You two are serious. I can see why my brother-in-love is so crazy for you."

"Yeah. I'm feeling like he's it for me."

"I love that. When you know, you know. Things were quick with Chi and me. It was just fifteen months from the day we met to the day we married. We got engaged on our first dating anniversary and married three months later."

"Wow, and so young. That's beautiful."

"Thank you. Can I also say that I look forward to finally having even teams? Girl, Gabby and I are outnumbered." She laughed again, and I laughed too.

I loved her infectious laugh and her low-key personality. Ella was beautiful. Taller than me, I'd say 5'6 or so. Slender with caramel skin, dark brown eyes, and black hair that sat right at her shoulders. It framed her heart-shaped face perfectly. No doubt she's been drinking her water and getting her beauty rest. Or maybe Sis just had some good genes. Her skin was vibrant and clear; in my humble opinion, she didn't need the minimal makeup she wore. Ella was classy, an eloquent speaker, sincerely confident, and kind. From where I sat, Malachi and Ella had something amazing, even all these years later, and I was glad to witness it. Live and in living color.

Gabe and Gabby were the perfect blend right between them. Gabe was physically built, just like Malachi and Micah. Tall and muscular. But he and Gabby had Ella's entire face. Gabby was gorgeous, just like Ella, and had her mom's dimples to match. I loved her natural hair she had in a twist out flowing freely just like her free spirit. Gabby was a knockout already at just twelve years old. But her girly innocence is what gave her charm.

"Hey, let's get together next week while Micah is in Glendale. The three of us ladies. Maybe brunch or something. Would that be cool with you?" Ella asked.

I beamed. "*Absolutely!* I would love to."

I was so excited to get to know Ella and Gabby and get closer. I liked both of them so much already.

eleven

DESTINEY

"Can I get you anything else, sweet darling?" Mr. Walker asked, taking away my empty plate. I love Micah's voice, and Mr. Walker's was quite similar. It was just as deep, with an extra layer of texture. Maybe gravelly is the word. If this were indicative of the way Micah would sound in the future, I could only imagine what pillow talk would do to me.

"I am stuffed, Mr. Walker," I said, shaking my head. "But thank you so very much." I'd just finished a generous piece of peach cobbler. The piece Mr. Walker gave me was so big that it was more like two pieces. I turned to Micah's mother, saying, "Everything was delicious." And man, was it! This woman could cook! Like *really* cook. Micah said his mom was a great cook, but he was being modest. He didn't allude to her being on this gourmet chef level. He mentioned on several occasions that she could bake a delectable dessert. And *oh my*!

Her peach cobbler was quite literally perfection. The peaches were cooked perfectly, and the sweetness was just right. The crust was also perfectly moist and flaky.

Perfection. I now knew precisely why Micah kept his ass in that gym.

"I'm so glad you could join us. You are so very welcome. Really." Mrs. Walker grabbed my hand and squeezed it gently.

"I'd love to help get everything cleaned up. Please." I stood, attempting to help collect some of the remaining dishes from the table.

"Nonsense! The men are on kitchen duty." Mrs. Walker laughed heartily. "I cooked up a storm, and you're our guest of honor." I sat back in my chair as Micah and Mr. Walker cleared dishes and returned the food to the kitchen.

"You heard the lady. Do not touch a thing," Micah said as he kissed me sweetly. It was just at the corner of my mouth. I turned my head in his direction, and he quickly stole another one right from my lips. My face grew warm immediately, but I couldn't hide my smile.

I heard Micah's light titter as he scurried back toward the kitchen with his hands full. Before disappearing around the corner, he looked back, giving me a mischievous grin.

He didn't need to steal it. I'd give him as many kisses as he wanted, anytime he wanted them.

But Micah knew me well and knew I'd be hesitant about kissing him in front of his parents.

And I was.

I felt a little shy, especially now, with his mother sitting across from me. It was just a little kiss, but... I was feeling bashful anyway, looking everywhere but at her, even though we were the only two people in the room. I couldn't even look up at her, let alone make eye contact. It was a fact that I was *absolutely* the only one making this a big deal.

I really should be used to this by now.

Unsurprisingly, the seasoned pair of Walkers was just as affectionate as the others.

And these Walker men looked a lot like their father. *Very* similar. Chips off the old block. Apples that didn't fall far.

Mr. Walker is a silver fox if I've ever seen one. He was bald too with a neat salt-and-pepper beard. Mostly salt. Micah's beard was fuller. Mr. Walker was about a shade darker than the brothers. Micah had him by a few inches. I'd say he was six foot even. Broad. Strapping. Looking great in his early sixties.

But anyway, this affection stuff was a thing around here. Naturally, *Mr. Malcom Walker* had his way of showing it. He was still sniffing behind his wife as if they were thirty years younger, least of all married more than thirty years. It was so damn sweet the way he kept Mrs. Walker's hand in his.

Multiple times this evening, I observed him bringing his wife's hand to his lips to kiss. He used gracious words. He spoke kindly to her, complimenting how delicious everything was, almost as if he was tasting her food for the first time. He expressed extreme gratitude for the lovely meal she'd prepared.

Lovely it was. An award-winning presentation with fine China to match.

These Walker men were the type who took great care of their women, showering them with love and affection. It was evident. Micah had been taking such great care of me, emotionally and physically. I saw the way Malachi handled Ella and now saw the way his father catered to his mother.

And as a side note, I love how Micah talks to his mother. The softness he shows her, the adoration he shows her, the affectionate way he speaks with her—all of this directly translates to how he handles me.

I could see precisely where the Walker brothers got all this from. They truly learned from the best.

Conversely, I thought of my upbringing. Dad did a great job providing for Daijah and me. In theory, he was an excellent example of what a provider and protector looked like from a father-daughter perspective. But since we lost Mom when Daijah and I were so young, and Daddy didn't date, we didn't have a firsthand example of him catering to a woman in this way.

This was a crash course if I've ever seen one.

"Micah tells me you enjoy a cup of tea," Mrs. Walker said, pulling me from my thoughts. I looked up to find her smiling warmly at me, and I was grateful for the distraction.

I gave her a smile of my own. "I sure do."

"How about we have a cup and chat while they finish up in there?"

"I would love to."

"Great. Head into the living room. I'll be right behind you, honey."

"Yes ma'am," I returned, doing just as I was told. I went to the next room and sat on the comfy sofa. Micah's parents still lived in his childhood home, and there was something so special about that. I loved their cozy house. It wasn't vast or extravagant. But his parents' house reminded me of my childhood home. It was inviting, with a nostalgic charm about it. I knew it was full of great memories, which gave me such a warm feeling. Their living room was modest, with lots of family pictures, new and old.

The focal point for me was the expansive bookshelf. Micah told me his mom was an avid reader, but this was beyond anything I had imagined.

This was something that could have come straight from Pinterest. The entire wall was covered in what had to be hundreds of books, with shelves from floor to ceiling. My eyes roamed row after row. I loved everything I saw, and many titles stood out to me. What was most intriguing were the classic urban fiction titles we all saw an aunt or older cousin reading. *Waiting to Exhale, God don't like Ugly, The Coldest Winter Ever, Milk in my Coffee*. Then I saw historical fiction titles like, *The Color Purple, Beloved, The*

Street, Their Eyes were watching God, I know why the Caged Bird Sings. Biographies, memoirs.

I saw various titles by Langston Hughes, James Baldwin, Eric Jerome Dickey, Carl Webber, E. Lynn Harris, Octavia Butler, Toni Morrison, and Kimberla Lawson Roby, among many others. I even peeped a few Chicken Soup for the Soul titles—I haven't seen a Chicken Soup for the Soul book in years.

"Here we are love." I turned toward Mrs. Walker's voice as she entered the living room with a tray carrying two cups of tea. She sat them gently on the coffee table in front of us. "I added a little sugar, but please tell me if you need more."

"I'm sure it's perfect. Thank you, Mrs. Walker." I pulled my saucer closer to me, inhaling the aroma. "Green tea and... lemon. Yum. This will be great."

Mrs. Walker's eyes grew wide with high eyebrows. "Wow! You haven't even taken a sip. That's impressive."

I shrugged lightly, chuckling. "Those notes stand out. Some tea blends are so complicated that I may only be able to pick out one layer. If that. My father is the *best* at it. He's a *tea enthusiast extraordinaire.* I get my love of tea from him." I smiled wide. "I've learned so much from him."

She nodded. "So I've heard. He seems to be a great man. Raising you so well... and your sister. Your mom would be so proud of the beautiful woman you have grown into."

I smiled. "Thank you. I miss her a lot these days. Especially..." I halted my words, unsure of how much I wanted to share. Also attempting to curb my emotions. I had been such a ball of feelings lately, crying at the drop of a hat. I didn't want to do that right now. That would be embarrassing. I looked across at Mrs. Walker, who was looking at me expectantly, her warm smile reassuring me to continue. Not wanting to leave her hanging, I said, "Just with everything going on, I guess," Shrugging again.

"Like falling in love."

I tried to keep my smile at bay, but it was useless. I cracked an enormous grin that spread across my entire face within seconds. She called it. And it wasn't a question.

Mrs. Walker laughed heartily, then took a sip of her tea. "My goodness. Look at you! That smile is all I needed to see."

I looked away again, embarrassed as usual, and Mrs. Walker continued, "I know the feeling, and it's nothing to be shy about. These Walker men are truly a rare breed." She paused momentarily. Then, "Glad you snagged yourself one," she winked at me, and my heart squeezed, "My Micah bear loves you, Destiney. And I love you for him, honey."

Beaming, I declared, "I love him too. So much. I don't even know when it happened, but it was easy to do. He's so easy to love," I sighed. "Micah is amazing. I've never been in love before. But this feeling is strong and all I can think about." By the way, that *Micah Bear* nickname was absolutely adorable.

She nodded, laughing lightly, "You're a woman in love. It's not something easily explained." She took another sip, and I took one too. It was a great cup. Herbal teas were typically my first choice, made from dried herbs, spices, flowers, or fruits. *But you could never go wrong with Green.* Best of all, green tea is so good for you. "Listen...you've done a beautiful something with my son's heart. I immediately noticed the change in Micah. In the best way. I'm over the moon for both of you. It really is a beautiful thing." She lifted her teacup. "Let's toast to new love."

"To new love!" I gently tapped my cup with hers, took a generous sip afterward, and thanked God for sending me my sweet Micah for the millionth time.

***

"So."

I peered to my left, meeting Micah's awaiting gaze. He wore the cutest smirk, so I gave him a lazy grin. We were headed to my house so he could drop me off. Unfortunately, I didn't want our time to end, but I needed to go home. It was getting late, and I had to be at the site in Roseville bright and early. We were about halfway finished, but the projections were concerning, so the plan was to make up some time. The crew would need to be on-site for an extended schedule for the next three days minimum. When the Artistic Director informed us that we were at risk of falling behind, I wasn't even surprised.

Becky's ass was to blame.

I'd had the most amazing time with my love and his adorable parents the past few hours. Mrs. Josette Walker is *gorgeous*, first of all. She had a classic beauty. Something akin to Claire Huxtable. Warm brown skin and black hair with scattered grey strands. Very few wrinkles. The years had been kind to her; clearly, she had been loved well.

It's a fact that well-loved women show up differently.

Mr. Walker called her his bride when speaking *of her*. When he was talking *to her*, he called her Joey. That was so cute that I could hardly stand it.

Mrs. Walker and I spent time chatting and getting better acquainted, and by the time we left, my heart was so full.

I wasn't even sure how I could say this so soon, but I really did adore that woman. I loved her kindness. I loved her hospitality. But her heart... it was so pure and open and genuine. I felt an outpouring of love and a gravitation towards her that seemed to come naturally. And somehow, simultaneously, it was as if she cared just as much about me, too.

Maybe it was maternal. I hadn't had my mother in the physical for close to twenty years. Maybe Mrs. Walker filled a void I didn't realize I had.

I couldn't call it... but whatever it was, it further confirmed that Micah was my one.

We continued cruising, and a tiny grin settled on my face, thinking back to the pinnacle of the night. Once the men finished in the kitchen, they joined Mrs. Walker and me in the living room, and the four of us laughed over the cutest baby pictures of Micah. I couldn't help myself as I cracked up at photo after photo. Micah was a good sport about it. Then there was one that had me so hysterical that I was laughing until my sides hurt.

Micah had to be about eleven or so and long and lanky with thick glasses and braces. He seriously looked like Urkel's twin! The only thing missing were suspenders.

"Mommy! You trying to scare her away or some-thing?"

Mr. Walker and I were in a laughing fit.

"Oh, hush Micah bear. She already loves you! No way a few old pictures will change that." Mrs. Walker was right. I loved me some him. But it was still funny. Micah gave me a smirk as I carried on laughing.

"I got something for you. I'll be having a talk with Mr. Evans; you already informed me you had an awkward phase," Micah said playfully.

"You wouldn't!" I was still laughing. *"Don't be like that baby."*

Mrs. Walker proudly showed me pictures from precious moments over the years. It was the sweetest thing seeing Micah and his brother Malachi when they were small. They were *adorable* little boys, beaming proudly at spelling bees, honor roll assemblies, baseball games, Christmas plays at school and Easter Sunday plays at the church. The Walkers were such proud parents. Rightfully so. They did a phenomenal job raising their sons, who now lead successful lives of their own.

Anyway, as we rode in silence, I thought about something else: I realized precisely why it was so easy falling for Micah. He was so much like his mother, and he was *incredibly* close to her. Apart from that, he was a lot like his father, and they had a great relationship as well. I loved seeing their dynamic. Micah had the absolute best of them both and had grown into this incredibly amazing man. A man who somehow, some way, for some earthly reason, chose to love me. That shit was bananas.

"Destiney baby."

"Hmm." I gave a languid moan with slow, fluttering eyelids.

Micah released a boisterous chuckle, "Look at you. Seconds away from a food coma." He drew out his laugh.

"Ain't my fault your mom kept stuffing me with her food. How could I say no to her. And it was *soooo gooood Micah*. Oh. My. Goshhhh." My eyes are shut now. The *itis* kicked in a long time ago.

Of course, it was no help that I was lounging comfortably in the plush passenger seat of Micah's Mercedes Benz. Being rocked to sleep damn near by the smooth ride. The temperature just right. Soft R&B whispering in the background. Micah called it. My ass was ready to knock out.

"Indeed. Mommy loves to cook. She's the best."

My response wasn't momentary, I was sleepy. "And... that peach cobbler...like...what the hell...never have I ever." I'd keep talking to Micah, we were less than twenty minutes from my house. Too short of a drive to sleep. We passed Micah's home on the way out. Mr. and Mrs. Walker lived halfway between Micah and Malachi's house, and I loved that they all lived near each other. "I loooove your mom." I really did. "She's soooo amazing." She really was.

"That she is. And she is already so fond of you baby. I believe she was before she officially met you."

"Yeah?"

"Indeed. Gabby girl informed her you had been over to meet them, sharing with her how much she enjoyed your company. So, Mommy was patiently waiting her turn."

"Aww. I'm glad it finally happened."

"It's a fair statement to surmise Daddy loves you too," Micah paused for a beat. Then, "He gave you a corner from the peach cobbler. In my family, the corners are *everyone's* favorite. You've already won him over."

A closed mouth smile slowly made its way across my face; my eyes still shut, "Aww. That makes me feel good… your dad is so awesome… and I love the corners too," After a brief pause, I said, "Theres only four corners. If everyone likes them how does that work out?"

"We be scrapping for them corners."

"Wow." My chuckle was low but vibrated deep in my belly.

"You still with me love?" Micah asked after we rode in silence for a little bit, lulled by Jodeci's smooth harmonies. The volume was so low I had to listen intently to make out the lyrics. "Come and talk to me." The epitome of a 90's slow jam classic. Micah reached over the console to take my hand in his.

"Yes baby," I absently rubbed my fingers with his. My eyes were still closed. I settled a little lower into the seat.

"I'm so glad they were able to meet you tonight. Finally, I knew they would adore you. Just like I do."

"I loved meeting them, too. They are wonderful. Really wonderful. You are blessed Micah."

"Thank you love. Indeed."

We cruised in comfortable silence. "Truth moment." Sitting up, I opened my eyes, glancing around. We were passing the Florin Road exit, less than ten minutes away from my house. I wanted to share something I had been harboring for the past few hours.

"Please do."

"I'm intimidated."

"Intimidated," Micah parroted moving his hand to my inner thigh rubbing softly. "Really?"

I waited for a beat, "Not in the way you're thinking."

"How do you mean?"

"It's trivial."

"Try me."

"Like. Okay…Your mom can cook. *Cook.* Ella can cook. Even Gabby can do a little something, something."

Micah remained silent as we cruised down the freeway.

"Micah," I called peering to my left to find him focused straight ahead.

"Yeah baby?"

"Oh my gosh. You heard me, right?"

"Yeah. Just waiting for the punchline."

"Micah." I tittered lightly, shaking my head. "You can be so silly sometimes. There isn't one."

He released that silly chuckle of his, then, "Okay. So…" He cleared his throat as he continued gently rubbing back and forth from my lower to upper thigh. What he was really doing was trying to calm my nerves. He was so aware, and he knew me so well. I didn't have to tell him. He likely realized I had been carrying this for a while.

Since Micah was such a sensitive being, he was hyper-aware of my feelings and constantly checking in on my mental. He had a way of handling me whenever I was in my head about something. I appreciated this so much and I loved him even more for it.

Truth be told, I loved everything he did to me and for me. Period.

The way he handled me in general.

In the meantime, I was starting to get excited because he was inching even closer to my pussy. I loved Micah's massive hands, and let me say, *his hands could cover a lot of real estate.* Micah was a man's man, with manly hands and meaty fingers. Yet somehow, he was always gentle whenever his hands were on me.

"I'm glad you told me baby." He pulled me from my thoughts with his comforting tone, "That isn't trivial. I get it, and I understand. I mean, Mommy and Ella throw it down." I looked over at him to find him already looking at me. After a second, he looked forward at the open freeway ahead. "So, here's the thing; I love my sis, but Ella couldn't cook like she can now when Mal first started bringing her around." My eyes grew wide, and my lips parted. "For real. After they graduated college and moved back, Mommy taught her. Ella is dope though because everything Mommy taught her; Ella made her own with a personal spin. Mommy can teach you. She wouldn't mind at all. It honestly comes with the territory. Spend some time with Mommy, you'll learn. Besides… I plan on keeping you around so… you'll be just fine." He captured my hand and brought it to his lips kissing it softly. He littered wet kisses all over my hand. "Also." Micah paused, waiting for me to look in his direction. Then, "Cook for me. All the time. I'll eat whatever you fix me. The more you cook the better you'll get. Just keep doing it baby. It's the best way to be great at something. Cooking is an art after all." He winked at me, and it was the most adorable thing.

Wow.

"That sound like a plan?" I nodded at a loss for words. "Everything good now?" He pressed showing that grin I loved. I nodded again, still unsure of what to say. Micah literally made me feel a hundred times better. I was anxious as hell, and Micah did what he did best.

Spoke life into me.

An issue that seemed so big in my world was really no biggie at all once he gave me his take on it.

That was Micah. Always calm. Sensible. Levelheaded.

He had a gift. Micah could seriously talk anyone off a ledge. Maybe his emotional balance will rub off on me at some point.

"You sure she wouldn't mind?" I asked finally. "I don't want to impose or barge my way…"

"Oh, she would enjoy that! Cooking and teaching are her happy places. And Mommy is *crazy* about you."

"Is she?" I smiled again. I adored Mrs. Walker. I really, really did. She was a dream, and I was convinced there was no one else in the world quite like her. It was no wonder Micah was so close to her. Not in a momma's boy kind of way either. He adores her. And I loved that.

"Yeah baby. She loves you so much already. You'll see more of her now that you've met. Don't be surprised if she asks to see you. *Without me.*" We both cracked up at that.

"That's so sweet."

"But who wouldn't love you? *My woman is amazing.* You should meet her. No doubt in my mind you'd fuck with her too."

Cracking up, I said, "You're something else." I squeezed his very toned left bicep.

"But you love me."

"That I do. With my whole heart Micah."

"Yeah? The *whole* thing?"

"The entire thing." I declared.

"I love you too Destiney baby."

We were sitting in front of my house now, turned in our seats completely facing one another.

"And likewise. You have my heart. I love you. *So.* My sweet Destiney baby. I'll give you whatever you need. Anything you want."

Damn.

Meanwhile he was still rubbing my thigh, and my panties were soaked. As usual. I changed panties multiple times a day now that we were hanging out.

"I have everything I need baby. You take good care of me."

"You already have gas for the week? I need to take your car around to fill her up?"

"Already filled up. I'm all set." I did not enjoy getting gas on a Monday morning with all the other procrastinators. Micah either and thanks to him, I acquired a habit of getting gas for the week before the weekend was out.

"Alright." Micah hadn't stopped rubbing my thigh. His hand was warm. They were always warm, and it felt so good. He'd been venturing higher, and things had already begun to wake up down there. I really needed to get in this bed, but suddenly, I wasn't so tired anymore. Before I could get lost in the moment any further, Micah got out of the car. I reached behind me to grab my purse as he walked around to my side. Opening my door, he was gentle as he pulled me to him, closing the car door behind me. Micah gracefully leaned me against his car and pressed his lips to mine as we quietly shared a few sweet kisses. Each kiss lasting longer than the one before. I wrapped my arms around him, and his arms came around me deepening our connection. He fed me his tongue and we hungrily kissed each other, sensual and unhurried. We kissed for a good while.

"Get inside baby." Micah managed to whisper, breaking our kiss for probably half a millisecond. His voice had fallen to that deeper register it would go to whenever things were hot and heavy between us. I fucking loved that shit. He told me to go inside, but he still hadn't let me go. Not that I wanted him to. I could feel his hardness as he pressed into me. My panties were already done for. We kept kissing.

"I don't like to be away from you baby." I pretty much whined into his mouth.

"You don't ever have to be away from me."

We were still kissing.

"Mmm...What do you propose?"

After several long seconds, "...I'm staying here tonight."

I shook my head gently but never disconnected our lips. Once I eventually broke away, I looked up at him. He met my gaze with low lids. I knew mine were just as low. "Baby. I have an early day that will be just as long tomorrow. If you stay here, we both know I won't be going to sleep anytime soon."

He released a boisterous laugh. "That so?" When he calmed down, "Tell me when I can see you again."

"When we break for lunch, I'll be able to chill with you. If you can get away, you're welcome on site."

Micah nodded. "Bet. Come by tomorrow evening beauty. I need you back in my arms expeditiously. Remember, my flight is late Tuesday morning."

I nodded, smiling. "I'd love to."

He nodded too. "Indeed." He kissed my forehead, lingered there, and then moved aside, leading me up the steps to my front door.

"About to hop in the shower, but text me when you get home?"

"Baby." Micah hung his head. "You just gave me a visual. Do not tell me you're getting in the shower if you want me to leave."

I laughed. "I'm sorry baby." We shared another sweet kiss, no tongue, which was a better idea.

If Micah had gotten started, then I certainly would have gotten started, and we would have needed to keep it going.

"I'll let you know when I get home, my love." He murmured against my lips.

"Drive safe baby."

I watched him drive off before I closed the door behind me.

I was *this* close to asking him to stay overnight with me. I don't know about Micah, but I wanted to go all the way. *Been* wanted to. For a while now. In true Micah fashion, he's been waiting on me, so I decided to bring this up for discussion when he returned from Glendale.

***

Mrs. Walker was so wonderful. Just the sweetest.

She joined Ella, Gabby, and me for brunch at Friends with Benedicts in Folsom. Folsom was a town about thirty minutes east of us. Ella picked me up, and the four of us rode out together.

I'd never been, and Ella highly recommended the place. It certainly lived up to the hype. I couldn't wait to take India and Daijah there. And maybe I was getting ahead of myself, but I couldn't wait to introduce them all.

Anyway, we had such a great time. We ate on the patio, enjoying the lovely early fall weather. Fall is my absolute favorite.

The food was phenomenal. We talked and got better acquainted. We drank mimosas and laughed until we cried.

And as it would turn out, Micah was right.

The very next week, Mrs. Walker asked me back, wanting to make plans for the following weekend.

While Micah was in Glendale, he sent me a screenshot of the exchange between him and her. It was the cutest thing.

Mommy Bear: Bring me my sweet girl next Saturday I'll need her help preparing Sunday dinner

Sure. What time would you like her?

Mommy Bear: About four

Indeed

Mommy Bear: Find something to occupy your time. She'll be busy with her Mommy in love, and we have lots to do

Do not go trying to steal my wife Mommy

Mommy Bear: Too late. I have decided I am keeping her

It was so funny too because right after the screen shot, Micah texted me saying, *Told you. I just knew you'd get invited without me*

I laughed too. Then smiled from ear to ear.

I missed the hell out of Micah while he was in Glendale and spending time with the ladies that meant so much to him helped me feel better.

I couldn't wait for my man to get home though.

twelve

MICAH

"I have good news and bad news."

As expected, Ellington's brows furrowed, then rose in alarm. I couldn't help myself and chuckled blowing my cover. "Don't worry, your job is safe."

I arrived in Glendale earlier this afternoon and I was onsite in our corporate office working on a few things before I had to get to some meetings. I decided to call Ellington in for a quick zoom meeting to give him an update. I figured this news would be best delivered in person, but now that it was officially official, I couldn't contain myself, deciding to tell him immediately.

A look of relief washed over Ellington's expression. He chuckled too. "Well, I'll take the bad news first boss. Then there's still something to look forward to."

"Fair enough." I nodded, chuckling. "The bad news is you are no longer reporting to me effective Monday."

"Oh. Uh… you moving on?"

"I am not. But you are."

His brows were back at his hairline. "How's that?"

"I'd like to offer you the System Manager of Program Development position, and you'll report directly to Charlie Simpson, the System Program Director." Ellington's eyes grew in surprise. "If you accept, the position will include a sixteen percent salary increase and a twenty-thousand-dollar sign-on bonus. You can counter. But I insured you received a generous increase with room to grow in the position."

His eyes had somehow grown even bigger.

"Wow! This is... I mean... I don't know what to say boss." He put his hands on his head. "I had no idea there was even an opening for that position. Actually," He laughed again, "I've never heard of that position."

"Well, there wasn't one. Not initially, anyway. I've been talking to our CEO about expanding the enterprise, and we will need a few more feet on the ground to make that happen. We discussed creating a few additional roles and responsibilities, which is how this position came about. When Larry asked if I had anyone in mind, I recommended you immediately. I know you'll be instrumental in moving us forward. You've already shown yourself worthy."

"Wow. I'm so thankful you mentioned me. I... I'm so appreciative of everything."

"It was all you and your hard work. It was an easy decision. You're my first choice. So, I take it you'll accept?"

He laughed, "Yes, I will!"

"I'm so pleased. Well, enjoy the rest of your week. I'm still available if you need anything while I'm in Glendale. I'll be back at the office on Monday, and we'll get you transitioned."

"*Great!* Boss, I sure wish I could shake your hand. Hug you, something. Thank you doesn't seem good enough."

"It's plenty. You're very welcome, E. Keep up the great work."

"Yes sir. Wait, What's the good news?"

"We'll be able to get together outside of work since I'm no longer your direct superior. You and the wife can come by and chill with my fiancé and me.

She'd love to meet your wife." Ellington really was like a younger brother. I'd told Destiney about Ellington. I told E about her, too. They'd even invited us to his daughter's first birthday party, but I couldn't accept it. Fraternization. All that. I didn't want to put either of our careers in jeopardy.

He smiled wide. *"Fiancé?"*

I laughed. "Almost. She's pretty special, and that's the plan."

***

After meeting with Ellington, I glanced at the clock. I had another half hour before I needed to head down the hall to the conference room for a meeting. That meeting would take us through to lunch. After that, we had a presentation and a couple of fireside chats, which would take us through the end of day one.

When I arrived in Glendale late this morning, I checked into my hotel and settled in just a bit before heading to the office.

I checked my email and learned I'll have to go to Chicago in early November. Our headquarters were in Chicago. I'd be there for eight days. They rotate locations, and last year, that trip was held at the corporate office in San Francisco.

I sighed.

San Francisco would have been *so much better*.

In my current role, I have to travel semi-frequently for work. At one point, none of that bothered me *too* much. I don't *love* sleeping in hotels. Or eating take-out for every meal. But it wasn't *all* that bad.
Back when I only had to think about myself. Literally. No plants to water. No pets to feed.

Now that I have Destiney, I immediately thought about having to be away from her again.

And I didn't like it.

So, I'd see if Destiney can join me on that trip since I have the exact dates.

I wanted her with me.

I smiled, thinking back on our earlier conversation while I was still at the hotel.

Just like clockwork, she called me on Facetime. I was expecting her to call me too.

"Hey Beautiful."

"Micah…" Her brilliant eyes were wide. Her voice cautionary.

"Yeah?"

"There's a ring on my finger." She held her hand up, and I saw the gold band flashing on her dainty finger.

"Yes. There is." I told her confidently.

"Pretty sure it wasn't there when I went to sleep…"

"I put it there. Before I left you this morning."

Destiney spent the night with me. I had to get to the airport early before she had to get up. So last night, I gave her a key and told her she could leave when she was ready.

Anyway, this morning, I got up and took a quick shower. After I was dressed, I got everything downstairs and in the trunk. I came back up a final time to kiss my sleeping beauty and then slipped a thin gold band on her left ring finger. She never woke up. Hardly stirred even.

*"It's not one of **those**. That's coming though. That's a placeholder. Like a pre-engagement ring. Since I have to be away from you, I need to mark my territory."*

*Clarity settled over her. "Micah. My goodness. You just..." She chuckled, shaking her head. "You just don't cease to amaze me." She smiled so wide it reached her pretty eyes. "It's **so** cute. I love it. Thank you."*

"You're welcome. It's a classic band for a classic beauty. And you can wear it even when you're working. It won't interfere. I just want something there." It was no biggie. The ring was fairly inexpensive. Fourteen karat gold. A thin band, perfect for her petite finger. Durable and would serve its purpose.

I was serious. I needed people to know my beauty was spoken for.

"Micah, it's perfect. It's exactly what I would have chosen for myself."

Destiney told me that due to the nature of their work, many people in the art space had alternative-style wedding rings. Some had silicone or ceramic rings. Some had tattooed rings. Some didn't wear anything on their finger; instead, they wore their ring on a chain hanging around their neck.

I looked around, researching, and decided this was perfect for my baby.

There isn't much classier than a simple gold wedding band. Only a select group of women can pull it off. It takes a level of class, confidence and self-assurance.

I certainly planned to purchase a beautiful ring for her.

In the very near future. Something she could wear now and then, on special occasions at least. When she wouldn't be handling chemicals and paints.

"I want to give you everything baby. Every little thing your heart desires." I told her. I knew she probably needed to hang up and get ready to head to work.

"Aww. You're all I need baby." She said. Destiney was reasonable. She didn't ask for much at all. But I was going to keep reminding her. I was here to make all her dreams come true.

Anything in my control. Anything in my power.

"You're all I need too baby. But don't you forget what I said love. Whatever you want is yours. And I want forever with you." I've told her that many times.

"I know baby. I love you, Micah. So much. I want forever with you too. My heart is yours, and I'm not going anywhere."

"I love you, beautiful Destiney." After a beat, "Oh sweetheart, I wish I was with you right now."

"Me too baby."

"I'll be back in your arms in three days," I told her.

"Can't wait baby."

After a beat, "I want to take my beauty out when I return Friday. Get some food and a drink or two. Can you swing that?"

"Yes, I can." She said sweetly.

"Indeed."

"Where are we going baby?"

"Hmm. It's going to be another lovely fall evening. Revival on J. That cool?"

"Oooh, you fancy. Hell yeah!"

We laughed.

"Well, I'll let you go beautiful. I'll text you later, but we'll talk this afternoon alright."

She nodded. "I love you, Micah."

"I love you, Destiney baby."

I was so in love with her. I missed her so much and had just been with her several hours before.

Many women fail to realize that if a man loved a woman, *truly* loved her, and wanted to do right by her, there is almost *nothing* he wouldn't do for her.

Especially if he was trying to wife her.

Jodeci said it best, "*whatever you want, whatever you need, my heart belongs to you. Whatever you need... there's nothing I won't do...*"

That was my current situation. And I didn't give a fuck.

***

"Somewhere along the way, folks started to lose sight of something." Malachi had my undivided attention. He sat silently for a few more beats. Then, "You want me to tell you what it is?" he asked me.

"Yeah!" I shot back.

He chuckled.

"I was just pausing for effect."

I shook my head and ran my hand down my face.

Mal and I were on the phone, chopping it up. After a long day, I'd finally returned to the room and showered. I had some dinner, and I spoke with Destiney briefly. She was back at her place, though I told her she was welcome to stay at mine. *Ours*. I didn't need to be there for her to stay there. I trusted her. But Destiney said India needed to get away from home, so she returned that way India could spend the next day or so with her. I'd had the chance to meet India, and she seemed cool. She reminded me a lot of Destiney, as a matter of fact.

"Well?" My voice was slightly annoyed.

"You only have to get it right one time," Malachi said. "It's really that simple. Ella is my forever, and I handle her as such. I took vows. Cultivating our friendship, prioritizing our relationship, and keeping our marriage at the forefront of my mind. I consider how everything I do will affect her and our children. The grass is green where you water it. It should take the pressure off. You found your wife, marry her. When you do, do *everything* you can to show up for each other daily."

"I see. You're making sense, brother." I replied. I understood the revelation. I'd seen it with Malachi, Ella, my parents, grandparents, even colleagues.

"And one more thing, baby brother. For now, anyway."

"What's that?" I asked.

"In my humble opinion, married sex is the best sex."

I said nothing as I regarded his statement. "You for real?" I lightly chuckled even though this conversation was not meant to be a humorous one. I always valued the marital advice Malachi shared with me. I was confident he wouldn't steer me wrong, and he was so open and generous with me. I didn't take it for granted.

"Nothing better," he continued, "Now, two types of people would argue with me. For the record, I don't give a fuck, and I'm saying it with my chest. But for the sake of this conversation, I'll tell you *exactly* who they are; a single person out here fucking 'round to fill some void and a married person who isn't prioritizing the shit that matters."

"I see." Just like before, he stunned me with revelations that weren't deep or complicated.

These sentiments had somehow been lost among so many people, and the institution of marriage suffered in the process. Everyone wasn't interested in marriage. I understood that. But *I* certainly was. Destiney was too, and she was the woman I wanted. Considering that, I regarded Mal's words.

"You think you'll get that good shit right now, *marry her* and see what I'm talking about. It's like fine wine. The intimacy deepens because you share it with your better half, the person with whom you experience everything. *Each time* you come together intimately you are aiming to please one another." He paused, "Sex is something the hookup culture has ruined. You don't even have to make it about religion. But once you know, you know."

We shot the shit a bit longer. Later, while I waited for Destiney to call me, I lay on my back, the TV watching me.

Before we hung up, I ended up telling Malachi we weren't quite giving each other the good shit.

But we were damn close.

"How's your wife doing anyway?"

"She's good. Missing her like crazy out here. By the way, we're still holding out."

"Good for you, baby brother. No need to rush. I'm getting enough for us both."

"Mal really?" He thought that shit was so damn funny. *"You play way too much man." Mal was still rolling. "Anyway, the tension between us is intense. Been messing around. May not be able to hold out much longer."*

*"No doubt. Listen man, if you can imagine... the moment will be **that** much sweeter. This shit is a marathon. A slow burn. Enjoy the ride and the time you're spending with your wife. Wait for the right moment. You'll know when it's time."*

I smiled at his term of endearment. Whenever Malachi spoke *of* Destiney, he referred to her as my wife. When he was talking *to* Destiney, he called her baby sis.

I didn't have to ask him why because I already knew.

My brother was manifesting that shit.

Malachi was so satisfied and fulfilled in his marriage that he wanted anyone who desired marriage to experience it.

Malachi was a *very married man* and proud of it. He promoted married life and believed in the infinite opportunities that *we could all get some*. Even for a seemingly lost ass cause like Raymond.

I thought over everything Mal said, and I couldn't agree more.

I felt like the time was near. Very near. And there was no doubt in my mind that it would be beautiful. I love Destiney *so much*. Madly. And loving her as much as I do would absolutely translate when we finally do.

I could imagine that sex within covenant is nothing short of amazing.

It seems there is something beautiful about being intimate with someone and knowing they will never give it to anyone else. To me.

Knowing they'll stay with you because they're committed to you.

Knowing they will come to you and no one else whenever they have the desire to be sexually fulfilled.

They want *you* to satisfy *all* their needs. They know you. They honor you. They want to please you, and you get to try again. And again, and again. And likewise. They get the same from you.

I wanted that. With Destiney. I can learn what she likes and how I can please her. She can learn from me.

I planned to make it abundantly clear to Destiney that should we take this next step, *no one* else can have her. Once I've had her, I don't want another man to have her ever again.

thirteen

DESTINEY

Fall was in full swing.

It was still relatively warm, which was typical for Sacramento. Fall temperatures didn't cool down completely until later in the fall season most of the time. Some fall days would still be in the upper eighties.

Aesthetically, there was no question. The leaves had turned. Pumpkin-spiced flavored cereal was back on the shelves. That was always the most telling. I absolutely love Pumpkin-spice Cheerios. And kids were back to school.

I wrapped up the project in Roseville. *Thank God.* It would be quite a while before I agreed to do something else like that.

I signed contracts for two shopping plazas in West Sacramento. I was excited because I hadn't done window lettering in a while.

Today, I worked at a cute coffee shop doing window art. They also had a chalk wall with their menu and prices, where I drew some fun fall designs. Leaves, acorns, squirrels, coffee mugs, teapots, and so on. It turned out adorable, I dare say.

The owners were a thirty-something earthy black couple who moved here from Philly. They had a great vibe and were a joy to work with. They'd only been in business for two years, but this was clearly their passion. They were vegan and used natural ingredients, serving vegan and non-vegan options.

I told them I was vegetarian, but I respect vegans tremendously. I don't think I could be one. I didn't tell them, but I love *real* cheese and *real* ice cream too much to be vegan.

Anyway, they were so kind to me. Though they were a coffee shop, they had an impressive selection of teas. Of course, once I learned that, we talked for a while. About tea and life in general. A generous offer was extended to me for as many lattes as I wanted while I worked. I didn't go too far with that. Before I was done for the day, I gave the wife of the pair my phone number. They were expecting their first baby in early January, and she wanted to get something painted in their nursery. It would be my pleasure to work with them again.

And I absolutely love cute coffee shops.

I always dreamed that I owned a bookstore with a coffee shop in another lifetime. Anything's possible. My next stop in the plaza was a consignment shop a few doors down, and I'd be there bright and early tomorrow.

Speaking of January, that will be a busy month. Daijah set a date. She and Julian would be married on the third Saturday in January. She didn't want anything extravagant, just a simple winter wedding. That seems so romantic. Roni and Vic will be her bridesmaids, and I'll be her maid of honor.

Soon, we'll be planning her big day. I was so excited for her.

Micah's birthday was also in January, and he'll be turning thirty-five. Malachi's is in February, and he'll be thirty-six. Micah told me that since they're eleven months apart, they are the same age for exactly twenty-four days, and during that time, they call each other "twin." Once Malachi has his birthday, they go back to calling each other brother. That was so cute. And I needed to think about what I would do for my man's birthday. He does so much for me.

When Micah got home about two weeks ago, I was so happy. I missed him so much. You would have thought he was gone much longer than four days.

I was spoiled. I knew that. And I was so attached to him. Seeing Micah as much as I had, then not being able to see him at all, was like ripping the ground from under me.

When he came home, we went to Revival in Downtown Sacramento.

Revival was a rooftop bar on the third-floor pool deck of an upscale hotel. Steps away from the Sacramento Kings arena. The ambiance is beautiful.

It was dark out, so the pool was illuminated. The lights gave a chill vibe. The Downtown Sacramento skyline made for the perfect backdrop. The decor was *lovely*. There was an expansive patio with indoor and outdoor seating options. A DJ too.

Anyway, Micah and I hung out for a couple of hours. Enjoying each other. It was so chill. We ordered a drink and some fries while we waited for our food. And the food was so good.

Anyway, this was the first time we'd had fries together, and it was so funny because Micah was teasing me about how I was eating my fries even though *he* was the one doing it all wrong.

Micah covered his basket of fries generously with ketchup. I made a face, and when he capped the ketchup, he caught my eyes as he leaned over to put it back.

I'll admit I had an expression that was part grimace and part disgust. He laughed, likely because he'd never seen that expression before.

I am incredibly expressive. Once, Micah told me I was one of the most expressive people he knew. But this one was new to him, I'm sure.

He studied me briefly, and I pretended not to notice. Then he looked down at his fries and then looked back up again.

*Finally, Micah said, "Oh, I get it. You're a dipper." He cracked up. "Good thing we aren't sharing these. **I am not** a dipper."*

"Clearly." I picked up the ketchup bottle, then moved one of the saucers on our table and squirted a small amount of ketchup neatly into the corner of the plate. I wasn't paying him any mind as I grabbed a fry, dipped it,

and took a bite. Then another. After eating a few more the same way, I finally looked up and caught **him** staring.

"What?" I asked mid-chew.

Micah shook his head. "You are the neatest French fry eater I have ever seen."

"Neat?" My brows were knitted.

Micah chuckled lightly. "Very neat."

"Why? Because I didn't squeeze half the ketchup bottle all over them?" I asked pointedly. "That is a lot of ketchup," I said. "More ketchup than fries." I made a face.

Micah guffawed at that. "It's not **that** much. Come on." He grabbed one, shoving it into his mouth. After another, he said, "ketchup is **made** for fries. Like peanut butter was made for jelly."

I shook my head. "Not that much. You ruined them. They're probably soggy now. Eww."

"They're perfect like this."

I shook my head again. "No way."

Micah continued eating his fries and said, "You're doing it all wrong anyway."

"What are you talking about?"

"The way you're dipping them. You can't get any ketchup on there doing it like that. It should be more like a scoop. And you only dip each fry once? What about the long ones?"

It was my turn to laugh. "Micah. Seriously? Why are you overanalyzing the way I eat my French fries?"

Micah was rolling at this point.

"Don't worry about what's going on over here. And for your information; there **is** such thing as too much ketchup. I can't eat them like that. One dip is all I need."

Micah was still cracking up.

"Micah." I playfully whined. "Stop laughing at me."

"Okay, okay. I'm just messing with you baby." He grabbed my hand across the table and squeezed it. "One last question though: you couldn't even squirt the ketchup in the basket with the fries? It had to be on a separate plate?"

"Oh my gosh," I said deadpan, rolling my eyes, and he was cracking up again.

"Okay baby. I'm done. I promise." Micah squeezed my hand gently. "You are so cute. I love learning all these quirky things about you." Micah said genuinely.

I did too. I loved everything about Micah.

Even the disgusting way he ate his French fries.

"I am absolutely crazy about you. Insane. I care about you so much. Even though you're a neat freak French fry eater."

I playfully rolled my eyes. "I care about you too baby. So very much. Even though you managed to ruin a perfect basket of French fries." I shrugged my shoulders. "Guess everything about you couldn't be perfect."

I tried to keep a straight face but lost my resolve just moments later, trying to stifle my laugh.

Micah shook his head. "You couldn't even keep a straight face. Maybe next time baby."

Some nights later something else happened. Well two things happened. Nothing major, but significant.

Micah and I were headed out to watch a movie and hang out. Once we reached the bottom of the stairs, instead of heading left toward the garage,

Micah stood in the entryway that connected to the living room.

He stood there silently for a few minutes.

"Are you alright baby?" I asked, standing beside him. He seemed to be in deep thought about something.

"Yeah." He took my hand. "Do you like this space?" He gestured around us. "I want you to feel at home and comfortable. If here isn't that we can look for another place."

My jaw dropped. "You just had this house built," I said in disbelief.

"Your comfort and happiness are my priority. I don't care. It's only a house. *You* make it a home. When I said I'd do anything for you, I meant that. Once we're married, we can move or have another house built. Whatever you want."

"Micah, I *love* this house. And I want to be with you, anywhere you are. That is home to me." After a beat, "This space could use a lot more color, though."

We both laughed.

"I saved that for you." Micah kissed my forehead. "In fact. You see that wall over there." He gestured toward a partition wall in the living room. It didn't even go to the ceiling but was super wide and very high. It was bare aside from the fireplace, which opened on both sides.

"Yeah. What about it?"

"I want you to paint something on it. Just blast that shit."

My eyes grew wide. "*Say whaaa?*"

He turned to face me. "I want you to paint something there."

My mouth formed into an *O* as I made my way over. I touched the wall. I looked up and down again. Then looked back at Micah and he chuckled.

"What are you doin?"

"Are you *sure*?" I asked.

"Positive. Why?"

I shrugged. "What did you have in mind?"

"You decide. You have full creative control. Whatever you're feeling, go with it. Don't worry about colors. I'll replace the furniture if I need to." He pulled out his wallet and gave me his Amex platinum. My eyes grew wide as he said, "Get whatever you need. As a matter of fact, keep the card. Use *that* from now on. *For everything.*"

***

"You good baby?" Micah asked me as he absently rubbed my thighs. I was on his lap, leaning into his neck.

"All good." I returned.

A few days later, we were at Malachi and Ella's. Micah and I had been here for the past few hours.

It was just the four of us. Gabe and Gabby were with Ella's parents for the weekend.

Currently we were sitting out on their back patio enjoying each other. I loved their patio; it was equally astonishing as their home was. An expansive awning covered it. There was a huge built-in barbeque pit with a cooking area and sink as well as a bar and prep area. The bonfire was lit, and a 90's playlist was going.

The itis was setting in for all of us, and Micah's lap felt pretty good right about now.

Malachi grilled salmon and corn on the cob, and Ella made a delicious broccolini and rice noodle stir fry ", especially for me," her words, not mine. Of course, there was plenty for everyone. I ate so much of it; I should be ashamed. Not only was it tasty, but it was colorful and cooked to perfection. The best stir-fry has the perfect crunch, and Ella understood the assignment. I loved the abundance of veggies, fresh ginger, and fresh garlic. She was chillin today, but this was my third time over here for dinner and all I know is Ella could cook her ass off.

"Here's your blanket Des." I snapped from my daze as Ella covered me with a throw blanket.

"Thank you, Ella." Micah and I both returned.

It was starting to cool off just a bit, and she offered to grab one for me when she went inside to get one for herself. I was still on Micah's lap, and he had been caressing me all over my lower back and my thighs.

Slow jams from the 90s had it so romantic out here.

We were in our own world, sitting across from Mal and Ella. We were all enjoying the moment, so there wasn't much talking. Surprisingly, when they'd gone into the house to get the food inside, they were only gone for a few minutes. Knowing how they got down, I didn't think they'd be back anytime soon. I hadn't even heard Ella come back until she covered me with the blanket.

I looked over at Ella when I suddenly heard a bunch of giggling. She was sitting on Mal's lap, and he had his face in her neck, telling her something. She continued giggling, and there were a bunch of movements underneath their blanket.

"Don't mind us baby sis. I'm extremely affectionate with my Queen. Micah and I come from the same stock, so as soon as he done acting scary, he gone fall right in line." Malachi said.

"Ain't nobody scary." Micah volleyed. With that, Micah took my face in his hands and kissed me passionately for several minutes. It was one of the most intense kisses we'd shared *by far*.

We kissed with so much fervor that Mal was whistling, Ella was squealing, my pussy started thumping, and my panties were soaked. I wished we were alone because we could have seriously taken it there.

"I see you baby brother!" Mal said when we finally broke apart. "Glad you got wit it."

I looked at Ella, and she wore a grin with her eyebrows high on her head.

I felt a little embarrassed, so I put my head down.

"Are you alright my love?" Micah asked me as he rubbed my back.

"Yes I'm fine."

"You good baby sis?" Mal pressed.

"Leave them alone baby. She's probably feeling bashful after kissing like that in front of us." Ella said. "Come on Des, let's go find some wine and have girl chat."

After pecking Micah on the lips, I followed her inside. We stopped in the kitchen, and she perused their extensive wine collection.

Once I slid the glass door closed, Ella giggled, "Des, that was making *me* hot! These men of ours are something else." She abruptly turned to face me. "Oh my gosh. I hope you aren't uncomfortable."

"I was a little bit, but I'm fine." I shrugged.

"Okay good. I think you know by now that this is a haven. You can be openly affectionate. You can enjoy him loving on you with no qualms, and you're safe here to show your man as much love as you want. Chi usually wouldn't make a spectacle out of it, but I think he was just giving Micah a hard time.

"Yeah, I figure that's why he asked if I was okay."

"*Yes*. Chi is protective of his *baby sis*. It's adorable, actually. I feel the same way. I never had a sister, but I love having one in you." Ella smiled, hugging me.

"Me too. I'm so glad we met."

Ella opened a bottle of rose and poured us both a hefty glass. Handing mine over, she said, "Let's toast."

Smiling, I asked, "To what?"

"Hmm… to our sexy men who adore their women and their reckless love for us."

"I'll toast to that."

I took a generous gulp, and I knew I'd be horny as hell by the time we left. I discovered that drinking wine at Micah's did that to me.

I decided I would ask him about lovemaking.

Tonight.

When we got home.

Ella and I made our way to the living room. After

grabbing the remote, Ella sat down next to me. "Let's see what's on Netflix."

I loved hanging out with Ella. She was so much fun to be around. We talked so much, and we laughed even more.

***

Ella and Gabby came out to *Chalk it up! Sacramento*, which was a huge turnout. Our squares looked terrific.

We drew a monarch butterfly perched on a sunflower. It was beautiful. India and I always had such a dope collaboration.

And Gabby was so inspired by all of the artwork she saw. I loved that. She'd been asking me millions of questions about art, and she'd followed a bunch of artists on the gram.

Once I saw her interest piqued, I bought her a sketchbook and colored pencils. I couldn't help myself. And Gabby was so appreciative.

Also, Ella and Gabby met Daijah and India.

Micah came out too and I was all smiles. Like a kid on Christmas.

fourteen

MICAH

"We don't have to sweetheart." I managed, grabbing both of her soft hands in mine.

Destiny stepped closer, eliminating the small space between us.

"You don't want to, do you?" I heard the slight air of disappointment as she peered at me with doe eyes.

I chuckled. "Does it look like I don't want to?" I was so damn hard that it was painful.

She chuckled softly. "I'm completely naked right in front of you, and I don't know when I'll ever work up the nerve to ask you again." She shook her head. "Please baby. Why won't you have me." It wasn't a question. She moved even closer, our bodies skin to skin, and my hard dick pressed between us.

"That's the thing. I want you so much. You have *no idea* how much." I ran my hand down my face. "But I want to marry you first. I respect you. I told you I'm not going anywhere."

Destiney searched my eyes. She placed her hand on my cheek and rubbed her thumb over my bottom lip. "I'm not going anywhere either."

Lifting her hand to my lips, I kissed her fingertips, studying her gaze for a moment. I was sure there would be a full moon tonight. Her sexuality was on full display. This had never been the case.

Where she was usually reserved, bashful, and slightly guarded, today she was hungry, eager, and open to explore. Finally, I said, "I only want this if you're sure. We can wait."

"I want this." She returned, resolute and without pause.

Still holding her hand, I lead her to my bed. "Lay down baby."

Climbing in on top of her, I positioned both of my hands on either side of her, slowly kissing up her neck, her chin, her cheeks, and her forehead. Her skin was soft and smooth. I gently kissed her lips, and she kissed me back. We kissed for several minutes deeply and passionately, our tongues dancing to their own rhythm. She spread her legs wider as I settled between them. I could smell her arousal stewing; meanwhile, I was still conflicted about taking this next step.

I took in the view of her naked body. She was a sight to behold.

"Beautiful Destiney. I love you baby."

"I really love you too Micah. So much." She returned sweetly. Her eyes were trained on me, her voice laced with desire. She smiled at me. I swear her smile was one of the many things that made my heartbeat for her so.

I held her gaze for a moment, contemplating. "So, you'll be my wife? Once I've had you, I don't want another man to have you ever again."

She grinned real big, "Not you proposing right now!"

"Deadass! I'm making sure we don't start something we can't finish. You can trust that I'm a man of my word; I want you to be my wife. Especially if we-"

"Yes, I will. Deadass." I couldn't even finish. She placed her arms around my neck, pulled me lower, and kissed me. The palpable yearning of her body emanated as she held onto me. I kissed her lips again, possessing the same fiery passion she had. We kissed for a good while. Kissing her was one of my favorite things to do. To that end, I was still contemplating. I cared for her so much, and being direct was the best way to proceed. I also needed her to be as comfortable as possible.

I sat back on my haunches. "Should we use a condom?" She looked away, likely embarrassed, and knowing her as the demure woman she was, I had a feeling it would happen. "Whatever you want to do is fine with me." I wanted her to make an informed decision. I was also stalling, if I was being honest. Deep down, I was hoping she'd change her mind. We could stop this as soon as she called it, even until the last second. She remained silent for a beat, processing everything.

"Can we?" She returned, now looking up at me. "Thank you for checking."

I gave a reassuring nod, "Absolutely."

I leaned over, reaching into my side table to retrieve a gold-foiled wrapper. Before strapping up, I kissed her shoulders and her neck. I wanted to make this a special moment for her. She told me it had been a number of years since she was intimate, so I knew I needed to take my time with her.

Unfortunately, a little pain was inevitable, but I would be gentle.

After sliding on the condom, I resumed kissing her all over. I tasted her to get her wet for me. I knew that would help when the time came.

"Baby," I said when I returned to my position on top of her.

"Yes baby?"

"Are you ready?"

"Yes." She replied without hesitation.

I began pressing into her slowly, giving her a moment to adjust to my girth. I didn't expect she'd be able to take all of me. Not this time.

Destiney was so damn tight. She felt like a virgin.

I'd penetrated her entry with just the tip when I felt a squirm beneath me.

I held her close whispering in her ear, "Relax baby, we'll take our time." Kissing behind her ear, I said, "I would never hurt you." She was so wet for me, but I needed to focus. I was on a mission to please every inch of her body the tender way she needed me too.

"Are you alright, my love?" I hardly moved as I gingerly whispered in her ear again, kissing up her neck and the side of her face. "You're driving this thing. Tell me what you need... whatever you want from me." I assured her, and I meant that shit. Destiney could have anything she wanted from me. I was deliberate in each move I made; as tight as she was, I wouldn't last long if I wasn't careful. I certainly didn't want to get carried away and cause unnecessary pain. She placed each of her hands on my biceps.

She ran her hands across my chest and said, "You're so big baby, but it feels so good." She spoke softly, looking everywhere but at me, and I knew she was feeling shy.

"Yeah?" I pulled out completely and entered her again, even slower this time, going just a little deeper; I gave her a minute to adjust to me again. "I want your eyes, Beauty." I kissed her lips, and as she peered up at me. I searched her languid expression for any sign of discomfort.

Kissing her forehead, I said, "You feel so good too. So tight around my dick." I was convinced long strokes would feel incredible, but now wasn't the time for that.

For the moment I would work on getting the two of us acclimated.

I gave her a little more, and she gradually opened up for me, getting wetter and more responsive. I continued to pace myself. "You feel amazing, sweetheart." I lifted her hips and slowly slid my hardness deeper into her slick pussy.

"My goodness, you feel amazing too baby." She said, our eyes still locked. After a few seconds, she began to look away again.

"Eyes baby." Regaining a burning gaze, we exchanged unspoken devotion and understanding, intensifying our connection. My passion and fervor for her directly impacted the intensity I felt. The conversation we were having with our eyes brought us greater intimacy. There were no words. Words couldn't explain it.

I was so fond of her.

I cherished her for so many reasons. I wanted her to be gratified far beyond anything carnal, and I would execute that. For now, my mission was to bring her as many orgasms as she could handle before I even considered my own climax.

Our slow lovemaking was bringing her to the edge; her sporadic whimpers and moans made it obvious, but I could still sense trepidation. I gave her more of me and maintained slow, deliberate strokes. She received me, gripping me like a glove.

"You ready to cum baby?" I asked in her ear. I kissed her forehead, knowing how much she loved that. "Let it go for me, and I'll make you cum again and again." I continued my slow, deliberate strokes. She continued to open gradually, and I entered her even deeper. Positioning myself close to her body, I could feel her breath on mine. I connected our lips again. Taking her lips into my mouth, deepening the kiss, and she sucked my bottom one passionately. Her soft hands were rubbing me with need. All over my back and all over my shoulders.

I roamed her body, letting my hands and tongue lead the way. I licked over her erect nipples, giving each one equal attention. I cupped her full breasts in my hands, running my thumb over her distended nipples. She responded by arching her back, and I discovered this had to be another one of her spots. I spent more time there.

"I'm about to... Micah...I'm..." She lifted her hips to meet my strokes, and I almost lost sight of my task. Regaining control I said, "Mmmhmm...go head baby, I got you."

***

I opened my eyes immediately when I felt Destiney's side of the bed cold and empty. I turned to the other side, grabbing my cell from the nightstand. It was hardly nine a.m. My restroom door was ajar, and I knew Destiney wasn't in there since the light was off. I pulled some joggers on and headed downstairs. When I didn't find her in the kitchen, I looked out of the kitchen window facing my backyard.

Not there either.

I headed to the office, where I knew she had to be.

I knew my baby, and I got the feeling she was trying to avoid me. How she would do that while she was in my house was a mystery, but still. I didn't want to make her any more uncomfortable than she already was.

Just the same, this needed to be addressed. *Expeditiously.* As TI would say.

There wasn't a damn thing Destiney needed to feel embarrassed about.

The sweet love she gave me last night... I was already thinking about indulging in her again. But I needed to pace myself.

I opened the door, and she was perched at the desk with her oversized sketchbook; she was working on something colorful. And *dope.*

But it seemed like a cop-out.

"Good morning, sunshine." I supplied.

"Good morning." She tossed over her shoulder.

"Are you alright?"

"Yes."

"Couldn't sleep in? You felt some inspiration this morning?"

She chuckled lightly, but it held no mirth. "Yeah. Seems that way."

"Hmm." I gave her a few beats. "Destiney baby?"

"Yes." She tried with all her might to say it casually. I saw right through it.

"Positive?"

She said nothing. She wouldn't look at me either.

"Destiney baby." I pressed. Ever so gently. I leaned into the doorway. "Can I have those pretty eyes? *Pretty please.*"

Slowly, she gave them to me.

Yeah.

She squirmed under my gaze, and I *knew* I was right.

"Baby?"

"Yes."

"Please come here."

Destiney capped her pen, placed it on the desk, and then rose to her feet. I gave her a reassuring smile as she padded toward me.

Taking her hands in mine, I held her gaze. She still seemed trepidatious.

"Do you regret what we've done baby? Please be honest."

"No." She shook her head gently. "I don't regret it at all. Any of it."

I nodded. "Indeed. I'm so glad you don't baby. And neither do I." I took a moment, then, "But I get the impression you're in that pretty head of yours." I caressed her fingers in mine, taking my time with this. I realized a while ago that this was the best way to handle her. "Like... maybe you're feeling bashful with me? Now that we've made love." She looked away briefly, but I gently used her chin to turn her face back toward me. "Would I be correct? I need your honesty."

Destiney nodded. I always preferred that she used words with me, but this would do.

I nodded too. "Indeed." I gave her another beat. "Baby." She looked at me expectantly. "How can I help you with that?"

She smiled warmly around a light titter. "Micah… I… gosh. This is *sooo* embarrassing."

"What are you embarrassed about?" I needed her to understand there wasn't *anything* she needed to feel embarrassed about. Had her warm body still been beside me when I woke up, I would be inside of her right now. It was clear she wasn't quite there yet. I could rock with her till she was.

She shrugged her shoulders, releasing a heavy sigh. "I don't know. I guess… because you saw me. You heard me. I've never done those things with anyone else. I feel exposed. I *swear* it isn't you. You were perfect. You knew exactly what you were doing. You are *incredibly good* at what you were doing. It's a personal problem." She laughed again. It was adorable.

"I see. So. Can I tell you something, Destiney baby?"

She nodded again.

"I loved everything I saw. Everything you blessed my eyes with. Every. Single. Thing. Your body is beautiful. You shared the most intimate moments and parts of yourself with me, and I do not take any of that for granted. At all. And I love the way you sound. Your voice. Your words. It was like the sweetest music in my ear."

I brought her hands to my lips, kissing them softly.

"I'll also mention that I have much more to look forward to. I'm patiently waiting for that sexy monster to make *her* introduction." Destiney's brows dipped, and I bit back my laugh. Trying my damndest to keep a straight face.

"Monster?"

I nodded. "Yep. You get good and comfortable. She's going to come out, and I can't wait to meet her."

"What do you mean?"

I smiled really big. "I've read that artists make the best lovers. I'm *convinced* you would love fiery. Fiercely. With an insurmountable passion. There's a depth to you. Your attention to detail. As sensitive as you are, you're hypersensitive and keenly aware of those around you. And their feelings." I was still kissing her fingers. "Your heart is big and open, and you give freely of yourself… aiming to please… you're emotional, and your soul is wide open to give and receive. And I don't mean freaky. *Not that I would mind*. But the level you're capable of going is far beyond that."

Destiney's mind was blown. I could tell. She swallowed hard and croaked out, "You sound so sure."

"I am *one thousand* percent sure."

"*Damn*. Alright then."

fifteen

MICAH

"Your dad is so low-key! Does he ever get angry?" Destiney asked me.

"Very rarely. That's Daddy. Low key like that pretty much all the time."

The moment could not be more perfect. The lights in my bedroom were dim. My playlist was going. We were lying in my bed talking, clad in nothing but undergarments. I was in my drawers, and Destiney was braless in a pair of black lace panties. She told me they were called hipsters. I asked her once, revealing they were my favorite style to see her in.

She had gotten to the point where she was comfortable enough to walk around in her bra and panties. Or only her panties... beyond just a few steps from the bed to the bathroom. A close second would be cheeky panties- she told me that too. One day, she walked by me in a pair; I noticed the difference and asked her. She's so cute because my revelation made her bashful. That didn't surprise me, and it was adorable. Anyway, and this is random, but I enjoyed the variety. Men generally wore boxers or briefs, but women had such a litany of options. My mind was blown because aside from granny panties and thongs, I was completely unaware of all the others. Apparently, they each served a specific purpose. Whatever floated her boat worked just fine for me.

I loved to see her in anything... *and* nothing.

"Yeah. That's where you get it from." Destiney said, pulling me from my thoughts. "Raising three knuckleheads was sure to ruffle his feathers at some point I bet."

I laughed. "Yeah. I mean, there were plenty of those, but he was never enraged like the Hulk or some shit." We chilled in comfortable silence for a beat or two. I was on my back, and Destiney was lying on her belly, her head resting on her arms, facing me. It was after midnight now, and we had been talking for hours, as usual. I loved talking to her. We could talk for hours. The subject was never a factor. And I was absolutely enjoying the view. Her soft, slightly toned body was a sight to behold. It was late, and her big, beautiful eyes were beginning to get lower. I loved her bedroom eyes. Destiney is such a lovely girl. She was simply stunning, and I was drawn to her like a gorgeous painting.

We spent the entire day together, and I enjoyed every second. Today was Saturday, and we both had the day wide open for once. Since Destiney was involved in so much community work, her weekends were always booked. Oftentimes, for weeks out. My weekends were a hit or miss. I would either be coaching or officiating most Saturday mornings and Sunday afternoons. But this weekend was all about her and us. No work, no distractions.

Yesterday evening, I picked her up, and she spent the night with me. This morning, as soon as she woke up, she let me make love to her. Then we made breakfast, and we made love again after we ate. That put us back to sleep. When we woke up in the late afternoon, we had lunch delivered- from two places. We had been eating on it all day. My playlists had been going for hours. So long they'd asked at least a dozen times if I was still listening. We didn't need to fix any dinner because we were still full off the lunch we had pigged out on.

I remember Destiney saying earlier that *I would starve at her house.* And that *I had a clean-ass fridge.* I was cracking up at her. She's so funny. I don't think she knows how silly she is sometimes.

"Yes, it's neat, but that's not what I mean. You have fresh vegetables. Fresh fruits. Water. Organic this, free-range that. Daijah and I are in our twenties, 'and we eat like it,' as my dad always says. You eat healthier than I do. In fact, it was a very common misconception that I must eat healthy since I'm vegetarian—jokes on them. I probably eat worse than people would even believe. I love carbs, first of all. And I do eat vegetables, but certainly not enough raw ones. I cook the hell out of my veggies."

I realized that subconsciously. I've cut back on the meat. When I cook for us, which is pretty often, I don't fix meat. When we go out, I may get some. I may not. Depends.

Our conversation had transitioned again, and now we were trading stories from our teenage years. I'd given her a run of the mill on all the foolery Malachi, Raymond, and I had found ourselves in. She'd shared stories of her own about her and Daijah, and we'd been cracking up.

Destiney perked up suddenly, "What's the most upset he's ever been? Give me a good one! I just know it had something to do with Ray."

Destiney was right. Anytime there was trouble, my dear cousin Raymond was at the center of it. Malachi and I were good kids. Thankfully, we were not corruptible because Ray would have fucked us up with his shenanigans and foolishness.

I thought it over for a minute. Truth be told, I was not always directly involved in the juicier stories. I'd just hear about it whenever Daddy got on Raymond and Malachi about it. According to Ray, I was too young to hang out with them even though Mal and I were only eleven months apart. I guess at that age, it made a big enough difference. Especially once they were teenagers.

Something came to mind, and a deep rumble rose from my belly. I cracked up for a while. *A good while.*

"What?! What?! Tell me!" I was still cracking up, and Destiney began to laugh, too, even though she had no idea what I was laughing at.

I shook my head. When I finally calmed down, I said, "Okay… so, the church we grew up at, Mommy and Daddy still go there. Well, the pastor has two daughters. One was Raymond's age, and one was Malachi's age. Ray was always chasing the younger one. Since we were kids, she eventually started to like him back, and by then, Ray was fourteen, Mal was thirteen, and I was twelve. But, with her being a PK (pastor's kid), she wasn't allowed to have a boyfriend. You know, they couldn't talk on the phone or hang out. They just saw each other at church, and that was pretty much it." Destiney eagerly nodded. "The pastor's wife was not fond of Ray. I never knew why, but I guess I can't blame her. Ray is out there. She'd tried to push her older daughter onto Mal for years, but he wasn't checking for her. Anyway, the pastor's wife was convinced Ray was damn near grown, and we *had* to be lying about his age. She knew he wasn't grown. But Ray was tall, stupid tall, so he looked older because of his height. Mal and I were tall too but not as tall as Ray. Ray was super tall when we were still kids. Like, he was tall as hell at thirteen and never really got much taller.

Mal and I gradually grew into our statures. Plus, we all had a deep ass voice, even back then. Honestly, I think she just wanted an excuse not to like him.

"Yeah."

"Okay, so Ray and the PK would sneak around a lot. Ray was always trying to devise these crazy ideas to get alone with her, and Mal would cover for him sometimes. Ray was wild, though. And he was like dead set on having sex with this girl. And eventually, it happened. He went to her house, and she snuck him in through her bedroom window. But get this. Her cousin was spending the night, and that nigga had a menage at the pastor's house."

"What?!" Destiney shrieked.

"Yup! Ray the real MVP for that one. I wonder if it was planned like that." I cracked up all over again.

"And they got caught?"

"No, they didn't. Ray slipped in and out without getting caught. Some time went by before it all came out. I think maybe a month or two."

"How did it get out?"

"The cousin wrote all about their menage in her journal. Her mom found it, who is the sister of the pastor's wife, and since she hated Ray so much, they took it to the pastor."

"Damnnnn."

"Yup. They demanded to have a conference with Mommy and Daddy. Then, the pastor spent the better part of the next few months preaching to our family indirectly about Ray's indiscretions. Since Ray had to sneak out to do the deed, Daddy was furious at Mal and me because he was convinced we knew about it. *I swear I didn't know shit.* Mal knew but never admitted to it."

"Yeah, I can imagine he was angry then."

"Oh yeah. It takes a lot to disappoint Daddy *that* much. And in this case, I was actually innocent. We were grounded for weeks. Couldn't go anywhere. No phone. No T.V."

"Shiiit. Ray would have been home free if it weren't for ole girl writing about it in her journal." Destiney chuckled, and I joined her.

"Right. Ray was a savage, though, having a menage at fourteen!"

"You ever snuck into a girl's window?"

"Naw. I was way too scared." I looked over at her. "You ever snuck a boy into your bedroom window?"

"No. Never." After a beat, "Snuck one through the front door."

My eyes grew wide as saucers. "For real?"

She nodded. "Yup. Daijah was dating a guy, and he came by with his cousin one night. They parked down the street and waited for my dad to go to sleep. He took forever, but once the coast was clear, we snuck them through the front door."

"Let me find out!" I laughed again.

"Nothing happened. We just made out. Definitely wasn't a menage!" Destiney laughed. After we calmed down, "You ever had a menage Micah?"

"I haven't. You?"

Destiney shook her head, "I haven't either."

"It's not something I'm into. I don't like to share. I want my woman all to myself."

"I feel the same way. I wouldn't want to share either."

Shifting gears, I asked, "So tell me, what's something you've always wanted?" She peered back at me with those low lids. Her beautiful face was mysteriously absent for a split second. But I saw it.

My brows knitted together in alarm. "You, okay?"

"Yeah… that question has me thinking of some things. That's all."

"What things baby?"

"You may not necessarily mean tangible stuff with that question… but my mind went there because you're such a giver. You spoil the shit out of me." She chuckled. "It's so sweet. I don't want for anything with you. I have everything I need. I'm content." She sighed before continuing, "But something I've always wanted… is something I'll never get. Not in this lifetime anyway."

"What is it?"

Destiney looked just past me. "It's… it's to have my mom back. To have her here again. I miss her so much. The older I'm getting, the more I wish she were here. Especially now that I have you. Meeting you, falling in love with you. I would have loved to tell her about you." She began to cry, and I immediately pulled her into my arms.

"Sweetheart, I didn't mean for this to be painful for you. I'm sorry." Things had shifted so quickly, and I felt awful about it. I rubbed her back softly, letting her be. I knew she probably needed to get it all out. We'd spoken of her mother many times, but this was the first time she'd broken down *like this*. Once she gathered her composure, she laid her head on my chest.

"She's with you in spirit always. You can still tell your mom about me..."

I felt her nod, but she said nothing. "Please tell her about me." I continued to hold her. This always broke my heart. I was so close to my mother. I couldn't imagine life without her. "Tell her how much I love you. I'm so into you. How happy you've made me. How ready I am to make you my wife and have babies with you." Then, "For what it's worth, we can share Mommy. You know how she feels about you. She loves you like a daughter. I'm actually convinced she loves *you* more than she loves *me*." Destiney chuckled, and it was music to my ears, and now I felt a little better about this. "You know it's the truth. But I don't mind at all." Destiney settled into my embrace, wrapping her arms around me, and we chilled in silence, surrounded by the slow jams, still whispering in the darkness.

She was quiet for several minutes, and I thought maybe she had fallen asleep. "Thank you for being patient with me... I just had a moment there."

"You can have as many moments as you need, baby."

"Thank you for caring so much about everything that is me. Even the things I'm still working through. I'll be honest... I kind of hide that part of myself away. You're so compassionate. Sincere and intentional." She continued, "No one's done that before. Just my father. No other man has done the things that you do, Micah. I appreciate you more than I can put into words. That's all."

I gently lifted her chin and kissed her forehead softly.

"Thank you for being vulnerable with me. I want to be here for you. I know we can work through things together. Feel free to open up with me, sweetheart. Trust me with your secrets. I'm not going anywhere else with them. I want to tell you all of mine too." I kissed her forehead again. "You're safe with me. *All of you* is safe with me."

She sighed. "My goodness Micah. Can you be any more perfect?"

"I'm *far* from perfect sweetheart," I told her without pause.

"Well, you just never cease to amaze me."

I was beyond amazed by *her*. We'd be here until the wee hours of the morning if I tried to put *that* into words. In the meantime, I settled with, "I just want you happy love. You're the most important person in my life now. Anything you need, you tell me."

"Alright."

"Baby."

"Yeah." When I didn't reply immediately, she looked up at me. Her eyes still held a tinge of red, but she was so beautiful. I'd like to think the change of events brought us even closer.

"I love you."

"I love you too."

"Can I kiss you?"

"Yes." I captured her lips, pecking them with soft kisses. I drew back, asking her, "Should we call this a night? What do you think?"

She silently nodded, and I lightly chuckled. "Way ahead of me huh?"

447

"I can't hang like you can. I'm always way ahead of you in this department."

I cut off my lamp, stopped my playlist music, and settled in, pulling her close to me. We both fell asleep shortly after.

sixteen

DESTINEY

The fact that Micah knew I called myself trying to hide from him was wild. Comical actually.

My man knows me inside and out. Forwards and backward. It's as sweet as it is ridiculous. In a good way, of course. I find it incredibly thoughtful that he has taken the time to get to know me. I've made an effort to do the same. Studying him like he is my favorite subject. And he is. Enjoying every moment of it.

But I was rolling when I really thought about it. Like, I was also thinking, damn, I didn't realize I was *that* easy to figure out.

And anyway, I really should have just stayed my tired ass in that bed. I was tired too.

Blissfully tired. The way Micah made love to me was like the shit I read about in my romance novels. But better if you can even imagine it.

Honestly, I never thought it would actually happen to me. My goodness.

So, that was several days ago, and since then, Micah had been sexing me silly.

I'm glad we were patient with all of this. Though it was very sexually frustrating at times. And we'd come close. Dangerously close. Many times. We talked about waiting- more than once. And back then, there were times I wondered if I could hold out. I wondered if he was thinking the same. Shit got creative before we finally got to the pinnacle. We'd done some simultaneous… masturbating. And mutual masturbating. I was getting better at stroking out his climaxes. I was damn proud too.

And Micah was so good to me; he took such good care of me. I didn't even think twice about it.

There were *many* things I was willing to do for him that I wouldn't have even considered for someone else. The way he affirmed me mentally, first of all.

The way Micah catered to my mind and my body. I couldn't even begin to explain it. And the care he took with me and my mental.

The way Micah handled me, the way he spoke to me.

Yeah. For him, I could absolutely be *freak nasty*. It was easy.

For Micah, I'd do it without a second thought.

I'm his woman. He's my man. Pleasing him was something that satisfied me, too.

I wanted to please him the way he had been pleasing me. Sometimes, I just didn't feel equipped. Was I even capable due to my lack of experience?

One night, I shared this with him. And Micah didn't make me feel bad. Instead, he promised to show me.

Micah always told me that he was so pleased with me. Even if he hadn't told me… he made it abundantly clear.

Micah told me he loved the way I tasted. And he was *always* wanting to taste me.

He would make me cum and then get ready to go back down and taste me again. I had to tell him I needed time to recuperate. Just yesterday, as a matter of fact.

"I need a few minutes, baby...after the way you feasted, I'm still feeling sensitive down there. Can we kiss for a while?"

"Hmm..." Micah chuckled softly. His bedroom eyes fixed on me. *"Forgive me, I can't get enough of your sweet pussy, my love."* Holding me in his arms, he kissed my lips. *"Your smell. Your taste. How wet you get for me. The way you sound."* He peppered kisses all over my cheeks and my lips. *"Love kissing you too."*

Yeah.

Everything happened organically. We were intimately familiar. And the fact that we'd gotten intimately familiar *before* we were intimate meant the physical intimacy was guaranteed to be explosive. Intimate isn't always sex. I think many people forget that.

I swear. Once we connected, we were catapulted into another dimension.

And... *fuck*.

His strokes. They were deep and slow.

His moans. They were deep and beautiful. Laced with pleasure and satisfaction.

Micah took his sweet time doing shit to me.

Like, I know it's commonly called foreplay, and anyway, it's like this *regard*. Revere. Esteem.

The esteem Micah has for me. Yeah, he loves me. But he likes me too. He's *so* into me. And he enjoys

450

being with me. I told him I felt the very same way. It's not what we're doing at all, though I have a blast with Micah. It's simply the fact that we're together.

He is neither shy nor selfish. From my head to my toes, Micah goes bananas.

I'd cum so many times before he even entered me. Sometimes my orgasms were so intense that I could knock out in a matter of seconds. Orgasms so powerful they tore through my entire body. And I would be spent. Ready to knock the hell out. That made me feel bad because I wanted to take care of him, too, even though I'm still trying to figure out how best to do that. I'm not on his level. Yet. I was learning a thing or two. And one thing about Micah: he wasn't shy about telling me. Teaching me or showing me.

And Micah is an extremely attentive lover.

He is attentive to me in general. But he spends an incredible amount of time pleasing me. And doesn't rush about it. Ever. Not in a hurry. Ever.

Head to toe. Rooter to the tooter.

Yup. I said it.

Micah is thorough. My *entire body* is his play-ground.

I was still coming down from *that* experience. I remember the night he went between my legs from behind, and my eyes grew wide when he spread my ass cheeks and started licking me there. It's hard to describe the feeling, but it felt good. I was so shy when he was back there that it was hard to focus on that, distracted by how good it felt.

And I've become quite acquainted with his fingers. His hands are large, his fingers are meaty, and he knows exactly what the hell to do with them. I've cum all over them. Plenty of times.

There's something else too. Several nights ago, when I fell apart in his arms, missing my mom, he took such care of me. As he always does. But Micah mentioned wanting babies. I was a bit taken aback at first. I noticed he hadn't mentioned kids since the hospital blow-up. I realized that it was likely my fault. He likely hadn't planned to mention them either, but the moment was so emotional that it may have come out inadvertently. I planned to tell him it was still a possibility for me. And I still want that for us. I get the feeling this will make him so happy.

So, like I was saying. Me hiding from my man that day... I was being *silly*. I can look back on that and laugh. Crack the fuck up at myself.

Because *now*, literally right this second, I want him. *So bad*. Right. Now. And I'm trying to figure out where he is. I figured he would have made his way back up to his room by now.

Who knew? I am doing the exact opposite of what I did after the first time.

Something about those tables. They always turn.

I grew impatient. Driven by desire, I made my way down the stairs in search of my man. Drawn to him like a moth to a flame.

When I arrived at his office, the door was open—it was always open. I found him at his desk, typing away on his computer.

"Hey."

"Hey love."

I leaned into the doorway. He didn't look *busy*, busy. Then again, I couldn't say I even knew what busy for him looked like. It was Thursday evening. When we spoke at lunch, he headed home, saying he would work from here for the rest of the day. And tomorrow. I'd been here about an hour. I came straight here from work and took a shower. It was close to six in the evening now. So I knew he'd be making his way out of here soon. We'd probably talk about what we'd do for dinner. I could have waited...but the now persistent pulse in my panties beckoned me to my man.

I was beginning to love having my clit licked, and my pussy played with. And feeling his dick inside of me. The strokes he delivered. His warm body on top of mine, the way he held me in his brawny arms. His deep ass voice whispering in my ear.

Yeah. Right about now, she was dripping and throbbing at the very thought of what Micah's tongue was capable of doing.

"Baby." It came out in a sultry whine, which I didn't mean for it to. That got Micah's attention because he immediately looked over at me.

"Yeah baby?" His tone even.

"You busy?"

"Not at all." Micah quickly closed his laptop and then turned to face me. "Are you alright?"

I nodded with a sweet smile. Now that I was here, I was silently battling within myself. Whether I would say anything or not. Directly. Without preamble. But I was feeling shy. I could easily just ask him if he's coming up soon. But damn it, I wanted him.

"Good." He mirrored my smile and kept his eyes expectantly trained on me.

"So, since you aren't busy. Uh… can we…can you…" I paused. Embarrassed, of course.

"Can I what, love?" He gently pressed after a few beats. His smile was gone, and now his face was void of expression.

"Umm. Will you…" Shit. "I'm going to text you."

I'm almost sure his smile grew. It was quick, but I saw it. Then he released his deep chuckle I've grown to love.

"Text me. Alright." He nodded. "I think I have my phone around here somewhere." After spinning back in his chair to face his desk, he moved a few papers around. "Here it is." Phone in hand, Micah turned back toward me. "Go for it, sweetheart."

I quickly composed and sent him a message. Partly because I didn't want to change my mind.

Mostly because I wanted him without delay.

When I heard his phone chime, I immediately had regrets. I felt exposed, open, and vulnerable. Those were good feelings with him because I knew I was always safe in his care. But I was bashful anyway. As freaking usual.

Micah silently read my message and looked up, but not before I looked down at the ground.

"Destiney baby. Look at me, please." When I wouldn't look up, he made his way toward me. Within moments, his warm hands cradled my face. He lifted my chin ever so gently, and I finally gave him my eyes.

He was smiling at me. His thumbs caressed my cheeks.

"You are so adorable."

I smiled too. That helped me relax. Got me out of my head. He held my gaze for a few breaths. Then, "You want *anything* from me. Anything at all. It's yours." He pressed himself even closer to me, and I felt the bulge in his joggers; the thin material pressed between my shorts didn't obstruct anything.

I felt all of it. All of him.

Micah was absently caressing my face. His right thumb ran over my bottom lip. The pulse in my panties stronger now. Damn.

"You hear me baby?"

I nodded.

"I need you to tell me you understand."

"I understand." I managed to whisper.

"Good. Now that we're clear." He kissed my lips hungrily. I moaned into his mouth as I felt him press himself into me. Growing harder. He broke our kiss. "You see how much I want you too." He pecked my lips. "I'll always want you." Another peck. "What can I do for you?" Peck. "Hmm?" He kissed me passionately. Our tongues found each other. His hands were around my waist, pulling me closer. My hands around his upper torso, our kiss deepened. After a good while, we broke apart again. "Tell me what you want Destiney baby?" He looked deeply into my eyes. His eyes were hooded with low lids.

I felt desired. I felt special. I felt safe.

Micah patiently waited for me to give him an answer. And when I did- uncharacteristically, I was blunt. Straight. No chaser.

"I want you to eat my pussy."

"Mmm." He nodded slowly. "I can do that for you beautiful." He had been caressing me all over, getting me going. Rocking himself into me. My hands were all over him too. He came down to my ear, "What else do you want?"

"I want your dick."

He nodded again. "I'll make love to your pussy with my mouth. Then I'll give you all of this dick. That sound good to you?"

"Yes. Please." I purred.

"Mmm. You sexy, sexy girl." Micah's hands were at my waist, and he slowly pulled at my shorts. "I want you right here."

"Okay." I was on the same type of time.

I wanted Micah. *Right now.*

He kneeled, taking my shorts and panties with him. I stepped out of them once they were pooled at my feet.

"I'm going to place your leg on my shoulder. Hold on to me so you don't fall baby."

And he did. Micah lifted my right leg and rested it on his left shoulder. I placed one hand on his head and the other on his right shoulder; no sooner than that did he start to lick me. It was seriously ridiculous the way he made love to my pussy with his mouth. *His tongue.* And Micah's flat tongue covered a gang of real estate. If he didn't cover it, he sought it out and found it. Wasn't nowhere he hadn't licked sucked or slurped. His arms were around me, securing me in place. And I needed it. I worried my leg would give out a couple of times. What he was doing felt so good. His dick game was wild, but his tongue game was unmatched. It seriously made no damn sense how well he could work that thing. I ain't been the same between the legs.

And he did that for a while. When I began to whimper, he returned to a standing position, capturing my lips again. While we kissed, he was unhooking my bra. He stepped back to pull both of our shirts over our heads. "Go to the couch baby."

I took my naked ass a few steps to the couch just as I was told.

Micah removed his joggers and was between my legs again moments later. Gently, he spread them, and once he reconnected to my center, I closed my eyes and sighed.

He took his sweet time. Licking my clit with a flat tongue. Then sucking softly. I rocked my hips, following his tongue everywhere he went.

It felt. So. Damn. Good. I didn't hold back my cries of pleasure. I couldn't if I wanted to. He was eating me up like he had something to prove.

"Mmmhmm. You like that baby?"

"Yessss." I drew out. "Oh my gosh."

"Mmm." He kept doing shit with his tongue. Nasty shit. Wild shit. His tongue followed every move I made. "Pretty ass pussy... is she all mine baby?" His lips were just a breath away from me. Then he was back. Lapping at me again.

"All yours." I purred.

Micah made me cum twice before his dick was inside me.

And his strokes were perfection. Taking his time, in and out, with precision. Now and then, he'd pull out and tap my pussy with his dick. I fucking loved that. His dick was heavy, and he'd hit the perfect spot each time.

"You never have to ask for something that's yours, Destiney baby." He was still stroking me. Deep and slow. Looking at me right in the eyes. "You bring me my pussy whenever you feel the need. It's *always* a good time." Damn he felt good. "I'm asleep...wake me up. I'm on this computer... I'm in front of the TV. I have a book open. Come. To. Me... you hear me baby?"

"Yes." I managed as I felt another orgasm coming.

***

Saturday afternoon, I was sitting at the kitchen island engrossed in my sketchbook. It was a peacock feather—just the outline. I used a black pen on an off-white page and made thick lines, thin lines, and curves. I planned to add color later. I *love* peacock feathers.

I also had a napkin generously piled with hot Cheetos right beside me. Occasionally, I'd toss a few in my mouth and keep going.

Micah walked into the kitchen and, after a moment, "That's incredible."

I looked up briefly, smiling. "Thank you baby." And then I was right back at it again.

"Okay..." Micah began. Then paused.

I finally looked up at him. He was planted at the counter on the other side of the island. Facing me. I ate a few more hot Cheetos, waiting for him to continue.

"How are you eating those without a glass of water?"

My brows dipped. "They aren't *that* hot."

Micah shook his head in disbelief. "Them damn things. You see Chester breathing fire, don't you?"

I chuckled at that. "Maybe for people who don't eat them often." I nodded at him.

"Fair enough. You aren't worried that red stuff is all over your fingers?"

I shrugged. "This isn't important."

His eyebrows went up in surprise. "It looks important. I love it."

"Aww, thank you baby. But no, just trying to keep myself balanced. Sketching helps me do that. Think of it like a therapy session."

"Makes sense," Micah said. He turned to open the fridge, taking out fresh produce. Then moved the blender over.

"It's a good thing I love you. This could have ended so badly just now."

Confusion etched his face as he looked over at me. I bit the inside of my cheek to maintain my poker face.

"You don't interrupt an artist at work, Mr. Walker." I schooled my features but could feel a slight grin trying to show itself. When Micah turned completely to face me, I cracked up laughing at his cocked eyebrow. "I'm kidding. I'm just letting it flow." Hopping off the stool, I went to him, wrapping my arms around his body and kissing him on his chest. "If I'm ever in my zone, you would know it. When possible, I'd tell you beforehand."

"*Oh*, I get it. Never interrupt a master at work." He playfully jested, kissing the top of my head. "Tell me your wife is an artist without telling me your wife is an artist."

"Definitely one of those."

We both cackled.

"I love you Micah," I spoke into his chest.

"I love you, Destiney baby."

I faintly heard the buzz of my phone. Since Micah was facing that way I asked him to check it.

"Indie the bestie is asking *can I come over?*"

Turning to my side, I reached for my phone. Instead of texting her back, I called her on speaker.

"Best."

"Hey Indie. I'm not home. Everything okay"

"Yeah. Just need some fresh air." She sighed.

"Okay." I pecked Micah's lips as he released me and left the kitchen. Likely giving us privacy.

After hanging up with India, I found Micah in his bedroom. He was sitting on his bed, and I noticed he'd changed into workout clothes.

"Baby?"

"Yep?"

"Do you mind taking me home? India needs me."

Micah came to pick me up a few nights ago, so I didn't have my car.

"Of course. Is everything okay?"

"Yeah. She's just needing an escape." I mentioned Indie's situation in passing.

"Okay.

"I feel bad baby. I hate to disturb you."

"You're not baby. I was just about to work out. I can do that when I get back."

I snuggled up, kissing him. Micah held me in his arms and lay back, and I straddled him. After a beat. "But you look so *comfortable*."

"I mean. I can drive you, no problem. But you can take the Benz."

"What if I don't come right back?"

"I have my Range if I need to go anywhere." Right. Micah has a clean ass, all black Range Rover he takes around the block now and then.

"If you want me to take you home, I can. Just let me know what you need." He kissed my neck. Then, "Honestly, she can come here too." He shrugged.

"Aww. You're so thoughtful." I thought that over.

"I have an idea. Maybe we can go out to Homegrown. Solomon said the band would be playing tonight."

"That's a great idea. She'll love it." I rolled off Micah to grab my phone. "Let me check with her and see if she's down, " I texted Indie.

I draped Micah with my arms and legs, and he turned towards me, taking me into his arms. A moment later, Indie replied affirmatively.

"I'll take the Benz. Later on, we'll come back, and we can go from here. Will that work?"

"Works for me." Micah's lips were back on my neck, gently littering me with his kisses.

"Mmm. Indie is pretty special for me to leave your arms and this impossibly comfy bed."

He let out a lazy chuckle. "You're a great friend. I hope her situation gets better soon."

"Me too baby."

I untangled myself after kissing Micah's lips a few times. I rose from the bed, and he did the same, rounding the foot to meet me. We held each other for a while.

When I descended the stairs, he was right at my heels.

"You hurry back to me baby." Micah had to adjust the seats considerably due to our height difference. He kissed my forehead, then my lips. Then he stepped back as he pressed the button to lift the garage door.

"I will. See you in a little bit."

***

HomeGrownSol delivered a good time as usual. We chilled, grooved along with *Smoke*, and had some of their bomb-ass food and a few drinks. I was so glad I could get India out. At least then, she could forget about shit, even for just a couple of hours. Her parents were dealing with chronic medical issues. They've been extremely challenging lately—specifically, things with her mom.

And apparently, she and her boyfriend weren't in a very good space either. India told me they were on somewhat of a break right now. They've taken a few breaks before, but India said she's feeling like they were done. Like *done*, done this time. And she seemed content with that- on the surface, at least. They dated for over two years, so she may be harboring hurt feelings.

Still, I wasn't going to pry. She'll come to me when she's ready to talk about it. India could always come to me, and she knew that.

Micah was with us too, but he hung back some. And Micah introduced India to Solomon during their break. Anyway, we stayed for their whole set, and just before we left for the night, Solomon handed Micah a handful of tickets to the *Colour of Music Festival,* which was happening next month. Micah said it was a great time, and he'd been there before.

Colour of Music is an eighty-piece masterworks orchestra and the only all-black Orchestra on the West Coast. I read about the festival once Micah mentioned it, and was fascinated.

The orchestra is an acclaimed ensemble composed of some of the top classically trained musicians in the country. All of them are of African descent. Musicians who have trained at some of the world's most prestigious music schools, conservatories, and universities. Many of them playing since their early childhood.

It sounds amazing. The festival would be over nine days with various performances, and the passes Solomon gave us were good for the entire festival. I gladly would have paid for mine had I known about it. This was an annual festival, and I planned to support them in the future.

Solomon was incredibly generous in sharing them with us. They would be put to great use. *I love the arts — not just the visual arts but also the performing arts.*

Art is all around us. Everything begins with a picture — everything we see. Our daily luxuries were once an idea someone had to draw or design.

The arts use math and science. The arts are history. Foreign Language.

The arts are all these things.

Anyway, I couldn't wait to go.

seventeen

MICAH

I am so very in love with Destiney Evans, soon to be Mrs. Destiney Walker or Evans-Walker. Whatever she wanted to do, I was good with it.

My ass was drowning in this shit. Her love for me and my love for her was overwhelming. In the best way. The feeling was incredible.

I'd been in love once before, and I missed that. I could admit that. Honestly.

And not only did I miss it, but I had been craving that connection for so long. Being wanted by someone and wanting them just as much was a beautiful thing.

No doubt our connection has intensified.

Especially after we started lovemaking.

But it's more than that. So much more.

I loved being in her company and having her in my arms. Destiney told me she loved lying under me and being with me, too. She didn't want to be *anywhere* else.

I'm a happy man.

I keep telling her how beautiful she is. And she is. So very beautiful.

Last week, I asked her to come by. She'd gone to dinner with Daijah and India, so I had to pick her up. I went to the restaurant to meet them once she told me she was about ready. I pulled into a parking spot near the entrance and waited for her to come out. I happened to look up at the exact moment they emerged and *damn*. They were all attractive women, but Destiney stood out to me. *Of course.*

I loved the way she moved.

She was so fucking sexy, and if I was doing my job right, she had grown to believe it.

Yeah.

My woman was incredible. Her talk, her walk. Her kind, gentle spirit. The effortless way she made me feel.

I continue showing her how much she means to me. I felt compelled to do so as her man. Reminding her at every opportunity. Destiney was so very special to me.

And her unassuming innocence was adorable.

I was so glad she was mine. I thanked God for her.

I'm never letting her go.

Speaking of lovemaking, I've thought back to that night.

The first night we made love.

It was just as beautiful as I thought it would be.

But it almost didn't happen.

Destiney came to me, put herself out there, was open and vulnerable and I managed to get her upset at me.

We came in from Mal and Ella's. Took a shower. Together. Then we were in my bed, and we'd been kissing each other for the past half hour. Things had gotten hot and heavy as usual, and it was all good in my hood. For now, I knew this was as far as things would go, and I was just fine with that. My baby was a phenomenal kisser, and I could kiss her soft ass lips all night long.

Our kisses were wet and sloppy. Our tongues were quite familiar by now, dancing to their own rhythm and making love to one another.

So, we came up for air, and imagine my surprise when Destiney said, entirely out of nowhere, "I'm feeling like I want you to make love to me."

It wasn't dark in my room; my bedside lamp was on to the lowest setting, and I found her sweet doe eyes trained on me. I knew her nerves were all over the place, and she was shy, but I was so proud of her for sharing her desires.

"You sure you're ready for that?" I asked, not missing a beat.

I also regretted that as soon as it left my lips.

Destiney glared back at me. Her brows knitted.

I knew she probably felt a slight sting of rejection, but it wasn't that at all.

It wasn't a question of whether I wanted to. I suppose I didn't think she'd be ready right now. We seemed to be enjoying what we'd been doing. With our mouths. I didn't want her to think we had to do this just because that's what typically happened next. I could have come up with something better though.

"What does that mean?" she snapped.

Okay.

That was the first time she'd used that tone with me. But I couldn't blame her.

Destiney turned away from me, so I leaned over and kissed her cheek, speaking softly in her ear, "I'm not trying to upset you sweetheart, just want to make sure." I continued kissing her cheek and her neck. "I'm in no rush. I'm ready whenever you're ready." I planted another kiss on her neck and then leaned back on the bed.

She exhaled a frustrated breath.

She was probably irritated now, and I likely turned her off.

I saw her cover her face with both hands, so I cuddled behind her and held her in my arms, rubbing her softly. I heard her sigh again, but louder this time. She wasn't pushing me away, so that was a good sign. Still caressing her and kissing her shoulder, I repeated, "We don't need to rush this baby. I'm here for the long haul. Ready whenever you're ready."

And I was thinking about what I'd just said.

It was mostly true. I was ready if she was too. I wanted her **bad**.

But. I wanted to do this right. Marry her before we take this step.

"Destiney baby?" She still hadn't spoken. She still hadn't turned back towards me.

I studied Destiney like she was the most intriguing subject; to me, she was. I made it a priority to be in tune with her. I already knew she was in her head. And I certainly didn't help responding the way I had. I sensed an internal battle, likely a mixture of nerves and embarrassment.

I ceased rubbing her and said, "I want your eyes, baby. Look at me, please." I gave her a beat or two, and she turned to face me. I regarded her. Eyes on eyes. Her expression wasn't very telling, but she didn't appear angry.

I spoke gently, "Tell me, baby. Tell me **exactly** what you want, beauty."

"I want you. Micah. I want you inside of me."

"I want to be inside of you too baby. But only if you're absolutely ready."

"Yes, baby I'm ready." She quickly replied. "I've never felt more ready."

I nodded. "You're sure?"

"Yes. But…"

"But what baby?"

"I don't really know…I'm not sure what **I** need to do. For you."

I released a light titter. There she goes again with this. My adorable, sweet, thoughtful Destiney. I kissed her forehead. I kissed her lips. Then, whispering in her ear, I told her, "Do whatever comes naturally to you. Whatever you want to do. You'll be fine. You sexy girl."

I stood from the bed, then put my hand out for her and brought her up towards me. "We won't need any clothing for this." I began undressing her. Since we'd just taken a shower, Destiney was only in a t-shirt and panties. But I removed them both. Then I removed my t-shirt, basketball shorts, and boxers.

She stood before me. I stood before her. Both of us were naked as the day we were born.

"We don't have to sweetheart." I managed, grabbing both of her soft hands in mine.

Destiney stepped closer, eliminating the small space between us.

"You don't want to, do you?" I heard the slight air of disappointment as she peered at me with doe eyes.

I chuckled. "Does it look like I don't want to?" I was so damn hard that it was painful.

She chuckled softly. "I'm completely naked right in front of you, and I don't know when I'll ever work up the nerve to ask you again." She shook her head. "Please baby. Why won't you have me." It wasn't a question. She moved even closer, our bodies skin to skin, and my hard dick pressed between us.

"That's the thing. I want you so much. You have no idea how much." I ran my hand down my face. "But I want to marry you first. I respect you. I told you I'm not going anywhere."

Destiney searched my eyes. She placed her hand on my cheek and rubbed her thumb over my bottom lip. "I'm not going anywhere either."

And now here we were.

Been sexing each other like it was going out of style. I was pacing myself, and my baby was keeping up too.

We've made love all over this house.

A few nights ago, she came looking for me. Wanting some of my "good shit," as she likes to call it. She's so cute because she came all the way to my office but got too nervous to ask me at the last second, deciding to text me instead.

Beauty: Can I have you baby?

My baby was asking for it, and it was so sexy. And sweet. And just like her to text it to me. She was adorable, but at the same time, I didn't want her to ever feel bashful about anything she did with me.

And the other night, I'd let it slip that I wanted babies. And I do. However we could make that happen. Surrogacy. Adoption. I was open.

Mal and I had a conversation about kids just a few days prior, and I think it came out since it was fresh on my mind. The moment was so emotionally intense. Destiney didn't acknowledge it right then, but I got the feeling it was coming. I was ready to talk about it whenever she was.

But yeah. Mal and I were reminiscing about when he and Ella first had Gabe and later when Gabby burst on the scene. Rocking our world.

"It would have been something special if we could have raised our kids together. Real close like we were." I said to Mal. I'd stopped by his house to shoot the breeze. On the way out to the car, I saw a few kids playing in the front yard across the street. "Your kids will be grown by the time I have some... If I have some."

*"You'll have children baby brother no doubt in my mind." He stopped at the railing surrounding his wrap-around porch. "You'll have a sitter. Gabby would love to watch the kids for you and baby sis. Then you can go out whenever. You know Ella and I didn't have that. Mommy would keep them a lot, but we weren't trying to wear her out too much." Mal said through a chuckle. "That Gabby was such a crier, remember? **My Gosh.**" Mal shook his head. "My baby was **always** crying."*

We both fell out laughing.

"My baby came out crying and didn't stop that shit for like three years."

I shook my head.

"I don't know why I thought they would both be super chill like Gabe was," I said with a chuckle.

*"Yeah. Gabe was **super-duper** chill. He was the easiest baby in the world. Dude was always chilling. Hardly made a peep, even if he needed to eat or be changed."*

I nodded at the memory. "Yeah, and he's still like that. Mature as fuck and cool as a cucumber. Gabe being so low-key may be why you guys had Gabby so quick."

"Hell yeah. Ella always said, if we'd had Gabby first, that may have been it!"

I roared with laughter at that.

Lately, something hadn't felt right in my spirit, and I didn't like how I felt. The more I mulled over it, the more I realized I was conflicted with something. Something major. It wasn't even deep. But it was complicated.

After sitting with my thoughts, I figured out what was giving me pause.

I wasn't all the way all right with having sex with Destiney. Like this. Outside of marriage.

Hear me out. I *knew* if we had intercourse, we would create a soul tie. Not that I took issue with that. I knew Destiney was my forever. But just the same, I know how I am and how easily I attached myself if something like that happened.

Generally, men can differentiate sex from feelings and relationships. Typically, women confuse the two.

Men can sleep with a woman and not even think of her again.

Women can't do that. A select group of women like to say they can, but they're lying, mostly to themselves. It's biology. Men and women are not the same.

Also, men can guard their emotions and feelings the same way women are with their sexuality.

But the caveat is that *I* have issues separating the two. I'm man enough to admit that. I would only be physical with a woman I deeply cared about. A woman I loved.

As much as I enjoyed making love to Destiney -and we did it a lot... man, it was like once we started, we couldn't seem to keep our hands off each other. Continuing to connect with her outside of the institution of marriage didn't sit right with me.

I wanted to wife her. Needed to. And not *solely* so I could sex her.

That was my dilemma. And I would work that out.

***

I pulled into the gas station to fill up. We were about seventy miles away from Pismo Beach. A coastal town just outside of San Luis Obispo. We were making great timing. Pismo Beach was a four-and-a-half-hour drive southeast of Sacramento.

For the most part, we'd been doing what we did best, conversing. Destiney had fallen asleep forty-five minutes ago, so I'd been cruising to the music and enjoying the beautiful scenery. The Central California Coast was breathtaking. The water, the beaches, the beachfront homes.

I surprised Destiney with this quick getaway just last night. I told her to pack a bag, and we'd be away for a few days. She mentioned having a few days without any commitments, so I was quick about asking my assistant to block my calendar and set this up.

She was so excited. I felt the same way.

While Destiney was asleep, I listened to the radio. Eventually, I turned on SiriusXM since the stations were so spotty out here.

Eventually, choosing *SiriusXM Love*. It just felt so right. I'd been driving more than two hundred miles with the love of my life right beside me. Just the two of us.

Then the Isley Brothers "For the Love of You" came on, and I got to thinking… it was crazy how much a love song spoke to your soul when you were in love.

It was as if every love song was about your special someone.

> *Driftin' on a memory*
> *Ain't no place I'd rather be*
> *Than with you*
> *Loving you*
>
> *Lovely as a ray of sun*
> *That touches me when the mornin' comes*
> *Feels good to me, yeah*
> *My love and me, well*
>
> *Smoother than a gentle breeze*
> *Flowin' through my mind with ease, soft as can*
> *be*
> *Well, when you're lovin' me*
> *When you're lovin' me*
>
> *I wanna be living for the love of you*
> *All that I'm giving is for the love of*
> *you*
>
> *Paradise I have within*
> *Can't feel insecure again*

You're the key, well, and this I see
Oh, I see

Now and then I lose my way
Using words that try to say
What I feel, yeah
Love is real
Our love is real

Yeah.

I couldn't have said it better.

I am so in love.

Once I cut the engine, I leaned over, kissing Destiney's forehead, then her cheek. She stirred just a little as I softly spoke in her ear, "I'm going to fill up and grab something from inside. What can I get you baby?"

"Purple Skittles." She languidly spoke with her eyes still closed.

"Purple Skittles. Okay."

As I opened my door, Destiney said, "Blue works too. Red is a last resort."

I looked over and saw that her eyes were still shut. I chuckled, "Okay baby."

After getting the pump situated, I headed inside the store. I only needed some jerky. We had plenty to drink in the cooler I had in my trunk. After grabbing her Skittles and paying, I went back to the car. I placed the bag on the backseat and returned the pump to the cradle.

"How much longer?" Destiney asked as I settled inside.

"About an hour or so. Everything good?"

"Yeah. Debating if I should go pee or not." She sat up and removed her seatbelt. "I better."

**

"It is beautiful out here," Destiney commented, letting her window down. We were on our way again once she used the ladies' room.

I nodded. "Indeed. I'll bring you back when it's a little warmer." The coast was beautiful any time of year, even during October, but the spring and summer were amazing. Also, we'd be able to go to the beach. It would be too cool to get close to the water right now.

"I just want to be with you Micah. You can take me anywhere."

"You got it. Do you have a passport?"

She shook her head. "Never needed one."

"We'll get that taken care of." I'd since tore open my jerky and ate a few pieces. "Also, I planned on tonguing you down, but now I wonder if you'll let me after having all this red meat in my mouth."

Destiney roared with laughter. "That wouldn't bother me. You kiss me anytime you want."

"*Oooh, lucky me.* I love kissing you."

"I love kissing you too baby."

We continued cruising down US 101-South. Traffic picked up a bit more recently, but it was a relatively easy drive.

"Should be about twenty more minutes," I told Destiney once we'd exited the freeway. We only had a few miles until we reached our Airbnb. We passed through the quaint beach town nearing our destination. No doubt coastal towns are charming.

Prime ocean access. Beachfront homes, seafood restaurants, and tiny shops.

"Micah, thank you so much for bringing me out here. *I'm so excited.*" She squealed, dancing in her seat. Destiney reached over, grabbing my hand. "I love this. This aesthetic is giving me so much life right now! The landscape even seems serene. So glad I brought my sketchbook. I can't say I'd get tired of the sound of these waves either."

"You're welcome baby. Thank you so much for joining me." Destiney may as well get used to this. I'm setting the standard, and I was going to show her something. I love her so much. I'd give her the world. "I lived right on the coast for four years. I never grew tired of it either."

***

We settled in at our Airbnb. The house was quaint and cozy, like a small cottage. High on stilts, the back of the house faced the ocean, the beach just a few feet away. And the view was amazing. There were two bedrooms, one bathroom, and a tiny kitchen with a breakfast nook. This would be a perfect home for us for the next few days.

I drove nearly three hundred miles, so once we got settled, I lay on the bed for about an hour. Destiney lay next to me, reading on her Kindle.

It was early. Hardly noon. We left Sacramento just before seven a.m. and missed all the traffic.

"Destiney baby?" I reached for her, draping my arm across her and around her waist.

"Yeah."

"We'll need to get some groceries. You coming with me?"

"Of course, I am."

I chuckled softly. "Indeed."

I was taking her to dinner tonight, but we will cook breakfast and dinner at home tomorrow, so I'd need to grab a few things. Fresh fruits and vegetables were a staple in my diet. I had a green smoothie at least twice daily, so I packed some essentials in my cooler in case I didn't find exactly what I needed.

"Anything in particular planned?" Destiney asked me.

"Besides chill with you?"

"Yeah." She released a soft giggle and gently nudged me with her shoulder. This was a king-sized bed, so we didn't have as much space. Not as much wiggle room. But we would make it work. I liked being close to her.

"As a matter of fact, I do. Two concrete plans. The rest is up to you."

"What did you plan?" Her eyes were bright in wonder. She placed her Kindle beside her.

"Dinner tonight. Wear a dress if you packed one."

She nodded. "And tomorrow?"

"Tomorrow, a scavenger hunt."

"A scavenger hunt?! *Really?!*" Destiney squealed in excitement.

"Yes. You said you'd prefer a scavenger hunt over an escape room. I think that would be a fun thing to do while we're here." I'd arranged one through *Let's Roam Scavenger Hunt,* a company I found online.

"Wow! *I can't wait!* I've never done a scavenger hunt before."

"Neither have I."

"So, this is a first for both of us? That's so special baby." Destiney leaned over and kissed me.

"Indeed. Our first trip together and our first scavenger hunt. I look forward to many more firsts with you, my love."

"Me too baby."

Later that evening, Destiney and I were about to head to our dinner reservations.

There was a restaurant just a few miles from us with great reviews. I waited for Destiney in the living area and stood immediately when she came out of the bedroom.

"Wow. Baby... you look... my goodness. You look amazing. Beautiful."

"Thank you, Micah." She smiled shyly. "I won't be overdressed, will I?" Destiney wore a sleek plunge-neck halter gown. It was long and elegant with a hunter and metallic gold floral pattern. She'd pulled her long locs from her face into a low ponytail. She looked absolutely gorgeous.

"I'm not worried about that. You shouldn't worry either. You look stunning." I took her hand in mine, kissing it softly

"Thank you, baby. You look *great*. You are so handsome." I was wearing a suit, so if we were overdressed, there would be two of us.

"I'm aight."

"Have you seen you?" She volleyed.

"Have *you* seen you?" I threw back, chuckling as I put my arm around her waist, pulling her close. "Seriously, you're very welcome." I took her into my arms. "Are you ready baby?"

"Yes."

"Indeed." We headed toward the front door. "Actually. One more thing. Sit down baby I'll be right back."

I went back to the bedroom, then returned with a small textured white gift box with gold lettering on the outside, wrapped with a white satin ribbon and gold star.

Destiney's eyes grew wide. I handed the box to her and said, "Open it, baby. We have time."

"Micah…"

"Go head baby." I sat down beside her.

She timidly untied the bow, slowly lifted the lid, and looked up at me with wide eyes. "This is beautiful."

"Not as beautiful as you."

Destiney closely admired the diamond tennis bracelet and matching necklace.

"*Dior?* I mean… Micah. This is… thank you baby. I love it." She placed the box beside her and hugged me. "Thank you, baby." She said again.

"You're welcome. You wearing it tonight?"

"*Hell yeah I am!*"

We laughed. Destiney was still wearing her Tiffany bracelet. She put her tennis bracelet on her other wrist. I helped her put on her necklace. It all came together nicely.

"Alright. I think we're ready baby." I told her, shutting off the lights in the living area. "Let's get some dinner."

The restaurant was a short drive from our Airbnb and right on the water.

We were just in time for our reservation, and the hostess offered to seat us any place we wanted. It was an open-air restaurant. So, anywhere was a great choice. There were tables out on the terrace with a fire pit. There were tables inside, bar seating, a lounge seating space, and for a more intimate experience, there were cozy booths tucked back into the far corner.

In the center of the restaurant, an older gentleman sat a grand piano accompanying a woman dressed in a red sequin evening gown. Her voice was warm and lovely as she serenaded us with a cover of "Breathless" by Corinne Bailey Rae.

"Micah, this is amazing." Destiney crooned once we were seated. We decided on an inside table just off the terrace and had the best of both worlds. Our table sat near oversized windows from the floor to the ceiling, giving us a wide-open view. The sun had set, and I loved the ambiance of dark water and the sounds of crashing ocean waves. "Thank you, baby. I'll probably say this the entire trip. You'd think I'd never been anywhere or something." We laughed. "I just appreciate you. And I love being with you."

"I love being with you too, sweetheart. You're so very welcome. Thank you for joining me." Our server poured each of us a glass of water and promised to return shortly with our drinks and to take our order. "I'll be thanking you for joining me many times over these next few days." I winked at Destiney, and she smiled at me.

"That's fine. I love you, Micah. "

"I love you too, Destiney baby."

This place was the perfect end to our first evening away together and Destiney's first night in Pismo Beach. The lighting in the restaurant was low. Each table had floating candle centerpieces. Destiney was already beautiful, but the glow of the candlelight adorned her elevating everything. She sipped from her glass of wine, nodding slightly to the music surrounding us. I couldn't take my eyes off of her.

She was my beautiful goddess. My reason. *My Destiney*. My love of a lifetime.

"What?" She asked sweetly once she realized I was staring.

I smiled, nodding silently. "You."

She kissed her teeth and then smirked. It was so cute. "What about me?"

I nodded again. Still silent. Reaching across the table, I took her free hand in mine.
Usually, I'm not the type to be at a loss for words. Even when things are difficult to articulate, I can still deliver *something*. But now? I was stuck. "I can't explain it, baby..." I spoke. Suddenly, growing emotional.

"Aww. *Really?*" Destiney's eyes bore into mine, and I knew there was a depth now. Feeling how I felt in this moment, I was convinced there was.

And I wanted her to see me. All of me. It was perfectly fine with me to reveal the deepest depths of my soul to her. To speak from my heart.

"For you, I'll try." I avowed.

"Okay." Her voice held a comfort that I appreciated so much. Being vulnerable with her was never an issue, but something was happening.

Destiney placed her glass on the table, then reached for my other hand.

Silent, I held her eyes. And we remained that way. The lovely voice serenaded us with another love song.

"I was beginning to lose hope." It came out before I could stop it. Though I didn't have a speech prepared, this wasn't what I planned to say. But I knew I could bare my soul with no judgment. She had a small smile, her doe eyes glowing in the candlelight, and it was all good in my hood. "Then came you..." Her smile reached her eyes. "You're the answer to my prayers. I believe you were meant for me and the proof that prayers are answered." I gently gripped her hands a little tighter. "Your love is so beautiful. *Our love* is so beautiful. You've made me so happy." I felt like maybe I was rambling. "I'm here for the long run, baby; you're it for me."

"Micah. That's..." I could see her eyes welling up. Mine had already. It was crazy because we always spoke about our feelings for each other. *All the time.*

But there was something about tonight.

Something about right now.

Something different.

Maybe it was because we were away together for the first time. Or the fact that a woman was belting out love ballads, and the mood was just right.

Hell, maybe it was these candles.

"Thank you for those words. I feel the same way. You've made me the happiest... I've never been so happy. I never imagined I could be so happy... and you make me feel so free. So safe. Secure.

Sexy…it's… I…" After a sigh, Destiney said, "I just love you, Micah. I love you so fucking much." She laughed, and a tear fell.

I chuckled. I understood her, undoubtably. My baby was feeling a lot like I was, growing emotional with so much to say and trying to find just the right words to articulate it. We'd established an unspoken understanding, and I knew her heart just like she knew mine. I gently wiped her tears. I was grateful for my long arms. She was sitting across from me. I usually preferred she sit beside me, but this was a sweetheart table.

Nodding, I returned, "I love you, my Destiney baby. I just want to keep loving you. Keep making you smile. Can I do that, sweetheart?"

"Yes, please. As long as I can keep loving you."

***

We returned to our Airbnb and immediately started getting changed and ready for bed. We showered before dinner so we could shower again in the morning.

The food was phenomenal. I had the Surf and Turf. Destiney had a Mushroom Risotto, and we shared a slice of cheesecake for dessert.

As I removed my clothing, I figured this was a good time to mention something I'd been thinking about. Now that we were intimate. And liable to be intimate again at any given moment.

"Baby?"

"Yes."

"We're all out of condoms," I informed Destiney. I loosened my tie to remove it. "We used the last one last night." I had been abstinent for two years, so I didn't have much of a stash, and we quickly depleted the small supply of condoms I did have. Once Destiney and I started lovemaking, we did that shit often, and honestly, it wasn't at the forefront of my mind to replenish them. I only want her. I'd be perfectly fine with shooting up the club raw. I knew she was my forever, but I needed her to be good with that. "I can make a run. But I was thinking since we're exclusive, maybe we could get tested; that way, we don't need to use them." Destiney had her back to me as she was removing her jewelry. "We can keep using them if that makes you most comfortable. But... just thought I'd mention it. You know." She said nothing. "Do we still need them love?" I quizzed after a few beats.

"Micah," Destiney said, her back still to me.

"Yeah, baby?"

Destiney turned to face me, and I was looking at her expectantly. She wore a small smile, but her eyes were glassy, almost like she was about to cry. *That* gave me pause, but I didn't have time to react. Finally, "We'll need condoms. I'm not on the pill. So. Unless you have a superb pull-out game..." She spoke evenly.

My brows knitted. *Pull-out game?* "Why would you need to be on the pill?"

She smiled wider this time. A tiny tear cascading. "Because. I could get pregnant."

My eyebrows promptly transitioned from furrowed to high on my forehead. "You could?" I walked around the bed to her side, sitting next to her.

"I thought… didn't you have surgery?" I smiled too. Couldn't help myself.

She shook her head. "I had surgery, but not the one initially planned. I only had my fibroids removed." She spoke through a tearful smile. "I can still have babies." Destiney beamed as tears rapidly fell. I knew these were happy tears. I was growing emotional myself.

I loved this for her.

For *us*.

And as thrilled as I was to hear this news, it was only the icing on the cake.

"*Wow*. That's great, baby. *So great!*" We kissed slow and passionate for a long time. When I pulled my lips away, I pressed my forehead to hers. I needed to set the record straight.

We haven't spoken of children since our infamous conversation that day. And aside from letting it slip those nights ago, I avoided broaching the topic altogether. It seemed Destiney was moving the same way, as she never brought it up either, even after my slip-up.

But there was something I needed to tell her. And there was no time like the present.

"Sweetheart. Whether we had children of our own, had children through other means, or decided not to have them at all, I would still want you. Make no mistake, children with you would be a bonus for sure…" I gently held her face in mine, wiping a lone tear. "But you're all I need, Destiney baby." I kissed her softly.

Destiney looked up at me. Eyes on eyes. Her beautiful face held a glow and spread into a smile. "I know that, Micah. I knew that then. At the time, I was an emotional mess. You'd expressed your desire to be a father from the beginning and... I felt you would have been settling with me. You know?" She sighed. "We could have talked about it. I'm sorry. I wasn't thinking logically."

"I understand. That was an emotional day, baby."

"Micah?"

"Yes, love?"

"I trust you."

"I trust you too."

"So, it's all right with me to continue if, at some point, we don't have any condoms. I know you'll take care of me."

My mind started to process what she was saying, and I could surmise what she meant. Knowing Destiney, she was too bashful to say it directly, but she got her point across.

I'm a straight shooter, in any case.

"You mean you'll have my babies, Destiney?" I quizzed.

"Yes. I will."

"Indeed. I've seen a future with you from the beginning. You're my forever, and I want you to be my wife before we have babies."

"You're my forever. All of that is perfectly alright with me, too."

"Yeah?"

"Yeah."

I captured her lips again. "So. You tryin' to play this pull-out game or what?" I teased, murmuring against her lips.

Destiney's giggles were muted when my lips returned to hers. Her sweet tongue was in my mouth. Mine was in hers, and we fell right into our rhythm. Her dainty hands were around my hardness, and it wasn't long before she was moaning with need. She lay back on the bed, bringing me with her. When my fingers found their way into her panties and I discovered how slick she already was, I knew it was game time.

eighteen

MICAH

"So, what's up with India though?" Solomon asked me.

Sol, Mal, Ray, and I sat on the back patio at Mal and Ella's. Talking and having a few beers. The sun was setting, but it was still early.

I raised my eyebrows. "What's up with India? What do you mean by that?" I asked, the surprise evident in my voice.

"What you so surprised for?" Ray said. "Shorty is bad!"

India was beautiful. Stevie Wonder could see that. I was surprised to hear Sol express interest in someone. I didn't even realize he'd been stealing glances at her. We'd been here most of the day, and he was just now saying something. He was subtle as hell with that. Like me, Sol had a long-term relationship that had gone south some years ago, and he'd taken a step away from the dating world.

"I didn't realize you were back out here. You swore off relationships." I replied.

"Fine as she is, my ass would come up off the bench too," Ray said.

Everything with Ray has been pretty chill lately. At least for the time being. That was always a good thing. It was nice to have him around. If anything, we could always count on him to make us laugh.

Solomon nodded. "Yeah. I certainly didn't set out to meet someone. But India is beautiful. I mean, *damn*."

"Destiney is beautiful with a beautiful ass friend. The fuck are the chances of that." Malachi, you ain't bout to be known as the only one with a badass wife on your arm." Ray chimed in.

We all cackled. Malachi has been with Ella for years, and from day one, everyone was captivated by Ella's beauty. She seemed more beautiful as we got older too.

"Well, you've already been introduced to her," I told Sol.

"Gone in the house, she's still in there I think." That was Malachi.

"Sol man, you been out the game so long, you done forgot how to talk to a woman?" Ray said.

We all laughed.

"I know how to talk to women fool!" Sol said. He looked over at me. "She seeing someone? Does she have any kids?"

I thought back on what Destiney mentioned. "Pretty sure she's single, and as far as I know, no kids," I said.

"Hmm," Sol said, nodding his head. He threw back the last of his beer, then placed the bottle on the table, sitting back in his chair.

"Nigga you need to move a little faster than that. She's single, no kids and she *that* fine? Shorty ain't gone last. Better get yo ass to it!" Ray said.

Sol rolled his eyes, and Malachi chuckled. Ray wasn't slick. That was code, meaning he planned on shooting his shot. I wasn't stupid.

"Ray, you can forget it. That's Destiney's friend, and I wouldn't allow it."

"Man, what you talking bout?"

"I'm serious. Stay away from India, Ray." I gave him a look.

Malachi shook his head. "Don't do it man. You know you're still out here playing way too many games."

"Even if it ain't me, ya'll know what I'm talking 'bout." Ray spat.

I glared at him a second longer. "Long as it ain't you," I said finally.

Mal and Sol thought that was so funny.

"Well, that's my queue. Let me go find my wife. It's about time I gave her a few more kisses. Maybe I can give her something else since yall niggas ain't leaving no time soon. I'll be back."

We all laughed. Malachi and Ella fucked like some damn rabbits. I was surprised they only had two kids. She had to have gotten her tubes tied or some shit. I wasn't mad. She had been his wife for nearly two decades, and they'd managed to keep the fire burning. It was a beautiful thing, and it gave me something to look forward to.

"I'm gone head out man, but I'm going to ask India for her number before I leave," Sol said, standing up. I stood with him and slapped his hand. "Aight, man. Be good."

Sol went inside, and I sat back in my chair, finishing the last of my beer. I didn't mind getting between Destiney's legs myself. I pulled my cell phone out and texted her.

Ready to get out of here baby? I sent the fire emoji too, and Destiney knew what that fire emoji meant.

I leaned back in my chair as she replied.

Beauty: *Your place or mine?*

I'll sleep at her place tonight. Since I work from home, it will be easier for her tomorrow morning. I couldn't wait to get her home. I was going to make sweet love to her. In the shower and her bed. I could feel him waking up already.

Yours

Beauty: *Give me ten more minutes I'm talking to Gabby*

Indeed

"You done?" Ray asked irritably as I was putting my phone back in my pocket.

"Man, stop. You quit being nasty and you can get   you   one   too."
"I tried! You and Malachi are blocking me."

I smirked and gave him a knowing expression.

"You know you ain't ready to settle down and be serious with anyone." Ray looked off in the distance. After a while, he said, "All this shit is just sex, man. That's it. Shit is getting old. I do want to settle

490

down. But women play games too." Ray let out an exasperated sigh. Now, my interest was piqued. It was seldom that he got serious when it came to this topic. "Can I tell you something, cousin?" Ray was being vulnerable, which was rare as hell.

"Of course."

"I was sleeping with this chick off and on for some months. But then, I realized I was developing real feelings for her, which is something I *never* do. Like ever. I told her how I felt, and she told me she felt the same, so we decided to be exclusive. I was serious about that shit. Honest to God. I cut off everyone else and was only seeing her. I figured we could build something, maybe have a future. We even talked about moving in together. Well, I found out recently that she's still out there doing that same shit. I saw her coming out the washeteria hugged up with some nigga she was fucking. She'd been lying to me the whole time about all of it." He shook his head and then placed his face in his hands.

"Damn cousin. I'm sorry."

"I'm nothing like you and Malachi man. I wonder if I'm even capable of all that love and marriage and family shit."

"Sure, you are. It's all about timing. Sometimes, we meet the right people at the wrong time. Or the wrong people at the right time. Keep saying you will, and you'll find your person at just the right time."

"It's more than that. Ella and Destiney, they're perfect. Like a calm to a storm. The women I meet have so much emotional baggage."

"Everyone has some sort of baggage, Ray."

"Yeah. But older women have a different set of issues. Man, I outta get me some young snatch. They seem like the perfect type of woman. You got her right, man. That's what the fuck I'm trying to get."

"She's right where I want her," I spoke. "I wouldn't change a thing about Destiney. She's absolutely perfect for me." I couldn't help but smile. "When we first met, I had this idea of how I thought our relationship would go, but she got me all the way together man. She taught me so much. The proper way to court her. Patience in my pursuit." I rubbed my chin.

Ray furrowed his brows. "She the one that wouldn't see you for some months, and yall was just talking on the phone and shit?"

"Yes. The same woman. I unlearned all my bad habits. We spoke so much and learned one another inside and out before we even held hands. Let alone kiss or have sex."

"Wow."

"Maybe you should try doing things differently in your next pursuit. I don't think age necessarily has much to do with it. It's the person."

nineteen

DESTINEY

"This is going on my 'to be read' list! It's ever-growing, but I don't mind. I'll get to all these eventually." Gabby giggled. She did some clicking on her iPad, updating her Goodreads account.

I laughed. "It's the same for me, Gabby. Let me know when you're ready for that one. I have a copy I can pass you." We had been discussing *Jubilee* by Margaret Walker. African American historical fiction was a great genre, and Gabby was slowly embarking on her discovery.

I laid back on their comfortable couch, trying not to doze off. I was beyond full, first of all. We'd been having a great time at Malachi and Ella's for the past few hours. Eating Ella's delicious food, drinking, and enjoying each other's company. I hung out in the kitchen with Ella when Micah and I arrived, catching up with her and offering my help if needed. I took a quick FaceTime call from India, and Ella extended an invite to her. India's schedule is quite hectic, so I didn't expect her to be able to come on the fly. Surprisingly, she could. Before India headed out, Micah's friend Solomon came in, and they spoke briefly. Ironically, Micah had mentioned the cookout to him as well. They're both single, so I knew exactly what time it was when Solomon pulled his phone out and handed it to her. India was gorgeous, and I noticed the subtle glances he'd been giving her. Solomon seemed like a nice guy, and I was sure she'd fill me in if anything became of it.

Now, it was down to just Gabby and me hanging out in their living room, so we spent time bonding. I'm only about fifteen years older than Gabby, and she was seriously like the kid sister I never had. Gabby was such a sweet girl. Intelligent. Beautiful inside and out. Super silly. Gabby got it honest because Ella was much of the same. They

were both so much fun to be around. My relationships with them both meant so much to me already.

For the past hour, Gabby and I nerded over
books. I loved many titles across many genres, romance being at the very top of my list. I accidentally
minored in African Diaspora Studies in college. I say
accidentally because that's precisely what it was.

I needed to choose an elective for the upcoming quarter and decided on an introductory course
on African American Literature. I love reading and
figured it would give me a break from my intense
linguistics courses. It was not at all what I expected
but in the best way. Every damn thing blew my
mind, and I *adored* my professor. As the quarter pro-
gressed, I was enamored with so many titles. The
game changer was when I discovered books from the
Harlem Renaissance Era, and that was when I knew.
I couldn't change my major so late without adding at
least another year before I could graduate; however,
I was able to squeeze in a minor. *Cane River*, *Not Without Laughter*, *Blacker the Berry*. *Passing* by Nella Lar-
son was another one Gabby and I talked about. It had
grown in notoriety since the Netflix film, but I read
the book several years back and enjoyed it.

Micah and Ray were still on the back patio.
Not long ago, Malachi came in and pulled Ella to him
from her seat on the couch, and they made out in the
living room. Those two were always kissing. Not
pecks, but that heavy kissing. It always cracked me
up because Gabe and Gabby didn't pay them any
mind, yet many kids their age got squeamish when
they saw their parents being affectionate. I think one
reason was that it was an everyday thing for them. I

believe parents should show love and affection in front of their children. Hugging, kissing, holding hands, and even flirting create fond memories of your parents in love. I think it brings children security. It certainly beats the alternative of having memories of parents fighting all the time.

Once they came up for air, Malachi led Ella out the front door. They had an expansive porch complete with a swing and rocking chairs. The sun was beginning to set, and I was sure it was a romantic vibe out there. This wasn't even the first time. Earlier, Malachi quickly scooped Ella up, tossing her over his shoulder, and moved through the living room toward the stairs. I heard him smack her ass as Ella cackled.

"*Chiiii!*" Ella drew his name out. She was in a fit of giggles. "We have company baby!"

"Yall carry on. We'll be back. Or maybe we won't. I'on know yet." Malachi declared, strolling up the stairs with ease. With one arm, he held her securely, and with the other, he rubbed Ella's ass and thighs, giving it an occasional smack. Sounds of Ella's excessive laughter floated behind them. India and I shared a glance and fell into a fit of giggles.

Micah texted me about being ready to get going, and I was ready too.

"Alright Gabby girl. I'm going to grab your uncle so we can get out of here." I gave her a tight hug.

"Okay. Alone time with you is the best. We talk about so many things!"

"I enjoy our chats too love."

"I'm going to ask Uncle Micah if I can come by this weekend. You'll be there, right?"

I smirked. *I damn near lived there,* but I wouldn't tell her that. "Let me know when you're going, and I'll be sure to be there too."

"Okay!"

I'd already given her my cell phone number, and we occasionally texted one another.

I headed toward the back patio to tell Micah I was ready to get home. I was just about to open the screen door when I heard it. "Man, I outta get me some young snatch. They seem like the perfect type of woman. You got her right man. That's what the fuck I'm trying to get."

"She's right where I want her." I heard Micah respond. I stopped abruptly mid-step, and my breath was caught in my throat.

I couldn't believe what I heard. My heart dropped as I quickly spun around, walking straight past the kitchen and out the front door. Tears began to flood my eyes. *Right where he wants me?* The fuck does that even mean. Was his goal to get a young, innocent, naive girl to groom or some shit? I tore through the front door, almost colliding with Malachi and Ella as they returned inside.

"Destiney!" Ella exclaimed.

Seeing how upset I was, Malachi gently grabbed my arm. "Hey, Baby sis. You okay?"

I nodded quickly as the tears began to fall, and I didn't bother to wipe them.

"Why are you crying?" Ella asked, reaching out to me. I broke away from her and kept walking toward my car.

"Micah know you leaving? Why isn't he walking you out?" Malachi's voice dipped in concern. He tried to grab me, too, but I broke from his grasp.

"He doesn't know." I managed and continued down the driveway to my car.

"That's aight, I'm out here anyway," he said as he and Ella followed closely behind me.

I didn't respond. I jumped into my car, slammed the door, and sped off before I strapped in my seatbelt. I began to cry hysterically as the floodgates opened. I could hardly see as the tears fell freely from my eyes. I felt terrible for the way I'd treated Malachi and Ella. None of this was their fault. I hopped on I-5 northbound, ready to get home and into bed.

I knew he was too good to be true. I knew, at some point, the other foot would drop.

Everything had been going so perfectly that I had finally let all that go.

My heart was hurting. I heard my phone ringing. Glancing over, I saw it was Micah. He called again twice more. A moment later, Ella called me. I ignored her call but would text her once I was off the road.

Then, I would block Micah's number.

He can try that grooming shit with someone else.

twenty

MICAH

I called Destiney for what seemed like the hundredth time… but it went straight to her voicemail this time. Either her phone was off, or she blocked me. I was so confused.

We'd all had such a great time at Malachi's house.

Or so I thought.

Mal and Ella were great hosts, as always. We ate good, of course. Sol and Ray came through, and India joined us. It was great seeing her again. She was dope, and she and Destiney had such a great friendship. I loved that for Destiney.

Eventually, the men had all gone out to the patio, and the women spent time in the house for a while. Destiney was chilling with Gabby once India took off, but I knew she'd be ready to head home soon. It had been a long day. I planned to follow her home once she was ready. Sol had already headed out. I was sitting on the back patio with Ray, shooting the shit, when Malachi came in with Ella on his heels to alert me of what had occurred moments prior.

"What's going on with your wife man?"

"What are you talking about?"

"She left." I heard Ella say.

"Left?"

"She said you didn't know she was leaving. But she seemed pretty upset. Baby sis was crying." Malachi continued, "She wouldn't tell us anything. She just got in her car and sped off."

I stood immediately and headed into the house. Malachi, Ella, and Ray followed.

Now, I was confused as hell. And worried. Why would she be crying? And why did she leave without telling me? We planned on leaving together; otherwise, I would always walk her out. I grabbed my phone and called her. It rang through, eventually rolling to voicemail, so I called her again.

"You think somethings going on with her family?" Ray asked.

"I'm not sure. Seems she would have told me." After getting her voicemail again, I texted her, asking if she was okay and asking her to please call me as soon as she could. I knew she was still driving, but I was sure she'd get back to me once she was off the road.

"I'll try to call her too," Ella said, placing her phone to her ear. I grabbed my jacket and put my shoes on.

"Thanks Ella. Let me know if you hear from her before me." I wasn't even sure why I said that shit.

"Of course." She replied.

I hugged Malachi and kissed Ella on the cheek. "I'm out of here. Let me try to figure out what's going on."

"I'm out too, cousin," Ray said as we slapped hands.

As soon as I cranked up, I headed toward Destiney's house. I needed to get to my baby and make sure she was okay.

I made it to Destiney's house in record time and saw her car parked outside. I was somewhat relieved but even more confused, as I'd called her several times since leaving Malachi's. I sprinted up the steps and rapidly knocked on the door. I heard the locks disengage, and a few moments later, Daijah greeted me.

"Hey Micah." She seemed okay, so it was likely that there wasn't a family emergency. That was good news.

"Hey Daijah." I stepped forward but halted abruptly once I realized she wasn't inviting me in. "My apologies. Do you mind if I come in? Destiney and I were over at my brother's house, and she suddenly left in tears. I've been calling and texting her, but she isn't responding.

Daijah slowly shook her head. "She doesn't want to see you right now."

"She doesn't want to see me? Why not?" I exclaimed, then immediately felt terrible. My volume was too loud for comfort, and my tone was unfriendly. I wasn't the type of man to raise my voice to any woman. I took a deep breath and then exhaled. "I'm sorry for raising my voice at you, Daijah."

"No harm done." She reassured me.

"Do you know why she doesn't want to see me?" If anyone knew, Daijah did. She and Destiney were closer than close. Just as close as Malachi and me.

She paused for a moment. "It's best if the two of you talk about it."

"But she won't answer my calls."

"I promise you will at least get a text. I'll go back to her room right now and make sure."

"Thanks, Daijah. Have a good night." I said, turning to head back to my car.

"You too." She said to my back, closing the door softly.

She doesn't want to see me.

This shit is bizarre.

twenty-one

DESTINEY

"Are we really back here again?" You can't just ignore him, Des. That isn't fair. He has no idea why you're even upset with him. How do you expect him to fix it if he doesn't know what he did?" Daijah had come home right behind me, and I filled her in on the latest. We were in her room, and I was lying across her bed on my stomach. I hardly ever came into her bedroom these days because she was hardly home. She was lying right beside me on her back.

"He should know! How is that okay? *I have her like I want her*?" I imitated, pissed all over again.

"That's all you heard?"

"Yes. Well, aside from what his idiot cousin Ray said. I don't like him at all, Daijah. He's such a manwhore. He's always on these sexual escapades and dealing with multiple women at one time. He and Micah are nothing alike."

"That's his cousin. We got crazy ass cousins too. Hell, everyone does. But they don't have any bearing on who we are as individuals."

"Okay," I said, returning a blank stare.

"You just completely missed my point." Daijah threw up her hand and huffed loudly. "Since you're in your feelings, I'll let that slide." She sat up next to me. "You just said Micah is nothing like Ray, right?"

I nodded.

"That means there's more to be considered. You only heard *some* of the conversation. Just because Ray said that, that doesn't necessarily mean Micah agreed. He likely refuted Ray's stance, but you walked away before you could hear it. If Micah were that type, we'd know it. And I'm willing to bet you'd have a different opinion had you heard the entire conversation."

I considered Daijah's words. She had a point. Micah mentioned several times that Ray was a wildcard, but they tolerated him since he was family, loving him just the same. Malachi and Micah were close to Ray, Micah a little closer; nonetheless, Ray's lifestyle choices did not appear to have any bearing on Malachi's or Micah's in the grand scheme. They didn't even seem to have the same ideals and convictions.

"You see what I mean?" Daijah asked, bringing me from my thoughts.

"Yeah, I guess I do," I replied. Daijah was probably right. Knowing Micah, he likely didn't even agree with Ray. He was literally in the middle of a thought and pissed; I stormed off.

"Please reach out to him. I felt so bad. He stood on the porch looking like he lost his best friend."

I hung my head.

"I can text him, but I'm embarrassed at how I reacted."

"So, tell him that part too. Tell him everything."

I probably wasn't the best person for a relationship with Micah. I handled this situation like a damn teenager. He didn't deserve that, and I didn't deserve him. Who was I kidding? It was best I stopped while I was ahead.

I may need to end things with Micah.

twenty-two

MICAH

I got up to use my ensuite restroom. Just as I was washing my hands, I heard my phone ringing. I flew back into my bedroom to see it was Malachi. I sighed.

"Brother."

"Hey man. You talk to her?" Mal asked me.

"Not yet. I think she blocked me."

"Okay. I wanted to tell you that she texted Ella earlier. Ella just saw it though; she's never glued to her phone. Never knows where the thing is half the time."

"Really? What did she say?"

"Just that she's sorry for storming off and ignoring us when we tried to see about her. She didn't offer anything else. Ella figured she'd share if she wanted to talk about anything more, so she didn't press."

"Well, I'm glad she heard from her at least." I felt a little better about that.

"Yeah."

"I'm so confused man. I wish she would at least tell me what has her so upset. This is our first official argument, and whatever it is, she has completely shut down from me."

"You ain't cheat on her, did you?"

"What? No!"

Malachi chuckled. "I already knew the answer to that. I was just messing with you, man. But seriously, I'm sure she will come around eventually."

"You think so?"

"Yeah man. I can't think of anything that could be worse than that. She'll come around."

"Thank you, Brother. I love you man."

"I love you, baby Brother. One more thing. I won't keep you."

"What's that?"

"Romance the *hell* out of her. I know you already have been. You've learned from the best."

We shared a light chuckle.

"But seriously. You have her address. You know what to do."

"I gotchu."

"Try to get some sleep, baby brother. Everything will work out."

"Thank you brother. Goodnight."

"Goodnight."

I tried calling Destiney again just to get her voicemail. I let out an exasperated breath as I rolled onto my back, staring at the ceiling. I doubted I would get a wink of sleep tonight. I closed my eyes momentarily, hearing a light chime from my cell phone on my side table. I ignored it, keeping my eyes closed, trying to clear my head. Whatever it was, it could wait. I knew it wasn't my baby anyway.

Daijah said she'd make sure Destiney texted me, but that was hours ago. Maybe she didn't mean tonight; perhaps she meant eventually.

I'd give Destiney a couple of days. Three at the most. I was moving in if I still hadn't heard from her after that. Making an executive decision.

We were *not* going to have a repeat of last time.

No way, no how.

No sir, no ma'am.

twenty-three

DESTINEY

"Destiney!"

I looked up toward the voice just as Neeka excitedly waved, making her way toward me from across the produce section.

Great. I mumbled to myself, sighing inwardly. I didn't feel like talking to anyone, least of all Neeka. Yet and still, I remained in place, figuring I'd see what she wanted and then be on my way.

I stopped at the store on my way home from work. I only planned to be here for a few minutes tops. I could carry my items and didn't even bother getting a basket.

I needed more than the small bags of tomatoes, limes, and avocados in my hand. I hadn't been grocery shopping for my house in ages.

This store, in particular, was the one I frequented the most.

Back when I needed to.

Hanging out with Micah and being at his place so much meant I didn't have to.

But. I'd been back at my place for the past couple of days.

Just me. Daijah practically lived with Julian. Hell, up until three days ago, I was living with Micah damn near. I even had a key to the place.

Anyway, returning home meant I needed to cook for myself again. Last night, I had cereal for dinner, which was fine. I didn't feel like having anything else. The night before last, I had rice and spicy lentils. I eat lentils pretty often. They're a staple for me; they have lots of protein, and I always keep bags of dry lentils in my pantry. Micah even had a few bags for me at his house.

Micah.

Luckily for me, India was coming over tonight, and we'd be making tacos. Even though I didn't have much of an appetite, I loved taco nights with my best friend, and I was looking forward to it. Sometimes, we made them with black beans, but tonight, we were making them with *Impossible Ground Beef.* You cook and season it just like actual ground beef. It's pretty good. I still remember what real ground beef tastes like, and it's one of the best meat substitutes I've had. I've been a vegetarian for almost a decade and tried many.

Earlier, Indie told me she wouldn't be able to stay the night; she'd need to get back to her parents. But we'll try to link up again in a couple of days.

And speaking of a couple of days, I swear these past three days have been the longest three days of my freaking life. I was losing my mind.

Missing Micah.

"Hey stranger!" Neeka said with a plastered-on smile. "Haven't heard from you in a while. New man must be keeping you busy."

I stood there, silent. Deadpan. Looking Neeka in the eye.

I usually would have eagerly embraced Neeka and then filled her in on everything going on in my life. I didn't say a word. My silence was deafening and awkward. I guess she felt she needed to fill the space with something. "I mean. You've been *super distant*." She was right. Neeka and I didn't talk daily, but several weeks had passed since our last conversation. We last spoke when she came to my house those weeks back. Ordinarily, I would have texted her by now. But I didn't bother to text her after that. Nor did she text me. Honestly, we'd only talk when I reached out first, anyway. Neeka continued, "I assume that's the reason." She cracked up. I didn't find shit funny, and her laughter was excessive, in my opinion. I'm guessing she was cracking up at herself, which was fine. I laughed at myself *all the time*.

Before I realized it, I started to laugh too.

At her.

Directly.

Neeka must think I'm stupid.

And at some point, maybe I was when it came to dealing with her wack ass.

I shouldn't have ignored all those red flags.

She was *never* my friend. Yet I treated her golden.

My desperation for a friendship with Neeka had me turning a blind eye to shit that most people wouldn't have tolerated.

"The phone works both ways." Her eyes grew wide at my even response. I know *that* took her off guard. I'd never spoken to Neeka like that. I didn't talk like that ever.

Fucking glass house. She can dish it, but it doesn't seem she can take it. It looked as if she almost clutched at her imaginary pearls but caught herself. Also, she'd suddenly stopped laughing—not a trace of a smile or mirth anywhere. I think right after I started laughing, suddenly, whatever she was laughing at wasn't so damn funny anymore.

"I'll need to get going. India's meeting me at my place."

"Really? What are you guys cooking?" She assumed we'd be cooking tonight, and she was right.

She used to be invited to these. But I ain't forget the last time I invited her; she had some fuck shit to say about my clothes.

"*Tacos?*" She asked, eyebrows high when I said nothing. "*I love Indie's tacos.*"

"Me too. Bye Neeka." I said dryly. I turned to walk away without a second thought.

And I walk fast.

I was wearing a busted pair of sneakers covered in blotches of paint, so I got away from her faster than she could keep up. Neeka was impeccably dressed in her usual pencil skirt, tucked-in blouse, and pumps.

Anyway, the conversation was over. She was fishing, and I wasn't biting.

"Destiney, wait!" I stopped. Why? I don't know. But I didn't turn around. I was in the bakery section now, closer to the front of the store, which was a bit crowded. People busied themselves around us with their shopping carts and children. I honestly didn't want to hear anything she had to say.

"I don't have any plans tonight." Neeka offered once she was facing me. "Can I come by? I'll bring wine with me."

My eyebrows were high on my head.

That's bold as fuck. And desperate. I shook my head. "Honestly, Neeka, tonight isn't a good night."

"A good night for what? It's only me. Me, you and Indie. That's typical." She shrugged. Yeah, she was desperate. And eager. It was evident in her voice.

Meanwhile, I thought over just how blunt I would be with her.

I sighed. "It's not a good night for *you* to come over. I am anxious as hell whenever you're around. You're too much."

"Too much? I'm just being me." She chuckled at that. And I said nothing as she waived dismissively. "I'm your friend. Y'all are my girls, and I am *way* overdue. *Been bored out of my mind!* So, what time should I come by?"

I looked at her square in the eye. "You aren't invited Neeka. And you aren't my friend." Her eyes ballooned. Her lips parted. She wasn't getting it, so I needed to say it. "*I've* certainly been a friend to *you*.

I was so nice to you. Too nice honestly." I shrugged. "A friend wouldn't speak like you've spoken to me. Or treat me the way you've treated me. I'm doing myself a disservice, giving you access to me." I gave Neeka half a beat, then, "And I know you're fucking Tyler." I lied.

I didn't know. But Neeka confirmed India's suspicions when she began to stammer.

"I... wha..." She snapped her mouth shut; her eyes narrowed to slits. "Tyler doesn't even belong to you!"

I slowly shook my head, rolling my eyes. Wow. *That's* what she chose to respond to?

"I need to spell it out for you, Neeka. Fine. It's not that ya'll are fucking. It's the way you choose to move about it. Sneaking around like that?" I gave her an incredulous glare. "Why hide?" I shook my head again, shrugging. "Friends wouldn't do that shit either. *We dated.* Why would you even... you know what? Never mind. Bye Neeka."

I turned to continue toward checkout, determined to leave everything right where it was.

Neeka caught me on the wrong day.

Or maybe it was the right day. It had been three days since the ordeal at Malachi and Ella's house, and I wasn't in the mood for Neeka's bullshit. Regardless, that conversation needed to happen a long time ago. I'm not sure I would have been so outspoken about that if I weren't in my feelings over things with Micah.

I've dealt with many toxic women. *Frenemies.* Plenty. More than I care to admit. Allowing women who are lackluster friends and just plain awful towards me into my life and my space was *my bad*.

But it's disgusting.

Repulsive how people think they can treat someone any way they feel like and then just sweep that shit under the rug as if it never happened and *then* be buddy-buddy in the next moment without even apologizing.

It didn't occur to Neeka to even hold herself accountable and ask *how* she's been a lousy friend so she can address it. And not the Tyler part, because honestly, that didn't bother me as much as how she treated me.

Neeka is toxic in general. And narcissistic. She invested too much time in the external, except for her academics and career. I'm no psychologist, but in my opinion, she never worked on developing her character. Or integrity. Neeka insisted she was looking for her husband, but the men she entertained only wanted to fuck her, so they'd never been able to tell her about herself.

And no man with sense would wife *that*. Not in *that* condition.

You can always tell when someone is speaking from a place of trauma. *Them motherfucker's* shine bright like diamonds.

You can hear when someone is projecting their feelings and opinions on the world because they are louder than everyone else—the loud minorities.

That's Neeka.

If she committed to seeing a therapist and did some serious work internally, she'd be okay.

But seriously fuck Neeka. I drove away from the store, pissed the hell off at her *audacity*.

I'm not the problem she is.

I'm like the mafia. It's hard to get in with me. My circle is curated, so when you're in with me, you are in. Like *in*, in. I am loyal. To a default.

Sometimes, I wonder if that works against me. Like, perhaps I've created a monster.

I realized I have a problem as it relates to people like her.

For the right people, I'm *exactly* the way I should be. Me.

***

I stepped inside and headed toward the kitchen. I dropped my backpack by the door and then placed my sack of groceries on the counter beside the roses I received yesterday.

Beside the roses was a sunflower arrangement I had received the day before.

They were so beautiful. The red roses were too, of course, but the *sunflowers*.

I'd never told Micah that sunflowers were my very favorite flowers.

And I love sunflowers. I love how bright they are, their big, beautiful boldness. They look like little suns, ready to lift your spirits. And when they were delivered two days ago, I cried all over again. Despite how ridiculously immature I was, Micah still thought enough of me to send my favorite flowers.

I barely hung my coat up when I heard my doorbell ring. I didn't think Indie would be here for another hour, but she knew she could come early if needed. I went to answer the door, and to my surprise, it was an *Edible Arrangement*.

After signing for my delivery, I thanked the driver and placed them on my counter. A note was attached, just as there were with the other two deliveries.

I'll always be yours, my Destiney baby. I love you. - MW.

***

"Neeka is wild. She doesn't even know what the hell she wants half the time." Indie said. We were sitting on the couch with some Tyler Perry movie on. I don't know which one. I was hardly watching.

When she first arrived, we'd briefly spoken about her and Solomon. Indie said he seemed chill, and she'd been chatting with him casually. She mentioned liking him a lot and seeing a future with him, but she was transparent about her recent break-up and wanted to be fair to Solomon. He was a good guy and didn't deserve her on some rebound shit. I respected that.

It was a trip too because Indie and I were both single for once.

We were *never* single at the same time.

Well, Indie was never single. Not for long, anyway; she was a serial monogamist. She's only had two boyfriends in the seven almost eight years since I've known her, but both of those relationships were years long. Before her most recent ex, she dated a guy she'd been with since high school. They dated for close to five years.

And I'd never been in a relationship.

This was my one and only, and… anyway.

I filled Indie in on what happened at the store earlier. And she was off on her tangent. Which often happened when Neeka did something to piss her off.

"I'm proud of you for standing up to her. I know she was flabbergasted." Indie chuckled hard at that. I did too. "I think she did well for herself, objectively speaking. If those things matter to you. But she leads with that."

India was right. Neeka is young but has accomplished a whole lot. She's a couple of years older than me but has a great career in Public Health Administration. Super smart. She skipped a grade, so she graduated from high school at sixteen and had two master's by twenty-four. She made great money, had nice things, and traveled the world.

But her conversation was limited, and somehow, regardless of the subject, she brought everything back to *her*.

Neeka was Neeka's favorite subject. She seemed one-dimensional on a good day. She only spoke about her academic and professional accomplishments.

"She's okay, I don't think she's a knockout." India said. She was still going. I was hardly listening if I'm honest. Neeka's ass wasn't my concern. "She likes to think she's the most beautiful thing you've ever seen. She's above average but her attitude makes her look bad. And that attitude and personality will repel a man every time. It seems some women who are high achieving have a harder time locking down a man. That's probably one of the reasons she doesn't have a man. She seems scattered and unsure of herself at times. She makes it seem that she has so many men that want to date her. Yet no one seem to want commitment. They just want to fuck on her. Like *all of them*. She used to say she didn't want anything serious but as of late, didn't you notice she's been commenting about wanting a husband? We *are* getting older so I could see why she change her tune."

India stood from the couch returning to the kitchen. Her words floated behind her. "I am so over that topic. And I really need to be nice." After a beat, "These flowers are beautiful Best." India commented. She was still back in the kitchen. Helping herself to thirds. I was stuffed, sprawled back on the couch, but I would probably have at least one more taco once I let my food go down.

I didn't have much of an appetite earlier, but I was ready by the time the food was ready.

"Yeah, they are." I sighed. "You see that fruit in the fridge? You're welcome to as much as you want. I can't eat all of it. Daijah may not be home anytime soon." That Edible Arrangement was massive. I'd already eaten quite a few of the chocolate dipped pieces. The pineapples were my favorite. Even then there was so much left of it.

"Sure, I'll have some." A few moments later, India put two plates on the coffee table then returned to her spot on the couch. One plate was covered with fruit, and one had two more tacos.

India could eat me under the table, but she always remained thin. "You know Des... there may not be too many more of these." Indie said, pulling me from my thoughts.

And they were on Micah. Naturally.

My response was delayed when I absently asked, "More of what?"

"I read his note. You broke things off with him and he's still fighting for you. Sending you these gorgeous flowers and expensive ass fruit." Out of my peripheral I could see Indie shaking her head. "I'm saying this out of love, Best. Micah may get tired of this. You don't want to lose him for good, do you?"

I hung my head.

Of course, I'd told Indie about the portion of the conversation I heard.

The night everything happened, I sent Micah a text message. Which I'd shared with Daijah and India too. They wanted to bite my head off for going overboard. Anyway, I did block him that night too but only for a couple hours. I thought that was a bit extreme after talking things over with Daijah. So, I unblocked him and sent him a text message. It was pretty late by then. I figured he'd gone to sleep. I wasn't expecting a response that night but after some time, Micah called me. I was still up so I answered his call.

I told Micah about the portion of the exchange I heard between him and Raymond. Micah went on to explain further and of course, it was taken out of context on my part.

Micah apologized profusely and despite that, for some damn reason, I stood firm on my brilliant idea to end things.

And since then, Micah has been sending me flowers. Beautiful flowers.

For the past three day's he'd also sent me *good morning, thinking of you, good night* and *I love you* texts.

The entire first day I left him on read, but by day two- yesterday, I was even more beside myself and replied to each one.

Good morning.
Thinking of you too.
Good night.
I love you too.

Micah hasn't tried calling me again. Anyway, I was such a mess behind this shit.

And it was all my fault. Again.

All of it. And I thought my breakup with him was apparent, but Micah wasn't giving up on me so quickly. On us. And I'm happy he wasn't. I miss him so much.

Why couldn't I have just gone to him, instead of rushing to conclusions?

Worse than that, making an impulsive decision. This misunderstanding could have been cleared up immediately if we'd just had a conversation.

I needed to handle myself better. Micah is a grown ass man and behaves like one. My lack of experience in relationships always shows itself at the worst times. It's embarrassing as hell. I wanted my man back and planned to call Micah as soon as India left.

And. Indie was right; this was strike two.

I'd be out of his life for good at strike three. No doubt in my mind.

***

I'm sorry baby.

India helped me clean the kitchen, and then she had to get going.

After shutting everything down in the front of the house, I headed to my bedroom to shower quickly.

I planned to call Micah as soon as I got settled. By the time I finished moisturizing my skin and settling into bed, I had received a text message from him. I figured he may be saying goodnight. He apologized. I sighed.

Micah had no reason to be sorry.

Desperately needing him- needing to reassure him, I called him. It rang once, and then I immediately felt the familiar comfort of his voice.

"Hey baby." His voice. It was smooth. It was familiar. And despite myself, it made me smile.

"Hey."

We were both silent for a beat.

"I'm sorry."

"I really am sorry."

We spoke at the same time.

"No Micah. I should be the one apologizing. *I'm* sorry. *I'm so sorry.* I'm sorry I didn't come to you." I was getting emotional, and, in a minute, I would surely break into an ugly cry.

"It's alright. I can see why you felt the way you did. Ray can have such a shit mouth. And I absolutely could have said that better than I did." He sighed heavily. "But... can we promise each other this won't happen again, and we'll always talk to each other first?"

"I promise baby." I avowed immediately. "I'm embarrassed as hell and angry at myself for how I reacted."

"No harm done beautiful. We learned from this, and now we can move on. I love you, Destiney baby."

"I love you too Micah. So much." I felt relieved. Immensely. And damn. I missed him.

The line was silent for a few beats.

"What are you doing baby?" Micah asked.

"Laying down. Talking to you. What are you doing?"

"Laying down, talking to you."

"Hmm."

"You tired baby?" He volleyed.

"Not at all."

"Same. I want you. I want to see you. I need to."

I glanced at the time. "It's late. Almost eleven."

"I need to put my eyes on you. Be near you. Hold you."

Same. I felt my excitement rising. "Baby... *please* be careful getting here."

"Let's talk while I'm on my way to you."

"Okay."

"Hang on about to change."

"Alright."

I heard shuffling. Then, "I've missed you so much beauty."

"I missed you too handsome."

I heard him moving about, then I heard the jingle of his keys a moment later.

"Alright. I'm headed your way baby."

I heard the garage door. "Can't wait. My days went so slow without you." I whined.

"Mine too sweetheart. It was torture."

I groaned. "It was like being cut off from everything that mattered."

"Same for me baby." I heard the car engine. After a moment, Micah said, "Don't take you away from *me* again. I need you."

The sincerity in his voice pulled at my heart-strings. I knew he wasn't trying to make me feel bad, but I did anyway.

And I needed him too. Even over these three days, the longest three days of my life, I needed him. "I need you too baby," I said finally. "Never again."

"Never. Ever."

Silence cruised through the line. I heard him quietly breathing as he listened to me do the same. I didn't even hear the radio on. "On the freeway now."

"Get to me safely."

"Indeed." Silence. "Baby?"

"Yes?"

"I've dreamed of you."

"Have you really?" My heart tripled in size.

"Indeed. You are the woman of my dreams. All my dreams include you."

"My gosh. Micah...I can't believe how sweet you are to me. And your words... they...you are *everything*."

"I'm just a man in love. *So very in love*. I love you, Destiney baby."

"I really do love you too Micah. So much."

"You mean so much to me."

"You mean the world to me."

More silence cruised through the line.

"Almost to you."

"Yeah?" My heart rate picked up.

"Yeah."

When I heard a groan, my pussy started to pulse. The groan was low but heavy and laced with desire, and I heard it loud and clear. I was on that same type of time.

"I'm here baby."

I got up from the bed and headed down the hall. I heard his car outside, and Micah was sprinting up my walkway when I opened the front door. He picked me up swiftly and began to spin me around. I tightly wrapped my legs around his waist as he hungrily kissed me with passion and fervor. I kissed him back just as eagerly, sensual moans emitting from us both.

He finally broke our kiss. Holding my gaze, he asked, "Can I make love to you, sweetheart?"

"Please do." I returned without hesitation.

Our lips connected again as he carried me to my bedroom, closing and locking the front door behind us.

He gently placed me on my bed and immediately began unbuttoning my pajama top, holding my gaze with low lids, undoing each one. After the final button, he gently pushed each side over my bare shoulders, peppering wet kisses down to my erect nipples and back again. I moaned in response.

Standing straight, he pulled his t-shirt over his head, tossing it to the side. I saw his dick print, and I reached for the waistband of his sweatpants, pulling them down. I was greeted with a head glistening with pre cum. My mouth watered as I went to lick it off the tip, but Micah gently pushed me back.

There was a subtle shake of his head. "Not yet." Going to his knees in front of my bed, he pulled my silk pajama bottoms and my panties over my legs as I lifted off the bed. "Lay back for me baby. I'm going to take my time with you."

Doing as instructed, my legs fell open as he settled between them. I would get my turn to please him eventually.

And I wanted to. Desperately. I wanted to make it up to him. Show him how much I missed him.

Micah had other plans.

"Mmm." He spoke against my pussy as he inhaled and rubbed my slick center with his fingers. She was throbbing for him.

"Damn... my pretty pussy was looking for me."

I groaned in anticipation. "You have her spoiled."

Micah lightly chuckled. "I'm here now baby." He inhaled deeply, speaking into my pussy, "Mine." Moans low and gruff, Micah swiped his tongue, and I damn near came right then. He rubbed my clit a few times and began to French kiss my lower lips, his tongue and fingers alternating inside of me; I started rocking my hips, getting lost in ecstasy. I cradled his face in my hands, watching him and spreading my legs as wide as they could go. In moments like this, I wish I was a little more flexible. But Micah made it work. His tongue reached everywhere it needed to. I gently caressed his jaws with my thumbs, enjoying the sweet torture his tongue was putting on me.

Knowing him, he'd want to get a few orgasms out of me before he took his first. I was good with that too.

We were finally reunited, and it felt so damn good.

twenty-four

MICAH

"Fuck… Destiney baby…You hear how she's talking to me?" I said between licks, sucks, and slurps. "Mine," I said it again.

"All. Yours. Baby." She purred. I could feel her orgasm rising as she continued to grind on my face. It wouldn't be much longer from here. She'd already come on my tongue a few minutes ago.

I made my way up her body, leaving a trail of kisses, and slowly pushed into her. I loved eating her, but I needed to feel her. I leaned close to her ear as I stroked her slowly, telling her all the ways I planned to love her. Confiding in her while making love to her was one of the best times to share my heart with her.

The energy surrounding us was just right. We were connected in the most intimate of ways, consumed with emotion, vulnerability, and passion. I maintained my pace, determined to slow stroke her to oblivion. She felt so good, but I concentrated.

This was not the time to fuck her. Maybe round two or some shit.

"Destiney baby?"

"Yes…"

"Does it feel good my love?"

"Yes... you know just what I like... you take good care of me. She's so happy."

"*Hell yeah,* she is. You hear how she's talking to me. She's so *loud.*" My chuckle was a deep rumble. "I hear you baby. I like it too." Destiney was so wet that the sounds of her wetness filled the room with each move I made.

Destiney got *incredibly wet.* It actually blew my mind.

Wetter than water. Shit was sexy as fuck.

I placed my hand on her clit, rubbing it a few times. My fingers slid back and forth with ease.

Destiney giggled.

"*Oh,* you're ticklish here too baby?" I asked her.

"Shit. Guess so... maybe a little bit." She giggled some, and it turned to a moan.

"Hmm." I spent some time there with my thumb. Rubbing her. Pressing her button. My baby liked that.

Yeah. I was already certain, but this confirmed everything. Laughing like we were doing, while we were lovemaking. Destiney was *absolutely* my wife.

I kept stroking her. *Slow.* Savoring her. I wasn't going any faster than this. I told Destiney I was taking my time and I was serious.

"*You sexy girl.* My beautiful Destiney baby." Still stroking her. "You mean the world to me. You're so special. I'm going to prove it to you every day for the rest of my life." I spoke closely in her ear, moving slowly and deliberately. Pulling out for just a second, I sat back up on my hunches, stroking my hardness.

Destiney watching me with low lids. Looking like a beautiful fucking masterpiece.

My dick was oozing precum and glistening with her essence. Her fat pussy was swollen and gushing with a delectable combination of her juices and mine. I slowly pushed back inside. "Fuck baby, this is a beautiful sight." I was about to bust just watching the way my shit looked sliding in and out of her slick opening. I was back in her ear again. "I can't wait to marry you baby."

"Hmm." Her faint moans were sexy as hell. "I can't wait to marry you either baby."

She was so wet. And she was so tight around me. She could take all of me now, and I filled her to the hilt.

"Baby."

"Mmmhmm."

"You almost there love?" I asked her.

"Yes."

I was close my damn self, but I needed her to go first.

Stroking her a few more times, I said, "Give it to me, baby. I got you." I'd be right behind her.

Later when I finally turned her loose, her mouth was around me, sucking my soul from my dick.

"Mmmhmm. That's right. You sexy girl." She was pleasing me so damn good, and I wanted her to know it. I learned Destiney liked praise, which kept her out of her head. I had no problem hyping my woman up. She loved it when I spoke to her low and slow. My voice was already deep but huskier when I got in her ear. Pillow talk with her was for anytime and everywhere she was. Not just between the sheets.

She continued sucking me, and she'd gotten pretty good at this. I'd told her so too. A few times.

I lifted myself into her slick mouth as I hummed. I knew she liked that.

We both enjoyed this, and that was the goal.

A deep rumble escaped me, and she moaned too. Destiney told me she loved it when I did that.

And anyway, we still had a few things to talk about.

And we would.

"Yeah… suck your dick baby."

Once we were done with this.

***

I stirred from my slumber, realizing I had dozed off. Deciding to try to get some sleep, I went to plug up my phone, and my heart skipped a beat when I saw a notification that Destiney had texted me more than an hour ago. I quickly opened the message, and just as quickly, my heart sank.

Micah, I am sorry for ignoring all your calls and texts. I heard a portion of your and Ray's conversation earlier, and I came to a conclusion that is likely not even correct. Based on how I have handled myself tonight, it doesn't seem I'm the right person for you. Relationships are just not in the cards for me. I don't deserve you, and I hope that you will forgive me.

I called Destiney immediately after reading that message. It was pretty late by then—maybe close to midnight—but Destiney answered my call.

And we talked about it. And I apologized profusely.

And since then, Destiney has uttered her embarrassment. Many times.

Truth is, I'm the humiliated one.

I have no clue why I needed to say what I said to Ray. The way I said it. Worse, my baby had to hear that.

Terrible.

I wasn't happy with myself. At all.

Mature men are extremely self-correcting. Inward looking. And the thing with inward-looking individuals is that we're always working to make ourselves better.

We can't help it. Like literally.

We know our value.

We know people hold us in high esteem, and we hold ourselves in high esteem. We are working to fix our issues *immediately*.

We will apologize *immediately* or fix things *immediately*.

We always represent our best selves in any space we're in.

Beyond that, I had Daddy and Malachi continuing to hold me accountable.

We hold *each other* accountable.

I expect to be called on my shit.

"Man, you fucked that one up yo." Or *"Man, I told you blah, blah, blah."*

And I was. As expected, Mal told me about myself. Called me on my shit.

After I spoke with Destiney and discovered the issue, I called Malachi and told him the next day.

"Nigga what?!?" His voice was octaves higher. *"I'm inclined to believe you are joking with me. I just* **know** *you lyin'."*

I snorted a dry ass chuckle. *"Wish I was brother."* I shook my head. *"I had one too many beers or something. That doesn't even* **sound** *like me."*

"No doubt." Mal chuckled himself after a beat. *"I would have walked out too, baby brother. Please tell me you cleaned that up."*

"I did. And I'm making it up to her in every way possible."

"Yo ass had better. Give baby sis whatever she wants."

A languid cackle left me in spite of myself. *"So that's it?"* I posed flippantly.

It was rhetorical. After that fiasco-of-a-blunder, there wasn't a damn thing Destiney couldn't ask me for.

For Destiney, I was willing.

"It's a start. The first order of business is to figure out **whatever** *the hell it is you need to do to get back in her good graces."*

"I'm already knowing, and I'm already on it." I returned.

Destiney seemed most concerned that her in-experience made her unequipped for a relationship with me. This being her first official relationship, she didn't feel she was cut out for it, and then there was our age difference.

I understood. But I disagreed, of course.

"Destiney... no..." I said the word firmly be-cause I needed her to understand. I shook my head profusely, though she couldn't see me. This would likely be one of the few times I would ever tell her

no. *"And I mean this respectfully, sweetheart. We aren't breaking up baby if you need a day or two. Space. That's fine. But we're not walking away from each other."* I'd told her. *"We're not just throwing all of this away. All the time we spent working this thing out, getting it just like we want it."*

No one is going to come behind me and step in and benefit from my hard work.

I'll be *damned.*

It wasn't going to happen.

I continued, *"We've gotten this to a great place. We built this beautiful thing together, and you had everything to do with it. Experienced or not."*

And I did give her space as much as I hated to. I gave it to her because that's what she needed.

And I continued to check in with her, missing her like crazy. Her laughter and energy were sorely missing from my home—our home. Her scent permeated my bedroom, and I spent all my time there, lying where she usually did, using the pillow she always used.

And I texted her.

And I sent her two floral arrangements.

When I perused the site and tried to decide, roses were an obvious choice, but that was too easy.

Destiney inspired and made me feel so many emotions; I wanted to step outside the typical. Sunflowers were a perfect choice because they reminded me so much of her. Destiney was like a ray of sunshine in my world. Her smile overtook her entire face. I was putty in her hands whenever she graced me with her smile.

"Everything feels so right with you. Micah." Destiney said, pulling me from my thoughts.

We were lying in Destiney's bed. I was on my back; she was on my chest. Her long, gorgeous locs splayed across the back of her naked body. It was dark in her bedroom, but her thin drapes let in the bright moonlight. My eyes followed the winding path of her body. A path my hands traveled many times. Her peaks and valleys. The rise of her plump ass. I loved her petite, curvy figure. Her naked body was alluring. She wasn't super trim or thin but fleshy and slightly toned. Soft and pretty. Lovely. Sweet.

I had my arms securely around her. Her arms were around me, too. It was late, after one a.m. now. We'd already decided neither of us was going to work tomorrow. We'd spend the day together. Not sure what we'd do, but I didn't care, just as long as I was with her.

It was completely silent until just a moment ago. We'd typically have music, but not right now.

"Like, my life has completely changed. In the best way. Since meeting you, I have seen everything differently. Myself included. It's like everything was black and white before. And now… everything is in color. Vividly clear and beautiful. I'm so glad I get to be with you Micah. It seems so surreal sometimes. Laying with you right now. Being loved by you. As well as you love me. It's everything. You know? I never want to be apart. I love you so much." Destiney sighed a heavy sigh. "But love doesn't seem like a big enough word. The way I feel for you. It's a beautiful feeling. Something I can't describe. But my heart is yours."

I rubbed her back softly, processing her feelings and words for me. It was so sweet—all of it. "I'm the fortunate one," I was emboldened to say.

And I was. I don't know how I got her. But I did. Somehow.

Like my grandmother used to say, favor ain't fair.

"No way." I felt her chuckle against me. "I'm complicated. I am the *epitome* of self-sabotage. Men didn't get anything from me. My time or my attention. Occasional men tried to get at me, but it never went far." She took a heavy pause. "I used to think I wasn't deserving of a loving relationship. Until I met you. But I'm still learning, and I'm not so good at relationships. But I want to be better. I don't want to keep disappointing you. I may get on your nerves in the process... but I want to make you as happy as you've made me, if that's even possible for me. And I want to step outside of my comfort zone. And boldly take these steps. You've been so patient."

"Look at me, please." Destiney lifted her head from my chest as I told her, "You're doing just fine baby. You have no idea how happy you've made me. But let's discuss things. You can't make decisions for me, just like I can't make decisions for you. We can discuss them and make decisions together. I don't want you disappearing every time there's an issue. We can work through things together. I want to be here for you, but I need you to tell me when something's amiss. If you run away, I have no idea what's happening, and I can't be there for you. How can we grow?"

She slightly hung her head, looking away from me. "That's all I know how to do. Run away. Fight or flight. That's all I know."

"Baby." Destiney looked up again, and once I had her eyes, I said, "It doesn't have to be that way. Continue to show me how to love you, Destiney baby. If nothing else, I promise to take heed and give it everything I have. Everything within me. I've told you you're safe with me."

"I know." Her voice was small. Almost a whisper. Her head returned to my chest. "I need to tell you something."

"Anything. I'm all ears, my love."

"When I heard what I heard... which I know now I was *so* wrong about- but I didn't know that then... I was triggered."

I'd been rubbing her back. Suddenly, there was a shift in her energy. And I felt this tension.

That put me on alert. "Triggered?"

"Back when I was seventeen. There was a guy I knew. We were the same age, but he was much more sexually experienced than me... and he took advantage of me. It was my first sexual experience. He took my virginity." I heard her sniffle, and she started to wipe her face. Her head was still on my chest. But I wanted her eyes. At the same time, I tried to tread carefully. She was clearly speaking from a place of trauma.

"He took it?" My question was more of a statement. A statement I made as evenly as I could. "Destiney. *Baby*... were you...?"

She took a moment. A long moment. I heard sniffles and sobs. I felt her warm tears falling onto my chest. And I said nothing. Instead, I continued to hold her. Caress her.

I took a few deep breaths too because this made me angry.

"I mean. I don't think so. No. But I should have spoken up for myself." She was still sniffling but a little calmer now.

But me? My blood was boiling.

She gathered her bearings. "Anyway. I think that's what bothered me so much. It took me there. And I felt bad." She looked up. Her eyes were red and glossy. "Because I feel so safe with you. I was so frustrated with myself."

I held her in my arms. "You don't have to feel bad about any of that. Once we're triggered, our traumas show themselves whether we are ready or not."

"Definitely. And as much as I have wanted to leave that buried, I want to tell you everything. I want you to see me and know me. Inside and out."

"I want the same."

"I've never told anyone. Not even Daijah. I never spoken of it aloud. You're the only one who knows about that." She'd returned her head to my chest. I resumed rubbing her back softly. Trying to calm down. This shit with ol' boy had me livid. My chest was heaving in anger. I knew she could feel that my heart rate had picked up.

"Don't let this get you all upset," Destiney said, pulling me from my thoughts.

I was angry. I didn't know her then, but I was so very angry with that individual and what he'd done to her and taken from her.

"I'm sorry," I told Destiney.

Her eyes were on me again. "Micah. It isn't your fault. You have nothing to be sorry about."

"I'm saying it anyway. And I know it's not enough, but I'm so sorry. What you have is sacred, and he had no right to take it from you. Your virginity most of all."

"I appreciate your words and your heart."

"I mean it, love. Sincerely. Now that I'm a part of your life and you're a part of mine, I won't let any harm come to you. I'll protect you. I want to heal you of all of your hurts. Restore any insecurities."

"You're amazing."

"*You're* amazing." I thought about our conversation months ago when I told Destiney about the child that would have been. How much I grieved for them. I even shed a few tears. That's something I struggled with moving past. Especially now that I have the complete story. And Destiney encouraged me. *"Micah, your child is always with you, in your heart. And they're safe in the arms of Jesus. There's no better place for them. It's the only other place they belong"*. I appreciated her being there for me and not judging me. I've since gone to therapy to better process my feelings concerning that.

My hands were all over her body. Rubbing as low as they could reach and back up again. "You know I'm not judging sweetheart. But why do you think you never told Daijah?"

"She's very protective of me. Even though I'm the big sister. And I know her. Somehow, she'll feel like she's to blame. I don't want to put that on her. None of this is her fault."

"None of this is your fault either."

"Most days, I can believe that." Destiney shared.

After a beat. "Have you talked to anyone about that? A therapist, a counselor?"

"I'd been to a few support groups. Years back. But that's the extent of it. I probably could benefit from seeing an actual therapist. But since I'm self-employed, I'm underinsured. I'd have to pay out of pocket, which can be pricey."

I waited a moment. Then I gently told her, "Find a therapist, love. I can request my assistant send me a list of some of the best in the area. Once you've found one, make an appointment at your earliest convenience. Use the card I gave you. Please."

"I promise I will. Thank you."

twenty-five

DESTINEY

"Baby."

"Yeah baby."

I sighed. Looking over myself in the full-body mirror in Micah's walk-in closet.

The outfit I had in mind didn't come together the way I wanted, so I changed into something else. Then something else. Then something else. This was my fourth outfit change, and I was no closer to being ready. I peered down at my cell phone, noting the time. I was going to make us late. I just needed to be comfy and casual. And cozy. We were closer to winter now, and temperatures had dipped.

We planned to meet with the crew: Daijah, Julian, Malachi, and Ella. India was coming out too, and she told me she'd asked Solomon to meet us. They'd been spending more time together. I could tell how much she liked him. Micah said Sol shared that he was really into her, too.

I love wine and a good conversation, and I looked forward to going out.

Tonight- if I could get myself together, we'd go to *Wine & Graze Taproom*. I'd never been, but Ella suggested the place. It's in the Delta Shores area of Elk Grove. I peeped at all the pictures on Yelp, and it was right up my alley. It looked like a chill, grown-ass vibe and comfortable atmosphere. Like a very sophisticated bar & lounge. There was music, flat screens everywhere, and plenty of comfy couches. Each person pays a flat fee, and there are self-pour taps with wines, beers, cocktails, and even coffee. The menu had typical bar options, and the food looked pretty good. If you want something lighter, you can build your own charcuterie board, which can be as small or as large as you like, with options to share with everyone.

"You alright?" Micah asked in alarm as he entered the closet. He was likely concerned because I took too long to respond. And he'd been ready a long ass time ago. He looked great. Wearing dark-washed jeans and a navy cardigan over a crisp white button-up. He was barefoot, but I saw the all-black Timbs he'd pulled out. Micah cleaned up very nicely, but I loved his casual look, too.

"Can we stay here?" I asked with a flustered sigh.

"We can do whatever you want to do." I saw him come up behind me in the full-body mirror I was still facing. He moved my hair aside and kissed my neck. My eyes fluttered.

"You always say that."

"I mean it baby. You're driving. I'm just along for the ride."

Chuckling, I asked, "But what do *you* want?"

"You." He lifted my hair, kissing my neck on the other side. This was an open kiss, so he left a wet mark.

"What do you want to *do*?"

"You."

"Besides that." I had just an element of frustration in my voice. He was so sweet, but this was burning up our daylight. Also, I was just a tad bit on the edge. I haven't been feeling very well.

I decided to keep that part to myself, though.

Micah tittered lightly before releasing me and sitting on the ottoman he kept in his closet. "Why do you want to stay here baby?" Micah asked in earnest.

I released an exasperated sigh. "I'm just in a funk. I didn't have the best day. And I don't like the way this fits." I shrugged my shoulders absently. "None of that made any sense, I'm sure."

"I get it baby. But first of all, you look great."

My smile spread as I looked down and back up at myself in the mirror. I had some high-waisted leather moto leggings on. A cropped slouchy sweater. It was one of my favorites. Dark grey with an embroidered tiger's face on the front. Lots of details and colors. I received compliments each time I wore it. White cami underneath. I'd probably wear my low-top, all-black vans. This was it. I felt good, and my man said I looked good.

"Your body is great baby. It's perfect, actually."

"Ain't nothing perfect about me," I said playfully, giving him a sincere smile. My sweet Micah said that all the time.

I stepped over to the built-in shelves in Micah's closet. Not long ago, he surprised me with an elegant emerald jewelry box. It had a glass lid, and the top opened like a chest, with various slots for smaller pieces. Two more layers, pulled out in the front like drawers for bigger pieces. It was so chic, and I was so grateful for it. I was beginning to acquire quite a collection. My man just kept decorating me. He'd given me a gorgeous pair of solitaire diamond stud earrings with the jewelry box. I hadn't taken those off since I put them on.

"I still think you're trying to get me fat." I joked sarcastically.

"What you mean?" He glared at me with a mischievous grin.

"We eat good. Often. Between you feeding me, taking me out. Mommy's. Ella stuffing us with her bomb-diggity food... I've probably gained ten pounds."

Micah laughed. "You're exaggerating baby. But you can work out in my gym anytime."

"I'm on my feet often, so I'm constantly in motion. I've realized that's not good enough for all this eating I've been doing. Somethings got to give."

"You're perfect for me baby." He stood again and came behind me. Turning me to face him as he wrapped me in his arms, he said, "If you want to get out, let's go. If you want to stay here, we can do that too. You look beautiful regardless."

"I'm all good now baby. We can go." I went up on my tiptoes, kissing him softly. "And I love you, Micah."

He pecked me a few times. "I love *you*, Destiney baby."

***

We had a great time at *Wine & Graze*. Stayed for a few hours. I'd definitely be back.

Micah and I were the last ones to arrive. I was sure we'd beat Mal and Ella. We'd met them many times before, and they were always fashionably late. We all knew how they got down.

Anyway, when we first arrived, everyone was coupled up. It was like a quadruple date. Eventually, the men congregated around one of the screens to watch a football game. We ladies sat around a nearby table and had girl talk. Laughing so damn much, of course.

Looking at them, I considered how thankful I was for these ladies.

I was. Truly.

And I loved each of them dearly for different reasons.

Day, my dearest sissy and very best friend. My sibling bestie. And always my voice of reason.

Indie, the bestie. My twin flame. A protector of my spirit and the calm to my storm.

And Ella, my sister-friend. Ella loved me and wished me well from the beginning, and she was quickly becoming so *precious* to me.

These ladies were my *tribe*, and they meant the entire world.

A chorus of *thank yous* sounded as our server delivered our charcuterie board. It was right on time. The four of us immediately began to dig in. We'd already started drinking since the beverages were self-pour. I had a sweet red wine in my glass, which was paired perfectly with the chocolate and cashews I started munching on. We also had crackers, pepper jack cheese, feta cheese, strawberries, and blueberries.

The ladies carried on chatting about something, but for a brief moment, I was distracted. I looked to my left to find Micah already looking at me. I smiled big and bright, and Micah did the same, winking too. I felt warm all over as he mouthed, *"I love you."*

Mouthing, *"I love you too,"* I blew him a kiss.

It was slight. A subtle gesture. I didn't make a show out of it. Just a little something Micah could see.

And anyone else paying attention.

Apparently, everyone was.

So, I surmise Micah was caught in the act. After our brief exchange, Malachi said something to Micah and all the men cracked up. Then, the sweetest chorus of *"Awws!"* broke the spell I was under. And I realized I'd been caught, too.

"You two are *so freaking adorable*. Hella sweet." India said, taking a sip from her glass. She had a red wine as well. Something drier than mine. Indie didn't like sweet reds as much as I did. "I love it Best." She was sitting right beside me and leaned into me, snuggling up close. "I am *so* happy for you!"

"Me too! I absolutely love Micah for you." That was Daijah. She had a white wine in her glass. The only one with white. Until recently, I used to drink white exclusively. I've gradually switched to red since Micah has so many wine selections. "I'm just glad you figured yourself out. Got out of your own damn way. Cuz… I love you, my dear sissy, but *oh my freaking goodness.*" Daijah shook her head, chuckling lightly, and everyone joined her. Even me.

"Me three!" That was Ella. She sipped from her glass of rosé. Her favorite. I was bound to learn that detail since we often chatted over a glass of wine at Ella and Malachi's. "Des, you are *perfect* for baby bro. He's so happy. Love looks amazing on him. And it's no wonder. We knew there had to be something about you when he started telling us about you."

I couldn't help but smile. "I'm happy too. *So happy.* I love my man something fierce. He's amazing. Quite literally."

Ella nodded. "Oh, absolutely. I know a thing or two about the Walker men." Ella offered playfully, sipping from her glass again.

"It was the same for us Ella. Destiney never took anyone seriously. But then this guy named *Micah* came riding in on a horse. Sweeping her off her feet." Daijah said with a smile.

"*Right!* I knew there was something about him when she wouldn't stop talking about him." India chimed in.

"It be like that!" Ella said, laughing. "You ladies already know."

We all shared a laugh. "I love the way he looks at you." Ella continued.

Daijah and India nodded in agreement.

"Aww. So do I." I smiled again. Glancing over at Micah, I saw his back was to me now. The guys were focused on the game and having a lively discussion.

"Also, Ella, that lipstick is hella cute," India said. It was. It was a deep maroon, which looked gorgeous against her complexion.

"Thank you! You're poppin' too, boo!"

India laughed. "Thanks." Indie was wearing a scarlet red lip, which was her typical go to. It looked amazing against her complexion.

I took another sip of my wine. I was getting close to needing another glass, and I debated whether I'd get the same one or try another. I counted six different wine options. The next one would be my last. I wouldn't need more than two glasses.

"So, ladies," I began. Six expectant eyes looking back at me. Each of them drank from a stem wine glass. I had a stemless wine glass. I discovered recently that I'm not a good match for stem glasses. For some reason, I keep knocking my glasses over. Micah bought a set of stemless glasses for us to drink with at his house. I continued, "I need help planning Micah's thirty-fifth birthday." Nods of approval and words of confirmation sounded from each of them. "I'll probably do something at his home. It's the perfect place for it."

"Absolutely! What did you have in mind?" Daijah asked.

"Something small and intimate. That's his thing. He wouldn't want anything big and extravagant."

The girls nodded.

"Some food. Some music. Some drinks. A cake. Maybe a few decorations."

They continued nodding. "And his boys. Micah is guaranteed to have a good time as long as they're in attendance."

The girls agreed.

Micah had a tight circle around him. A *brotherhood*. A kinship.

Malachi, of course. The dopest big brother there ever was.

His childhood friend Solomon. His boy Tyson from college. His good friend Ellington from work. I'm sure he wouldn't mind having Ray there. And Julian, who'd been warmly welcomed to the pack.

And speaking of Ray, I didn't have any issues with him. I didn't take anything he said that day personally. Micah assured me Ray's comments weren't directed at me, and I trusted that.

But Micah was easy to please. He'd have extreme gratitude for just the thought.

I planned to invite Micah's parents, of course. As well as my dad and Ms. Natalie.

"What's on the menu Des? I'm glad to help with that." Ella offered.

"I love you, Ella, but no way. Not this time." I shook my head. You get a night off for once. You are always cooking for everyone for something or other, which we appreciate, by the way! I told Micah before we got here that your food is *bomb diggity!*"

Daijah and India laughed.

Ella laughed too. "Thank you! Are you sure though? You know I don't mind. I'll take that off your hands, no problem."

"I know. But really, not this time. All you need to do is show up and have a good time. Just like the rest of us."

I planned to have the food catered so everyone could come and enjoy themselves without worrying about the food. Since the party wasn't until January, I still have time to decide on the specifics.

We moved on to something else, and I looked down at my phone when it vibrated next to me.

I smiled at the text message I'd received from Mrs. Walker.

She is so sweet—just as sweet as she could be. I love seeing her and spending time with her. I sent her a screenshot of a pasta recipe I saw on Pinterest, asking if she'd like to try this next.

Mommy Josette: I'd love to! How about next week?

It's a date

Mrs. Walker has already asked for my help with the coming holiday meals. Ella and Gabby will also help. Thanksgiving is swiftly approaching. We still have a few weeks, but it will be here before we know it. Then, of course, there is Christmas and New Year's.

I've been over multiple times helping Mrs. Walker cook different things and learning so much from her. We cooked homemade lasagna not long ago, and I was too juiced that day. I love lasagna, but

I haven't had any in so long. I hadn't had any home-made entirely from scratch, ever.

And I was her proud sous chef. Her ambitious student. Eagerly soaking in everything I could. She's a prolific teacher. During our time together, we always learn more about one another.

So, it turned out that Mrs. Walker taught middle-grade English for the Sacramento Public Schools for over thirty years. Now that she's retired, she frequently volunteers with Friends of the Sacramento Public Library.

Suddenly, her love for books, stories, languages, and literature made sense. It was the sweetest thing to learn that we have a shared passion for those things, too. Mrs. Walker listened intently when I shared that my degree is in Linguistics. Many of my upper-division classes were cross-listed for English. I told her I always felt like the English and Linguistics majors were like fraternal twins. Many of the same courses were required. She found my observation funny, and after laughing heartily, she agreed. If you know, you know. I was *almost* an English major.

A course in Social Linguistics is what sold me. It's quite fascinating.

Mrs. Walker mentioned that she was surprised that I didn't have an art degree. Micah proudly shared pictures of my work with her. She told me she was so impressed. Considering I was self-taught.

I took a few art classes throughout my childhood but none in college. I told her at the time, I didn't think I could do art full-time and make a decent living. I figured I'd get a "real job" and do art for fun.

I couldn't have been more wrong. And it's truly amazing how God has continued looking out for me and providing for me. I've been working independently for nearly a decade now, but with plenty of work to do, I hardly have to look for work. I'm often approached, and sometimes, I have to turn things away because my schedule just doesn't allow it.

I'm not just surviving but thriving in the art space, and I'm so very thankful. I get to do what I love, keep my bills paid, keep myself fed, learn, grow, and network. I met my bestie, India.
It's why I can take on many volunteer positions or community gigs.

God is good all the time.

And all the time, God is good. *For real.*

Mommy also mentioned in passing that I should consider taking an art class or two at community college.

Because why not?

She planted a seed.

And yeah, I call her Mommy now and then. It slipped once, but it felt so natural. She certainly has been a mother to me these past few months. And she smiled so big at that. I did, too.

And I'm such a fucking crybaby. Of course, I cried right there. Right then. Happy tears.

Yeah.

And Mommy calls me her *sweet girl.* Mr. Walker calls me *sweet darling.*

And something else, I thought I knew how to chop and slice vegetables, but there was a much better way to do it. And yes, turns out there is a difference between cutting and slicing.

Mrs. Walker told me that cutting veggies roughly the same size ensured they cooked evenly and at the same rate. I learned to julienne carrots for the lasagna. We made one meat and one vegetarian. It was a deep pan too. We took the vegetarian one home, and it took Micah and me days to finish it. And it was even better the next day, too. Pasta is always better the next day.

We made a triple-layer caramel cake another day. It was scrumptious. I don't bake much, so I learned a thing or two, like using brown eggs as often as possible. For some recipes, let the eggs, milk, and butter get to room temperature to ensure they blend cohesively.

And we met Ms. Natalie some months ago and we've gotten together with her and dad a few times since.

She's *wonderful*. Dad is so happy. They're just adorable, those two. She seems just as fond as he is. I learned that she and Dad had a similar story and shared a similar pain.

Ms. Natalie was a widow. She lost her husband about six years ago in a tragic work accident. My heart broke for her hearing that. She has one grown son between Daijah's age and mine. He's currently stationed in Germany, and he'll be home sometime next year. We're excited to meet him.

***

India and I were starting our second week of working together. Working with Indie has always been a great thing.

A community theatre was putting on a few productions for the Christmas season, and we'd joined the Design Team to get the sets painted. We were formally hired as *Scenic Artists*.

The Set Designer, Mrs. Rose, was super talented and a visionary. I was beyond impressed with her. And the crew was dope as hell. They were a bunch of black hippie artists with *enormous* talent.

This was the first time India and I would work with a crew made up entirely of people of color.

Scenic Artist was something brand new to put on my resume. It was my first time doing scenic art, and I was learning so much.

It wasn't as straightforward as just painting the sets, though we'd do that, but rather creating visual illusions. We'd be painting on backdrops, and the scenery painted would create perspective. This week, we painted faux surfaces: rusty metal doors, a colossal pile of stones, weathered wood grain, and a graffiti-covered brick wall.

We had an important job. Production costs can be very high when using those materials. Scenic artists can paint them on plywood instead at a fraction of the cost. Also, when it's painted, we can add additional details using different brushes, colors, and techniques. For example, we can use paints to create a rusty, aged, or worn look.

We'd be committed for at least the next six weeks. It would pay modestly, but I was perfectly fine with that. The experience was priceless. I appreciate the opportunity. And I love coming to work every day. I was having so much fun.

And the theatre was a hidden gem. Tucked away off the main road in a converted warehouse. You'd never know it from the outside.

The dear and delightful Dr. Giselle, founder and Artistic Director of the Village, is a beacon in the community.

Dr. Giselle is amazing. A Goddess.

Nearly seventy-years young and still teaching acting and dance.

A D.C. native and Spelman woman with a Degree in Theatre. She's graced many stages as a professional actress over the past five decades. A playwright. A thought leader. Industry expert. Fostering the black theatre continuum.

She has a theatre company based at the Village called *Imisi*, which roughly means inspiration in Yoruba. It is open to all ages and skill levels. She's created a space for young and mature black talent to grow and thrive as black actors, encouraging discovery, creativity, and scholarship.

Dr. Giselle welcomed India and me with open arms. Gushing over *her* excitement to work with *us*.

That's sweet and everything, but *we're* the ones so fortunate.

"Girl, I forgot just how huge this house is," India said as she stepped into the front door of Micah's home. India came here once before, but we didn't hang out here very long. That was the night we went out to *HomeGrownSol*.

She removed her shoes and left them by the front door. She never wore shoes inside, even when people insisted she didn't need to remove them. Her Indian culture wouldn't allow her to. I was already barefoot. Honestly, I've implemented no shoes inside since we first became friends. I've found that it stays much cleaner when you don't wear shoes in your home.

"Thanks, on *Micah's* behalf. It's a really nice house. Nicer than any place I've ever imagined spending this much time in."

India came by to assess the wall Micah wanted me to paint. We'd been off work for a few hours, but she went home first to check on her parents. Thankfully, they were doing much better these days. I wouldn't have bothered her with this request if that wasn't the case. This would take a while.

Micah asked me weeks ago to paint something on his wall, and I wanted to get started. That way, it would all be done in plenty of time for his birthday. The wall was expansive, so I asked India for her expertise and help. It would take much longer if I did it all myself. Besides, when India and I collaborate, we make fucking magic. I wanted to capture that here. I wanted this to be some of my best work yet.

My man deserved it. He took such care of me, and my mental health was of the utmost importance to him. He was serious about me seeing a therapist. Ms. Laurie, his assistant, sent me an email the following day. After some research, I found an amazing therapist. She was a black woman in her late forties. She was a woman of God, a wife, and a mother. A

Howard University alum, H.U. regalia tastefully decorated her office with crimson and cream Greek letters.

But all of that was secondary.

Dr. Jemma Robinson was a whole vibe. Trust-building. Inquiring. Compassionate. Kind. And she gently shared pearls of wisdom with me.

She shared one about relationships and striving to be the best version of ourselves for the person we care about.

*"We're the best **we** when **I'm** the best **me**."*

That had to be the most profound thing I'd heard in a while.

At the moment, I saw Dr. Jemma, and she insists I call her that every other week. That was a great cadence for now.

India stood in front of the wall, looked up and down, and touched it just like I had. I remember that puzzling Micah and he even chuckled about it. For an ordinary person, maybe it was odd, but there was a method to the madness. The wall was our canvas, and the texture of the wall would tell us how we would need to prepare it to receive the paint.

A great mural begins with the surface it's painted on.

"Stucco. And there's a glossy paint on top. Okay, so this will definitely need to be primed," India said.

"Right."

"How high up were you thinking?" She asked, looking up again.

"Probably seventy-five percent. Micah said this is an eight-foot wall." The wall didn't reach the ceiling, but the ceiling in this portion of the house was ten feet high.

She nodded. "We'll need two ladders."

"Yeah."

"It will cover the entire width?" It was approximately fifteen feet across.

"Yes."

She nodded again. There was an electric fireplace on both sides of the wall. That would save us a significant square footage of painting.

India walked around the partition wall, returning on the other side. "We're painting both sides?"

"*God, no.*"

We both cackled at that.

"Girl... I love you but *shit*. I was bout to lose it."

We laughed all over again.

"Since you won't let me pay you, please tell me what we can do for you instead. This will be a lot of work. We'll already be painting all day at the Village Theatre. So, after work won't be practical. Not every day. This will likely be a weekend thing." Micah still wanted to pay India. I agreed. And we would. She was crazy if she thought for a second we wouldn't.

"That's what I'm thinking." India nodded. "We can do occasional days after work. Once a week maybe. That gives us at least three working days a week. Let's put tentative dates on the calendar week by week and play it by ear. We can always move the weekday slots."

"Good idea Best. Let's sit down so I can show you the sketch I came up with. We can talk colors too." India followed me to the kitchen island.

Eventually, Micah came down to say hello and thank India in advance for agreeing to work with me. He also made dinner for us and then headed to his office. India and I watched part of a movie, and then she had to get going. I'd see her at the Village tomorrow bright and early.

When Indie left, I took a shower. Micah had already taken his, and he lay in bed reading when I finished my skin moisturizing and face routine.

I sighed heavily when I finally lay down beside him. I'd be asleep in two-point-five seconds, I was sure.

"You good baby?"

"Yeah. Just tired. It was a long day." I cuddled up beside Micah, and he closed his book and placed it on his side table. He also lowered the lamps to the lowest setting.

It had been a long day, but I still wasn't quite feeling very well. It came and went in waves. It's hard to describe exactly how I felt, but it wasn't my normal self. I hadn't mentioned it to anyone since it was sort of infrequent. In fact, I felt fine all day. It wasn't until I got in the shower that I began to feel sick. "How was your day, baby?"

"Good. Thank you love. Busy, but productive."

Micah had me in his arms from behind. He snuggled closer to me.

"That's good." I yawned. "I love your bed. I get such great sleep." I said absently as I closed my eyes.

"It loves you too."

I was tickled at that.

Micah held me tighter. Moments later, his hands were beneath my shirt and had risen to my bare breasts. He gently rubbed over my nipples, and they peaked immediately. My nipples are super-duper-sensitive to his touch. It felt nice. His firm, warm hands always felt nice wherever he ventured.

"I have no problem expressing myself." Micah began.

My response was a bit delayed. I was tired, and his gentle caress put me deeper in the zone. His deep timbre in my ear would do it every time. My breasts were in his hands. They were a perfect fit. He cupped each one, his thumbs still grazing my nipples. "I know baby."

Micah moved my locs to the side and kissed my neck. After a faint moan, "I have no problem expressing my appreciation either... no problem complimenting you. You're my good thing, Beauty. By now I expect you're used to it. Me complimenting you."

A slow smile made its way across my face. He couldn't see it. And anyway, I wondered where all this was going.

I didn't have to wonder too long.

"I have a confession... I've never told you this before, but I'm telling you now..." He kissed my neck again. He never stopped. He'd literally been kissing there the entire time. "I'm convinced that you're the best sleeping companion."

"Am I really?" I pressed languidly.

"The *very* best."

"How so?"

"That's easy. You're the *perfect* little spoon."

A boisterous chuckle came up from my belly. I wasn't expecting that. My silly Micah could always get a laugh out of me.

Micah laughed too. "I'm serious. You aren't a wild sleeper. You're soft." Kisses. "You smell nice." More kisses. "You don't snore either. This bed is nice and all, but I've gotten some of the best sleep *ever* sleeping with you."

"Wow. Well thanks baby."

"Mmmhmm."

"You're the perfect big spoon," I told him after a beat.

"Thank you, love." Micah reached back and cut the lamps completely off, then settled back in. "Baby."

"Yeah?"

"Real quick before you knock out. We're having a Holiday Gala for work in a couple of weeks. Will you be my date for the evening?"

"I'd love to baby." I turned to face Micah. Finding his lips in the darkness, I kissed him tenderly. "Absolutely. Positively. *Definitely*." I settled in his arms again, facing him now.

"Great." Micah kissed my forehead. "It's a formal event. Black tie. I'll be wearing a tux. Take the card and get yourself an evening gown. I'll wait until you get it to coordinate my tie and pocket square."

"Alright baby."

"High heels... one of those tiny purse thingies..."

My light titter floated into the darkness around us. "It's called a clutch."

"A clutch huh?" His chuckle was light, but I felt it. We were so close. I felt his every inhale and exhale. His massive hands were in my shirt again, wrapped around my bare back. Rubbing and kneading my skin. Something he was so damn *spectacular* at, by the way. "Some earrings. A necklace if you want..." His voice was slowing down as he started drifting. I was right behind him too. "...maybe nails. Toes. Or whatever else... get it, sweetheart."

"Thank you, baby."

"Thank *you*. Goodnight, my love."

"Goodnight.

twenty-six

MICAH

"Man, the fuck Lewis was doing! Fumbling like that."

"Right," Mal uttered.

We were die-hard football fans. Me, Daddy and Mal. The game was on, and Mal and I were watching it while shooting the shit on the phone. I could get to Mal's house from mine in eight-minutes flat. Sometimes, when the game was on, I would go by to watch it or vice versa, granted we weren't busy with something else. I continued, "He knew we needed those points. Leave it to him. Fucking Lewis."

"Exactly."

"We're up this season. Guess we may have a shot at the championship." We knew we weren't rooting the best team, but we were loyal fans, nonetheless.

I continued my sports commentary until I realized I had been carrying on for a while, and Mal was quiet. That was never the case whenever we talked about sports. "Mal?" My brows dipped. I had the call on speaker, so I glanced down to see if it was still connected. It was. "Mal?" Maybe he'd accidentally muted or something. "Mal?"

"Yeah."

"Everything good?"

"…Yeah… baby brother… umm…let me…let me call you back…"

"Mal, for real? You couldn't wait for us to hang up. Man, I swear!"

Shaking my head, I went to disconnect, but not before I could hear Mal chuckling, "My bad, dude…"

I shook my head again but couldn't help myself as I chuckled, too.

I tossed my phone beside me on the couch and laid back to continue watching the game. About an hour went by when I felt it vibrating beside me. It was Malachi calling me back.

"You better not be calling me in the middle of nothing man."

"Quit hating nigga. When my wife climbs on top of me, I'm gone rise to the occasion. Literally and figuratively. She wants it, she can get it... *Touch-down!!!! You see that shit man?"*

"*Yes!* That's what the fuck I'm talking about!" I cheered right along with Mal. It was a great play. Perfectly executed.

"What you needed though? You said you wanted to talk about something."

I lightly sighed. It was the irony for me.

That is what had me calling my brother in the first place. I'd initially called Mal to get his advice on something, but since we both had the game on, it was easy to get distracted.

I had the place to myself so I could speak freely. Destiney was out with Daijah looking for a dress for the Gala in two weeks.

Anyway, there is absolutely no doubt that Destiney is the woman God had given me.

My wife. The mother of our future children.

Knowing that I wanted to do right by her. I have to. I'm convicted.

I haven't been okay with continuing to make love to Destiney outside of the covenant of marriage. It's almost like I feel as though I'm violating her. And she deserves better.

I prayed for her, and here she was. Continuing to connect with her this way just made me feel guilty. It was hard to explain. Beyond that, there was nowhere I could go mentally to escape the integrity and morals Mommy and Daddy raised us with. The more I tried to drown it out, the louder that damn voice was in my head.

I really need Destiney to be my wife.

That way, I can make love to her.

Or fuck her.

Whatever she wanted.

In peace.

Being in my damn head so much has gotten me in a funk plenty of times. Like, I've mastered Destiney. I'm *very* in tune with her. But she's in tune with me too. I worry she may already be sensing something.

"I stopped initiating. But we still engage because *she's* initiating now."

I explained all of this to Malachi. The very best I could.

"I see." I knew Mal was processing it all. I let him rock.

I already felt relief just getting this off my chest. I'm glad I decided to run my situation by my big brother and pick his brain about it. I didn't think he'd see my position any differently.

Where I hesitated was bringing it to Destiney.

For fear of her feeling rejected. My baby is sensitive. Her feelings are fragile.

I quickly added, "Instead of denying her, I figured I'd just stop entering her. But that only worked once."

I knew what Mal was silently thinking, so I offered, "I try to hold out and give her a *few* the other way, hoping she'll be good with that, but she'll still ask me. I can't say no to my baby. A couple of times, she put that nigga in herself."

Mal chuckled at that. "I see." Then, "You need to talk to her about this. Like yesterday. If you hold this in and continue doing what you've been doing, baby sis will notice. She likely already has.

When she notices, she'll convince herself something is wrong with her or your relationship. Getting ahead of the situation and discussing your position would be much easier, especially if you want to avoid hurting her feelings. Women notice these things because they're extremely sensitive. Even the most confident women have a level of sensitivity regarding this. If you fumble this, and she brings it up, it will be from a place of hurt or exasperation. I guarantee you. It won't be pretty."

I understood. "Yeah, I see what you mean. I need to figure out the best way to present this. She may feel shafted or even rejected. That's the last thing I want for her. I never want to hurt her. Even unintentionally."

"Right. Bring this up for discussion expeditiously, baby brother. Do not let this ride because it will cause a greater conflict than it needs to be. I believe she'll understand as long as you explain well. Make it make sense to her. That way, there won't be any room for feelings of rejection."

"Right. Appreciate you man."

"You got it. Always."

I will bring it up for discussion as soon as I can get my words together.

Mal had a great point; Destiney may have noticed the shift already and was possibly already in her head about it. I will bring it up soon.

I just hoped it wasn't too late.

***

I'll be headed out to Chicago right after Thanksgiving and be gone for eight days.

I'd go to Destiney's father first, but I planned to propose as soon as I returned from Chicago.

I hated that Destiney couldn't join me. She was just as disappointed. She wanted to come; she'd never been to Chicago. I'd been once, and it would have been pretty cool to show her around. I told her I'd be glad to take her there when her schedule allowed. She was committed to a community theatre project and was so excited about this gig. She'd been given tickets to some of their matinee shows, and we planned to check them out together once performances started.

I enjoy the magic on stage. As a kid, I was a thespian of sorts, eagerly participating in small productions at school and church.

But these days I prefer to experience the sights and sounds from the audience.

Especially musical theatre. I saw Hamilton twice. And the Lion King in San Francisco.

Life-changing.

So, I had it in my mind to ask Destiney to marry me in the coming weeks.

The guys and I talked about it when we were at Wine & Graze.

Malachi, Solomon, Julian, and I huddled around a tall table, watching a football game on an oversized flat screen. We'd been clowning around, drinking beer, and pigging out on a massive platter of wings.

The women, Destiney, Daijah, Ella, and India, were sitting around a booth just a few feet from us.

Looking regal and classy. All four of them. Chatting, laughing, sipping wine, and snacking on cheese, berries, chocolate, and nuts.

It all started because I got caught stealing glances at Destiney.

My baby is so beautiful. My goodness.

In a crowded room, I would always search for her. The guys were cracking jokes at me, but I knew it was all in jest. These men adored their women just as much as I loved mine.

Well, except for Sol. But I knew he was making something shake with India.

"You're staring again man." Mal teased, taking *another swig from his beer.*

I shook my head, chuckling. I couldn't help myself. I wouldn't even try.

"She wifey or what?" Sol asked, slapping me on *my shoulder.*

*"She is **certainly** wifey."* I returned. Resolute. *Without pause.*

"When you asking her?" Julian queried.

"Soon man. Before the end of the year, for sure."

I proceeded to show them my phone. I had been looking over some rings I had in mind for her. I narrowed it down to a few styles, and I'd get Daijah's expertise before I made a final decision. I'll likely ask her to meet me at the jewelry store.

The guys hooped, hollered, and whistled with wide eyes and high brows. I nervously looked at the women, but they were preoccupied and chatting away. Not paying us any mind. They probably thought we were carrying on about the football game.

"Shiiiittt! I need some sunglasses for some of these." Sol joked. *Gesturing his hands in front of his face as if he was seeing something bright and blinding.*

We all cracked up at that.

*"No doubt!" Mal said. "I see you baby brother. These are **genteel**!"*

I didn't mind their playful banter.

Julian nodded once he'd had a look. "She must be worth it, man." He'd just gone through this himself when he proposed to Daijah early this year. We didn't know him then but were excited about their upcoming nuptials. January was just around the corner.

Julian was my newest friend, but he was swiftly becoming more like a brother. Such a solid dude. Mal and Sol fucked with Julian too. They met Julian for the first time some weeks back when Mal and Ella hosted a game night.

And Destiney shared with me how well Julian treated her.

I appreciate that. Tremendously. More than he knew. I certainly make an effort to treat Daijah just as well as I treat Destiney. I know that mattered a lot to her. She and Daijah were inseparable and extremely protective of each other.

"She's worth this and so much more." I declared. "She's priceless."

***

Tonight was the Holiday Gala.

This year, it was being held at the Library Galleria. A premiere event space in downtown Sacramento.

There would be a live jazz band as our entertainment for the evening, an open bar, and a plated four-course meal.

That all sounded nice, but I got the feeling the food would be subpar.

For some reason, these events always failed miserably with food selection.

Everything else was always top-tier. The venue, the décor, the entertainment.

But the catering was always a miss. Never a hit.

Such a damn shame.

I didn't eat fast food, but every blue moon and tonight, I wasn't above rolling through a late-night drive-through if necessary. The Wendy's closest to me was open till one a.m.

I also secured a driver for the evening so I could drink to my heart's content. I didn't plan on being sloppy drunk around my working constituents, but I didn't want to have to think about driving tonight.

I was dressed and ready, hanging out at the kitchen island, waiting for Destiney. I'd cut the television off not long ago; I knew she'd be making her way down here soon. Daijah came by to do Destiney's hair and to help her get ready. She'd taken off about a half hour ago.

I glanced at my watch. We were doing pretty good on time.

My phone illuminated on the kitchen island beside me. It was a notification that our driver had arrived. He was punctual, and I appreciated that. The company I booked through were friends of the family, and they gave me a great price.

I gave him a quick call, assuring him we'll make our way out soon. He'd been paid to be our driver for the rest of the evening. I planned to tip him handsomely too.

I entered the living area and sat on the couch as I faintly heard my bedroom door open. I stood immediately.

Destiney descended the stairs like a literal angel. Floating. Taking my breath away.

From head to toe. Everything was just...

I felt like Johny Gill. *My, my, my.*

Destiney was striking in her gown. This was my first time seeing it. I only knew it was navy once she told me what color I needed to get for my tux. And the navy blue looked stunning against her chocolate skin.

Anyway, Destiney was luxurious. Exquisite.

The top was a tailored fit. Following her every curve like a second skin. Sitting tastefully close to her body. Perfectly lining her chest and waist. Sheer at the top. Boat neckline. Elegantly embroidered gold details with beads and sequins. Graceful sheer three-quarter sleeves.

It was a floor-length gown. Finished with a flowing skirt. The perfect touch of allure. This gown was *so her.*

She wore gold heels, which I saw peeking out as she continued descending the steps.

I loved her locs too. They were freshly re-twisted, and it looked like they had taken two locs, stranding them into one, with all of them pinned and draped to one side.

I approached the stairs to meet her, immediately taking her into my arms. Embracing her close.

"Hello, beautiful," I spoke into her ear. Lining the side of her face with kisses, then kissing her forehead. I remained there for just a moment, taking in her scent. I could smell a subtle grapefruit, or maybe it was mango coming from her hair. Her hair always smelled nice; she used shea butter all over her body, including her hair. I loved the way it mixed with her natural pheromones and the body oil she used.

But tonight, she was wearing a different scent.

Something I hadn't smelled on her before.

I liked it.

It was warm and spicy with notes of musk and amber.

My hands remained at the small of her back. I never disconnected us as I stepped back to get another look at her.

"Hello handsome." Destiney returned. She seemed shy. Just a little. She was likely extremely nervous since she'd be meeting many people tonight. I'd make sure she felt safe. And comfortable. "I'm so glad you like it, baby." She told me.

I took her hand in mine and gently lifted it above her head. "Turn around baby." Destiney gave me a twirl, and I loved everything I saw. Wow. "I *love* it. Thank you for being my date. Last year I went alone. I would have skipped if I could. But I'm expected to attend as a VP."

"I'm honored to be your date, baby. Thank you for all of this. Everything I'm wearing." She looked down at herself.

"You're welcome. You look great baby. And you smell amazing."

"Thank you baby. And for that too. It's a new perfume I picked up. For special occasions." She gave me a wink.

"I love it baby."

I brought Destiney back to me, kissing her forehead again. Then her neck. Finally, her lips. We kissed a few times. Pecks at first, but then we began to get carried away.

"We should get going, baby," Destiney said, breaking our kiss.

"Yeah. Before we don't." I chuckled.

We headed toward the front door, and I picked up the plastic container I'd left sitting on the coffee table.

"Do you mind pinning my boutonniere on me?"

"Of course, I don't mind, baby."

I'd gotten Destiney a matching corsage. White rose with baby's breath.

"I haven't seen one of these since prom."

I snickered. "People still wear them. Weddings, of course. Most formal events, really." After she'd pinned me, I placed her corsage on her wrist. "Have I told you how much I love seeing my pretty wife wearing pretty things?" I asked Destiney. I kissed her hand.

She gave me a sweet smile. "No, you haven't baby."

"Well...*I love seeing my pretty wife wearing pretty things.* Or nothing. I like seeing that too."

She giggled at that as I opened the front door, allowing her to step out in front of me. We seldom ever entered or left through the front door. Always using the garage to come in and out. I paused to lock the door behind us, and before I could get the key in the door, Destiney was squealing behind me.

"*Micah!* Oh my gosh, is this limo for us?"

I was worried for a second. I almost dropped my keys. Destiney squealed so suddenly and so loud I thought something had happened.

I locked the door and met her as we descended the walkway leading to the sidewalk.

"Yes baby. We have a limo for the night."

"Aww, Micah, this is so sweet. I've never ridden in a limo before. Thank you for this baby."

"You're welcome love. I'm glad." Our chauffeur had since exited the limo and waited for us at the passenger door. After Destiney and I got settled inside, we were on our way.

***

We were having a *ball* at the Gala.

Ellington and his wife Jayla had been hanging with us most of the evening. The four of us chatted extensively during the cocktail hour. Jayla is lovely. She and E seemed to be tailor-made for each other. This was my second time meeting E's wife. I met her briefly once before when she came to the office to take Ellington to lunch. She had their cute little one with her that day. Jade was so adorable. The perfect mix of them both. Just precious.

Once dinner was served, E and Jayla sat beside us at the same table. The banquet table seated ten, and a few others from our department, and their dates sat with us, too. We enjoyed our meal. They had a vegetarian option for Destiney. I was sure to mention that when I submitted my RSVP. But the food wasn't half bad. Better than I expected, actually.

Destiney and Jayla took to each other right away. Since Destiney is considerably younger than me, she and Jayla were around the same age. At one point it seemed Destiney and Jayla forgot Ellington and I were there. Chatting like old friends. E and I laughed about it.

Anyway, Destiney met dozens of people this evening. My boss, some colleagues, and a few direct reports of mine. They were all so glad to meet her.

And speaking of my boss, I'd heard that E was doing phenomenal work in his new role. Since Ellington no longer reported to me, I wasn't exactly privy to his performance. Of course, I wasn't surprised to hear that. We wouldn't be talking about work this evening, but I'd be sure to tell him to keep up the great work next week.

I'd managed to avoid Erica. So far. And anyway, I hadn't seen her at the office much, which was a great thing. But I knew she would be here. There was no way she would miss an event like this.

I was on high alert to stay away from her. And keep Destiney away from her.

I'd heard that some transplant from another department would be her date. He probably agreed to it because he hadn't heard about her reputation.

Or maybe he didn't care. Either way, it wasn't my business.

The five-piece jazz band was great. They called themselves *The Flipside*. There were two ladies and three gentlemen. They played jazz covers during cocktails and dinner. After dinner, the dance floor was open, and the band did jazz covers of modern songs. Destiney and I danced quite a bit.

We were in the middle of a mid-tempo jam when Destiney alerted me that she needed to use the ladies room. Since Ellington and Jayla were still dancing Destiney didn't want to interrupt them, asking Jayla to go with her. I always noticed that ladies went to the restroom in twos. Or in groups.

"I'll escort you baby, no worries."

I hung out in the hallway. Not long after Destiney went into the ladies room, I felt the unmistakable presence of someone.

"Ahem."

I lightly sighed, obliging her. Expressionless.

"Micah."

"Erica."

I saw her once the dance floor opened, and people began congregating. She wasn't dancing, though. More so, walking around. And talking to people who were trying to dance with their spouses or dates. Victor steadily followed her around. It was funny because he looked pathetic.

We exchanged pleasantries when I saw him at the bar earlier this evening. That was it. But the dude had a smug expression on his face. I don't know who he was trying to fool.

Victor, looking smug, was hilarious. I think he thought he was doing something with Erica on his arm. It's obvious when a man isn't used to dealing with an attractive woman. They do all sorts of *clown shit*. Pandering is one of them. Agreeing to anything just to feel accepted.

Meanwhile, Erica was treating Victor like a damn doormat. Hardly acknowledging his presence. I was embarrassed for him.

She looked great, I'll admit. And just because I wasn't going there with Erica didn't negate that she was an attractive woman. But that was the extent of it.

She was an attractive woman on the outside.

Beauty was only skin deep with her.

And Erica didn't hold a candle to how gorgeous my woman was. Destiney was beautiful inside and out. I noticed all the fawning these men were doing.

According to office gossip, Victor had pursued Erica since he'd transferred into our department.

Months ago. Erica never gave the poor guy a second glance.

I guess she needed a date, and he was available.

Victor looked comical even now. Standing behind Erica like a lost puppy.

Just then, the door to the lobby swung open. As Destiney emerged, I saw the look Erica gave her. Erica whirled her head my way. She was so swift that I was sure she'd get whiplash.

"Alright Micah. I'm ready." Destiney told me as she linked her arm in mine. She didn't even seem to notice Erica standing there. And good for her. Erica wasn't even worth the energy.

"Indeed. Let's get back to our table. I think dessert is being served now."

Erica reared her head back as if her death glare wasn't enough. And she stood there, continuing to glare at Destiney for another moment.

"Wow." Erica drew the word out. Then, "So *this* is why you're not giving me a chance? You've been keeping company with... with... *her?*"

I didn't appreciate the infliction.

Destiney and I had already taken a few steps. We were almost to the door leading back to the reception. But I was putting an end to this shit. Right now. Once and for all.

"Erica. *I will not* stand here and allow you to disrespect me or my woman. I have already explained that we will not be more than colleagues. Should you allude to anything further *again*, I'll have you relieved of your duties. *Effective immediately.*"

Her eyes grew wide.

I turned to Destiney. She was looking at me expectantly with that beautiful smile that I love. "Shall we, baby?"

"We shall."

Just as we exited the hallway to the ballroom, Destiney stopped and turned back toward Erica, who was still planted in the same place. Her mouth was agape. Victor still standing there, looking... *confused?* Hell, I didn't know.

"You know Erica. It isn't very becoming of you to be so nasty." Destiney spoke in her usual tone.

Light. Airy. Pleasant. The voice I fell in love with. "Then you're steadily pursuing a man who has already made it clear he isn't interested. You've been informed of this two years ago. No woman of class should do such a thing. Especially in front of your date." Destiney shrugged. "You're a beautiful woman." Erica's expression visibly softened. And if you could believe it, I saw the faintest trace of a smile at the corner of her lip. "Have a good evening," Destiney said, commencing her stroll, her head held high.

I was so proud of my baby.

Speaking of class, after Destiney was insulted, she handled Erica like a *class act*.

And I was confident that this Erica shit could finally be put to rest.

twenty-seven

DESTINEY

I really needed my sister.

I felt something off with Micah, and I trusted that he would come to me about it. That was his M.O. The thing was, though, he still hasn't, and it's been a couple of weeks now.

We had a great time at the Gala last week.

An amazing time.

I'd never been to such a fancy event before. It was nice.

Satin drapes hanging from the ceilings. Banquet tables galore with elegant place settings. Astonishing centerpieces.

Everyone seemed to enjoy the flowing drinks. The bartenders were top-tier. I had a bomb-ass white sangria.

I felt beautiful. Rode in a limo. And when Micah and I arrived, we had such a good time.

Good food. Great company. We Danced.

I met a host of people from Micah's department. Everyone was so friendly.

Well, except Erica. When Micah and I returned to our table, I sent a condensed version to the group chat with Day and Indie. The next morning, I called them on FaceTime and brought them up to speed. They were *rolling*.

I'd already told them about Erica when we had that run-in months ago.

I get the feeling she won't be trying me anymore.

As Tamar Braxton would say, *"girlfriend needed to get her life."*

She was too pretty to act like that, especially at this age. She had to be in her thirties. Too old for that. Erica reminded me of Neeka. They didn't resemble one another, but they were the same type. Pretty and pretty *damn* confused. Acting ugly because they're frustrated with their lives since they aren't bearing the fruit they want.

Acting out certainly won't fix *that* problem.

And anyway, I finally met the famous Ellington. Micah is a huge fan of Ellington. E's a good guy.

He's about ten years younger than Micah. So, I'm just a couple of years older than Ellington and his wife.

I loved meeting his wife, Jayla. She said they were college sweethearts. Both of them are from Sac but met up at Chico State. About an hour and some change north of here. They've been married for just over three years now. They're a complementary couple with a lovely dynamic.

But seriously, Jayla is the folks for real. We spent the majority of our time hanging out and talking. A few ladies at the gala were shocked we were meeting for the first time.

Jayla and I talked about making plans to get together. We may invite the guys. We may not.

I'm kidding.

And Jayla showed me pictures of their beautiful baby. Jade is just about a year old. *So cute.* And such a happy baby. Chubby cheeks. Bright glittering eyes. A mound of dark auburn curls on her head.

Anyway, I assumed that we would finish the night when Micah and I got home. And just because we didn't, that *ordinarily* wouldn't cause me alarm. We didn't make love every night.

Sometimes, Micah would be too spent. Or I would be. But this had been happening for a while. Weeks.

Micah didn't seem to want me.

And that scared me.

But he did give me a massage. Man. It was so relaxing.

As soon as we stepped in the front door. Micah knelt to remove my shoes. After his shoes were off, he carried me upstairs. Once we were in his bedroom, Micah got me out of my dress, bra, and panties. Sent me to the tub to soak in oils and bath salts. After that, I took a quick shower, and as soon as I got out, he met me with a plush bath towel. Dried me off. Then he brought me to his bed and got to work massaging me from head to toe.

Micah laid me on my belly first, straddling me. Then he rolled me onto my back. I felt his warm touch on every inch of my body. I told Micah a long ass time ago that he had the skills of a masseuse.

I moaned so much that I moaned my ass to sleep.

So, I was home alone, lying in my bed. I showered and did my moisturizing routine a while ago, and now I was relaxing. Or at least trying to. My head was about to explode.

Micah was going to pick me up in the next two hours, and we'd head back to his place.

And I knew Day would make me feel better. I texted Daijah when I got out of the shower, asking if she could talk tonight. Of course, I didn't need an appointment, and I could call my sister anytime, but since she was with Julian, I wanted to be considerate. I knew the conversation wasn't going to be quick. She was the same with me now that I was seeing Micah. She'd text ahead if she ever needed to talk.

On the rare occasions she came home, if she saw Micah's car parked outside, she'd let me know she was home and asked if it was alright to come in. She didn't want to walk in and catch Micah and me in the middle of something. I would do the same if I ever came home and saw Julian's car.

Daijah replied a few minutes ago, saying she'd give me a call shortly, and as promised, she was calling me on Facetime about fifteen minutes later.

"Hey Day." I chirped. I propped my pillows behind me as I sat up against my headboard.

"Hey Des." She was just as peachy, looking vibrant and beautiful as always. I told her so, and she brushed it off after thanking me, saying I was beautiful.

She always said that, and she was so sweet about it. "Hold on sister." Daijah leaned over and then returned to view, sitting in bed. "I needed to mute this TV. We're binge-watching some Hulu series."

"Yeah? How is it so far?"

"Pretty good, actually. You know I'm not much of a TV person, but this one has me hooked."

Daijah and I weren't much into TV. Growing up, we watched a lot of black sitcoms, but as we've gotten older, we both prefer to read or watch a great movie now and then.

"That's what's up. Text me so I can add it to my list. Not sure when I'll get around to it, but..." I shrugged my shoulders. We both laughed. She already knew how it went.

"*Exactly!* Julian didn't think I was serious when I asked him to pick us something to watch. He was too juiced to start this new series with me."

"You probably made him turn on them damn subtitles."

"*And did*! They stay on, thank you very much." We were both cracking up again.

577

For some reason, Daijah insisted on watching everything with captions. She's been doing it for years. Daijah could hear just fine, but she said it helped with making sure she didn't miss any of the dialogue. I guess I could see that, and after years of practice, I hardly noticed them anymore. Julian probably had the hang of it by now, too.

I've heard that people who don't watch with subtitles regularly would often get caught up in reading the subtitles and miss the action happening. Or read them moving their mouth. Only a people watcher would catch that. For the record, I am *not* a people watcher, but Daijah is, and she would point that out anytime she saw it.

She saw Neeka doing it during a girl's night when we watched a movie and nudged me, gesturing in her direction. It took a few minutes for me to realize what she was showing me, and all I could do was shake my head.

Once our laughter calmed, Daijah asked, "So, what's up, Des? Everything, everything? It's just you, and I. Julian is in the living room. I told him we needed to chat."

I nodded and sighed at the same time. Asking her about this would make it all real.

Part of me felt like maybe I was imagining things, but yesterday left me no doubt. It was hard to explain it even.

Forging ahead, I figured that whatever I said and however I said it, Daijah would understand.

She always understood me.

Thankfully, Daijah spoke fluent Destiney.

"Somethings off with Micah and me, Day. Whenever we're intimate, I literally have to ask him to penetrate me."

Daijah had a confused expression. "*Ask him*?"

I nodded. "Yes. But not in a sexy way. I'm literally saying, "Please put it inside." I have to ask him because, for some reason, he's avoiding that part. I tried holding out to see what would happen but realized he wouldn't do it if I didn't ask."

"Hmm." Her brows were furrowed. "And this is new?"

"Yeahhhhh." I dragged the word out. Confused as hell. And anxious. "I mean... initially, he waited for me to be ready. But once we started going all the way, it was fair game. Lately, though, it's like... I don't know. I feel like he's holding himself back. Emotionally and physically. There's like a block." I huffed. "That probably didn't make any sense."

"No, I follow you, sister." Her brows were knitted as she silently pondered. Then, "Do you think he's having an issue getting hard?"

Shaking my head vigorously, I responded, "No. No, no. Not at all. He's hard as hell within seconds. All we have to do is kiss, and he's ready to go."

Daijah nodded. "Maybe he's worried about finishing too soon?"

I shook my head again. "Micah doesn't have that problem either."

"Okay... maybe it's something at work? Or with his family? And he can't compartmentalize. Know what I mean?"

"I know what you mean. But family or work stuff seems like something he'd come to me about."

"Yeah." Daijah nodded in understanding. The two of us were both silent for a beat. "Well, Des, I am just as confused as you. *But you know what I'm going to say.*" She sang that last part and looked at me knowingly.

And I did. She never wavered in encouraging healthy communication. I appreciate that about Daijah immensely. "Talk to him about it."

"Yeah… I'm just hesitant."

"Why?"

"I mean. There's the "don't ask the question if you don't want to know the answer." And that's how I'm feeling. This whole thing is making me anxious. Shit Daijah. What if he's having sex with someone else, and he doesn't need it from me anymore? I know I'm not the most experienced. Sex with me is probably vanilla."

"*Woah!* Where in the hell is this coming from? Are you kidding me Des?" Daijah jested. "We both know that isn't it."

"What else could it be? We went from ravishing the shit out of each other to nothing. We were so connected before. He always wanted eye contact. It made the moment so much more intense. Now… he's like in his head someplace else. Certainly not in the present with me. Not even looking at me. What the hell is going on with him?"

"I don't know. Why don't you ask him?" Daijah said sarcastically. She stood up, going out of view. "One second, I have to pee really quick." Once

Daijah was back in view, she said, "Talk to that man Destiney. Talk. To. Him."

twenty-eight

MICAH

Destiney was at my place. We were about to have lunch and planned to take a walk before the sun started to go down. It would be too chilly once it got dark.

I loved neighborhood walks with her and the quality time it afforded us. This had become a sweet moment with her that I always looked forward to. So, this was an excellent opportunity to talk things over. My talk with Malachi was almost two weeks ago and I knew I was pressing things waiting as long as I have. We'll discuss things today for sure.

We made grilled cheese on honey wheat with pepper jack and provolone and a delicious salad with spinach, arugula, avocado, walnuts, and strawberries. I hadn't tried strawberries on salad until Destiney introduced me and I love it.

Recently, I've cut back on meat even more than I had. These days I only eat chicken and fish. Red meat is very infrequent. Destiney never made it a big deal, and she had no issue coexisting with carnivores, but I welcomed the change. I could eat a little cleaner.

We'd eaten and cleaned up and were hanging out on the couch. I noticed Destiney was a little quieter. Not talking much while we were eating. She also seemed distant. She usually sat extremely close to me. If she wasn't in my lap. Right now, she was on the other end of the couch.

I wasn't even surprised. Mal was right. I shouldn't have waited to bring this to her.

The TV was on, but neither of us was watching.

Destiney had YouTube on with someone cooking something, and she was pretending to watch, but I peeped at her earlier. She was distracted. She'd been consumed with cooking channels on YouTube since she'd spent time with Mommy learning to cook different things. Mommy even gave her a few cookbooks, and Destiney was excited about them.

I had my laptop in front of me, checking a few things to prepare for my trip out to Chicago. I flew out three days after Thanksgiving. About a week away.

I hated that Destiney couldn't join me.

I looked over at her again, and I sensed some tension.

The way she sat, arms folded. Her absent gaze.

I sighed inwardly. Despite my plans to talk to her about this when we took our walk, I had the feeling we wouldn't get that far.

Something was up with her. I'm pretty sure I knew what it was, but she wasn't doing a good job masking it. Though she was trying, I knew her.

I studied her. And something was amiss.

We needed to talk right now.

I closed my laptop. I could do this later.

I walked over to the kitchen island and placed my laptop there. I returned to the living room and asked Destiney, "You alright love?"

She was silent for so long that I grew nervous. I made it back to the living room, and I sat on the couch right beside her. "Baby. Everything okay?"

Destiney sighed. "Honestly?"

Urging her forward, "Please do."

"I don't know if everything is okay. You tell me." She tried to say it evenly, but I heard the emotion there.

I nodded.

I grabbed the remote, turned off the TV, and then moved to sit on the coffee table directly in front of her. I held her gaze for a moment. She never wavered.

"Alright love. What's giving you doubt?"

She looked away from me briefly, and I could see gears shifting. When her eyes were back, she said, "Micah. Is there someone else? Are you cheating on me? Are you sleeping with someone else?"

I drew my head back. My eyes grew wide as saucers, and my mouth dropped open.

"No," I said firmly and definitively. I wasn't expecting *this* at all.

Where would she get the idea that I was cheating on her?

"We're being honest with each other. Please tell me the truth, Micah. I can handle it."

"That is the truth. Destiney, I wouldn't cheat on you. I *couldn't* cheat on you." My tone was pleading.

She crossed her arms, shaking her head slowly. "Then why don't you want me anymore?"

Ah. There it was. "I do want you baby. You're all I want. For the rest of our lives."

"Micah." Her tone was deadpan. She chuckled too, but there wasn't an ounce of mirth. "I don't feel like you want me. You never want to make love to me anymore. *You used to want me.* I know I'm not the most sexually exciting. I know I'm not the most experienced. But I thought... you said... we would learn together..." Destiney sighed an exasperated breath. She was absolutely on the verge of tears.

Meanwhile, I felt terrible.

Horrible.

Awful. Mal was right, and I could kick my own ass for this shit.

"You don't seem to want me anymore, and I get the feeling you're getting it from someone else," Destiney said after a moment. This time with an ounce of confidence.

"No baby. I swear. It's not that at all." I was frantic but told her in the most comforting tone I could muster.

I wanted to hold her, but her arms were still crossed. That told me she didn't want me any closer to her.

I needed to fix this immediately.

"Destiney baby."

When she wouldn't look at me, I leaned in closer. My lips were just a whisper from hers. She hadn't pushed me away, so that was a good sign.

"Destiney."

She looked everywhere but at me, and I couldn't blame her. Her heart was in my possession.

She'd given it to me hesitantly but willingly, and *I messed up*. That was my bad. I was going to fix this.

"Destiney, my love…" Placing my hands into the folds of her arms, I gently brought them down. I captured her hands, threading her fingers in mine, grateful she allowed me to. "Look at me, sweetheart. *Please*. I need you to know something."

She slowly peered up at me, and I saw her eyes pooled with tears.

Fuck me man.

I was supposed to be so much better at communicating. I'd caused her distress, and we could have avoided all this.

I needed to do some serious damage control.

"Baby. As God is my witness, I'm not seeing anyone else. All I see is you. You're the woman I want. You're it for me. *Please* believe that."

I took a moment to gather myself so I could make the rest of my dilemma make sense to her.

"So. Making love to you." I felt the corners of my mouth lifting and I didn't try to stop them. I couldn't even if I wanted to. A cheesy grin was across my face in nanoseconds.

"Being intimate with you is a privilege beyond description. You're a queen, Destiney baby. I don't take you for granted, and I don't take this lightly. You please me above and beyond anything I could describe. Your body is perfect. Your taste, your smell. The way you express your love for me whenever we come together. You satisfy every single one of my needs."

I'd been absently caressing Destiney's fingers, and she'd been caressing mine. That, coupled with the things I'd begun to express to her, was getting a rise out of me.

This wasn't the time for him to be bricking up, but he didn't know the difference.

Clearly.

After a moment, "Lately, I've felt conflicted." I gently told her. As I expected, her eyebrows were high on her head. "Baby. I love you, and I care about you. You are precious to me. And the truth is, I haven't felt right about being intimate with you outside of a covenant. Without a ring. I want to make love to you, but you deserve that within the covenant of a marriage. I wanted to talk to you about it. I was trying to figure out how without you feeling like I don't want you anymore or I'm rejecting you. That couldn't be further from the truth. I'm sorry for causing any stress or hurting you. I should have just come to you. I'm sorry baby."

Destiney nodded. I said so much to her, and I'm sure she needed to process it. So, I continued caressing her soft fingers against mine. I was semi-hard, too, still. I knew she could see it since I was wearing basketball shorts. Nothing was hidden in those.

"Where do we go from here baby?" Destiney asked me sweetly, around her adorable smile.

"That means you believe me? And you forgive me?"

"Yes baby. I believe you, and I forgive you." She leaned into me, kissing my lips softly. "I'm sorry for waiting until I was so upset about this to say anything. I was in agony, and all I had to do was ask you about this."

"It isn't all on you love. We both could have said something sooner."

"I understand your hesitation. But we can discuss anything and everything. Let's say something right away next time."

"Indeed." I moved from the coffee table back to the couch beside her. Pulling her toward me. She nestled her head into my side. Her favorite place to be when we were sitting on the couch.

I was glad to have her there. And glad this was finally off my chest. And I was so glad she felt better now.

"So, baby."

"Yeah?"

"You never said. What happens now?" Destiney asked.

I sighed lightly. "Well. I think we should abstain. Now that I've tasted you, it won't be easy. No doubt about that. But... the next time I make love to you, I want you to be Mrs. Walker."

"Mmm." I felt her vibrations in my side. "You've awakened the monster, and now you're putting her back in hibernation." Destiney playfully jested.

I released a boisterous chuckle. "We can do it. I know we can."

"We absolutely can." After a beat, she asked, "When are you planning to marry me?" We talked about marriage too many times to count. I told her she was it for me. I told her I wanted her for the rest of our lives plenty of times.

"Tomorrow."

"Micah. You haven't even officially asked."

"I assumed you'd agree." My tone was serious but laced with sarcasm. "And not just so I can get back in that pussy. Though that's a part of the reason. I want to spend the rest of my life loving you. You're all I need, Destiney baby." After a beat, "If I had a ring, and officially asked. What would you say?"

"I'd say yes."

My smile was wide. Hers too. Big, bright, and beautiful, reaching her celestial eyes. I could see every single tooth in her mouth. "Yeah?"

"Mmmhmm. *Yes.*"

Somehow, my smile grew even wider. "Yes?"

She giggled just a little, "Yes Micah. Absolutely. Positively. *Definitely.*" She murmured the last part as I connected our lips.

After many kisses, I pulled her back into my side, and we settled on the couch again. Destiney turned her cooking show back on, and I shut my eyes.

Content. Grateful. Excited. All the things, really. I hated that I'd have to be away from her, but I was already making plans in my head for when I returned. My first order of business was getting her a ring.

twenty-nine

DESTINEY

"Best. You okay?" India asked. Her brows knitted, concerning eyes surveying me.

I took a few steps out of the ensuite to my bedroom, and India stood to meet me.

I love Indie. She truly is the best.

So present.

Always there for me.

She just got me. Understood me. Never needing to explain shit- she just knew.

I flopped back on my bed. Stretching out a little. "Just not feeling well." I huffed. "And I miss Micah."

India sat beside me on my bed. "I know you miss Micah." She had her purse on her lap. I think she was digging around for something.

Anyway, I shut my eyes.

"When is he coming back?"

"Five more days." I groaned. I was barely halfway through these eight days, and I was already suffering extreme withdrawals.

For some reason, the few days before he left, I felt extra attached to Micah, and being away from him now felt *brutal*.

It occurred to me the other night that it was the conversation we had a few days before he left.

Yeah.

It was absolutely the conversation we had.

I can't even describe my feelings hearing Micah bear his heart to me.

Well. Relief initially.

I'd convinced myself, which is completely ludicrous, that he must have been cheating on me. I went to the most extreme rationale. But Micah talked me off that cliff.

And he's so good at that. Good to me.

He continues to prove himself.

How much he loves me. How much I mean to him.

He's taught me and *continues* to teach me what love is. I really didn't fully know before him.

He cares for me so deeply, loving me exactly the way I need him to.

A way I didn't even *know* I needed.

Effortlessly.

I love him so much. Words just can't explain.

So, I missed my man. *Something serious.* Micah keeps saying that he misses me, too.

We'd been texting and FaceTiming as usual, and though it helped, it wasn't the same.

India stayed at my place last night and will stay again tonight.

We were in full swing of our creative groove, working away at the Village, which was going well. The sets looked amazing.

And we'd been working away on the mural at Micah's house.

The wall had been primed with eggshell white, and then we outlined oversized leaves on it, some of them overlapping. The eggshell white was the perfect background color, as it was a warmer white that would make the brightly colored Monstera Delicios leaves pop in contrast.

We started adding color yesterday. Some of the leaves would be outlined, and some would be painted completely. Adding the color was my favorite part. I love to see the vision come to life, and adding the color does just that. Of course, I also love going to the art supply store, looking through all the color palettes, and picking out the perfect shades. I love the fun names they have for the various colors, too. It always seemed like the coolest job to be able to come up with the names for the endless hues of colors, like the names of the various scents at Bath and Body Works or Victoria's Secret.

So, we were working with four colors: a deep hunter green, a bright goldfish orange, a refreshing aqua blue, and a gleaming rich black. These colors were complementary, and I knew it would look great once we were all done.

The plan was to go back to Micah's in a couple of days. But that all depended on how I felt. I still hadn't been feeling well. It was growing worse. For the past few days, I've been feeling nauseous. Yesterday morning, I threw up.

Last night, I'd finally broken down and told Indie. Up until then, I hadn't told anyone. Partly because it wasn't unusual for me... once upon a time. Back when I had my issue of blood, I was constantly feeling sick.

Off. Tired. In pain. Not myself. And I just dealt with it.

Not nauseated though.

"Try not to focus on that too much," India said, still rummaging through her purse. My eyes were still closed, but I could hear it. "Just look ahead." She told me in a comforting tone. "Your man will be home soon."

"Thanks Indie."

"You said Day would be home tonight, right?" She asked after a moment.

"Yeah. She said she'd just be stopping by though." I put my arm over my eyes. "Girl, what are you looking for?" She was still searching.

"My phone, but I found it."

I lightly shook my head. Indie carried a canvas tote, as most artists do, and sometimes, foolishly, she tosses her phone in there. I love India, but she really shouldn't do that. That tote of hers has a million and one things in it, just like mine. And it's always so hard for her to find anything. I've called her phone so many times only for her to retrieve it ringing at the bottom. I knew better than to ever put anything important in my tote.

A moment later, I heard Daijah's chipper voice. "Hey Indie!" India had called her on speaker.

"Hey Day. You headed this way yet?"

"Pretty soon. You guys, okay?"

"Yeah, we're good. Just need some clarity on something. Do you mind making a pit stop?"

"Sure don't. What do you need?"

"*I* don't need anything. But *Des* needs a pregnancy test. Make that two, actually."

I sat up fast, "Indie, what are you talking about?"

"A pregnancy test?" Daijah and I spoke at the same time.

Indie carried on with Daijah just like I wasn't there. "Destiney revealed she hasn't been feeling well the past few weeks. Feeling nauseous recently. Since we know she's been fucking on the regular…" She looked at me knowingly, "*It's quite possible Des is prego.*" Indie sang that last part.

"Des, why didn't you tell anyone you haven't been feeling well?" Daijah asked.

"I don't know. Just didn't think it was a big deal. I'm used to it."

"That was *before*," Indie said.

"After surgery, you said you've never felt better." Daijah pointed out. She was right.

"Precisely. Now you're feeling nauseous. Girl, you should have said something. We need to know. We were just drinking. Smoking hookah too."

That freaked me out. My eyes grew wide.

"When was your last period?" That was Daijah.

"It was several weeks ago," India's eyes ballooned. "But I don't have a period every month," I quickly added. "It's not quite monthly, but getting there."

My doctor said it can take a while for my cycle to be normal post-surgery, if at all. Some women never have a monthly cycle, which can make conceiving difficult when they are actually trying.

Were we trying?

No. We weren't really.

But… we weren't exactly *not* trying either.

We'd pretty much stopped using condoms altogether. Honestly, and now that I think about it, maybe that was incredibly irresponsible of us. Of me. Especially if I smoke hookah and drink on occasion.

"I'll grab a few tests..." I tuned out whatever it was Day and Indie were talking about. I had to think for a second.

Micah picked up a few condoms while we were in Pismo Beach.

We used those.

Then we got home and started playing the pullout game.

And Micah, being as thoughtful as he was, asked me if I was okay with that. Beforehand.

I was perfectly fine with that. I loved the way he felt.

He said he loved it too. And he'd been pulling out in time.

But since I'm not on any birth control, I guess there's always a possibility. Even if Micah pulls out. It only takes one.

Just one determined swimmer.

Wow.

Maybe I am pregnant.

Holy shit.

thirty

MICAH

"Hey brother," I said after I tossed my suitcase in the back seat and climbed into the front passenger side of Malachi's truck.

"Baby brother. You looking good. Feeling good?"

"Yeah. Glad to be back."

"Yup. Glad to have you back. Thank God for traveling grace." Mal pulled away from the curb, merging into the bustling airport traffic.

"Indeed. Thank you for picking me up."

"Of course. I got you baby brother."

The traffic flowed, and soon, we were on the freeway, making our way toward south Sacramento.

"So, how'd everything go? Productive? Accomplished?"

Mal asked. I was away on business for eight days.

"Yeah. I got to meet our new CEO. Had a few fireside chats with some counterparts in our neighboring regions. Appreciate the perspective. Things are looking well fiscally. Glad to be back though. It's too cold in Chicago for me."

Mal laughed. "No doubt." He sounded just like Daddy saying that, too. *No doubt* was their *indeed*. They both said it all the time. "We're just California boys, that's all." We both chuckled at that.

"Right!"

"I went up there a few times with the team." Mal played basketball when he was at Morehouse. "Couldn't get used to that. They don't call it Windy City for nothing. I think they get just about a month of an actual summer up there."

"Yeah. And long winters. Not my forte."

"Shiiiittt. Mine either."

We cruised through traffic, which, thankfully, wasn't too bad. The airport was just north of Natomas. It's about thirty minutes from our neck of the woods, but with traffic, it may take longer. I was okay with that. Hanging with my big brother was always a vibe.

"The kids okay?"

"Yeah. I meant to tell you, so Gabe had a group assignment he worked on earlier this week and his partner had to come over at some point so they could practice their presentation, which came out phenomenal by the way. Proud father."

I nodded. "*Very* proud uncle."

Mal nodded too. "So, it turns out his partner is this girl. And I am *certain* Gabe is sweet on her."

My eyes grew wide. "Oh yeah?" I chuckled at that.

"*Yes*. My boy was fumbling and stuttering. They were practicing, and he couldn't even get through his presentation." Mal and I were cracking up. "His calm and cool demeanor was nowhere to be found. That's what gave it away. He's *absolutely* got a sweet spot for her."

"Sounds like it. Nephew has a crush huh?"

"Man…" Mal rubbed his beard absently. "He's definitely smitten. You know Gabe. Not much else would throw him off his square."

We both cackled.

"I didn't want to make it a big deal, you know. But we talked about it. Gabe said they were just friends and that she was a cool girl. Smart. Friendly. He thinks she's pretty." Mal chuckled again. "She seems like a nice girl. So. All that sounds good to me."

"Damn." I shook my head. "We getting old brother."

"I'm saying. Gabe's going on fifteen. Gabby's going on thirteen. It's wild too. They aren't much younger than Ella and I were when we met."

"Right! Now that's bananas."

We cruised in silence for a few beats.

"Mommy and Daddy straight?" We usually shared the task of looking in on them, but I knew Mal was good for holding down the fort by himself.

"Oh yeah. Everything's straight at the blue house. G-squared and I went by yesterday evening as a matter of fact." (*G-Squared* were Gabe and Gabby girl). Mal looked over his shoulder as he veered into an open lane. "You planning to go by today?"

"Yeah, I need to run a few errands, so I'll stop by on my way out." It was hardly eleven a.m.; I took a red-eye flight out yesterday and flew directly back. Thankfully, there weren't any delays, and I was home early enough to have the rest of the day.

He nodded.

"How's my sis?" I was sure to look to my left when I asked. A silly grin made its way across Malachi's face just like I knew it would. It was the same grin I'd seen for the past 17 years.

"She's perfect. Can't wait to get back to her." After a beat, "Was in the middle of something and had to climb out my good shit just to come scoop yo ass."

"Mal, really?"

Of course, Malachi thought that was so funny. A deep rumble made its way from the pit of his belly as he filled the truck with his laughter. All I could do was shake my head.

"You gone find out baby brother. Believe me." Mal said once he calmed down.

I already knew.

This had been the longest eight days of my life, and I missed the hell out of Destiney. I couldn't wait to get back.

To see her.

As much as I appreciated Mal picking me up, I wished I'd arranged for her to greet me. But being so far away and for that long gave me room to consider my next move.

And it was time.

Before leaving for Chicago, I picked Daijah's brain on the best type of ring for Destiney. I narrowed it down to two, and when I couldn't decide between them, I asked Gabby girl to help me decide.

I knew Destiney would have loved either of them, but I'm glad I could ask Gabby girl. She was the reason I'd met Destiney.

So, I arranged to have a few things in place by this evening.

On my flight home, I mentally prepared what I was going to do for her and what I was going to say to her.

I wanted it all to be perfect.

I planned to visit Mommy and Daddy, then pick up a couple more things and get showered. After that, I'd pick up my baby and bring her home.

Yes. *Home.* With me. Where she belonged.

I was so fortunate to have secured a huge favor from Janelle, co-owner and executive chef at HomeGrownSol. Janelle graciously agreed that I could hire her to come and prepare a meal for us. I requested a few of Destiney's favorite things on the menu. She always raved about the roasted red potatoes with Brussels sprouts. And the roasted stuffed zucchini. The zucchini was delicious. Made with fire-roasted tomatoes, breadcrumbs, parmesan, mozza-rella, basil, and garlic. Destiney loved it. We'd gotten it to go a few times.

We'd have some sweet wine. Candles. Also, picking up some flowers. Destiney may even want to soak in the huge ass tub in the master. I knew it would come in handy someday. I'd never used the tub, but I got the feeling Destiney would get plenty of use out of it. I had a stockpile of spa essentials for her.

Most importantly, I have already asked Mr. Evans for Destiney's hand.

I went by her father's home the day before my flight to speak with him.

"You take care of my baby. Give me your word that you will. She is precious to me and her late mother. Should you no longer wish to, you bring her back to me. Whole. Better than the way I am giving her to you." Mr. Evans *spoke sternly. Much sterner than he's ever spoken with me. But I was perfectly alright with that.*

I stood up straight, looking slightly downward into her father's eyes.

Sticking my hand out, I said, "You have my word, Mr. Evans. I will take the best care of Destiney."

He shook my hand firmly with a smile that reached his eyes.

"Call me dad."

"Baby brother?"

I looked over at Mal. "My bad… just in my head."

"Damn right." Mal cackled. "You thinking of your sweetheart?"

I grinned, and he cackled all over again. "You don't even have to answer that."

"Tonight is the night, brother," I revealed.

"Oh yeah? *That's* why you're in your head over there."

I chuckled. "I want things to go perfectly. Just running over it in my mind."

"That's all you had to say. I'll be quiet."

"You good big brother. I need the distraction." I was a ball of nerves.

"I know you. I'm sure you thought of everything." Mal chuckled. "Everything's handled. All you have left to do now is ask."

I nodded. "Yeah… you think she'll say yes?" I didn't plan on asking Mal that question, but I couldn't help myself. I wasn't too proud to reveal my feelings. We always spoke with complete transparency, after all.

"I think she'll say yes. You two…" he smiled, shaking his head. "The love I've witnessed growing between the two of you. It's explosive. She adores you, Micah. And likewise, you've shown her your heart and that it beats for her through your words and actions. It's been beautiful to witness. You did well, brother. Baby sis is good to you and for you. I think she'll say yes."

I felt better just that quickly. "You'll be the first to know," I told Malachi.

"I'll be here, baby brother. Looking forward to hearing the good news. Celebrating. Everything to come."

"Indeed."

I knew this was right.

It felt so right. And I knew this was what we both wanted.

Now, we'll make it official.

thirty-one

DESTINEY

Today was *everything*. Quite literally.

I was so happy my man was back.

He came to get me. And he took me *home*. To his house.

It's a fact that his place has been like a second home for me. And I've spent more time there than anywhere else. And that's just the way I like it.

So, we got home, and I don't know how or when he managed to pull it off, but Micah had the most romantic evening planned for me.

It was *everything*.

I stepped into the front door—Micah was right behind me—and was greeted with the beautiful sight of rose petals. At Micah's encouragement, I followed the trail, and the delicate pink rose petals led us from the front door to the dining room table.

The table was covered with a black satin tablecloth, more pink rose petals, lit candles, and two elegant place settings.

Then, I noticed the striking arrangement of sunflowers.

Even more striking than the last one. Bold and bright in a gorgeous vase.

I turned to Micah, looking up at him. He was right behind me and already wearing a knowing smile.

My smile was wide when I said, "Micah. This is all *so* beautiful."

"*You're* beautiful," He returned.

I fell into his arms, and he held me for a long time. Micah doesn't cease to amaze me. Ever.

I'd read about the sweet, romantic gesture of rose petals. I read all about them in my romance novels. Plenty. Seen them in the movies too. And honestly, I didn't think it would happen to me.

And...I was feeling emotional, but I didn't cry. I just held onto my man, momentarily losing myself in his sweet embrace, not wanting to sever our connection. I surmise he felt the same. Micah held me just as securely.

After a few moments—I don't know how many...softly, close to my ear, Micah said, "Been telling you love...anything for you baby." He spoke in that deep register I love so much—the one that gets me going every single time. And I held him even tighter, nodding silently.

My man is fucking amazing.

Micah loosened his grip but didn't let me go completely. "Sweetheart, there are some people here I'd love for you to meet."

I looked up at Micah in surprise. Then I looked just past Micah, and only then did I realize two women were moving about in the kitchen. Both of them dressed in a black chef's coat.

I briefly—only briefly—forgot that I was consumed by the savory scents of fragrant food when I entered the house. The delectable aromas emanating from the kitchen were even richer now.

My senses told me something delightful was being freshly prepared.

"Destiney baby. Meet Mrs. Janelle Bailey. The illustrious Executive Chef and co-owner of Home-GrownSol."

My eyes grew wide. My jaw dropped.

This is Janelle? *The* Janelle?

How did he get her?

That restaurant is *always* bustling. They probably were *right now*.

And she was *here*? *In Micah's kitchen*. Preparing a meal for *us*.

"Lovely to meet you, Destiney. Please meet my daughter Naomi, Sauté chef. She's been my right hand this evening." She smiled proudly as she shook my hand; Naomi followed suit, smiling shyly. She appeared about sixteen or so. Pretty, just like her mom.

"Sooo nice to meet you, Janelle. Naomi. I am fanning out right now. I *love* your food! Micah has got to be sick of me. He's *always* ordering something for me from HomeGrown."

"Hey, I don't mind at all. I'll usually get something for myself while I'm at it." Micah said.

We all shared a laugh.

"I appreciate all of the vegetarian options, too," I told them excitedly.

"That's what I love to hear! I'm so glad you enjoy it. " Her warm smile reached her eyes. Janelle continued, "Good food is great for the soul. I hope you find tonight's meal just as delicious."

"I'm sure we will! It smells great," I gushed.

"Your dinner is ready. Please be seated whenever you're ready for us to serve you," Naomi politely offered.

"Excellent. We'll go wash up and be back momentarily," Micah promised.

The guest restroom was just down the hall, across from the office. We both headed that way, and Micah pulled me to him just as we turned the corner.

"Hang on...give me those lips, baby." Micah gently backed me against the wall, and we kissed sweetly at first, but it quickly turned passionate. I started pulling away. Well, I was trying to, but Micah had a grip around my waist. "Where you going beauty?" He murmured against my lips, "...I'm not finished." His hand descended, and within seconds, he was inside my already damp underwear, and his fingers were moving just past my lower lips.

"Micah..." I moaned, trying to keep my voice down, "Baby..." He had two of his thick ass fingers inside me, and it felt so good. Not only had I missed him, but I missed this too. We'd only shared a few sweet pecks when he came to pick me up earlier. And this was nice. Mostly. I knew we were outside their line of sight, but I was apprehensive. Kinda paranoid. My moans were growing slightly in volume. And I was distracted because I didn't want either of the ladies in the next room to hear us.

"Ssshhh. You trying to blow our cover?" Micah teased, speaking against my lips. He was stroking me with his fingers. "*Fuck.* Baby, you are slippery." His thumb was on my clit, gently rubbing...driving me fucking insane. "You like that sexy girl?"

"Yeah baby. I love it." Just that quickly, I'd released my reservations. Enjoying the strum of his fingers. They'd get an eyeful if they dared to come down this hall.

I wouldn't worry about that right now.

"Go head baby," Micah said, "Give me one right here. Right on my fingers." He was gentle yet persistent. Rubbing my clit with fervor. His tongue was *all up in* my mouth. Kissing me deep, slow, and nasty.

As if on command, I came undone, feeling an intense wave of pleasure making my eyes flutter. As I reached my peak, he swallowed my moans. Which absolutely would have given us away. I'm glad Micah's lips were still on mine.

"There it is," Micah praised. I loved that shit.

His fingers went into his mouth, where he sucked them clean, then kissed me again, and I tasted myself all over his tongue. I loved that shit too.

"Go on upstairs and get cleaned up, baby. I'll use this restroom and head back. I'll tell them you'll be a few more minutes."

"Alright." My voice was contented. And blissful.

I went upstairs to get a fresh pair of panties. These were done for.

***

So, dinner was absolutely delicious. Somehow, it tasted even better than it did at the restaurant.

First, they served Caprese avocado toast as an appetizer. This wasn't something on their menu. I'd have ordered it if so. Micah must have made a special request. He knows how much I love avocado toast. And it was so good. Perfectly toasted baguette topped with avocado, mozzarella, and heirloom tomatoes. Fresh basil. Fresh cracked black pepper. Olive oil drizzle. *Mmm!* The fresh pepper and fresh basil gave it a rustic flavor. For Micah, there was Italian turkey stuffed with portobello mushrooms.

Janelle made my most requested entree for my main course. I was so pleased. And I don't think I'll ever get tired of the balsamic Brussels sprouts. Micah had pan-seared Sea Bass over a bed of wilted mixed greens.

The food was stellar. Marvelous.

Janelle and Naomi quietly made their exit once they served us dessert. Each of them placed a generous slice of red velvet cake covered in light whipped frosting in front of us. Micah and I really could have shared a slice, and every bite was rich, moist, decadent, and heavenly.

Throughout the evening, Micah and I raved about the superb food prepared. We were thankful and delighted our chefs set the time aside for us. I was beyond satisfied with all three courses.

When we took our dessert plates to the kitchen, we discovered it was cleaned and restored to the tidy condition Micah kept it in. There was almost no trace of them there. Aside from the Tupperware, they packed the leftover food in. And there was still plenty for a filling lunch tomorrow.

I leaned against the counter, sipping from my glass of water. I was so full at the moment—past full.

Lunch was the furthest thing from my mind, but I was emotionally full, too. My heart was so full. Yeah.

I closed my eyes, enchanted with the tranquil sounds of the soft music that had been playing, when something else occurred to me: I'm so glad I wasn't feeling too sick today. And able to keep my food down. I'd thrown up a couple of times, and that would have ruined everything. It would have blown my cover, too.

"Did you enjoy yourself, love?" Micah asked. He washed our plates and forks and then placed them on the dishrack.

I nodded eagerly, giving him a contented smile. "Thank you. I have. Today was *so*… it was everything, Micah. You're so thoughtful, baby. I'll remember today for the rest of my life."

"Indeed. I'm so glad to hear that. I missed you so much, baby. I could hardly wait to get back to you."

"I missed you too, Micah."

I could cry because I was so overwhelmed and appreciative of this man.

My man.

He continues to remind me of his thoughtfulness.

I don't travel often, but when I do, I'm exhausted once I get home. Micah did all of this for me after traveling the last several hours. It was the thought behind it all for me. He was so thoughtful to do this.

He turned toward the fridge and began loading the food.

During dinner, I extended my gratitude to Micah at least a million times. In true Micah fashion, he insisted it was no big deal, but I insisted that it really was. I told him I would have been just fine having peanut butter and jelly.

"Baby," I called.

"Yeah?" He moved a few things around but turned toward me when I didn't answer immediately. "Are you alright?"

I nodded with a lazy smile. My lids were low. "Thank you. I am."

"Good." He turned back toward the fridge. "Need anything, sweetheart?" He was likely wondering why I called out to him. He had checked in with me a few times earlier when I turned down a glass of wine with dinner. He didn't press, but I knew he would be bringing it up soon.

"I need you," I lulled.

"Do you?" His voice dipped. Micah turned back towards me, closing the fridge behind him. His lids low now. Just like mine.

"Mmmhmm." I placed my glass on the kitchen counter beside me and took a few steps towards him. Eyes on eyes, we were pressed together, body to body.

"Mmm. Tell me what you need, beauty."

I went for his belt buckle, then the zipper on his jeans, freeing him from his boxers. *Damn.* Micah was already hard as a rock. I stroked his hardness, then dropped to my knees. I could show him better than I could tell him.

"*Mmmmm.* I see."

"I missed you baby." It was muffled. I had his big dick in my mouth, after all. I commenced sucking, taking as much of him as I could. Giving it my very best.

"I missed you more… so glad to be back, my love…" Micah's fingers were threaded in my locs. Gently cradling my head in his large hands. Murmuring my encouragement and his pleasure. "There you go beauty. Damn, you suck me so good."

I pressed my hands against the cool fridge on either side of him. Anchoring myself for leverage as he began to stroke my mouth. Gladly relinquishing control.

My mouth was wet and slick and sloppy. I could taste his precum as he glided in and out like a hot-ass knife through butter.

Micah's strokes were slow and measured at first. Then, growing erratic the closer he got.

I fucking loved that shit.

"Destiney… beauty… you want this baby?" Micah didn't even have to ask.

I pressed myself closer. He understood my silent agreement.

When he released inside of my mouth, his beautiful sound surrounded us.

Micah helped me up, kissing my lips, my neck, and my chin.

"Thank you, baby. I needed you, too," He told me.

"*Always a pleasure,*" I said in a flirty tone. Winking, I turned back to the counter, tossing back the last of my water. I washed my glass and placed it on the dishrack.

"You're so damn sexy," Micah told me, smacking my ass.

I yelped in surprise. Rubbing my ass at the mild sting. He was heavy-handed, but I liked having my ass smacked.

"Thank you handsome."

Micah nodded, taking me into his arms, and leaned us against the counter. After kissing my neck softly, "How about we take a shower, and I'll give you a massage?"

"*Yes, please,*" I returned, pecking his lips sweetly.

"You got it baby. Head upstairs and get the shower started. I'll be right in behind you."

So, Micah gave me a massage. He's the best at them, and I was appreciative and excited. I loved being intimately close to him, as close as possible, considering we weren't making love right now. And this was good enough for me. It was perfect. We may have stopped having intercourse, but the intimacy hadn't gone anywhere. It was still living and breathing between us. I'd argue that we've gotten closer in these last few weeks.

And now we were *finally* dressed for bed.

That massage had me so relaxed that I would be down for the count soon.

But I needed to tell him the news first.

I'd been counting down the days while Micah was in Chicago. More than two thousand miles away from me.

Obsessively at first.

But then I thought better of it. Bearing in mind how much more difficult things could have been.

If Micah had been deployed or something, it would have been months, *not days*… with no guarantee he'd even return alive.

I had an *enormous* respect for military wives. No way I could do it.

That reality check got me through just fine.

I busied myself with work.

And the mural. Indie and I made significant progress.

In between time, I sipped ginger ale and kept ginger candy nearby, combating the nausea.

Yet still feeling a strong gravitational pull. Still longing for Micah.

I desperately wanted him home.

Not only because I missed him but I was grappling with the news.

The news was like a burning secret. Fiery. Scorching. *Ablaze* like an ignited flame.

Like a blaring alarm.

A declaration fighting to reveal its presence.

The news, warring to free itself from the containment of my lips.

Micah and I had been texting and talking on the phone, of course, and I came dangerously close a few times.

I wanted to tell Micah as soon as it was confirmed.

But I was sure I should share this with him in person.

And I couldn't wait. I was so eager to share this with Micah.

I sat on my side of the bed, checking in with Day and Indie. I shared a few pictures from the set-up downstairs in our group chat, and they asked a million questions. They also asked if I'd told him yet, and I said I was about to. Micah was in the walk-in closet, and I was sure he would be making his way out of there any minute. I promised I'd fill them in with all the details tomorrow and then wished them a good night.

I plugged up my phone just as Micah walked out of the closet.

"Can I talk to you?"

"Baby, I need to talk to you."

We spoke at the same time.

Micah was beside me in seconds. "Of course you can, baby, " his voice was laced with concern. "Everything okay?"

I nodded, "It is. I promise."

"Indeed. Well, you go first. I can wait."

"Okay."

Then, several moments went by. And I said nothing.

This was not how I imagined this would go. Because suddenly, and out of nowhere, I was nervous. I don't know why. Considering just hours ago, I was bursting with this news. Now I was feeling shy.

"Micah," I turned toward him. Looking into his expectant, warm brown eyes. He nodded, encouraging me to continue. He held his hand in mine, threading our fingers. "Micah," I looked away, but he was with me. Caressing my fingers. Patiently waiting for whatever this was.

"Yes baby? What is it?"

I took another beat, then, "I'm pregnant. I'm… we're…having a baby."

Micah's eyes were wide. His smile was even wider. *"Are you? Really?!"*

I smiled too. My eyes were filling up as I nodded silently.

"Baby! You're having my baby?"

"I am." Growing emotional, I sniffed, but my smile reached my eyes.

Micah moved to his knees in front of me. Lifting my shirt, he wrapped his arms around my waist, pressing kisses against my belly. His chuckle was deep, *"That's why* you didn't want wine with dinner."

"Yeah," I giggled at the ticklish sensation of his beard on my skin.

"Have you seen a doctor?"

"Next week."

I felt him nod against me. "I'm so happy baby." I would have known even if he hadn't told me. Micah's joy was evident as he continued scattering kisses all over my midsection. I closed my eyes, holding his head in my hands. He never moved from the floor in front of me. Rubbing my lower back, softly kissing me.

I couldn't help myself as I asked, "You promise you're happy, Micah?" I knew how much he wanted to be a father. But I also knew that he wanted to be married first.

I felt the same way, honestly.

Micah looked up into my eyes. *"So happy baby. I wouldn't lie to you."* I believed him. "How are you feeling?" He quizzed.

"I'm happy too." My tears finally fell, and Micah wiped them away. Holding his eyes, I continued, "But I know you wanted to be married before kids."

"Yeah." Micah nodded. "Which confirms I'm right on time with this."

My brows were knitted, "With what?"

Micah reached into his pocket, pulling out a small black velvet box. He opened it, and I gasped when I realized what it was and what he was doing. He took my left hand in his. "There are few things in this life I'm certain of…" He pressed my hand to his lips, "But when it comes to you..." Kiss. "Me. Us." Another kiss. "I am certain. I am so confident. Be my wife, baby. Will you marry me? Tell me you'll be my wife."

"I'd love nothing more than to be your wife, Micah. Yes," I replied through tears.

"Yeah?" He grinned.

"Yes baby."

He slid the rose gold diamond ring on my finger, and I peered at it in awe. Admiring the intricate details.

It was beautiful—an oval cut diamond in the center. Pavé set diamonds on the halo and along each side of the band.

Gorgeous. Radiant. Breathtaking.

I fell into Micah's arms. Right there on the floor. Kissing all over him. Holding him tightly, just as tightly as he held me.

"I love you, Micah."

"I love you, Destiney baby. I'm never letting you go."

Epilogue

One year later

"So, you ready to be an uncle?"

I remember when Mal first shared the news that they were expecting.

He was so proud.

I was too!

The question had caught me so off guard that I was stuck for a second. We weren't even on the subject. I don't recall precisely what we were talking about, but it wasn't remotely related. Anyway, the moment I realized what he was telling me, I looked up and saw a big Kool-Aid smile.

"Sis is pregnant?" In a matter of seconds, I was sporting the same smile.

"Yeah man. I can't believe it."

"Wow brother. That is great news! Congrats!"

"Thank you, baby brother."

I hugged him tight. "You already tell Mommy and Daddy?"

"Not yet. You're the first and only person we've shared this with. Do me a favor and keep this between us, baby brother."

"Your good news is safe with me."

"No doubt. You've always been that."

"Of course."

"We'll tell everyone at the end of the month. Ella wanted to see her doctor first, get her official due date and all that jazz."

I nodded. *"Get ready. Mommy is going to be over the moon. She'll probably start buying stuff before you even know what it is."*

We both cackled. I continued, *"I don't know why you're so surprised anyway. The way you always pouncing on my sis."*

"Aye man! My wife takes care of me. What can I say."

Months later, there was another moment I won't forget as long as I live.

It was a moment so very special to me.

I came to the hospital to meet my brand-new nephew, and when Mal placed him in my arms, he proudly introduced us, and that's when I learned my nephew would forever have a part of me, too.

"Baby brother. We're thrilled to introduce you to our son. Gabriel Micah Walker."

My eyes grew wide, *"You serious man?"*

Ella looked on proudly, *"You better believe it. We wouldn't have it any other way. You introduced us, remember?"*

I sure did remember that, but this was huge. My brother gave my name to his first-born child, a son who was already his pride and joy, a physical representation of his infinite love for his wife.

"Wow. This is... I am so honored. Gabriel is beautiful." And he was. Content and alert, his soft brown eyes looking right at me. I held Gabriel close, growing emotional. *"Nice to meet you, Gabriel Micah Walker."* I chuckled because I couldn't help myself. *"Has a nice ring to it."*

"We thought so too," Mal said.

"Indeed." I looked up at my brother and over at my sister-in-love. "I'm so proud of you. Both of you."

"Thank you, baby brother."

"Thank you."

They replied simultaneously.

I decided that day, right at that very moment, that should God bless me with a son, I would give him my brother's name, too.

***

I entered the room quietly to find Destiney sleeping. Making my way to the bed, I watched her sleep peacefully for a while.

I watched her sleep constantly, but I could pinch myself now.

I know this moment is real, but sometimes I still can't believe it.

Destiney is my heart. In human form. My heartbeat. Sharing this space and making a life together is such a beautiful thing. I express my gratitude every single day.

For years, I had been searching. For her.

And now, here we were. I'm her husband, she's my wife, and we're making memories we can cherish for the rest of our lives.

Destiney and I were married eight months ago. Our engagement was short—something we both wanted. We set a date, exactly a month after Daijah and Julian's nuptials and just *ten months* to the date we met.

Wild. When you know, you know.

Destiney was a beautiful bride. I remember when she entered the church on her proud father's arm. She neared me, and it was as if everyone else- everything else had disappeared.

As if time stood still.

For the briefest of moments, nothing else existed. Only my soon-to-be wife. When Destiney descended the aisle and we locked eyes, it was a moment of significant vulnerability. An unspoken connection. For us both.

I released tears of joy, trying with all my might to collect myself, and my big brother and best man comforted me.

"This is your moment, baby brother. Look at her. She's your wife. Everything you prayed for."

Malachi's firm, reassuring hand on my shoulder reminded me that he was right beside me and always would be. I knew this full well. He didn't need to tell me.

Like an angel, Destiney floated towards me. And all I could do was thank the good Lord above for his favor. For his sovereignty. For the best thing to ever happen to me.

The aisle was fairly long, and I saw Mr. Evans speaking to Destiney as they came into view. I couldn't hear him, of course, but seeing this sweet father-daughter moment between them was so special.

When they finally arrived at the altar, he said, "Are you ready, princess?"

Nodding, Destiney said, "Yes. I'm ready Daddy."

After firmly shaking my hand, Mr. Evans lifted Destiney's veil, kissed her forehead, and joined her hand and mine before taking his seat.

That was when Destiney grew emotional and Daijah, her matron of honor, helped make sure she didn't ruin her makeup, whispering encouraging words of her own.

Destiney was perfect—she couldn't have looked more perfect.

My wife had the wedding of her dreams. No expenses were spared. She wanted something intimate yet elegant and got exactly what she wanted.

The day we said 'I do' will forever be one of my proudest moments and no doubt one of the happiest moments of my life.

I continued to watch her sleep. She's never been more beautiful than she is right now.

She lay on her side with a body pillow propped between her legs. Lately, this was the only position she could sleep in comfortably. Her swollen belly had been growing and stretching, making room for our precious baby, and Destiney was such a great sport about it.

We've been waiting with such excitement for our baby to arrive.

We're about halfway there. Destiney officially made five months a couple of days ago.

We decided to keep our baby's gender a surprise.

It's been easy to do. We were just so grateful for this miracle.

We were pregnant late last year, but sadly we miscarried. It was an early miscarriage. A week after we confirmed the news, it was over.

And then we took some time away. We unplugged from everything else, focused on looking after each other, and took care of each other.

And I waited patiently for my wife to tell me when she was ready to try again.

And we did.

Then Destiney told me she was pregnant again, and I was elated.

This time, cautiously optimistic. But *so* happy. And grateful.

Leading up to that moment, we'd been trying ferociously. But not saying so out loud. Trying not to make it a thing. It was unspoken, but the synergy between us didn't require that we spoke it aloud. We both wanted this so much. And we both knew we'd have to stay the course.

When you have a few things working against you, *trying* to get pregnant is not fun, if I'm honest.

We had the challenge of irregular ovulation. So, we had to make love even when we weren't feeling up to it… if you catch my drift…for fear of missing the window. Taking a day off was a risk.

Anyone who had trouble conceiving the traditional way knows exactly what I am talking about.

Now, make no mistake. I love my wife. I'll always want her. I'll always desire her. But it got to be a lot for her. I knew that. And I wanted this *for* her so much.

But it finally happened.

I think back to the day she shared the news with me. I always smile at that memory.

I hovered over Destiney's belly, littering her midsection with kisses, trying to manifest shit if I'm honest… I'd been trying, with all my might, to put a baby in her. I was sure to plant my seeds deep inside each time we came together. Placing a pillow under her hips. Reminding her to lie still and relax afterward. Let things take root.

And I was anxiously anticipating her telling me when it happened.

I was trying to be patient at the same time. I knew the situation was delicate, and I was sensitive to that.

"Is there a baby in here yet?" I asked her in jest, trying to lighten the mood. It had gotten to be a little heavy around here. Looming thoughts. Negative tests. Tears. Doubts.

I made my way up her body, kissing her neck and along her cheeks. Then I spoke softly in her ear.

"Wife...I've been planting seeds deep inside of you...I'm gone keep doing it. I'm giving you everything you need to grow us a beautiful baby." I kissed behind her ear and along her neck. "That okay with you sweetheart?" Two more kisses.

Destiney peered up at me with low lids, and I knew my plan was working. I was getting her ready for me. Ensuring she stayed out of her head would help, so I had a job to do.

I placed her hand on my hardness. I was ready too. She stroked me through my joggers. I needed these out of the way, along with her shorts and panties. I groaned. "Like right now, I'm ready to plant some deep inside of you, baby."

"Husband," Destiney's voice was soft. Laced with need. But there was something else there, too.

However, I was unsure of what exactly.

I moved away from her neck, sitting back on my hunches. Eyes on eyes. Her lids were low, but I couldn't read her expression otherwise.

"Yeah baby?"

Destiney took my hand and gently placed it on her belly.

"There's a baby here right now." She smiled wide. That angelic smile of hers I love so much.

I smiled so big. "Is there really?"
She nodded silently. "Just confirmed today."
I took her in my arms. Holding her. Kissing her.
Then I went back to her belly, littering more kisses there.

Now, here we were.

I'm sure I was biased, but I didn't know a more beautiful pregnant woman. My wife is so beautiful—breathtaking—and she's all mine.

Speaking of miracles, I was so amazed watching her grow our child. There was something ineffable about seeing my wife carrying my offspring. Utterly indescribable, having the privilege of witnessing her grow a life from a seed I planted. And as you can imagine, I've grown even more protective of Destiney. My primal instincts are in overdrive.

And Destiney was so cute. Her skin was glowing. Her hair was growing.

She had been feeling less beautiful lately. She told me she felt as big as a house and was miserable, but I found her to be delicious.

And pregnant pussy was my shit. Yeah. I said it.

I had a salacious desire for my wife that I couldn't explain. Yep. That pregnant pussy had a vice grip on my shit. I was always wanting to be inside her. She gushed for me without me needing to touch her. She was too uncomfortable to get on top now, but we did it from the back just fine. And if I wasn't entering her from behind, I was eating her. I spent so much time between her thick thighs, eating to my heart's content. I was delighted when I discovered how much her nipples had darkened and how much heavier her breasts were in my hands. I looked forward to having my wife back but was fine rocking with this for a while longer.

Oh, Daijah is pregnant, too! She and Julian are expecting a little princess, due any day now.
Destiney and Daijah have grown even closer during this season. It's been so special. God has continued to bless us beyond anything I could ever imagine, and I am so thankful.

I was still beside the bed, admiring how beautiful Destiney looked carrying life.

Destiney is so precious. So lovely. *My good thing.*

Everything. Exactly what I need. More than I could ever want.

And this was love. An insurmountable love.

Immeasurable, vast, endless.

Unconditional. Absolute.

A love, sweet like honey.

Indeed.

The End

By way of Thanks

I am beyond grateful for the opportunity to share this story and for the courage to put my tongue on the page and write what feels most authentic to the characters and most natural to me. To God be the glory. Always!

This story was a true labor of love, and there are a few very dear people who made it all possible.

JM, your friendship has been a wonderful surprise. My middle child is why we met, as you were his preschool teacher, and you have been a part of our lives ever since. He'll be thirteen this year! Thank you for rocking with me on this journey, holding me accountable, and graciously reading every version of this story. Your encouragement and support have been unwavering. Thank you.

PR, you've been such a gem all these years. I was a brand-new mom when we met. My firstborn was weeks old, and can you believe he'll be fourteen this year? I love that we mark our years of friendship by his age, LOL! I am so blessed to have you! Thank you.

My sisters, who beautifully embody the spirit of Destiney's sister, Daijah. I love you and I love our tribe. I'll always be proud of you! Thank you for believing in me and my writing when I was twelve and still believing in me today. Thank you for always showing up for me. I'm so grateful for your encouragement, as it truly helped me finish this story. I couldn't have done this without you!

My babies, I've never grown as much as I have since becoming your mom. Everything I do is for you, and everything I do well is because of you. I love you three with all my heart. Thank you for allowing me to write.

My husband, I can't adequately express how much you mean to me and there aren't enough ways to say thank you. But truly, thank you for being my support. I appreciate you beyond words. This story has taken me on an incredible journey, pushing me beyond what I ever imagined at times. I'm grateful for your constant encouragement along the way. I completed this first draft on our fifteenth wedding anniversary, and I fondly remember you joking about being such a wonderful husband for letting me write instead of taking me out. My love, you are wonderful for many reasons, and I love you fiercely. I always will. Now that we—yes, we— have finally accomplished this, you can take me out anytime, baby!

For the ones who fell in Love: a word for the Collector

I released Chasing Destiney on my thirty-seventh birthday.

I chose that date because, truthfully, this story was a gift to myself. I had finally done something I'd always dreamed of, and no other day felt quite right. As many of you know, and some of you are just now learning, Destiney has been with me for a long time. I first started writing her story in seventh grade. Though the plot has evolved, Destiney grew up with me. Now, twenty-five years later, I've brought her story full circle.

When I wrote Destiney and Micah, I simply set out to tell a story about two people who weren't necessarily searching for the same thing but somehow found everything they needed in each other. I never imagined how many people would see themselves in their love. The passion, the fears, the quiet unlearning of old patterns to make room for something real, beautiful, and transformative. To know that their journey has resonated so deeply and even reached readers across the world has been humbling, and I'm deeply grateful.

The readers who fell hard for Destiney and Micah's story and reached out asking for more, *this Collector's Edition is for you. Yes, you!*

I won't say this is the last you'll hear of them—you'll see them again in another story I'm working on—but in the meantime, I've written two bonus chapters *exclusive* to this edition. One takes

626

place during the Chasing Destiney era, when everything between them was still fresh and electric. Their
connection was intensifying, their feelings already
taking root. They weren't official, not yet, but Micah
knew Destiney was different. This chapter captures
the moment he posed a gentle, quiet question, the
kind that only comes from a man who's already imagined a future. The second chapter is set during the
Destiney Fulfilled era. By then, their journey had
deepened. Their intimacy had become more raw and
more sacred. In the middle of a tender, physical moment, Destiney reflects on what that closeness
means, how deeply Micah sees her, touches her, and
caters to her body, and her spirit. This chapter speaks
to a love that's been earned, that runs deep, that
stretches wide and becomes something infinite. Nur-
tured by trust, shaped by growth, and chosen again
and again. Limitless and beautiful.

Thank you for holding space for this story.
Thank you for believing in characters who are messy,
bold, sensitive, imperfect, but real.
Destiney and Micah are so very precious to me.
I'm grateful they've become that for you, too.

xoxo,
Vivienne Paul

p.s. If you've been curious about Destiney's best
friend *India*... just wait until you meet the man who
sees her *soul*.

Bonus Chapters

MICAH

One of their early moments. They were still building. Taking it slow, but Destiney was different, and she was already pulling him in.

"So, question for the panel." I waited until I had her eyes. "Would you like children of your own someday? A mini you running around?" I wore a smirk, and Destiney peered back at me. Not quite expressionless. But she said nothing.

Destiney and I were on FaceTime. Doing what we did best. Conversing. We'd had dinner, taken showers, and now we were relaxing and settled into our nightly conversation. It was my favorite time of the day. Especially after a day like this one. Work was ridiculously hectic today. I was so glad to be done. But we always talked at the end of the day. Even just briefly. No matter how long it was. Or how tired we were.

Anyway, I was sure tonight would be like most of the others and our conversation would flow well into the late hours... and she'd eventually fall asleep on me. I was good with that. I loved being the last voice she heard. I loved that she was my last voice.

She still hadn't responded to my question, and as I intently peered back at her, I could see gears shifting. I just couldn't get a read on her expression.

We've spoken of children plenty of times.

I often spoke proudly of Gabe and Gabby girl. Their various academic and athletic accomplishments.

I spoke of the children I coached. Especially the ones who made significant strides on and off the court. Some of them came from broken homes without much to look forward to. Those children had my heart.

And likewise, Destiney spoke of the children she worked with in her community efforts. She beamed with such jubilation, sharing the progress they had made on a project. Or the ones whose talent and promise shone like bright lights among the rest.

Overjoyed. As if these children were hers.

That always struck me. In the best way.

Then I realized it. This was a direct question. A direct question I'd never asked.

Finally, she said, "That was a loaded question. I can't just respond simply." She had a tight smile.

And there was a pause. On my part. But I found my voice. "Tell me more Destiney baby."

She sighed lightly. Looking away from me. "Well, for starters, I don't feel comfortable bringing a child into all my mess. And I'm a mess. A mess of feelings and a mess of anxiety. I can't even articulate the shit." Her eyes finally met mine. By the sudden change in her demeanor, I knew she observed the level of concern in them.

I didn't urge her forward. I was patient with her. Offering her the comfort and peace she seemed to need in this moment.

629

The silence between us wasn't awkward or uncomfortable. But it was a little heavy. I knew she was processing whatever she was trying to work out.

"I'm scared, Micah." She revealed. Her voice was so small it was almost a whisper.

"Scared?" My brows knitted. I opened my mouth slightly but decided not to say anything else, for now, and quickly pursed my lips together again.

Now my gears were shifting.

Couldn't help myself. I'm a fixer.

I wanted to know where, why, and how, so I could figure out what.

Who scared you? What can I do? Where is this coming from? How can I fix this?

"I worry... what if I'm not a good mother. I'm so screwed up." She laughed without mirth. "My trauma. My anxiety. I have so much work to do."

Ah.

"And I'm also afraid that I won't be here to raise them. I lost my mom... when I was so young. I know what that does to a child... I don't want that to happen to an innocent child. Wouldn't wish it on my worst enemy."

I gave her a few beats. Before I said, "I understand. And I wish I could promise that nothing will happen to you." I sighed heavily. Gently proceeding, "What happened to you. Daijah. Your mom. Your dad. It was so very tragic... but I don't want you to move through life worried about that. It's not good for you. Therapy would help tremendously with that."

She nodded. "I should seriously consider that. And I'll be honest with you, Micah... I never entertained the concept of having children of my own. Ever, I don't think. But lately, getting to know you, I've warmed up to it. You've made me feel safe to do so." She smiled after that.

"Yeah?" I smiled too.

"Yeah. Truth moment... there's no one else I'd want to go half on a baby with." She had an adorable giggle, and I chuckled myself.

Nodding, I told her, "That would be amazing when the time comes."

"Compelled to agree." She beamed.

I waited several beats, "Destiney. I'm so into you; I would go half on so much more with you. I'd go half on a whole life with you—no hesitation." I volleyed playfully. I was serious as fuck though. But I wanted to keep things light.

"Aww. That's so sweet, Micah." She beamed even brighter.

Later that evening, after we'd said our goodnights, I lay in bed thinking over our conversation. And I thought about children naturally.

The potential of my own and the children I had been blessed to meet over the years. Working with children is a thankless job. Educators especially.

Mentoring was something I felt strongly about as well. That's one reason I volunteered as a coach. I was an official, too, but I liked coaching a little more. I've been a big brother a few times as well.

I grew up watching my father mentor and coach hundreds over years. And I saw the differences he made. He coached our baseball team for years when we played Little League. When we got to be teenagers, he mentored many of the kids at the church, some of our teammates, and classmates. Acting as a father figure.

As chair of deacons, he oversaw the junior deacons in training, which Mal, Ray, and I were a part of. We didn't have a choice, but one thing it instilled in me was a heart to serve others. My heart to serve has taken me far in life. I truly find fulfillment in that.

My father is a great man. I dare say. He taught Mal and me everything we know. He made an honest living driving garbage trucks and worked hard providing for us. I appreciated that so much. And though neither of us was in the blue-collar profession, Mal and I were both great with our hands and didn't trip about busting our knuckles doing something outside. My hands were callous as hell. I have colleagues whose hands I shake, and it felt as though they had never used a shovel a day in their lives! I couldn't believe that shit.

Anyway, most of our friends took to Daddy right away. He's cool as a cucumber, pretty much all the time. A man of few words. Unassuming. Laid back. Easy to chop it up with. He's always been low-key, and Mal and I got it honest. My nephew Gabe was a chip off the old block, too. Anytime Daddy got riled up, you knew it had to be serious.

When it came to taking care of business, like school and family, Daddy didn't play around with any of that. Specifically, our relationship as brothers and our family unit.

At the very top of that list was our personal relationship with God.

Something else I always appreciated was that Daddy handled Mal and me as individuals. As similar as we are, we are fundamentally different at the same time.

To most outsiders, we seem incredibly similar, and we are. But there are distinctive nuances there that set us apart. Anyone who knows us intimately can see it. Almost like identical twins. A quick glance and it's damn near impossible to tell them apart. But people who know them well, spend time with them, learn who they are individually, could tell them apart with their eyes closed.

Daddy took the time to see us and handled us accordingly. He met us exactly where we were and was patient and graceful through the process. He knew what worked for Malachi wouldn't work for me. And what worked for me wouldn't necessarily work for Mal.

We are both sensitive, but I've got Mal beat in that area.

We're both incredibly expressive, but Mal has me beat there.

Malachi was always great at articulating his thoughts, his ideas. His feelings.

His sensitivity shows in his word choice and his attentiveness. He's excellent at reading the room. It shows in every space he dwells, really.

And he's the best when it came to helping you feel better after a fuck up. He didn't waver either. Ever. That shit is one of my brothers' superpowers.

I struggle with that sometimes, depending on the situation, but I was great at pretending I don't.

And that was mommy's doing. She always encouraged us to talk through our thoughts and to use our words. Even when it's difficult.

"Our feelings matter, but our choice of words matters most."

When we were younger and we struggled articulating things verbally, she'd have us sit with our thoughts and then write them down.

I left mommy many notes back when we were kids, if I needed to talk to her about something, but I didn't quite have my thoughts together. At her encouragement. Many times.

I always left it on her nightstand, folded neatly and slid beneath whatever book she was reading. I wouldn't tell her I left her a note, but after she discovered it, she would come find me and we'd have a talk.

Mal and I both kept journals in our younger years and writing in them was a part of our daily routine.

I recall one day; Ray caught me by myself and was teasing me about keeping a "diary" and "writing in diaries was shit girls did."

That thought hadn't crossed my mind, so I was confused at that. And since Ray was older than us, I believed it. One day, Mommy found out I hadn't been writing and asked me about it. When I told her, she immediately encouraged me, insisting it's not true at all. Men keep journals, and there's nothing wrong with writing down your feelings or your prayers.

I learned Daddy had one, he wrote in it now and then.

I found out a couple years ago that Mal still kept a journal. He didn't journal daily, but he wrote often.

I took a few years off and realized what I'd been missing once I picked it up again.

When everything happened with Ayesha, I was back to writing daily. Between journaling and therapy, I was able to better manage my feelings.

Anyway. I settled in, ready to knock out. But my mind kept circling back to what Destiney told me. And that one statement lingered. It had a hold on me. Destiney said she would go half on a baby with me. After having never considered having children of her own. That was huge.

She said it teasingly, but her words were sincere and significant. And. I could not stop replying that.

I had a playful tone when I shot her my comeback, but I would be honored to start a family with her. More than babies. Everything.

Marriage. A home full of love, laughter, and security.

Protection. Provision.

Everything. The sleepless nights and early mornings with the babies she gives me. The feedings, the diapers. The quiet moments in between.

Yeah. I'd give her all of it.

And I know it was soon. It really was so soon. We were still learning each other, still peeling back layers.

But somehow, I already felt like she was the one.

The one I could build with. Grow with.

The only one I'd want to have the early mornings and sleepless nights with.

And if God said the same…if life let me have her…if she chose me…

I would not dare take a single moment for granted.

DESTINEY

One of the nights that reminded her just how deeply she was already his. She let herself feel all of it, sinking fully into the sweet, secure love they built.

So, Micah had me spoiled, and that is a fact.

After years of abstinence, I was now used to his toe-curling, soul-snatching feasts. Served on the regular.

Micah's head game. His mouth work. Lip service.

My goodness.

We still hadn't gone all the way, but we'd been using our mouths just fine. Micah was always tonguing me like I was his favorite dessert. Licking me like he couldn't get enough. Always putting in work with that mouth of his.

Then hold me like I was his whole world.

Yeah. He had me spoiled.

When he was in Glendale, and it was only four days, mind you, I seriously had no idea how bad I would suffer going without it. Like, I was climbing the damn walls or something.

Things had been awakened in me, and being away from Micah left me feeling on the edge. Like, I was way in my feelings. Snippy and shit.

I was seriously trying to figure my life out. Because we haven't even had intercourse yet. And here Micah was calling my body *a temple*. Making a whole meal out of me. That shit threw me. In the best way.

Yeah.

When Micah was in Glendale, I found myself scrolling Amazon late one night. I was desperate for some kind of relief. I told Micah on FaceTime how much I missed him, and I was aching for his mouth on me. He talked me through a release. I used my fingers and that deep voice of his. Steady, telling me exactly what I needed to hear.

But still.

I figured I could get a vibrator to help take the damn edge off till I had him back.

That quest turned into a damn headache. Because eventually, I was down a neon rabbit hole (pun intended) of pure chaos. I gave up, and I decided I'd ask Day and Indie.

I knew they'd get me right.

But I had a plan. And I was going to go wherever Micah did. Whenever possible. And I would try my damndest. All I needed was my iPad and my sketchbook.

I was so glad to have Micah back when he returned. And that dry spell was in the distant past.

Life before him period was in the distant past. Especially now that I was with him all the time.

Micah and I settled into something so easy. Something real. We were together all the time. Living life side by side and I loved this so much.

And speaking of, we were falling deeper. Each passing day.

He brought me into his world. I brought him into mine.

Micah and Julian got close real quick. And kicked it like old friends from the jump.

And I had breakfast with his mom, just the two of us, all the time. I simply adore her, and she loves me back. I feel her love for me every time we are together. It's been so special, and I don't think I realized how much I missed that maternal comfort until I had it with her. That mother-love energy I haven't felt in close to twenty years. And she gave it to me freely and gracefully.

Yeah. I couldn't recall life before Micah. And I didn't want to. Didn't even try to.

My life felt normal again.

My cycle had finally calmed. I wasn't bleeding between cycles. No excessive bleeding, and I didn't have to worry so much about an accident. I felt so free.

My energy was back. The peace in that was utterly indescribable. I was so damn thankful.

Yeah.

And anyway... right now? At this very moment, I was loving on my man

With my mouth.

I made my way down, took him into my mouth, and gave him all that love back. Slow. Wet and intentional. I was locked in. Focused. Loving on my man with my mouth. The way he always loved on me.

He was thick. Long. And heavy. Hard as hell. My lips were slick with spit. My jaw was working slowly and focused. And I took my time because he deserved that.

Micah always took his time with me. He made sure I felt cherished. And sexy.

So this was for him. But truthfully... I loved it too.

Especially the way he responded.

Oh my gosh.

His voice went deep as hell. Every moan released. Every uttered curse word. Every low growl... I felt it pulse through my body. Straight to my pussy. Micah didn't hold back. He never held back. He was always vulnerable, and that was everything. He wasn't just receiving; he was praising me constantly. Telling me how much he enjoyed what I was doing. The way I made him feel. Told me how good I was. The way I focused while I pleased him.

Like right now.

"You feel incredible, baby. You taking your time with this. *Mmm.*"

His voice. That low, reverent rumble. It only showed itself when we were like this. And. It wasn't performative. It was honest. And real. And it made me want to give him even more.

And I knew I had gotten better. I wanted to. He made me feel safe and sexy. And capable.

Micah didn't rush me. Never pressured me. Only guided me. Lovingly guided me. Affirming me with his patience. That shit did something to me. It still did. The first time I had my lips around him seemed like ages ago.

So, hell yeah, I gave it my best. Every single time.

"You like this beauty?" He pressed.

"Mmmhmm." *Fuck yeah, I liked this.*

"Mmm. Damn you feel so good... Enjoying this as much as I am?"

"*Mmmhmm,*" I emphasized it more that time.

Micah moaned low and deep. His large hands cradled my head. Gently. With care and control. His fingers threaded in my locs. Not guiding but holding.

Micah's eyes were low. Locked on me. Watching me work. "You sexy girl... that pretty mouth, those sweet lips. Look at you, baby. Pleasing me so damn good."

I looked up for a second, a moment ago. And his gaze was dark. And hungry. And proud.

Yeah.

My man was proud of me.

I closed my eyes quickly, but it wasn't because I was shy or embarrassed. I was focused. Honestly, I'm not bashful anymore. Not with him. Not about this. I was all the way in it now. Committed and present. Giving my man my best because he always gave me his.

Whenever he was pleasing me, it was like worship to him. Like joy. I was always in bliss from that kind of pleasure. Floating and shit. He was so good at it. And when I started getting better at this, he noticed. And told me so. Praised me for it. And he emphasized that it wasn't just the act, but because of the way I loved on him through it.

My mind was blown when he said that.

"You sexy girl... I feel every bit of that." He murmured. His breath had grown ragged. I knew he was inching closer. "*Mmm.* You know what you're doing to me, baby?"

Oh, I knew *exactly* what I was doing.

Trying to focus but his hard dick was in my mouth. Heavy and decorated with flaring veins, I could feel with my tongue. Each time I slid down and eased back up again, I could feel them, and I felt the tension building.

Micah caught his breath. His grip tightened slightly. His breath was ragged. He spoke in a broken rhythm now.

"Mmm... bout to fucking cum Destiney baby... fuck...all for you. Just tell me where?"

Micah always asked me that. He never assumed. Ever. I appreciated that more than I could say. But that was Micah. My sweet Micah. So thoughtful. Always considering me. Checking in with me. Even the smallest things. Like how I liked my tea, or if I needed a minute when shit go to be too much in the world outside. Or with difficult clients at work. But in the bedroom, his care for me amplified. He was hyperaware of my body. Of my every breath. My sighs. Everything.

"Baby... where?" Micah urged again. His voice was thick with need. And restraint.

Breaking away for just a second, I found his eyes, whispering, "In this pretty mouth. Go head." Micah always called my mouth pretty. He said it every time I did this for him. Like he needed to make sure I knew it.

Micah gave me a quiet chuckle and a beat later, he released a sound that made my pussy pulse. And I felt him. Hot and thick, coating the back of my throat. But fuck. She was pulsing with need.

And it always happened like this.

His sounds did things to me. The deep, guttural rumble he gave me when he let go.

Oh. My. Gosh.

He didn't even have to say shit.

But. When he did… it was just as potent. Every time we did this shit with our mouths. With our lips and tongues and hands. Fingers.

Getting lost in the ecstasy of heat and care, I came undone from more than just the physical.

It was so much more with him.

With Micah, it was everything.

If you enjoyed this Collector's Edition and these bonus chapters, I would be so grateful if you'd please leave a review on your platform of choice. Your continued support means the world to me! Thank you!

About the Author

Vivienne Paul is obsessed with a sweet, sappy black love story, and most days—with a cup of tea or glass of wine in hand—you'll find her reading or writing one.

A Northern California native, she's a wife and a mom embracing life's tender moments and its beautiful chaos.

In the time between, she's an occasional artist and amateur chef. She is currently writing her next book. Follow her for updates on upcoming titles.

IG: vivpaulwrites

vivpaulwrites@gmail.com

www.ingramcontent.com/pod-product-compliance
Lightning Source LLC
Chambersburg PA
CBHW021931110726
47901CB00003B/790